MW00714806

Thanks

APK

Stays Crunchy in Milk

Adam P. Knave

Stays Crunchy in Milk
by Adam P. Knave

ISBN-10: 1894953-592
ISBN-13: 978-1894953-597
Trade edition. This book is also available in a limited edition
hardcover, signed and numbered.

Published in Canada by Creative Guy Publishing
Vancouver BC Canada

Edited by Lauren Vogelbaum
Cover and interior art by Renato Pastor
©2009 Renato Pastor

Library and Archives Canada Cataloguing in Publication

Knave, Adam P., 1975-
Stays crunchy in milk / Adam P. Knave.

ISBN 978-1-894953-59-7

I. Title.

PS3611.N38S72 2009 813'.6 C2009-902168-4

Stays Crunchy in Milk

Adam P. Knave

creative guy publishing

vancouver | canada

For Fezzik and MacKenzie.
Two close friends who were there every step of the way.

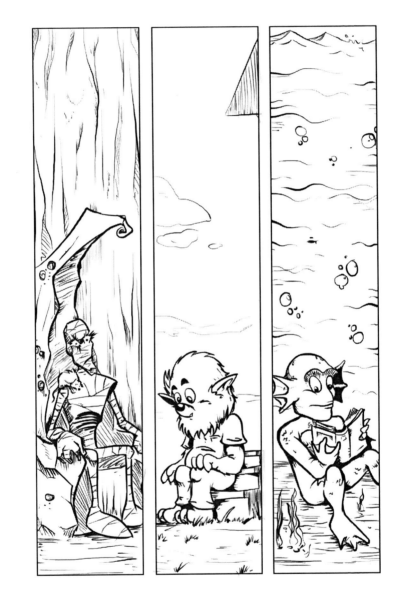

PART ONE
The Known World

"To be matter of fact about the world is to blunder into fantasy—and dull fantasy at that, as the real world is strange and wonderful."

—Robert A. Heinlein

1 • The True Curse

THE SUN ROSE. The chocolate river flowed steadily on. The rays of the sun shot down across the syrupy water of the lake and bounced off of it, blinding nearby animals for full seconds at a time. Thick brown clouds hung in the sky above the dazzled, blinking animals. The clouds seemed too heavy to float, and yet they never drooped.

A large, chocolate-colored pyramid ran along the bank of the river. The sun shone on, trying its best to light the structure. It did a reasonably good job on the outer parts, but the light never pierced the pyramid, not even a little. Candles of dark brown wax lit the interior. The wax never ran, leaving the candles looking the same one day as the next, reaching back as far as anything could remember. They gave off an almond scent that filled the corridors. The air, already thick from the general lack of ventilation, only suffered more for it.

Bats flew along the heady passageways. They flapped leathery wings and chased both each other and the rats that scurried around the pyramid not giving a damn about bats unless they were currently being chased. One bat left her pack and took off down a hallway. After a while the bat considered going back, but couldn't be bothered to make the decision.

Eventually the bat swooped out into a large chamber and settled on a milk chocolate sarcophagus etched with hieroglyphics both senseless and purposeful. The bat's landing was perfect, ten points on the nose, but still caused the slightest of sounds. The vibrations shuddered into the tomb and woke that which lay inside.

The lid of the tomb shook, rumbling as it worked itself loose. The bat took off in a hurry. A body consisting only of dark brown bandages sat up and stretched arms that fairly dripped with loose ends of linen, broken and torn. The immortal, wise, and sugary Choco-Ra climbed out of his tomb and sighed deeply.

He was, as always, tired. Those stupid bats, he thought, always had the worst timing—though it wasn't like there was a particularly good time to be awake.

Choco-Ra stretched his limbs, the bandages creaking with distress. His long, thin frame unbent and he stood tall in his bedchamber, considering all the things the day could bring. His eyes shone a bright, pinpoint red in an otherwise pitch-black gap in the bandages around his face. Might as well, he decided firmly, face the day.

After closing the lid of his sarcophagus, Choco-Ra started the long walk toward the upper chambers. The pyramid was his, and he was the only thing inside it. The only thing except for the vermin that infested every inch of it, that is. Choco-Ra didn't mind them particularly. He had trained some of them, as much as he could, to be servants and helpers, though he gave in and controlled them directly at times. Life was, he reflected, lonely as always.

As he sat down on his white chocolate throne, inlaid with peanuts and almonds, Choco-Ra pondered his next move. Being an immortal mummy didn't leave one with a lot of needs, nor a grand amount of available sleep. The combined effect tended toward a profound and dismally deep boredom. Which was, he thought with a grin that twitched the bandages around his mouth, nothing new.

He could go fishing, perhaps. Cultivate the garden? Neither left him with a spark of interest. There were only so many choco-trout to catch when you didn't eat, and who really cared for a variety of arum when you couldn't quite smell them? He also realized that, today at least, he just didn't damn well care what he did.

Which meant, he realized as he picked a rat off the floor

and scratched it behind the ears, that he really should get the hell out of the pyramid and do something for a change. Eternity wore on every last nerve he had some days. Weeks. Months. Decades.

Depositing the rat on the floor gently, he stood and looked around his throne room. It was devoid of furniture, and there were only a few musty, dripping paintings of his ancestors to serve as decoration. For the millionth time he decided to do something about that. When he got back, of course.

Choco-Ra wandered down hallways and switchbacks until he came to a small locked door. He patted himself down for keys, knowing full well he possessed no pockets. He used the magic word, regretting the lack of the simple fun of a physical key.

The room was small and dark, and the mummy stooped to fit his six-foot-five frame inside. His eyes shone brighter, illuminating the room. Keys he might not have, but flashlights he didn't need. Along every free surface and stacked on the floor were backpacks, bags, candles, shovels, and other equipment he'd collected over the years, having decided that it might come in handy for a trip.

Choco-Ra selected a light brown backpack and stuffed it with candles, matches, a small spade, a compass, and a few maps. He knew the way to his destination as surely as he knew his way around his own pyramid, but it never hurt to be prepared.

Something, some strange and unknown urge, was pushing him out faster than he was used to. There was no cause for the rush that he could figure. He had no reason to hurry. Still, he felt a tightening in his chest. It was new, though, and therefore interesting. The spring in his step told him a lot, too. He couldn't work out why he felt the need to hurry up and leave, but his body was full of raw urgency. Brushing off what he kept calling simple jitters, Choco-Ra wandered back along hallways, off to see his three friends.

The thought froze him in his tracks. Three friends? Where had that come from? He only had two good friends, and yet he knew there was a third. He knew it deep in his bandages. The information was pure and true—it just didn't fit with reality. Two, not three, and yet three was the number he knew to be right.

Confused and, now more than ever, raring to get moving, Choco-Ra pushed open the large stone door to his pyramid and gave his kingdom a lingering look. He didn't know it, but it was the last time he would set eyes on the chocolate lands of his youth.

2 • The Shifting Fruit

STRAWBERRIES BLOOMED EVERYWHERE. To every side of every thing, there were strawberry plants. They sat next to the trees and next to the lake. They sat, frankly, in places that strawberry plants can't normally grow. A few grew to the right of the large stone wall that surrounded a small, normal-looking pink house.

The trees had green leaves and brown bark, but the wood underneath was a bright, cheerful pink. The stones all had a pink-and-red hue to them—still basically stone-gray, but with a strong suggestion of pink to come.

The moon above was shaped like a strawberry, although certainly a moon-colored one. Despite the presence of a moon in the sky, sitting amongst stars which, yes, glowed faintly pink-and-red, the sky was somehow light. Not quite day, nor dusk, the light had the quality of noon in the moonlight.

Birds of all colors swooped between the trees, and butterflies of every shade fluttered from flower to flower. The occasional pink squirrel ran around at the usual breakneck speed. An owl hooted loudly at a robin. Animals both diurnal and nocturnal found themselves awake, neither group seeming to especially care about the discrepancy.

An owl, one not distracted by other birds or various scampering things, flew over to the stone wall. It sounded off loudly. Inside the house someone, in response to the noise, stirred. He was short, only reaching five-foot-seven on a good day. He loved being the height he was, though, having realized early on that finding a bed big enough to really sprawl out in was quite easy. As he woke up he stretched, the tips of his toes curling and uncurling. They didn't even reach the foot of the bed, and he smiled at the sensation of a good, languid stretch.

He turned and looked out the window to try and see what time it might be. The place was as timeless as ever, giving him no good idea at all. Getting as much of a hint as he ever did, Wereberry sat up and let his feet fall over the edge of the bed.

His feet were covered in thick pink fur. Gnarled pink claws poked out, drumming along the floor as he wiggled his toes. The fur continued up his legs. It went up and up, covering, truth be told, every inch of his frame. Wereberry sat in bed, covers thrown aside, and ran a hand over his face. His muzzle was long and sharply angled, almost like a hawk's beak. His ears sat upright, at attention, and tiny, extra-sensitive hairs along the rims waved with little currents in the air.

Something, he realized, had changed. It was being communicated to him by every inch of his body. The way the air moved, a hint of a scent, the sound of leaves falling. It was all, ever so slightly, off. If he hadn't spent the better part of his life in the Strawberry Glade he could have easily missed it.

Wereberry considered his options. He could run and hide. He could always, he thought, bring the problem to Choco-Ra. Ra wasn't always right, but he had a better batting average than Were'. Maybe he could wander over to the Lagoon, he thought, and have a talk with T.C. Except that T.C. would back the hiding plan, and that didn't feel right.

The werewolf paced the confines of his bedroom and considered further. There was no sense in rushing, he decided. Whatever had changed had gone ahead and changed without telling anyone. Given that, why would it hurry up and play its hand? No, he resolved with a firm shake of his head, it made no sense at all to go rushing out, waving your arms and yelling. Not yet.

That decided, Wereberry took a long hot shower. He used his special strawberry-scented shampoo in preparation for whatever it was he was preparing for. Shaking himself dry in front of a mirror and combing out his fur, he had time to reflect that really, going out and looking for trouble only ever got you trouble.

It was only when he sat down for breakfast that another thought occurred to him: if something felt wrong to him, chances were that it was wrong in a wider area. If that held true at all then Ra would come looking for him. If, he continued the chain of possible events, Ra was going to come for him, he would bring T.C. before T.C. could hide too well.

All of which boiled down to more people for breakfast, or possibly lunch; time to raid the cabinets and lay out a spread. Sighing lightly to himself, he moved around the kitchen. He had already made breakfast, so he continued to eat it in stolen bites between preparations for a big picnic lunch.

He liked company well enough. When he was truly honest with himself, he admitted that he loved it. Even so, making a big lunch took time, and Wereberry found himself quickly losing the morning to preparing for the afternoon.

Owls hooted outside. Birds sang. Squirrels chattered. The moonlight shifted subtly, confusing all of the animals nearby. Wereberry sniffed deeply and sorted the smell of lunch, parsing the changes around him.

Something was not only changed, it was still changing. Worrying that he should have done more than simply pack up some sandwiches and a cheese plate, he loped out of his front door. The Strawberry Glade still looked mostly the same. There was simply an edge of impending otherness to everything.

He stood outside, tapping one foot, the claws clicking loudly on vaguely pink stone, and waited for people to arrive. He really hoped now that they would. They had to, he reassured himself. They simply had to. If they didn't, he would have to go all the way to Ra's place, carrying lunch, and when he got there it would already be time for dinner.

He stood, and tapped, and waited.

3 • Just Under the Surface

CRICKETS CHIRPED UNDER A DUSKY SKY. Frogs croaked and hopped. The lagoon swirled languidly with a multitude of colors. If a rainbow ever melted, it might just end up looking like the lagoon did on a normal day.

Along the bank of the water, large trees sat in bloom and fruit of all kinds hung from their branches. Some was the kind that didn't usually grow on trees, but that was just fine by the monkeys that lived in the area.

The abundance of fruit lent the entire area a redolent smell. It was cloying and rich, full of all sorts of clashing fruitiness. Grapes collided with apples and pears. Oranges and tangerines fought a silent war against bananas. Fruit chaos ensued. There could be no clear winner on this battlefield. No one even seemed to have an upper hand. Evenly matched, each tree seemed determined to pump out as many fumes and molecules of scent as possible. If they couldn't win, they could at least annoy each other to death.

Which would have worked if trees could smell each other. Since they couldn't, it was only the population of the lagoon that suffered, except they had gotten used to it. It lent the whole affair a senseless edge that wasn't lost on at least one person.

The Creature From the Fruit Lagoon sat at the bottom of said lagoon, watching the almost-but-never-quite-navy sky swirl above him through a haze of other colors. He had no proper name. No one had ever called him Bob, say. The closest he came to a name was either The Creature From the Fruit Lagoon, which was fairly lengthy, or T.C. He didn't like the name T.C. but it beat having people use a preposition as your first name, he had decided ages ago.

T.C. had sensed the change early. Living at the bottom of a body of water made someone notice the air. When he had surfaced that morning, he knew instantly that something was off. So he dived back down and sat along the bottom to think on it. He wasn't, he was sure, hiding. He might have been holding back, or... no, he knew he was hiding from the change. T.C. didn't like change, as a general rule.

No good cause for that; he was just one of those people that enjoyed the status quo more than the unknown. He did not, he knew deeply, hide out of fear. He hid out of reluctance.

That wasn't going to hold him down for long, though. He cared too much about his friends to sit and ride out a burst of change without checking in on them. T.C. decided to hold off a while first. He couldn't avoid change, but he at least could deny it sometimes.

Suddenly, a rock broke the surface of the lagoon and drifted down toward his head. The monkeys would pitch the occasional rock but when the second, third, and fourth followed, T.C. knew it wasn't monkeys.

He surfaced quickly, seeing Choco-Ra standing on the bank. The old mummy held a few more stones in his hand and was about to lob another one out when T.C. surfaced.

"T.C., I thought I might find you down there," Ra said, his voice deep and gravelly.

"You say that like you solved a great mystery, Ra." T.C. climbed out of the lagoon and stood next to his friend. T.C.'s leathery, blue-tinted skin glistened with moisture. He tried to not drip on Ra.

"Well, no. I just came by to ask—"

"If I had noticed something off about today?" T.C. interrupted. "Yeah. I was just about to—"

"Continue to sit on the bottom of your lake and think about it," Ra interrupted right back.

"Unfair. And it's a lagoon, not a lake. Look, whatever is

off, it's big, and I'm not sure what the hell it might be."

"Neither am I." Ra looked T.C. in the eyes, the two of them close to each other in height.

T.C. stretched his webbed hands while he chewed on that. If Ra had no clue, then it was going to be an interesting day. His gills opened and closed with a flutter of nervousness that he bit back. He closed his solid black eyes and tilted his head back.

"What does Were' say?" he asked, eyes still closed.

"Haven't gone to see him yet. I thought I would pick you up first."

"Because you thought I was going to hide all day otherwise?" shot T.C., a slow burn of anger rising.

"No," Ra said with a rumbling laugh, "because you're on the way."

"Do you want to grab the bird, too?"

"Not really," Ra said, "I don't think this concerns him."

"How do you know, though, when you already said you don't know what this is about?" T.C. challenged. Ra was considered the de facto leader of the three friends (even though T.C. kept thinking the number four), and he could get a bit egotistical about that.

"All right, fine. I just don't like the bird."

"Honest enough. Why couldn't you just say that first?"

"I don't know. Maybe he was... I don't know. I just didn't," Ra admitted, shaking his head.

"Fair enough. So what are the chances Were' is on his way here? Or even to your place?" T.C. asked.

"Slim, I would guess," Ra said. "I was going to bet that he was at home, waiting for us. He wouldn't want to miss us, after all."

"So you think he feels the same thing," T.C. said as a matter of fact.

"Yes. We both do. I'd wager he does, too. Makes an amount of sense."

"Sure. Let me grab some things and I'll be right with you," T.C. said. He dove back into the lagoon without waiting for a reply.

Down along the bottom, T.C. opened a chest and pulled out a shoulder bag. He stuffed it with a net, some self-sealing bags, a big bottle of moisturizer, and a few books. He surfaced slowly. He didn't want to drag out his departure but he also didn't relish rushing things. Choco-Ra stood on the bank of the lagoon, petting a small red lizard. The lizard, sitting on the branch of a tree, welcomed the attention.

T.C. hoisted his bag and clapped Ra wetly on the shoulder. Ra scowled and shook his head, but didn't comment. The two walked out of the lagoon, side by side, in silence.

4 • ...And Four Makes Three

WEREBERRY SAT ON HIS FRONT STAIR, eating a sandwich. There was only the one stair to sit on. He had considered building a full-blown stoop when he first moved in, but it felt like too much work. Three stairs would have three times the chance to cause trouble that one did. The one stair never caused him any trouble.

Lunchtime drifted along leisurely. Soon, time would slip right past it and he would have to consider hunting down Ra himself. A hunt wasn't what he wanted, but he started to gather the desire as best he could.

Wereberry stood and opened his door. He grabbed the basket with the rest of lunch and set it down on the kitchen table. He started to unpack it, in between bites of his strawberry-flavored cheese sandwich.

As his tongue flicked the last crumbs from his muzzle he heard footsteps approaching. Two separate sets of footsteps, in fact, once he bothered to really listen. They didn't seem to be in a hurry. They didn't seem to be much of anything, outside of two people taking a stroll.

Laughing to himself, Wereberry quickly repacked the basket. Of course that was the way things worked, he thought; once you give up on something it comes around anyway just to make you think twice the next time. He stayed away from a thought train concerning the futility of it all, generally being much happier than that. No, Wereberry just repacked lunch and jaunted over to the door as quick as one of the jackrabbits he occasionally chased. The important thing now, in his mind, was not being caught out at second guessing himself or his friends.

Choco-Ra and T.C. walked down the long and winding path to Wereberry's house, still side by side. They weren't, the werewolf noticed, talking. Hell, they weren't even looking at each other. If he didn't know better, he could've easily guessed they were strangers who just happened to be on the same road and walking at exactly the same pace. Which, though it would've been rare and kind of amusing to see, was certainly not the case here.

Waving to get their attention, Wereberry jerked a furred thumb over his shoulder and wandered around the side of the house. He set the basket down on his backyard table and started to slowly unpack it. Before he finished getting everything out and onto the table, his friends caught up with him.

Still silent, they sat down, each in front of a pink paper plate. Wereberry wanted to say something. He felt like his chest was going to burst if this silence gag went on much longer, but he also sensed the weight of it. The heaviness of the moment settled across the table like a stone. T.C. and Choco-Ra allowed it to encumber them easily, but Wereberry visibly fought at it.

Sure he could feel it, and that it was somehow right, but he really wanted to just shout and dance and do anything, anything he could think of, to break the moment and move past it. Instead he grabbed another sandwich and bit into it.

"So," Ra offered, "where do we go from here?"

"We have to figure out why we're all convinced something is wrong, what it is, I guess," T.C. said, waggling half a sandwich in one hand for emphasis.

"You do know what we're talking about," Ra asked Wereberry, "right?"

"I guess so, inferring from, like, two vague sentences, sure," Wereberry answered.

"All we have is vague right now, Were'." T.C. said. "Come on, what do you expect?"

"Answers, generally," the werewolf replied, "but those—"

"Are hard to come by, harder to prove," Ra finished for him.

Choco-Ra froze as soon as he stopped speaking, drumming his fingers on the table. Something about the phrase bothered him. He'd heard it before, and he was sure the others had, too. He just wasn't sure where or when.

"When have I heard that before?" asked Wereberry.

"Haven't you said it before?" T.C. asked, knowing that it wasn't true.

"No, the other one did," Ra said. His voice was low when he spoke. He hunched over the table and glanced between his friends. "There was a fourth, wasn't there?"

"Yes," Wereberry said quickly.

"No," T.C. said at the same time.

They looked at each other and then at Choco-Ra.

"No," Wereberry said, sounding unconvinced.

"Yes," T.C. said quietly.

"Exactly," Ra put in, "the problem, and exactly why we're here, I'd guess."

"So this other person, this other one," Wereberry said, dropping the last of his lunch and rubbing his temples, "he—"

"She," Ra insisted.

"She then, yeah, you're right, Ra," Wereberry realized with a nod. "She is what we're missing and who said that phrase and, and what?"

"And she's the one who left," T.C. said.

"Left where? When? Why, and for that matter, who was she?" Ra asked, growing angry. His eyes glowed a bright red and his dull, rounded fingers started to scratch uselessly at the surface of the table.

"Great," T.C. said. "That's what got us all up this morning. We don't have the answers, Ra. Can we deal with that and just ignore it, or do we do something about it?"

"We have to find out!" Ra fumed.

"Do we, though?" asked Wereberry. "We didn't know any of this yesterday for a reason, possibly. Hell, I don't know. Maybe we did know it yesterday. The point is, it didn't hurt us not knowing before, so I don't see why we have to set fire to things looking for answers now. We just found out. Maybe some time to plan first, and then we can decide for real."

"Or maybe we have to act now to do whatever it is we're going to do," Choco-Ra said, trying to regain his calm. "Acting now, and decisively, could be the best way to go about this. I want to find her, and find her now."

"Both ways have risk. The deciding factor is the fact that she could be in trouble," T.C. said.

"If it was one of us missing we wouldn't hesitate, would we?" Wereberry asked.

"Of course not," Ra said.

"Then you're right, Ra. We find her. Now." Wereberry stuffed the last of his sandwich in his mouth and chewed.

Choco-Ra nodded. T.C. nodded. Wereberry nodded and chewed. They were in agreement and something about that felt right to each of them. Though they all felt the same satisfaction of apt behavior, they all felt it for different reasons. T.C. felt that a united front had a better chance than a bickering group going forth unsure of itself. Wereberry felt more confident because, though he hadn't said it, the more they talked about her the more something in his brain itched. It was an itch he had to scratch, no matter how cautious he might want to be. Choco-Ra felt relaxed and calm now because he could feel, deep inside him, that this was a purpose that he had been waiting for. Even if he hadn't known it before that very second.

Separately, they were together. The rest of lunch was eaten, by the two of them that ate, in silence. It wasn't the same weighted silence that had started the meal, but a comfortable silence. The silence before movement.

Wereberry cleared the table, moving unhurriedly. Already

thinking forward to what he would pack and how he would leave his house, he absently stuffed the last of the sandwiches under the plates, squishing them. T.C. and Choco-Ra sat back from the table, watching. Neither of them bothered to speak, not to point out the strange packing techniques Wereberry engaged in or anything else. They had each faced the same problem, and though they had dealt with it differently, they both knew one thing: it had to be dealt with alone.

Leaving home was never easy. No one pretended otherwise. Not when the uncertainty of return hung so heavily over each action. They weren't even sure where they were going yet, much less when they would return. If they would. If they could, even, after all was said and done. Such goodbyes were too private to share, even with your best friends.

Wereberry stood in his kitchen and thought about the future. It shifted and folded in on itself while he tried to picture it. With the start of a headache already tugging at his consciousness, he sighed and set the basket of slightly ruined food down on the counter.

He ran a hand along the back of his neck, kneading his fingers against muscle and scratching along his own fur. It normally served to relax him, but this time it felt like a cheap ploy. Yes, definitely a headache coming on.

Nothing to be done for it. The only thing, Wereberry felt, was to do what he needed to do and worry about little things like headaches later. So he wandered toward the other end of his house and grabbed a backpack. He wandered around his house quickly, shoving things into it. He considered each option fully; he just refused to dwell on them so that he didn't give himself a chance to hesitate.

Soon enough the bag was half full. A nail clipper, grabbed off a pink stone sink, joined the mass of objects in the bag, and a comb, and then an extra comb followed it. A third comb found its way into the bag before he left to return to the kitchen.

Food filled the rest of the bag. Wereberry wasn't sure what would happen to the food he left behind, if they would be gone long enough for it to rot or not, so he took as much as possible.

Then he grabbed two tight-sealing kitchen baggies and crammed them full of strawberries, one baggie for dried and one for fresh but all extremely pungent, and gently packed them into the top of the bag before zipping the bag shut.

Pink backpack slung over his shoulders, Wereberry walked back outside. He stopped at the tree in front of his house and stroked its rough bark. Then he took a deep breath and walked to the back of the house to rejoin his friends.

"Do you guys need anything?" he asked.

Choco-Ra and T.C. stood as they saw Were' come into view.

"We're both ready," Ra said.

T.C. simply nodded. Both of them wore their feelings across their faces: open, friendly faces, full of understanding.

"Sorry I took so long," Wereberry started.

"Were', it isn't like we rushed either," T.C. said with a half-shake of his head. "You just didn't see us do it. Relax."

The werewolf nodded, his sense of guilt washing away quickly. He trusted his friends. If they both seemed to be bothered this little, then they must be bothered almost exactly that little, he reasoned.

"All right, so I am not the slowest of the slow," he conceded with a smile, "but it does leave us at a bit of a problem."

"What's that?" T.C. asked.

"We know what we want to do," Were' said.

"But not where to go or how to do it?" Ra ventured.

Wereberry nodded. None of them, at least, was stupid.

"I was giving that some thought while you were packing," Ra continued, "and I don't think she's in this land."

"In Wereberry's land, of course not," T.C. said, "that much is obvious." He laughed and shook his head when Ra started

21

to speak, "No, Ra, I know you meant the wider land. I just had to say it. Anyway, I agree. So we have to leave the land."

"The Jug can get us out," Wereberry said.

"What makes you say that?" Ra asked. As soon as he asked, however, he knew it was right.

"She told me, she told—she told all of us that before she left," Wereberry said, shaking his head. His headache was getting worse but he was determined to ignore it for as long as possible.

"She did, didn't she?" T.C. said in wonderment. "And since she isn't here maybe she was even right."

"She has a name, damn it," Ra insisted suddenly.

"I know," Were' said. He moved closer to his mummified friend and laid a soothing hand on Ra's shoulder. "I can't remember it either."

"It was...." T.C. trailed off, also lost.

"Cherrygiest," Wereberry said out of nowhere. A smile broke out across his muzzle, long and thin. It fell quickly as the next piece fell into his waiting mind. "And I loved her," he said sadly.

"We all did," Ra put in, forcing himself to not shake. Hearing her name and knowing that it was right set him off. Fear mixed with indignation and tingled all along his spine. It was bad enough that this was all an unknown puzzle, but to have it feel like something or someone had withheld knowledge from Ra's mind... that felt like the biggest betrayal he could remember.

"No, we all loved her, and we all love each other," Wereberry tried to explain, "but I loved her. I think she loved me the same way, but I don't remember."

"We'll find her," T.C. said.

"We'll try," Ra countered, not wanting to build up his friend's hope too high.

Wereberry nodded, but to which sentiment none of them, not even he, knew.

"We're wasting time," Wereberry said firmly, looking around, "so which way to the Jug man?"

"This way, I think," Ra said, pointing due east.

"Then we're off," T.C. said.

5 • Three Squared

THE THREE WALKED FOR A FEW HOURS just talking softly. Wereberry watched the land as the pink bled out of things and greens and blues took over. The light shifted, growing bright and strong. Trees stood taller and fields of corn and wheat could be seen blowing in the distance.

They stopped for a few minutes, sitting next to a warm rock with their packs set down into the soft green grass. A bird, bright orange, settled on T.C.'s bag and chirped a while, until Wereberry barked at it. The bird took wing quickly at that and Wereberry allowed himself a smile.

"Where are we?" he asked his friends. Neither of them knew for sure, and though Ra had a guess he kept it to himself.

None of them wandered around with regularity these days. They generally either visited each other or struck out at random directions and intervals, always making it home before too much time passed.

Rested after their initial push, they stood and shouldered their bags once more.

Wereberry took the lead, blinking against his headache. The pain started behind his eyes and spread quickly up along his forehead. Still, Wereberry refused to give in or acknowledge it, not wanting to give it power over him.

Behind him walked Choco-Ra. Ra noticed the obvious discomfort his furred friend was in and wanted to help. He just didn't know what he could do.

At the rear walked T.C. T.C. didn't really care if Were' wanted help or not; he was busily mixing a few leaves with a few herbs he carried to make a decent migraine cure. To be sure, he wished that one day his friend would admit that he got migraines and confess to them when they hit. He also knew it wasn't likely to happen. So, instead, he mixed up a solution and waited.

Before T.C. could deliver his cure, however, Wereberry's pain took a turn for the extreme worse. The cause wasn't a natural progression of his headache; it was, instead, due to a series of loud noises.

They rang out like explosions. They were, in fact, explosions. To be fair, they sounded far bigger than they were. All three travelers stopped and looked around. Ra alone sighed, recognizing the sounds for what they were.

"Relax," he said, "it's just the triplets."

"I didn't realize they were so close," Wereberry said, looking around.

"I thought this might be their land, but then I thought that it was rather further away than next door to you," Ra said.

"Hell, I thought it was to the north of your house, Were'," T.C. added, amused. They were fairly certain that the lands sometimes shifted a bit, but none of them knew why or relied on it happening. Besides, with their self-proclaimed lack of information, they chalked it up to ignorance rather than a changing landscape. Changing landscapes didn't make as much sense, after all. Except. Except that they knew their neighbors. They, each of them, knew plenty of folks across the lands. Yet finding their way around them proved difficult sometimes. A chain of thought started to form in T.C.'s head for later digestion.

Another series of explosions rattled the landscape. The wheat fields in the distance shook visibly. The clouds seemed to ripple a few seconds after the noise. Nothing stood untouched by the sound of the blasts, and yet the force of them didn't seem to destroy anything at all.

T.C. passed Were' a ball of mush.

"Swallow it," he whispered, "it'll make your headache go away."

"Thanks, T.C.," Wereberry whispered back, "but why are we whispering?"

"After a noise like that, doesn't whispering feel appropriate?" T.C. asked in another whisper.

"You're both just slightly deaf," Ra said.

"I thought it felt like I was screaming," Wereberry said, having swallowed the medicine ball.

Three small boys burst out of the tall grass to the side of the three wanderers. Each one was short, coming up only to Wereberry's elbows. They wore striped stockings that vanished into pointed booties at one end and loose denim shorts at the other. The shorts had striped shirts tucked into them and solid denim vests sat above the shirts. Each youth had a blond buzz cut topped with a tiny, wedge-shaped hat.

Although they were perfectly identical in look and dress, each one of them sported a different color. One was in the brightest of blues, the other in the brightest of greens, while the third wore stunning yellows. Each boy's eyes matched his outfit's primary color.

"What are you doing here," the triplets demanded in unison, "and why are you here together?"

"We're headed by to see—" T.C. started, cut off by Ra.

"We were just wandering, boys," he said deeply, "don't worry about it."

"Boys," the triplets exclaimed in unison, "we aren't boys!"

"Whatever," Ra said dismissively.

Three explosions rocked the land as the triplets jumped into the air. At the apex of their jump, each one was surrounded by a nimbus of light, the same color as their eyes and outfits, followed by a concussive sound.

BOOM!

POW!

BLAM!

The three noises overlapped and ran into each other, distinguishable only briefly before becoming an unavoidable mass of sonic annoyance.

"We're Boom, Pow, and Blam, the triplets of fun and adventures! We aren't boys!" They spoke in unison. They always spoke in unison. Only when they were alone and they were sure that no one, not even the smallest of creatures, could hear them did they speak separately and to each other.

"Yes," Ra said as the three boys landed, "we get it. We've met, even. Don't you remember?"

"Oh, wait," the triplets said, "you're that mummy that bores us!"

"Exactly," Ra said. His eyes glowed brighter.

"Oh wait, I have met them before," T.C. said, remembering when he and Ra had once wandered through the land.

"Well, I've never met them," Wereberry said, wishing his headache was already gone and not being subjected to explosions.

"Well we are very pleased to meet you, furry werewolf person."

"Right back 'atcha, triplets."

"Boom, Pow, and Blam!"

"Right, sorry. Very nice to meet you as well, Boom, Pow, and Blam," Wereberry said formally.

"Would you like the tour? We could give you a tour."

"We were just passing through," Ra said quickly.

"He's never been here before," the triplets said, "so he should get the tour at least."

"Let him decide," T.C. suggested.

Wereberry bit back a laugh. "I don't have time for a tour right now," he told them, "and we really were just passing through, but if I can I'll come back for the tour later, all right?"

"If you mean it," they said warily.

"I mean it," he assured them.

"Well... all right. Where are you headed?"

"East," Ra said, not wanting to give away too much information.

"We'll walk with you a ways then," the triplets insisted.

"Just please," Wereberry said, "no more jumping and exploding. I have a headache."

The triplets sighed and looked between themselves, considering, for a second. "Well, all right. Let's go east, we can give you the special east-only tour."

"That sounds just fine," Wereberry said, walking up next to the triplets.

Ra hung back, letting his eyes dim. T.C. walked next to Ra. T.C. had no real problem with the triplets; they actually seemed fairly fun-loving, but Ra appeared too cranky to be left alone. If he doesn't find support now, T.C. thought, what will it be like once this journey really gets going?

Ra sighed, glancing at T.C. in resignation. He didn't hate the triplets; he just had no patience for them. They rubbed him the wrong way. But it wouldn't hurt, he knew, to indulge them a little. So long as it wasn't him doing the actual, face-to-face indulging, that was.

The triplets walked quickly, forcing Wereberry to keep up with them. Ra and T.C lagged behind. They were fine with lagging behind, as it let them not have to hear the triplets go on quite as much.

"Over here," they said to Wereberry, "is the main wheat field." One of the triplets, the one in yellow, pointed. When Wereberry didn't look he got harrumphed at until he turned his head and watched the tall wheat wave in a breeze.

"It's very nice wheat," Were' said lamely.

"It is!"

"And over there," the pink werewolf asked, pointing, "is that corn?"

"Those are our corn fields, yes," agreed the three. They smiled widely and nodded to each other. Here was, they felt, someone worth giving a tour to.

The wind picked up as they continued to walk. It shifted direction constantly. Steady breezes were interrupted by gusts and gusts were redirected by eddies and whorls. Were' looked up and noticed the clouds didn't move. The hung where they were, looking painted onto the sky. The winds that he felt didn't seem to reach upwards much. Still, the wheat and corn and grass all swayed in time to the winds. The trees, regardless of how tall, did the same, leaves whipping this way and then that.

T.C. stretched his arms into the wind and looked at Choco-Ra. Ra's bandages, very slightly frayed, shifted with the gusts. Tiny loose threads drifted back and forth.

"I don't remember this wind," T.C. whispered.

"You didn't travel along the fields, then," Ra whispered in response, "they never seem to stop around here."

"Is there anywhere you haven't been?" T.C. asked.

"Of course," Ra said with a low laugh, "there are many more places I haven't been than places I have. Though, to be fair about it, I have spent a lot more time wandering than either you or Wereberry ever bothered to."

"Why, though? Not that it's a problem, or a... I'm just wondering."

"You have your lands, your animals. You relate to them, as our furred friend does. I control the animals around my home, when I want to. It's hard to think of them as companions when you can make them do anything with a thought."

"That's not really," T.C. thought for a moment, "nice, I suppose."

"No," Ra agreed, "it isn't. But it is the truth. I can't consider a being a friend when I control them absolutely. It lacks a certain give and take."

"I suppose. Still."

"You try it and then we'll debate the rightness of it."

"No need to get snippy, Ra."

29

"No need to get judgmental, T.C."

"Point."

"Thank you."

"But still…." T.C. continued.

While Ra and T.C. discussed free will and mental slavery amongst one's friends, Wereberry was making friends of his own a handful of feet ahead.

"What's with the wind, guys?" Were' asked, shielding his eyes with a hand and staring off into the wheat fields.

"It's how the air gets into the grain," they replied, "obviously."

"Wait, what? Air gets into the—"

"Grain," the triplets said, cutting Were' off. "Otherwise it wouldn't explode."

Wereberry took a step to his left, edging further away from the vegetation. He eyed it carefully, looking for indications of impending explosion. Nothing seemed out of the ordinary.

This, he thought, was the problem with traveling. Everywhere had its own version of normal. Exploding wheat could be as ordinary as strawberries, and you wouldn't know it until a local told you or you lost a foot in some horrible accident. At least they had warned him this time.

"All right, guys, I need to ask. Why does the wheat explode?"

"The corn does too," the triplets put in, smiling.

"You seem so pleased with that fact," Were' said, finding a smile growing across his own face. Their happiness was contagious.

"Well sure, it's the most fun ever," they explained, "and it isn't like it just explodes there in the fields. Not often, anyway. No, after we process it we make sure to trap the air so it can explode later!"

"Oh, well that makes more sense," Wereberry said, not feeling sure that it did, or that sense would have made anything better. He just thought it was the right thing to say. There was no particularly good way to say what he was really thinking: exploding wheat and corn, and processing it to ensure that it exploded, made about as much sense as trapping your fur in a glue pot.

"Exactly!" they exclaimed, running twice around the werewolf's body and then jogging ahead of him. Once there, they turned to face him and then leapt into the air.

BOOM!

POW!

BLAM!

Wereberry covered his ears a second too late to help and felt his fur blow backward from the force of the noise. He yelped, both in surprise and pain. Behind him Ra and T.C. winced, mostly because they guessed their friend's headache still hadn't left him.

"I thought," Were' said as his ears stopped ringing, "we agreed not to do that again."

"Sorry," they assured him as they landed, "but sometimes we can't help it. We think about the way the post-processed stuff just explodes and it makes us so happy and did you know it makes the same sound we do? How cool is that? Sure it does it quieter than us, but even so! It's like we get to have our own echoes! And we think about it and we just get so happy that we—"

BOOM!

POW!

BLAM!

ARGH!

Wereberry's scream matched up with, and became a new part of, the dissonance the triplets created. His fur stood on end and his hands clenched and unclenched. By the time they landed, Wereberry was working out how he could strangle three people at once. He knew if he only grabbed one or two, the free ones would start making a racket again.

T.C. and Ra were alongside Wereberry quickly. They each

rested a hand on one of his furry shoulders. They didn't exert any pressure; their hands just laid there, one slightly damp and chilly, the other a dry, scratchy fabric, waiting.

Were' took the hint and forced himself to relax. The triplets weren't worth his anger, and they didn't mean to enrage him, certainly. They were just happy. And when they were happy, they exploded. Which was, for them, perfectly normal.

T.C. looked at the triplets. They looked back, not understanding why Wereberry seemed upset. Maybe, they reasoned, he was angry because he hadn't seen the wheat and corn in its finished state and he was just jealous of them. That made a lot of sense. They decided that simply must be it.

"It's getting late," T.C. said, glancing at his bare wrist, "and you guys should probably get home. We're not far from where we need to go, I'm sure, so," he glanced at his wrist again, "yep, getting late. Thanks for the tour."

The triplets looked at each other, blinking. It didn't feel late, but then it never really did feel late, so that wasn't a good indication. And he had looked at his wrist with authority, which meant he must know something. It added up quite right and nice in their heads. They nodded.

"Well sure! Thanks for letting us give you the tour, the east tour at least," they said. "Just make sure you come back for the rest of it!"

"Oh we will," Ra said, "we will. But like T.C. said, we simply must be going."

"Sorry I didn't realize how late it was getting," added Wereberry, playing along.

The triplets nodded again and waved furiously. Their hands became little blurs as they kept waving while waking away. They ran and skipped into the distance.

"Oh, thank you, T.C.," Wereberry said when the triplets were out of earshot, "I don't think I could've taken another round of that."

"No problem. I didn't think it would work, but they

looked just excitable enough, you know?"

"Good thinking," Ra said, "I wish I had thought of that the last time I was here."

"No problem," T.C. with a chuckle. "So let's get going before—"

BOOM!

POW!

BLAM!

The noises sounded in the distance but still carried enough power that Wereberry covered his ears and added his part to the symphony.

ARGH!

6 • Tromping and Climbing

CHOCO-RA, T.C., AND WEREBERRY HURRIED quickly along the winding paths and wind-swept fields. Although Wereberry's headache had faded from a migraine to an annoyance, none of them wanted it to come back. They also knew that as long as they remained anywhere near the triplets, they ran that risk.

The land started to change again as they walked. The wheat and corn fields gave way to wide-open grassy land. The three friends walked happily on, glad for the change. The sky seemed a darker shade of blue above them. It still had the light quality of noon, but the sky itself ran darker, along toward late afternoon. Trees started to pop up sporadically along their way.

The trees became more and more numerous until they found themselves walking in a full-fledged forest. Here and there they spotted wide-open glades, half hidden through the trees. Ra noticed that each glade they passed had a single large rock sitting in it. The rock wasn't always in the center of the glade, but a rock was continually easily seen. The glades evened out and a path formed, off to their right.

Unspeaking, they dodged through the trees and stepped onto the path. Now that they were on what seemed to be a main thoroughfare, the glades became even easier to spot. Smaller paths that sat invisible from within the tree line lead off toward the clearings. They alternated sides, T.C. noticed. If a glade was seen to the left, the next one would be to the right, and vise versa. It was very carefully thought out. Too carefully.

"Guys?" T.C. asked.

"Yes," Ra said in answer, "it's a bit too regulated, isn't it?"

"I kind of like it," Wereberry said, "never a surprise in where a rock to sit on is. You always know which way to go to find a good clearing to think in."

"It's a bit," T.C. said, "too regular, though, don't you think?"

"Nope. Quite comfy. Reassuring, really," Wereberry said.

"No accounting for taste," Ra sniped.

"I'm sure the next thing we come across will be nothing but geometric shapes stacked on top of one another in no pattern what-so-ever," Wereberry said, "and there'll be no where to sit, and nothing to rest along. But it will look ever so interesting. Will that be better for you?"

"Much," Ra said, adding a sharp nod for emphasis.

"Now you're just trying to get a reaction," Wereberry said.

"Yeah, he is," T.C. agreed.

"Yes, I am," Ra agreed as well, "I didn't think to bring along any cards, much less a chess set. Boredom is a villain we must be wary of and fight off at all turns."

"Boredom? We haven't even been out a day," T.C. said.

"I get bored easily, I suppose," Ra admitted, "but you knew that."

"But it's fun," T.C. pointed out, "to get a reaction out of you, too."

The land continued by under their feet. Visually, nothing changed. As they went deeper and deeper into the land, however, the scent of fruit started to grow. Soon it piled up around them, thick and sharp. T.C. loved it but the others weren't quite as enamored.

They trudged on. Wereberry heard a noise. It wasn't a normal forest noise. He held out a hand and softly clicked his tongue. The other two stopped, turning to look at him. He touched his ear and scanned the area carefully, turning his head this way and that. After the twins, Wereberry had decided he wanted to know, if possible, about anything surprising before it happened.

The sound, he realized, was footsteps. Very heavy footsteps that sped up and then slowed down in a constant oscillation. He waved the other two in closer.

"There's someone coming," he whispered.

"Let's get behind a tree and see them before they see us," T.C. said.

"I can't imagine it's dangerous," Ra said, "but sure, why not?"

They moved behind the nearest tree, standing on the side opposite the direction Wereberry had heard the footsteps come from. By the time they got behind the tree, all three of them could hear the thumping.

The tree was wide and old. It didn't hide all three of them perfectly, but it did a better job than any of them had really thought it would. The thumping got louder and closer. As it did they could faintly hear a voice, except Wereberry, that is, who could hear it as clear as day when he concentrated.

"Where?" the voice was asking the air, "Where, where where? Somewhere, but where?"

The voice was high-pitched and filled with panic. The thumping hit the point in its cycle where it sped up, and soon the others could hear the questioning clearly, too. They could also, if they peeked, see the body that the voice and footsteps belonged to.

The rabbit was tall, at least Choco-Ra's height without even taking its long ears into account. Its white fur fairly shone against the other colors in the forest. The rabbit wore a short pantsuit, all of it a bright, blazing red. No hat topped his head and no shoes covered his wide rabbit feet. No, except for the color, he was dressed like a British school child of old.

"All right," Ra whispered, "there is no way this guy is a threat."

"You've never met him?" T.C. asked.

"I have," Wereberry said, "once."

"And?" T.C. asked.

"He's not a threat, just hard to talk to. Come on."

Wereberry stepped out from behind the tree, T.C. and Choco-Ra right behind him. The rabbit spotted them as they came into view and panicked.

"Tricked!" he screamed, "I've been tricked! Aaaaahhhhhhhhhhhh!"

"Relax," Wereberry said, "we didn't mean to trick you. We just wanted to know a simple direction."

"Oh, sure," the rabbit said, unconvinced, "like I don't know how this goes."

"I will regret asking this, but how what goes?" Ra asked. The unconscious wince that creased his bandaged face started with the first word he spoke and settled into place as he continued.

"I just want to find the basket. It's in a glade," the rabbit explained, "but you want to get it first, maybe to move it, maybe to have it yourself. I don't know yet, but why do you have to do that?"

"We're not—" T.C. tried to cut in, but the rabbit overran him.

"I know I'll never get it. I know that, and I don't want to look for it, I just can't help it. I have to. I can't stop looking. So why do you have to ruin it for me? Why, you guys? I don't even know you!"

"We met once," Wereberry said, sighing as the rabbit just continued on.

"I want to stop! I do!" His speech got faster and more excited with each sentence until it was almost a blur of sound. "It's this thing inside me, I have to get that basket! I know I won't, ok? I know it! But what would you do? Huh? No better than me, I bet! You wouldn't have it either! Well one day I'll get it! It'll happen! It will!" And with that the rabbit started to hop off.

"Wait!" Ra yelled, his voice deep and commanding. "All we want to know is where to find the Jug man. You know him?"

"Left!" the rabbit yelled over his shoulder as he took off down the trail. "Left left left! Left!"

"So he's left?" T.C. asked, looking into a glade. "Through a glade and then?"

"Left! I said go left! Just go left and keep going left! Left!" the rabbit's voice came back at them as he ran down the trail.

"You," Ra said to Wereberry, "have some strange friends."

"Yeah I do, but if you mean him," Were' said with a laugh, "I only met him once and he doesn't even remember me."

The three friends dutifully turned left off the trail and started to walk through one of the countless glades. They passed the obligatory rock and kept going past it. The forest claimed them and it was only when they were deeply mired in thick trees that they each, separately, wondered which left the rabbit had meant. It changed depending on which way you stood on the trail, after all. But they each figured the other two had it worked out, so each of them kept quiet.

The path grew harder and harder to navigate. Trees blocked every straight line they tried to walk. They found themselves picking singular paths through the forest, meeting up as best they could and trying to keep an eye on each other.

The sun started to go down and late afternoon took over. None of their internal clocks were set to the rise and fall of the sun, though their day had already been full of so many different settings of sunlight that it wouldn't have mattered either way. Except that in the darkening air, it was slightly harder to see that the ground cover was changing.

It happened slowly at first, with creepers and above-ground tree roots and the like. Then the trees started to thin out, both in number and in bulk per trunk. They were grateful for the change. Stepping lightly through the increasingly wild undergrowth had slowed them to a crawl, but with the extra space they were gaining they could move more easily, and together.

The grass started seeming taller while they walked. Soon each blade came up to their knees, and then their hips. Were' noticed that the blades weren't just growing tall; they seemed to have the same structure as they would if they were normal-sized, only bigger. Which made no sense, but he couldn't find a better way to explain it.

T.C. had a moment where he thought he might be shrinking. Maybe they all were, he thought, as he noticed that the grass was gaining on them steadily. The trees, too, were higher.

For his part, Choco-Ra just found himself feeling something he was unaccustomed to: small. It wasn't just that he was used to being tall, Ra knew; the experience was sapping something inside him. His position, his time, had lent itself to feeling big, no matter what was around him. But this, this made him feel small physically and mentally.

The land opened up around them, but they couldn't see it very well. The grass was up over their heads. They walked together, inching, finding their way. A large tree loomed ahead of them, and T.C., who was currently in the lead of the three, headed for it.

They reached it and, close up, the bark was deeply gnarled and laden with grave indentations. They each realized that all bark looked like this if you were as small in relation to it as they now were.

"We'll see better from the top," T.C. said, and he put out a webbed hand, hauling himself up.

The others nodded. Ra went next, bandaged fingers having a harder time finding secure purchase.

"Wait," Wereberry said, "let me go first. I can get the best grip in this. In fact, do we have something like a rope?"

"Nope," Ra said, lowering himself to the ground once more.

"All I have is a net," T.C. said.

"We can unstring it and use that. If we tie rope around ourselves we can climb, and if one of you slips I can hold on the best," Were' said, hand already out for the promised net.

T.C. handed over the net and Wereberry started to quickly dismantle it, undoing knots carefully with the tips of his claws and tugging at each length he freed. He coiled the rope as he went and soon had a thick coil around his shoulder, settling into his pink fur.

Each of them tied a harness around their bodies and tugged on the ends to ensure some level of safety. Wereberry didn't tell them that he could only really hope to support the weight of both of the others if they fell. There was no use he could see in worrying them.

Wereberry climbed up first, until the cord tugged sharply against T.C., who looked up.

"Come on!" Were' called back.

"Don't outpace us or you'll pull us free," T.C. yelled back, and he started to climb. The rough bark slid against his webbing and itched. A few handholds later and the webbing on both his hands and feet was sore. He hoped it wouldn't tear before they got to where they were going.

Ra struggled to keep up when it his turn came to start climbing. His hands and feet kept slipping slightly, but never all at once. They climbed further up. Ten feet. Then twenty. Up thirty and forty feet into the air, the tree standing tall above them, looking too thin to support its own weight but not even swaying the tiniest bit.

Choco-Ra's right hand grabbed for a piece of outcropping bark. His fingers curled tightly around it and he let go with his left hand. His right started to slip, and even as he reached for the tree with his left he could feel himself fall free of the tree trunk.

His weight hit T.C. with a jerk, tearing him away from the trunk as well. They both swung free, hitting the trunk but bouncing off of it before either could grab a new handhold.

Wereberry felt the sharp tug from below and didn't bother to look down to see what had happened. He simply dug in with both hands and feet as hard as possible. The bark shredded under his claws so he dug in fiercer, scoring the wood of the tree itself. He held fast and spared a glance down.

T.C.'s left hand bled slightly, the webbing torn. He grabbed the trunk on the next swing as tightly as he could but the slick blood along his palm made the surface too hard to hold tightly, and he swung free again.

"I can't get a good—" T.C. called out.

"Me either!" shouted Ra.

"Both of you just try to stop swinging so much," Were' pleaded. "I'll see if I can drag us up some."

Ra didn't see how that would help, but T.C. did. He had done a bunch of climbing, though nothing quite like this, and knew that if Wereberry could drag them up at all, they would come to rest against the tree again.

Wereberry pulled a hand free and reached up a few inches. The claws still anchoring him felt like they were running the risk of tearing free from his hand. He bit back the pain and pushed harder. His free hand dug in securely. Were' repeated the process with his other hand and they all rose a few inches.

The rope slowly stopped swinging and the tree came within arm's reach for both Choco-Ra and T.C. Both of them grabbed on as tightly as they could manage.

"There's a branch not far above me. Let's get to it and rest there a while," Wereberry said, starting to climb again. He didn't wait for an answer. Once the others felt him begin to climb they didn't bother to answer, either.

They reached the branch without incident. Wereberry sat on it, straddling it between his legs, and helped haul the other two up to join him. The tree suddenly shook. All three friends grabbed at the branch they sat upon. Their hands and legs clutched tight as the branch shook again.

Except it was obviously not just the tree that shook. The world, it looked like, shook every few seconds, a thunderous shake that rattled everything they could see. A noise preceded it. A soft noise, but booming in the bass. Each hit was followed by another tremor. T.C. looked behind them and yelped.

"Giant!" he whispered, not daring to nudge Ra or Were'.

Both of them turned as well and saw him. He stood at least sixty feet tall and had skin as brown as a tree. He looked nothing like a tree, however, if you discounted the relative sizes involved. His brown skin was smooth, almost shining, and around his body he wore a tunic made of bright yellow and red leaves, the colors of autumn.

Uncannily, the giant spotted the trio on the branch and he laughed mightily, "Ha! Ha! Ha! Gigantic!" The raw power of his voice was almost enough to send them spiraling off their branch.

7 • Large and in Charge

"AT LEAST MY HEADACHE FADED," Wereberry said as the giant clomped closer to them. He covered the distance to the tree quickly, huge strides swallowed up by his extraordinary legs.

"Small favors, and all that," T.C. said.

"Has anyone ever even heard of a giant around here?" Ra asked.

None of them had. None of them particularly wanted to, either. Nor were they excited to have heard of one now. The giant stood in front of them, peering down at their branch retreat.

"Now where do you small ones come from?" he asked, voice booming. Wereberry dug his claws in. T.C. wrapped tighter around the branch and Ra followed suit.

"Could you please," Wereberry asked, "turn down the volume before you kill us?" He tried his best to sound calm.

"Ha! Ha! Ha! Gigantic!" the giant said, lowering his voice some. "You don't belong here. I know everything that belongs here and you aren't on that list. You'll come with me."

"We're fine where we are," Ra said, fearlessly.

"You don't belong, so you must come with me," the giant repeated. He reached a hand out and scooped them up, tangling them up in the rope that linked them all together. "You are three but bound together? Why are you bound? Criminals?"

"No, we had to climb the tree–" Were' started to explain.

"Criminals! Now I know you have to come with me." The giant walked away from the tree, the three friends in his hand. The land sped by quickly under them. A few times the giant passed by a tree close enough that those in his hand worried he might smash them into it by accident. Or on purpose, they couldn't be sure which it would be.

After about twenty minutes of jostling, swinging, swaying, and high-speed relative movement, the giant set them down in a clearing. The dirt underneath them seemed more wonderful than anything ever had. They quickly undid the rope that bound them together. T.C. shoved it into his bag while all three of them looked around.

"Now you'll go to jail until I can find out where you escaped from, criminals!" boomed the giant.

"We'd rather not," Ra said shakily.

Wereberry sat on the ground, recovering his balance. T.C. stood near him, willing the world to stop spinning. Choco-Ra stood proudly, his equilibrium recovered. He was sick of being pushed around. In his own lands he was the supreme ruler, and he wasn't good at taking orders from someone else.

"I didn't give you a choice," the giant pointed out.

"He's right," Were' said, standing.

"I don't recognize his authority," Ra said testily.

"I recognize his size, Ra," T.C. said, "and his size tells me he'll pretty much put us where he wants. For now, all right?"

"For now," Ra agreed.

"Ha! Ha! Ha! Gigantic! You will stay until I decide you can go free," the giant thundered. "You don't dare escape!"

"Of course not," Were' said, "we wouldn't dream of it. Ignore these two. We won't escape."

The giant nodded and knelt down in front of them. He pointed to his left. A small box sat there. Small by the giant's standards, but fully big enough to comfortably seat five. The walls were metal bars as was the only door, which sat open.

"Get in," the giant commanded.

Wereberry shrugged and walked into the cage, followed by Ra and T.C. The giant closed the door behind them, pushing it with his index finger. Once it was closed he grabbed the edge of the door and the nearest bit of cell bar between his thumb and forefinger and twisted. The metal bent easily, sealing the door firmly.

"That's why we went along with him," Were' said, nodding at the twisted metal.

"You can't escape," the giant said, standing. "I will be back soon to tell you what I've found of your plans, criminals." He strode away, thundering footsteps receding quickly into the distance.

"All right, he's gone," Were' said turning to Ra, "what's the escape plan?"

Choco-Ra laughed softly, "Easy. These bars are too small to let us slide through right now, but any of us could escape this place." He looked at Wereberry, "Given about, what, a day? You could slip through quick enough. And you," he smiled at T.C., "could probably wedge yourself between two bars and exert enough steady pressure to bend them wide enough to get through."

"Sure," T.C. agreed, "but?"

"But I can get through now," Ra said, and he walked over to the bars. Sucking in a deep breath, his bandages tightened around him, decreasing his size incredibly. Half his original width, Ra slipped sideways through the bars with ease. Once on the other side he let go of the breath he had held and his bandages loosened again, returning him to his original size.

"Nice trick, Ra. Very nicely done," Were' said. "Now what about us?"

"Now we work together. T.C., wedge yourself between two bars. Were', grab a bar on one side of him, I'll get the other."

They did as he asked and once in place, Were' and Ra pulled while T.C. pushed as hard as possible. The bars he was wedged between groaned briefly and then bent wide. T.C. dropped to the ground and walked clear of the cell. Wereberry followed behind him quickly.

"So why did you have to be outside the cell when we did

that?" Were' asked Ra.

"I didn't."

"Then..."

"To see your face," Ra said, looking around them to see what he could see.

"Oh, priceless. Next time more escaping, less showing off, ok?" Wereberry asked, feigning annoyance.

"Deal," Ra said over his shoulder. "Now, all we have to do is make a break for it."

"Wrong," Were' said, "this place is obviously too big for that. We'll need to find some landmarks and a place to hide. We hide out when he comes looking for us. Then when he moves on, we advance and hide again. If we stage our escape, we can increase our chances of making it."

"I like it," admitted Ra. "T.C.?"

"It makes sense, but I can hide out in the tall grass better than you two, so I'll scout when we have to switch locations, all right?"

"Good," Were' said, loping ahead some. "I can smell water this way, probably a good bet that's where we should go."

"I smell it too," T.C. said, "let's go."

The water was close by, and sure enough there were huge patches of grass near it. There were also gigantic pea pods sprouting up from the ground. Some of the pods were empty, having opened early, while others sat plump and ripe.

"Are you thinking what I am?" asked Wereberry. His companions nodded. Were' and Choco-Ra slipped into a pod each, pulling them closed once inside. T.C. sealed them with a bit of mud from the bank of the wide lake they were near. Soon the pods looked just as ripe as the ones near them.

That done, T.C. slid into the lake. He was glad for the chance to sit in water again, and sank to the bottom gratefully. The lake bed was muddy and chilled, just the way T.C. liked it. He sucked in a huge amount of water, pushing it back out through his gills, refreshed. Lying on the bottom, he watched the sky and listened to vibrations, waiting.

Wereberry slowed his breathing as much as possible. He wasn't a fan of tight places, but he wouldn't admit he was afraid of them, either. It wasn't terrible, he reminded himself a few times. Just dark, and close, and stuffy. Anyone can survive dark and close and stuffy. Ra probably felt the same way. At least T.C. was in his element. Still, Were' told himself, they wouldn't be here long and he would be fine. Ra, he knew, had to be just as annoyed as he was about the situation. Just ready to burst free and leap out of there to find a much better, and roomier, hiding place.

Inside his pod, Choco-Ra leaned and listened. The damn darkness reminded him of his sarcophagus. Sound muffled and light cut off, he felt almost at home. A sudden tiredness hit him like a hammer. He fought to stay awake, but quickly lost track of time. An hour went by, or a minute, or some combination thereof, and Choco-Ra fell into a deep slumber.

Time passed. T.C. sensed nothing much at all. A few fish swam around him, curious, but otherwise the day was the day. So he sat and waited, almost aching to swim around the lake. He didn't. He felt that the bubbles and eddies stirred up would deviate too far from the entire plan of hiding.

So instead he lay on his back and watched the sky through the depth of the water. His gills flexed dreamily. He packed his torn webbing in some cool mud and settled down for as long a wait as necessary. He assumed the others were doing the same, just biding their time and getting comfortable.

At least, he thought, no one was currently chasing them, yelling at them, or running around them, much less exploding. A baseline had been established for T.C., and he was more than happy to be above it for a while. This trip had only started, he knew, but he missed sitting and relaxing all day. So while he could, and without forgetting that he was supposed to be paying close attention, he relaxed as much as possible.

T.C. stretched his limbs, arching his back and feeling the

tug of each muscle along his bones. It felt good. He flexed his hands and feet and watched the sky. Soon, he planned on surfacing. As little as possible so he wouldn't be seen, but he had to taste air to get a good gauge of its currents and to find out if the giant was after them yet.

Something broke the surface of the water before T.C. could start to get up. T.C. blinked and tried to burrow under the mud without actually moving. He tried willing himself deeper, which worked about as well as he thought it would: not at all.

The figure that dove into the lake swam down, exploring but, T.C. judged, not coming right for him. It was a person, that much was clear. He seemed to be a smaller version of the giant, with the same brown skin that almost shined and tunic of autumn leaves wrapped around his body. Except this guy was the same size as Choco-Ra, only slightly taller than T.C.

T.C. stayed as still as possible while the intruder, who probably had more claim to the lake than T.C. did, floated by above him. He was obviously playing, free-swimming and diving and soaring under the water. T.C. ached to join him, but it didn't make sense to join an unknown for a playful romp when you were already being hunted.

The figure swam closer. T.C. tensed. He was seen. He knew it a second before it happened and could do nothing. The figure saw him and raced back up for the surface in alarm. T.C. saw no choice but to follow.

He beat the stranger to the surface, leaping straight out of the water and landing on the muddy bank of the lake. When the brown man surfaced, he saw T.C. and froze where he was. Looking back into the water, he couldn't make up his mind— either there were two bluish mermen, or one very fast one. He decided that a merman could easily outswim him, so it must be only one. Two would be an invasion, and coming down on the side of no invasion certainly helped his choice.

"Uhhh, hi?" T.C. ventured, smiling.

"Who are you? Where are you from? Why are you here?" the smaller brown man—no, brown boy, T.C. realized—asked nervously, spitting out the questions rapid fire.

"You can call me T.C. As for what I'm doing here," T.C. waved his hands around some, searching for the right phrasing, "that giant, he captured me and I escaped. He thought I was a criminal but I was just passing through."

"Alone? Why?" the youth demanded.

"I just have to get to the other side of this land, that's all. Appointments to keep. Alone." T.C. didn't want the boy to know about his friends. If he was recaptured, at least Ra and Were' might get a decent-sized getaway window in the confusion.

The boy circled T.C. carefully, looking him over from every angle. T.C. stood still, glad he had come up on a side of the lake away from the pea pods where Ra and Were' were hidden. The boy continued his examination, keeping a distance.

"I should call Gigantic," the boy said.

T.C. felt a chill run down his spine. "You don't have to do that. Look, just walk away and I can be on my way and he never has to know."

"No, he'd be pretty mad at me for that," the youth said.

"What's your name, kid?" T.C. asked. Maybe, he reasoned, the kid needs a friend his own size. If I could get on his good side, T.C. thought, maybe he'll change his mind and take a risk.

"I'm Growth," the boy said, holding out his hand before realizing that might be a bad idea and dropping it back to his side quickly. "I'm Gigantic's partner."

"His partner? Not his son?" T.C. asked.

"Naw, he's raised me since I was really tiny though. I'll grow up to be as big as he is, someday, I'm sure!"

"I bet you will," T.C. agreed. "So Growth, why does Gigantic think that anyone who comes through here is a criminal? I mean, he didn't even give me a chance to explain."

"He worries about the crops a lot. But you're really just passing through?"

"I am." T.C. worried. If he admitted he had two friends with him now, then the kid wouldn't trust him. But if he didn't and was forced to leave them behind, he wasn't sure what he would do.

"Well, I can talk to him if you want, I mean if you really are just passing through alone and all," Growth said warily.

"I... look, about that alone part," T.C. started, feeling sunk either way, "I'm not quite alone."

"But you said—" Growth's face fell as he spoke.

"I know. But I had to protect them, you see? We aren't criminals at all," T.C. said, his eyes full of pleading for understanding. "We're just passing through. But I had to protect them. Now I trust you, though."

"You do?"

T.C. nodded. "You seem like a stand-up kind of guy. I think you'll do the right thing."

"What if that's turning you over to Gigantic?"

"I believe that you'll do the right thing, and that turning us in to be locked up isn't it."

"Where are they, then? Show them to me." Growth stood taller, crossing his arms over his chest. His face betrayed him, showing that he still wanted to trust T.C. and to help. At least, T.C. hoped so.

"All right," T.C. said, "they're on the other side of the lake. Want to just swim across?"

Growth nodded toward the water and T.C. jumped in, swimming slowly enough for Growth to easily pace him. They got to the other side and T.C. climbed out of the water first. He stood and waited for Growth, watching him, making every inch of his body posture submissive.

The pea pods sat lumpily, exactly as they were when T.C. had left them. He pried open Were's first. The werewolf fell right on T.C., unprepared for the change in pod status. Wereberry saw Growth and bristled, eyeing T.C.

"It's all right, I'll get Ra, you just make friends," T.C. said, already moving.

Wereberry eyed Growth and held a hand out to him. Growth took a step back, growing nervous. When the merman said he had friends, Growth naturally had expected others of the same kind. A werewolf wasn't something he had planned for, mentally. Even less planned was the sight of a mummy waking up from a nap. Ra stretched and blinked a few times, red eyes dimming and relighting as he did.

T.C. hurried back over to Growth after noticing the look in his eyes. "It's all right, Growth, these are my friends. Like I told you."

Growth nodded but kept his distance from the two recently emerged. Ra and Were' looked at each other, having no clue what the game plan was. Neither of them was particularly used to being out of the loop on a plan, seeing as how one of them always made the plans in the first place.

"Why don't you go explain to Gigantic—" T.C. began.

"The giant's name is really Gigantic?" Ra asked.

"Yeah," T.C. said over his shoulder, "and this is his partner, Growth. Growth, why don't you go explain the situation to Gigantic? He'll listen to you and we can be on our way."

Growth nodded again but didn't take a step toward moving. Wereberry smiled at him. Ra nodded and raised a hand in welcome. Growth nervously retreated to go find his large partner.

"T.C., what the hell is going on?" Ra demanded as soon as Growth was gone.

"You two weren't around, so I solved this, I think. I ran into Growth and he's sure this is all fixable. I trust him, mostly."

"Mostly?" Wereberry asked, skeptical.

"Hey, I did the best I could."

Ra moved forward, clapping his damp friend on the

shoulder warmly. "I'm sure it'll work out, T.C. It isn't like you're dumb, and why couldn't you solve this by yourself, huh?"

"Yeah," Were' added, "this one was yours, and you found an answer. Don't let us rattle you, we're just control freaks sometimes."

"Don't lump me in with you," Ra said with a grin.

T.C. started to laugh, glad things were back to normal, when the ground shook. It shook again and again, in huge, striding intervals.

"Guess we'll find out how good I was," T.C. said. His friends nodded as if they didn't have a doubt in their minds.

"Ha! Ha! Ha! Gigantic!" boomed the giant as he came into view. Growth ran along next to him to keep up.

"See, these are them," Growth said, "they really aren't criminals, I checked."

Ra wondered when they had been checked, but seeing the kid flash a slightly nervous smile toward T.C. explained it. Looks like The Creature was right after all. Good.

"Then why are you here?" Gigantic asked, standing over them. He loomed tall amongst the large pods.

"Passing through," Were' said.

"You said you wouldn't escape," the giant lamented.

"Well, about that," Ra started, only to be cut off by T.C.

"But we weren't criminals and Growth believed us, so we really did the right thing."

"I suppose," the giant said.

Growth, meanwhile, had moved closer to T.C. He smiled warmly, fighting down his own nerves, and whispered, "He hasn't been acting quite right recently. I'm not sure what's going on, but things have been changing."

T.C. gave Growth the smallest of nods. "Tell me about it," he whispered back, "and hey, thanks."

"Where are you headed to?" Gigantic asked them, finding some ease at seeing his young charge be friendly toward the strangers. Maybe he had been wrong about locking them up so quickly.

"The Jug man, really," T.C. said before Ra could give a far more evasive answer.

"That's far," Gigantic told them, voice lowering some, "I will get you there faster than walking! Ha! Ha! Ha! Gigantic!"

"No, that's fine," Were' said, "we'll walk."

"I insist!" boomed the giant. He didn't want these probably-not-criminals around for too long; they might turn out to be bad influences, even if Growth did trust them. One never knew, after all.

The giant reached down and scooped up the three friends in one hand, grabbing Growth in the other. He was careful not to squeeze. Walking across the lands, booming and rattling everything as he went, Gigantic carried them all back to what had to be his own house.

Around the back of his house he set them down. There, on a wide dirt circle, was a ball. It was broken in half and they could see heavy padding in each half.

"No way," Ra said, getting a bad feeling about where this was going.

"It's safe," Gigantic insisted, "sometimes Growth goes for rides in it. I'll toss you clear to the Jug man's home."

"Nope," Ra repeated, "I am not getting thrown to my doom in a big ball. No."

"Ra, he says it's safe," T.C. offered.

"It is," Growth said, smiling, "I've ridden in it a lot of times. You just lash yourself to the inside and wait for the thump."

"The thump?" Wereberry asked.

"It means you've landed," Growth said.

"Oh, that thump," Were' said softly.

"Not happening," Ra said again.

But Gigantic wasn't listening, or perhaps just didn't care if they wanted to go or not. It was safe enough and would get them far away. That was a good enough solution for him. Scooping them up swiftly, he placed T.C. in one half of the ball and settled the other two friends in the other half.

Inside, thick vines were secured to the deep padding. Quickly, not liking this one bit, Choco-Ra and Wereberry tied themselves firmly in place. T.C. did the same in his half. Gigantic picked up both halves of the ball and pushed them together. Before blackness enveloped them they caught a glimpse of each other, all strapped in and looking like they weren't getting back out. Ever.

Ra's eyes lit up brighter, the glow giving them some light to see by.

"So what do you think?" Were' asked Ra.

"Little to no chance of survival."

"But Growth said—" T.C. started

"He said it was fine for him. How strong is he? How hard to hurt? I have no clue, do you?" Ra asked, growing angry. "None of us do. We have no clue what will happen here. It might work, sure. It probably won't."

"Oh, Ra, you worry too much," Wereberry said, trying to sound nonchalant and light, "I'm sure we'll be—"

His last coherent word was cut off as Gigantic threw the ball as hard as he could. It arced up and away, trailing behind it the fading remains of three hearty screams.

8 • Poking Holes in a Concept

AFTER A WHILE THERE WAS A BIG THUMP. Dirt rose in plumes against a reddening sky. The ball rolled to a stop, resting against a brick wall. Light winds plucked at the dust and grit in the air, giving it a good spin. As the effects of the landing settled, the ball split open. Each half fell over, rocking back and forth gently. T.C. stumbled out of his half, falling to the ground hard. He coughed and sputtered in the dust. Choco-Ra and Wereberry appeared over the edge of their half of the ball. Wereberry climbed down, and almost made it before he, too, stumbled. He sat down heavily, wincing at the treatment to his short tail. Ra dropped lightly to the ground and stood, watching his friends.

"How is it you never lose your balance?" Were' asked, sounding offended.

"No inner ear, I guess, or something," Ra said with a shrug. He offered T.C. a hand up and then helped Wereberry.

"Whatever," Wereberry said, recovering quickly, "are we where we want to be?"

"No clue," T.C. said, looking around.

"I've never been here before, but I've never been to where we're going, either, so that's no help," Choco-Ra said.

The three travelers looked around, trying to get their bearings. They had rolled to a stop by a brick wall. The edges of the wall were ragged, either unfinished or only partly demolished. They couldn't tell which at first. Their scans of the area gave them a bigger clue.

There were broken and smashed walls of all sorts as far as the eye could see. There was space between them—often a good amount of it—but walls dominated the landscape.

Every white fence they saw had a wall of some sort nearby. Sometimes there were two or three walls joined, making an almost box. Some of those even had partial roofing. None of them were finished houses, though. And they all had large, gaping holes in the walls.

"What is this, a war zone?" T.C. asked.

"Too quiet for that," Ra answered quickly, "but I'd be willing to bet we're in the right place."

The other two nodded and the trio spread out, looking for signs of life, or of anything other than odd destruction. At first they found nothing. Brick dust and plaster debris draped the grass and dirt. Everything was simple and barren, as if whoever lived here had just up and left.

Wandering farther and farther from where they landed, though, the three started to hear some signs of life. Laughter first, then what sounded like skin on skin. Wereberry took the lead, with Ra and T.C. right behind him, heading off to the source of the noise.

Two people stood near a wall, under the shade of a tree, laughing and high-fiving each other. Were' could hear that they were congratulating each other over something. As they came within easy distance, Wereberry raised a hand in greeting.

"Hey there," he said, still moving, "Jug man?"

Both of the people turned to look at him. One of them was made out of glass, and filled with green liquid up to his spout. Arms and legs sprouted from the sides and bottom of his glass body. His wide and strangely non-descript face smiled. The person next to him was much smaller. He sported a slick suit and tie, dark sunglasses, and patent leather shoes, and overall looked like a jazz musician. He didn't wave, or even smile. He just looked toward the incoming strangers, expressionless and uncaring.

"Yeah, I'm Jug, Cool Man Jug," the glass, pitcher-shaped man said, still smiling, "What'chu want?"

"Hey, man," his shorter friend said, "weren't we busy?

Do we gotta deal with these folk? Who are they? Friends of yours?"

"Never met 'em," Jug said, "but they could still be friends."

"Yeah, we're friends," T.C. said, "and we were hoping you could help us out."

"Hey, the Jug likes helping people out. What'chu need?"

"A friend of ours passed through here, we think, a while back and—" Ra started.

"Nope," Jug said simply.

"No? But we're sure she came by and—" Wereberry tried.

"The man said no," Cool Man Jug's friend said. "Why would you make him repeat it?"

"Sorry," Ra said to the shorter man, "I didn't catch your name."

The trio moved closer to the two friends. The tree's shade hung over all five of them. T.C. took a small breath of relief; the rest of the land was too hot for him to really enjoy, but the shade cut things a bit. Enough.

"And we didn't catch yours. But fair, sure, I'm Smooth Wallop," he said, nodding.

"I'm T.C., this is Choco-Ra, and this here is Wereberry. We're looking for a friend of ours. Female, pink, kind of wispy at times?"

"No one's passed through here except me and Cool for ages. Sorry," Smooth said.

"She was looking for a way out of this world. She said she was coming to see you," Were' insisted.

"Then she didn't get here," Smooth said. "No one has."

"That damned bee did," Cool Man Jug said. "Remember? The bee came over here a while ago."

"That bee better not come back, either," Smooth said, frowning, "but they ain't talking about a bee. They're talking about a girl." He shook his head, lost in memory for a second. He really despised that little bee, coming all the way to them and demanding they help him break into some honeycomb hive that he had locked behind him. When they had tried to explain that they would just shatter it completely, even if they tried to be careful, the bee had flown off pissed.

"Yeah, I didn't see a girl," Jug said, racking his memory just in case.

"Me either. Sorry guys, we didn't see a girl."

"Maybe you forgot," Wereberry tried, "Listen, we know—well we're pretty sure—she came here. She said she would and we haven't seen her, so—"

"So you tried the whole rest of the world?" Cool Man Jug asked.

"What? No," Wereberry said.

"Then maybe she's somewhere else," Jug offered.

"He could be right," T.C. said softly.

"He isn't!" raged Were'. "She came here and got help and I want to know what happened. Now tell me, or—"

"Or what?"

"Or I'll break that glass jug you seem to be made out of." Wereberry tensed, his fur starting to stand on end. His claws seemed to shine in the light and he hunched his shoulders in.

"This isn't helping, Were'," Ra said.

"Neither is them denying it," Wereberry said, a snarl starting at the corners of his muzzle. He didn't want to fight but he found that he was completely overcome by frustration. He had to find her. He was positive that they could help and had helped her in the past. Wereberry tried to calm down but found himself fighting a slowly losing battle.

"All right, hey I don't want no fight," Jug said, frowning.

"Not like they'd win," Smooth added.

"Not the point, Smooth. Listen guys, I would tell you if I knew, I promise. But I haven't seen a girl and I have no clue what you want from me."

"Were', I think he's telling the truth," T.C. said, reaching a hand up to rest gently on Wereberry's shoulder.

The werewolf spun on his heel to face his friends. "Don't you get it?" he asked, "We forgot her for who knows how long. Maybe they did, too. She came here. They helped."

He couldn't believe this. Was everyone else mad? Couldn't they feel it? Didn't they just know that this was the answer, and that they had to get help, even if it meant forcing it? He tried to remind himself that this wasn't like him, that he didn't have this bad of a temper. Except, he realized, apparently he did if he was pushed hard enough.

"How do you know?" Ra asked. He didn't want to try to stop Wereberry if he attacked, but knew he would have to intervene somehow if push literally came to shove.

"I just do. Think deep in yourself, don't you know it, too?"

T.C. frowned and concentrated on what scraps of memory he had of Cherrygiest. Choco-Ra did the same, giving his friend every benefit of the doubt he could possibly extend.

Both of them looked up at the same time, blinking hard.

"She did," T.C. said.

"She was here," Ra echoed.

"And how do you know?" Were' asked, satisfied.

"I don't know. I just know that she meant to and that somehow she did," Ra said.

"I can't prove it, but I know it," T.C. said.

"I still don't remember this," Cool Man Jug said, "so I don't know how I can be a help."

"Yeah, come on, we were having a contest here," Smooth said, "before you showed up and started threatening us."

"Sorry about that," Were' said, shrugging.

"Yeah, look, we just need to get out of this world," Ra said, feeling foolish. What was outside of the world? Where did it go and how did one get there? He had no clue, but he was determined to just charge forward until he found answers.

"How?" Smooth asked, "I mean what does that even mean?"

"Well," Were' said, "you guys like to hit things, I'm guessing?"

The two laughed and high-fived. They nodded and Cool Man Jug winked at Wereberry, stepping up to the wall next to them. He pulled his arm back and smashed a fist through, screaming "Cool!" as he did.

"Hey, no fair," Smooth protested, "we hadn't started the competition yet!"

"I was just showing them," Jug said with a grin.

"Humph," Smooth offered, stepping up to the wall. With an incredibly loud WALLOP he slammed his hand through the wall, leaving a slightly smaller hole behind.

"Smaller," Cool Man Jug said.

"Prettier," countered Smooth. "See how well-formed and perfectly round mine is?"

"Are we going for size or form?" Jug asked.

"Whichever, I guess," Smooth replied.

Ra, Wereberry, and T.C. watched with a mixture of amusement and admiration. Wereberry felt a tinge of relief that he hadn't started a fight. Either of them could have put a fist right through him. He'd look mighty strange with an arm through his chest, he thought, never mind the problem of staying alive.

"Maybe that's it," Ra said. "Maybe that's it exactly."

"Punching holes in walls?" Cool Man Jug asked. He liked putting holes in walls. If that was all it took to make these three strangers go away then he would happily do it. Hell, he'd do it even if they weren't there.

"Except not in walls," Ra said. His eyes grew brighter as he spoke. "What if you put a hole in the world?"

"A hole in the world? How would that even work, man?" Smooth asked. He wasn't against the idea—in fact, he kind of liked it. He just didn't know how to.

"Maybe if you both punched at the same time—" Ra started to say.

"But hit the air, instead!" Wereberry broke in, excitedly. "Then you could push through whatever the world is and break a hole in it!"

"Wouldn't that just push air around?" T.C. asked. Smooth and Cool nodded in unison.

"Maybe," Ra admitted, "but then again, if they concentrated really hard and focused on breaking through to... whatever is on the other side of this... then maybe it would work."

"It's like the ultimate wall," Cool Man Jug said to Smooth. "Wanna try it?"

"Why not," Smooth said. "We'll punch the air and then we'll be done with this."

"No, you have to really think you're going to do it," Were' said.

"Okay then," Smooth said, shrugging, "we'll punch a hole in whatever it is that's here."

The two stood side by side, facing nothing but empty air. They took a few practice swings, counting so they could time their dual punch exactly. Taking a deep breath, they cocked their arms and let fly.

WALLOP!

"Cool!"

The air shuddered, visibly. Then it bent, and the empty space they were looking at seemed to break. It left a ragged white hole just hanging there above the field. All five of the gathered witnesses gasped. The hole closed in on itself quickly, making an audible pop as it finished snapping shut.

"That would be it," Wereberry said, his tone almost reverent.

"Are we sure this is right?" T.C. asked.

"You know it is," Ra answered without sparing a glance toward his friend.

Cool Man Jug and Smooth Wallop stood back, looked at each other, and laughed long and hard. They high-fived numerous times and Smooth even did a little dance. That had to be the best punch anyone had ever delivered. It also, Smooth realized deep down, felt familiar. Maybe these guys were right and this had been done before, but it made no sense. With a dismissal that seemed urgent and easy, Smooth shoved the thought away.

"Can you do it again? Maybe a bit larger?" Were' asked.

"I guess we can, but it doesn't feel right to do," Cool said. The same odd feeling nagged at him. Something was fundamentally wrong with what they had accomplished, and they both wanted to forget that it had ever happened, to say nothing of the chance that it had happened before, only to be forgotten.

"Please?" T.C. asked. "We'll be ready this time. Just open that hole again and we'll go through and you're rid of us."

"I guess we can," Cool Man Jug said. He didn't want to, but since they had already done it once, what could twice hurt?

"Wait, before you do," Ra said quickly, turning to face his friends, "are we sure about this? Really sure?"

"We have to find her," Were' said.

"We've come this far, I guess," T.C. said.

Ra sighed and shook his head. "This isn't another ride in a stupid ball. We don't know what this is or where it goes or if it's even right."

"You know it's right," Were' insisted.

"No, I know it feels like it's right but that I have no proof. That isn't the same. I want to find her as well, Were', but we can't be utterly stupid about it."

"We're not," Wereberry said.

"Look, if we go through, what happens?" T.C. asked.

"We don't know," admitted Were'.

Ra nodded. That was the crux of it. He was willing to go to the ends of the world for this, no problem. He thought he was willing to go further, but this might not be that. Risking everything on a chance that felt right but seemed wrong just added up to foolishness for him. But it felt so right.

Wereberry had no qualms. Yes, they could die doing this. Sure, they might regret it, and this might not even be the right move, and who knew where they could end up. But it felt right, deep in his core. That was good enough.

T.C. counted the ways their next planned move could be right or wrong. Wrong kept coming up the winner, but the arguments for it being right were more compelling. He was adrift in a sea of choice and chance. It wasn't how he liked the world to be ordered.

"Do it," Were' said, seeing the faces of his friends. He knew they wanted to say yes along with him but just hadn't caught up to doing it yet.

Smooth and Cool nodded and drew deep breaths. They took some practice swings and counted down. Ra looked at Were' and shook his head.

"You better be right about this," he said.

"You know I am," Were' said.

"I hope you are. I think you are," T.C. said, "but I don't know it."

"It'll do," Were' said gently. "Now prepare to jump."

After a few extra practice swings, Smooth and Cool gave a final count. Their arms swung forward in perfect unison.

WALLOP!

"Cool!"

Empty space broke again, slightly bigger this time. It was hard to look directly into, seeming to not be there even while it was. Their eyes, all five pairs, tried to slide off the hole, looking around it.

Wereberry took a deep breath and leapt headfirst into the space that could only be described as having no space. T.C. followed quickly, gritting his teeth. Choco-Ra dove in last, eyes shining as bright as possible against the enveloping whiteness.

The three vanished from the world. The hole sealed behind

them with a sharp pop. Smooth Wallop and Cool Man Jug quickly forgot they had ever even tried to punch through the world. They went back to their contest, all memories of the encounter vanishing swiftly.

INTERLUDE ONE

THREE FORMS DOTTED an otherwise blank space. The whiteness of it was blinding in more ways than one. There was nothing to focus on, so their eyes searched for anything other than themselves but found nothing. The space also glowed brightly, so even if they could've found something to see, it very well might have been obscured by the light.

Either way, they found themselves blind. They also found themselves floating. There was no up and no down. The void was absolute and in that absoluteness it was also finite. Their minds couldn't keep up.

Wereberry tried to speak but found that no sound came out. Ra floundered where he was, turning endlessly between his friends. Only T.C. found a way to deal. He tried to swim. He found it worked. He didn't know if he was really moving, but it felt like he was. He grabbed for Choco-Ra and Wereberry and had them hold onto his sides.

With his arms and legs free, T.C. swam in a direction he decided was forward. He kicked and pushed against nothing, and then did it harder. Gradually his sense of movement increased.

Ahead of them, for some value of ahead, there was a spot. It looked to Ra like a rainbow gone horribly wrong. To Were' it smelled like grass and trees. To T.C. it was simply where the current was headed. Not that there had been a current until he noticed it.

Regardless, T.C. headed for the spot. As they got closer, the spot grew. Soon it was near enough to touch. So T.C. tried to touch it. He stuck a hand out, seeing if he could move through the spot into whatever was on the other side. His hand met resistance.

He punched at it to no avail. Ra let go and kicked his legs, moving forward to the spot, and tried to punch it himself, meeting the same result as T.C. had. They tried to punch it together, with no result.

Wereberry watched them and let go of T.C. as well, moving up to join them. He noticed the spot had a definite edge. He could grab it and hold on. Bracing himself, he looked at the others and nodded. As one they punched. Their fists bounced off the spot with a shuddering, painful rebound.

They were stuck.

T.C. grabbed hold of the edge of the spot as well and studied it. It seemed rooted in space, relative to them, and was as hard as metal. He kicked it, fruitlessly, more out of frustration than hope of success.

Behind them the whiteness started to dim, and smoky trails started to appear. None of them noticed. The smoke coalesced into the start of objects. The beginning of the thought of a tree here, the slightest notion of a rock there.

Meanwhile, the three friends tried to break through, to escape what they had found themselves in. Finally Wereberry had a foolish thought. He moved around to the spot's other side.

His hand sunk into it easily. Laughing without sound, he waved at the other two furiously until they joined him. He showed them what he had found. They had been hitting the wrong end of the spot. The back of it. Whereas the front, which they now faced, was empty and open.

They had started to go through the hole when Ra noticed what grew around them. Now in front of them, the smoking shapes were quite readily visible. All three friends stopped to stare. Trees came into view. Some rocks were almost completely formed.

Grass and sky had just started to take shape out of the thick, milky smoke. They were, as yet, just guesses toward blue and green, but somehow all three travelers knew what the colors would become.

Ra pointed and started to let go of the spot, the hole. Were' shook his head and tried to tug Ra back. T.C. joined him. Together they caught Choco-Ra's legs and reeled him in.

Wereberry tried to speak, but still no sound came out. He wanted to explain, to shout. He couldn't. Left with no good way of communicating higher ideas, Wereberry found himself just shoving Ra toward the hole.

Ra fought for a while, trying to explore instead of escape. T.C. kept shaking his head, pointing at the hole.

The milky smoke grew thicker. Wereberry considered his options. He couldn't very well leave Ra here. Forcing Ra through the hole wasn't going so well either. And who knew, he thought, how long the hole would even stay open.

They might just be getting lucky, and that had to be taken advantage of. He tugged Ra's leg again. T.C. joined in, tugging the other one. Ra nodded and moved toward the hole with them.

They went through together, finding the hole just wide enough to accept them all side by side. A burst of color, smell, and sound flooded their senses as they entered the hole.

Behind them the milky gray smoke dispersed as slowly as it had formed.

PART TWO
Petty in Pink

"We would often be sorry if our wishes were gratified."

–Aesop

1 • A Landing You Can Walk Away From

SOMEWHERE FAR OVERHEAD, a bird chirped. It was a blue bird, and it sang clear and loud as it flapped through the air. It soared, occasionally watching the land below it. The hard brown perch of a tree branch tempted the bird down from the sky. It landed softly, tucking its wings in close to its body. The bird stepped from side to side a little, finding the perfect spot to watch the world from.

A flash of bright white light appeared out of nowhere, close to the soft green grass on the ground. The bird startled and flapped hard, lifting off. It had time to see three bodies fall out of the white flash of light before it faced the sky and resumed chasing clouds.

Clouds were the first thing Wereberry saw. He lay on his back and watched them drift lazily overhead. Having a world around him was a pleasant change. Wereberry rolled on his side and saw T.C. and Choco-Ra on the ground right next to him. They both seemed just as content to lie still for a moment.

After a time, the three friends stood and looked around them. The world seemed pristine, from the strong trees to the blue sky. It wasn't, obviously, paradise, but it could probably draw you a map and not be far off.

"What the hell were you thinking?" Were' asked Ra, breaking the serene silence.

"What do you mean?" Ra countered.

"Remember that big white... whatever it was that we were just lost in? That? Why were you trying to stay?"

"It was changing around us!" Ra said angrily, "and I wanted to find out what that was about."

"At whatever risk it incurred?" Were' asked.

"Guys, maybe we should fight later," T.C. said, shaking his head.

"No, he wants this out now," Ra said, "let's have it out now. You," Ra jabbed a finger at Wereberry's chest, "want to talk to me about untold risk? After you pushed us into the void in the first place?"

"We agreed to go!" Wereberry protested.

"No, you decided and we, T.C. and I, were on the fence. But you made up our minds for us."

"T.C.?" Ra asked.

"Well I was pretty sure we should go, but I wasn't fully—"

"See? So, sure, I wanted to take a risk. No bigger than the one you already tossed us into."

Wereberry turned and walked away from his two friends. He was mad. He was frustrated. He couldn't see why Ra didn't get that one risk was necessary and the other was counter-productive to their goal. He was angrier still because Ra was also right. He had meant well, but he had forced a choice on them.

"Were'?" T.C. asked as Wereberry walked away.

"I need time to think. I'll catch up with you guys later," Were' said. He continued to walk away, not even looking back.

"That's not good," T.C. said to Ra. "I really think we should stick together. We just got here. We don't know anything at all. I mean—"

"T.C.," Choco-Ra said patiently, "he'll be back. Or he won't. We're here, so we might as well get adjusted to it."

"We can't just abandon him," T.C. insisted.

"He's leaving us, if you didn't notice. Look, whatever, all right? You stay and wait for him. I'm going this way."

Choco-Ra started to walk away in the direction opposite the one that Wereberry had taken. He strode purposefully, letting his anger show in every step. He had every right to decide what they did, just as much right as Wereberry or T.C. He had more, the way he figured it. Neither of them had ever been a ruler. But no, that didn't matter, he fumed—they wanted to have an equal say in everything. Directions picked at random with a gloss of groupthink that really came down to who decided fastest.

That wasn't quite right either, Ra knew, but it felt right, and that would be good enough for now. To hell with them both. They could catch up when they wanted to. But he could find their missing person all by himself if need be. That would show them. It would show them... something. It'd show them that he had been the right person for the job all along and that they shouldn't ever doubt it, that was it. That was it exactly. Or at least, a nagging doubt chewed on Ra's consciousness, that was right enough to justify himself just then.

T.C. stood and watched his friends walk away from him. He knew he wasn't why they were leaving, but it still hurt him. They had started this as a group, and after one bad wave in the path they were ready to give up? He wanted to stomp his foot. So he did. Then he did it again. Finally he sat down and waited for a few minutes, hoping one of them would come back and be ready to think rationally again.

When that didn't happen, T.C. waited another while. The sun started to set. Hours had passed while T.C. sat and waited. Feeling helpless, he started walking. He went in a straight line from where he was, just walking off in the direction he happened to be facing. Directionless was how he felt, and it was how he acted.

The patch of grass the three travelers landed on sat there, not caring that no one stood on it anymore. It was once again an empty piece of land. Vacant.

2 • Exploratory Measures

WEREBERRY STOMPED OFF ALONE into the woods. The further he went, the less his anger mattered. A combination of pride and not wanting to give Ra an excuse to act smug kept him moving forward. He almost turned back a number of times but refused the urge. He was pretty sure the other two were right behind him, anyway.

The land dipped as he walked, leading him down into a shallow valley. As he entered it he heard voices. They were high pitched, but not painfully so, and they were singing. They sounded happy. Were' found his pace quickening. The idea of a group of people who were as happy as the sounds indicated excited him.

The grass hill leveled out, opening up into a small valley. Wereberry could smell water nearby, could hear the burbling of the water against rock. The scent and sound made him realize how thirsty he was, so he headed right for it. The singing people would wait long enough for a drink of water, after all.

Cupping handfuls of water from the stream, Were' slaked his thirst quickly and sat down along the bank of the small stream to look around. There weren't very many trees in sight. The few there were all looked to be oak. The grass was short, as if mowed regularly. Plucking a blade free from the ground, Wereberry noticed it didn't look cut. The grass appeared to grow exactly as high as a well-cut lawn and then stop by itself, content with the height it had achieved. Flowers sprouted up from the ground in regular little patches. Nothing looked tended or designed. It just all hung together in exactly the way someone would plan a garden of this size. Little randomnesses leant the land a natural air that it would have lacked otherwise. A rose in the wildflower patch, a lilac sitting all alone by a rock; these things made everything else make sense.

It wasn't designed then, just very, very pretty. Were' could deal with very pretty. He preferred it, as a matter of fact. The only thing that kept him from stretching out and taking a nap right there by the stream was those happily singing voices. They were still going at it, too. Wereberry stood up, adjusting his bag, and started walking again.

He drew nearer to the voices, and as he did he took in deep draughts of air. He smelled fresh-cut wood, the smoke of a cooking fire, some sort of tomato-based food, animal fur, and, of course, a lot of grass. The smell of food cooking was too much for him and he felt his stomach protest. Sure, life might not have been swell recently, really recently, but his stomach was right: you couldn't go on without fresh food.

The voices grew louder, rising to a crescendo in their song. Snatches of words came clearly to Wereberry's ears. They were singing all about how great life was, how much they looked forward to eating, and how wonderful their valley was to live in.

Wereberry felt a pang of suspicion enter his heart. They were almost too happy. No, Were' thought, that was Ra's cynicism creeping in. Too much time spent with that old bandaged grump had managed to get Wereberry doubting himself, he reasoned. Just because people were happy, he thought, didn't mean that something worse was at play. People could be honestly happy and content. It wasn't the end of the world.

A voice sang out loudly, carrying across the distance, "Hello, stranger!" Wereberry startled. How had they seen him? He hurried up, loping across the grasslands to reach the speaker as quick as possible. If they could see him, there was no point in strolling up and delaying lunch or dinner any longer.

The path took a gentle turn, a slow curve that Were' took almost without noticing it. When he came all the way around it, however, he saw a clutch of short, stubby animals. There were quite a few different species represented and none of them seemed to repeat. There was a panda, an otter, a very domestic-looking cat, a poodle, a giraffe, and a brown bear, all of them standing around a very large cooking pot. Each one of them had on different clothes, but visible on each was a wrist band. The wrist bands were wide, sweatbands really, and each had a different logo stitched on. Even from a distance the stitching was visible and rough.

Each one of them waved, which is when Wereberry became conscious of another fact: none of them had fingers. Their hands all ended in rounded-off blunt stubs with no digits attached. The hands bent in the middle, like mittens without thumbs, and none of the people around the pot seemed in pain because of it. But still, no fingers. Wereberry recoiled internally, suppressing a shudder. How did they work zippers? Hold forks? Survive?

Wereberry fought his small burst of sheer revulsion and walked closer, giving a friendly wave, very conscious of the fact that he had fingers. He hoped no one would break out crying. None of them did.

"Hey there, I'm Wereberry," he said, giving them a friendly smile to go along with the words.

"You're new," the panda remarked.

"Of course he's new, we haven't seen him before so he must be new," the poodle said.

"Yeah, I'm uhhhh, I'm new," Wereberry said, eyeing the pot hungrily, "and it's really nice to meet you all. So uhh, what's new then?"

"We were just about to have dinner," the giraffe said, "did you want to join us? You look hungry."

"I am," Were' admitted. "Thanks."

"No problem," the giraffe said, "I'm Bernie. That's Sam,"

he said, pointing at the panda.

"I'm Patricia," the cat said.

"Jennifer," said the bear.

"Kevin," the poodle said.

"Victor," the otter announced proudly.

"We're the founding members of," Bernie said, pausing for effect, "The Fuzzticuffs!"

They waved vigorously and Wereberry looked at the pot to avoid looking at their hands again. The stew boiled and bubbled nicely and Wereberry felt saliva rush into his mouth. He would, he decided right then, find a way to ask about their fingers after dinner. He didn't want to spoil his meal, and he didn't want to offend them and have them deny him a meal, either.

They set to, pulling bowls and spoons out of a hidden hutch near the pot. Initially, Wereberry refused to look at them as they gathered their belongings to eat, but raw curiosity overtook him. Their hands, he saw, bent deeply. They were like prehensile tails, except that they were hands. Shaking his head at the visual discrepancy, he took a bowl and spoon as they were passed to him.

Both were hot from their proximity to the cooking pot, and the heat was a welcome thing to Wereberry. He gripped the spoon tightly, letting the warmth spill out into his own skin. The bowl he gripped by the edge and waited.

Kevin grabbed up a ladle and started to serve each of them in turn, pouring huge helpings of stew into every bowl. The smells hit Wereberry even harder now that they were right up close to his nose. He waited, though, holding back until he saw what the prevailing niceties were.

There were none. As soon as the bowls were full people started to eat, scooping spoonfuls of food into their mouths, one after the other. They all ate like they hadn't eaten in weeks. Wereberry felt at home. He devoured his meal as fast as the others, licking stray drops from his muzzle as he went.

"So, what do you guys do around here?" he asked the group as his spoon hit the bottom of his bowl for the last time. He was full. He was contented. It was time, possibly, for a nap. But first he thought he should get a feel for the lay of the land.

"Whatever, really," Jennifer said, setting her own bowl down.

"Sometimes we play tag, or go down to the stream," added Victor.

"Hey, yeah how did you guys see me when I was so far away still?" Were' asked.

"That was Sam. He loves sitting in trees," Bernie said.

"Right," Wereberry said, "so aside from playing, what else goes on around here?"

"Not much, unless She needs us for something," Sam said. He curled up on his side, nuzzling the ground as he lay down. He sounded almost as sleepy as he looked.

"She?" Wereberry asked, "Who is she?"

"She's... wait, how do you not know?" Kevin asked. Victor nodded in agreement.

"I'm new here, remember?"

"No, no, new here maybe," Victor said, "but everyone in the world knows about Her. I mean, you can be new here but you can't be new to the world."

"Yeah, actually I'm pretty sure I can," Wereberry said with a laugh, "since I am new to the world. Well, this world at least."

"Impossible!" yelped Jennifer.

"Ridiculous!" echoed Patricia.

The rest joined in with cries of "absurd!" and "really just silly!" Wereberry sat and shook his head. These guys weren't stupid. However, if the shoe was on the other foot, Were' told himself, wouldn't he have said the same thing a while ago? Probably.

"No, you're right. I just say that to get a rise out of people.

But I did lose my memory a few days ago," he said, thinking fast. "Horrible fruit picking accident."

"Ohhhh," they all went. Except Sam, who had fallen asleep and was snoring softly.

"Yup, it was terrible, so remind me again? Who is she?"

"The Princess! You forgot the whole story?" Bernie asked.

"I guess I did. There's a Princess, huh?"

"Yeah. She came to the land one day—"

"So if she," Wereberry interrupted, "could come from a different land, why couldn't you buy that I did?"

"You're not a princess," Patricia said haughtily, "duh?"

"Fair enough," Were' said. He wanted to argue but he had gotten the memory story sold easily enough. Going back now wouldn't win him friends.

"Anyway," Bernie continued, "She came to the land one day and everyone was so in love with Her that they realized She was the Princess. So they gave Her a castle."

"She has a castle?"

"Of course, that's where princesses live," Patricia cut in, "duh?"

"Right, again, so sorry. Continue."

"She is all in pink," Bernie said, "and She haunts her castle day and night, decreeing things and protecting the lands."

"She... haunts a castle?" Wereberry asked. "And she has a thing for pink? And she... what's her name?"

"Princess," Kevin said, shaking his head.

"I might know her!" Wereberry exclaimed, throwing his arms up.

Victor and Bernie shot each other a quick worried glance. They raised their arms and pointed their stump-like hands at Wereberry. The wrist bands they each wore glowed brightly. Beams of color shot out along their arms, starting at the bands. The colors swirled, a rainbow of light, and splashed against Wereberry, who sat down quickly.

"Whoa," he said sleepily, "what was that?"

"You got a bit too excited there, Wereberry," Victor said. "So we had to calm you down."

"With that light show?"

All of them, except Sam, who still snored, leapt up happily and spoke as one, "You don't need fisticuffs when you have Fuzzticuffs!"

"Huh?"

"Well, we like to play and have fun and all that, but you can't get too excited, or angry," Patricia said, "but if you do, well the Fuzzticuffs can help you calm down and take a time-out."

"Is that what this is? I feel... well... fuzzy."

"Exactly," Jennifer pointed out.

"Yeah," Wereberry said, stifling a yawn, "so uhhh the Princess, she's your leader?"

"She's everyone's leader. She provides for us," Kevin told Wereberry.

"It doesn't look," Wereberry said, glancing around the area, "like she provides too well for you."

"Well, She is busy and there are only so many things to be handed out. She needs a lot of them for Herself, after all. But past that She takes care of us and we're fine."

"Oh, all right," Wereberry agreed quickly. He felt very agreeable. Very.

"Yeah, our bands used to be shinier," Patricia said, "but they got worn. She didn't have to replace them at all, right, but She did. And these are very colorful and functional."

Wereberry nodded. The blast was wearing off some; the time-out must not last too long, he figured, and he started to wonder again. Still, he kept himself as calm as possible. He felt no need to get blasted a second time.

So there was a Princess, and on the one hand she sounded like she could be Cherrygiest, but on the other she sounded kind of... petty. Could she even really be who they had all been searching for? Why not?

Wereberry considered the concept. He tasted it and chewed on it for a few minutes. The Fuzzticuffs took his silence as right and natural after a double blast, so they let him think and work things out. It could be her, he realized; there was no reason why it really and truly couldn't be. Sure this princess sounded a bit mean, but after she left her friends and no one came for her, maybe she was lonely. And being lonely and left to her own devices in a strange world where they made you royalty could turn someone a bit strange. Sure, why not? It made up his mind.

"I need to go meet the Princess," he said, nodding. He kept nodding his head, unsure of why he couldn't manage to stop. The blast had lingered a bit more than he had originally figured, he thought.

"Why?" Patricia asked, pondering the demand.

"Well, if she is as nice as you say she is, and I'm sure she is, then I want to meet her. Plus I think I knew her before."

"Before your horrible fruit picking accident?" Bernie asked.

"Yes, exactly that, before the fruit picking accident. Horrible, I know. Still, I think I knew her and if that's true, well then I have to get back and see her, don't I?" Wereberry felt a small pang at the idea that he could be stringing them along, but if he was right it was all going to be worth it.

"We can't just go to the castle," complained Victor.

"Why not?"

"Well... I mean... if we don't need anything..."

"We do, we all do; think about it, she'd thank you if I'm right. And if I'm wrong, well, no harm done, you just tried to help someone. Surely she'd appreciate that."

"I suppose," Victor agreed reluctantly.

"All right," Were' said, restraining himself from showing too much excitement, "then can we go?"

"I suppose we can after all," Bernie said with a smile, "but first we should nap and then have breakfast. It's a long walk

81

to the castle, after all. Plus we have to sing a few songs and then we have to go with Sam to find some new leaves. I heard he had an adventure in mind. But then we can go see the Princess, sure."

"Couldn't we," tried Were', "manage the trip sooner than later? Maybe after sleep and food, and singing can be done along the way really, but the leaves could certainly wait, couldn't they?"

They had to ponder that. Kevin woke Sam up to let him in on everything he had missed. They left Wereberry where he stood and wandered off a ways to talk it out. Wereberry didn't listen in. He could've and he knew it, but he also knew nothing he said would really affect their choice. All he could do was hope they felt like helping him more than finding some new leaves.

He also knew, in the pit of his gut, that the leaves would win. Wereberry thought about Choco-Ra and T.C. They hadn't followed him, at least not that he, or the Fuzzticuffs, had noticed. Which meant they had gone off and left him. To be fair, he had left them first, he knew. Still, they were off somewhere else, doing other things.

He wondered what they were doing. He hoped they were all right. He found that he resented them just a bit for not being here with him. He was also sure that they felt the same.

Sighing, Wereberry started to pace. He missed them. He was sorry that he had blamed Ra for being Ra and even sorrier that T.C. had gotten caught up in the middle. All he could do now, he thought, was go forward and make it better eventually. He could always find them, he reasoned. If the Princess was Cherrygiest, well then they would have the power of her station to help them search, and if not, he could and would do it himself.

The Fuzzticuffs wandered back to join Wereberry. He perked up as they drew near. He didn't want them to see him down; he wasn't sure if down was as bad as up to them. He also didn't want them to feel bad, no matter what they had decided. Either way, they'd already agreed to help him; it was just a matter of timing. He could wait if he had to.

"Well, we thought about it," Bernie said.

"And we talked about it," Victor added.

"These new leaves are really cool," Sam said happily, "you'll be glad we went and saw them. It'll be a good adventure, and then we can go on to the next adventure."

"The Princess?" Wereberry said, hoping no other adventure had occurred to them while they debated.

"The Princess," agreed Patricia. "We'll take you to Her, and you can let Her know how much we helped."

"Of course I will," Wereberry said. He smiled honestly. "And thank you guys for helping me."

"Why wouldn't we? We're the Fuzzticuffs," Bernie said seriously.

"Oh," Wereberry said, nodding, "there is that, of course."

"Did you forget already?" Kevin asked. "Was that fruit picking accident worse than maybe you think?"

"Oh, it was horrible," Wereberry said, nodding.

3 • Combing Through the Wreckage

T.C. WALKED AWAY FROM WHERE he and his friends landed, feeling glum. Unsure of what else to do, he wandered aimlessly. First a bit to the left, then a bit to the right, taking a turn here and there for no reason at all. He didn't care where his feet took him, so long as they took him.

It wasn't long before he could smell water. He was, he admitted to himself, feeling parched and dry. Reclaiming control of his meandering, T.C. headed directly for the water.

The lake was wide and cool. Grass grew right up to the very edge of the bank, where it fought with vines and creepers. Flowers sprouted here and there. Their colors made everything brighter and T.C. smiled. He judged the depth of the lake and then dove in headfirst.

Water engulfed his body, replenishing and refreshing him. He pushed it through his gills in big gulps. T.C. let himself sink to the bottom of the lake and looked up. Above him, past the water, was clear sky, dotted by the occasional flying thing.

In the lake itself, a few fish darted back and forth. Some of them were curious enough that they overcame their fear of the new and nosed up to him. T.C. grinned, watching the fish peacefully. His hand shot out, bubbles rising from the speed of the displaced water. When the hand returned to his side it held a fish. He raised it to his mouth and snapped it up, eating it quickly. The other fish still swam by, not seeming to notice that their numbers had decreased by one.

After a while, T.C. felt a ripple from the surface. He looked up and saw a tiny tongue lapping at the lake's water. The shape of the head that the tongue belonged to didn't really seem to go right. The head looked large and blocky, only in miniature. A younger thing, T.C. thought, or maybe it was just how the world worked here. He didn't know, but he wanted to find out.

As he sat up, he realized that was a new thought for him. Still, the last time he met someone that way it had worked out for the best. T.C. thought of Growth, of how glad he'd been for a new friend, and he smiled, his decision even firmer than before. His legs bunched under him, webbed toes gripping the silt of the lake's bottom, and pushed off.

He swam quickly to the surface, turning as he went. He burst out of the water, breaking the waterline at speed to get himself clear to the bank of the lake, far enough from the thing drinking to be out of range of it, but close enough to talk to it.

T.C. looked at the being near the water. The first thing he noticed was that it wasn't alone. The second was that it looked exactly like a miniature buffalo, except for the bright primary- and neon-colored fur.

They all, the whole pack of miniature buffalo, had different-colored fur. The colors didn't appear to repeat, either. Not fully. While there was a bright red one and a bright blue one, there was also a red and blue striped one, as well as neon blue and neon red.

T.C. didn't gape. He didn't shout or laugh. Instead, he raised one webbed hand and said, "Awwww, cute!" The buffalo turned as one and gave him a huge, collective smile in return.

"Hello!" squeaked the closest Buffalove, the same one that had just been drinking. His fur was a full, rich purple, and rumpled.

"Hi there," T.C. said, waving again. He hadn't expected such a high-pitched voice, but to be fair, he admitted to himself that had never run into multicolored miniature buffalo either, so who was he to decide what they should sound like?

The purple buffalo nodded and walked over to T.C., showing no fear at all. In fact, none of them seemed to be nervous or worried that a creature had just jumped out of their lake and waved at them. They acted instead, T.C. thought, like this happened every single day. And maybe it did; maybe they got a ton of visitors through here, he said to himself. It made him wonder if, by chance, the others were also here, having met the herd already. They could be hanging out back at whatever buffalo village existed, relaxing and having fun. It was, T.C. felt, entirely possible.

"I'm T.C., just got into town, you know how it is," T.C. babbled at them, "and I lost my friends. I was wondering if maybe you've seen them?"

"No," said a brick-red buffalo, "no one like you has come through here... ever, I think."

"They don't look like me," T.C. said quickly.

"Well," said a lime-green buffalo, "no one at all has been through here in quite some time."

"Oh," T.C. said. He sighed softly and drummed his toes on the ground, wondering what to do next.

"Do you want to look for them anyway?" the purple buffalo asked.

"But you said they weren't here," T.C. pointed out warily.

"We could be wrong," the brick-red one said.

"But... well, all right. Who are you, by they way? Do you have names, maybe?"

"We have colors!" a few of them shouted at once. "We're the Buffaloves!"

"The what-a-whats?" T.C. asked, pretty sure he hadn't heard them right.

"The Buffaloves!"

"What's a Buffalove?" T.C. asked reluctantly. He was fairly sure that there wouldn't be an answer full of deep meaning, but it was always worth a shot.

"Us?" tried a sky-blue Buffalove.

"Well, I can't find fault with that, I suppose," T.C. said, and he laughed. He liked these guys. They might appear to be fairly simple, but T.C. had a sense that was only because they were innocent, not stupid in any way. "So where do you think my friends might be if they're here but you haven't seen them?"

"Home?" guessed a purple-, green-, and yellow-striped Buffalove.

"Your home?" T.C. started to revise his thinking about their intelligence, but squashed that train of thought.

"Well, we like it—maybe they do, too. Come on!"

And so T.C. found himself walking along with a herd of brightly colored Buffaloves. He used the time to question the pack members nearest him. He found out that as a whole, they didn't have proper names—they used their colors instead. It lead to the occasional problem, they told him, when someone felt they were blue-green instead of green-blue. Those two, particularly, always got into trouble.

The Buffaloves told T.C. all about themselves. Their numbers (the herd was over two hundred Buffaloves at last count) and their love of being brushed and eating grass. T.C. understood the brushing. The Buffaloves had no way to hold a brush, much less use one. Their fur showed it, too. Many of them had tangles and mattes that didn't look happy at all. Sometimes they tried to hold combs in their teeth and brush one another, but it was never the same, and lots of places were very hard to reach.

Still, they did what they could and were as happy as possible, which was way happier than most people were on a daily, weekly, or even monthly basis. Their life was simple and they seemed to love everything and everyone that it included. T.C. was still taken by their cuteness, as well. They came up to his shoulder and as he walked, their huge, bushy, brightly colored manes brushed against him. They tickled, unintentionally, and every time the Buffaloves heard him laugh they laughed along with him, not understanding what he was finding so funny and not caring, either.

Eventually they came upon the Buffalove village. Low, squat huts made of mud and brush dotted the area. In the center of town sat a small pond, surrounded by bright green grass. Buffaloves walked all around, greeting each other, rubbing against one another, and occasionally try to brush each other.

T.C. poked around the village, sticking his head into doors and looking for Wereberry and Choco-Ra. He knew they weren't around, but he gave it a try anyway. The Buffaloves were endlessly helpful, though no one had seen either friend of T.C.'s. He didn't grow despondent, if only because he got exactly what he had expected to get.

Later, he watched as two Buffaloves tried brushing each other, combs held in their mouths. Neither one was getting anywhere good with the work.

"Want some help?" he asked them.

"You want to brush us?" one of the Buffaloves, an orange and yellow one, asked him, dropping his comb.

"Sure," T.C. said, and bent to pick up the comb. After he worked through the tangles of orange and yellow he worked on the other one, who waited patiently. That one, a black and green Buffalove, squealed with joy as T.C. worked. Soon, other Buffaloves heard about T.C.'s willingness to help and his deft work with a comb. He spent the rest of the night brushing Buffaloves right in the center of the village.

The next morning T.C. woke up, in the center of town, to find he had been resting against some Buffaloves. They slept on, leaning against each other, but T.C. got up and wandered around. He spotted the purple Buffalove again, his first new friend, and headed for him.

"I meant to ask," the purple Buffalove said happily as T.C. drew near, "where are you from, anyway? We've never seen a creature like you before."

"I'm from another world," T.C. told him plainly. "It's a whole different place. I came here with my two friends and we... got separated."

"I bet the Princess can find them for you," the Buffalove said. He pawed the ground with excitement.

"The Princess?" asked T.C.

"Yeah, She's wonderful! She likes to brush us. We don't all go at once, but sometimes She'll send for a small group to go to Her castle. And we'll sit there all day and be brushed and played with. She's even put bows in our hair before! Bows!"

"Wow, bows are pretty special, huh?" T.C. said, nodding. "She sounds like a nice woman, your Princess."

"She is, and She's not a Buffalove, of course, but She had Her friends come and help us build this village. We're not too good at building," the purple one said. He laughed, throwing his head back.

"That was really nice of her. And you think she could help me?" T.C. didn't want to get his hopes up, but he had to admit this Princess sounded too good to be true. And yet the Buffaloves seemed to, well, love her. T.C. couldn't imagine them loving someone who was unhelpful or horrible to them.

"She helped us, right? So She can help you, too. We can take you to Her," the Buffalove offered, "and tell Her you're a Buffalove, so She can help you like She does us."

"I don't," T.C. said, glancing at himself, "look anything like a Buffalove."

"You brushed us, all night, even though you didn't have to. And you like us. And you're nice. So maybe," the purple Buffalove said, growing more serious, "you aren't a Buffalove in the strictest sense, but you're one of us as far as we're concerned."

T.C. took a deep breath and then smiled wide. He liked these guys, all of them, from their tiny horns to their bushy legs. Each one, of every color, was just plain nice. It was refreshing and pure. T.C. found that he wasn't sure how he could find his friends, continue looking for Cherrygiest, and leave the Buffaloves behind. He knew he couldn't take them, and that they would offer to go if he asked, regardless, but it wasn't their trip. Still, he didn't know how he would leave them.

"All right," T.C. agreed, "we'll go and you can introduce me. But if she doesn't want to help me, then that's her issue. Don't make it a thing for yourselves. Deal?"

The Buffalove nodded. He turned to leave, without another word. T.C. sat there, unsure as to what would happen next. He decided he would find that out when it happened, and went to go try to nap a while longer.

T.C. woke up to a clutch of Buffaloves surrounding him. Some of them he knew, but a few were new to him. They stood around him peacefully, watching him without word or expectation. As he woke up, and startled slightly, they kept watching him, waiting. T.C. couldn't work out what they were waiting for at first, but he stretched, yawned, and thought about it as he stood up.

As soon as he did, they smiled and gave him a round of good mornings and hellos. He laughed and helloed each of them in turn.

"Do you want to leave, then?" asked the purple Buffalove.

T.C. was taken by surprise. Sure, he knew they would take him to meet this Princess, but he didn't think they'd meant this soon. Still, though putting it off might feel natural, even right to a degree, it wouldn't manage to achieve anything. So he nodded.

Ten Buffaloves walked out of the Buffalove village, T.C. walking beside them, comb in hand.

4 • Getting Hives

CHOCO-RA HEARD THEM before he saw them. They made little noises, bustling and scraping against trees and grass. They hummed as well, tiny pipsqueak voices that grated on Ra's nerves. He stood very still and scanned the area.

After leaving T.C. behind, Ra had walked a ways on a wide track before finding a small, semi-hidden path. With a shrug of his wrapped shoulders, he decided to take it. It ended up opening into a tiny clearing. The clearing was where he stood now, just at the entrance, listening.

"Scut this," he heard a voice say. Ra wasn't sure where the voice had come from, exactly. It had risen up to him, he knew that much. But past that he couldn't tell. He looked around the clearing again.

Tiny hedges, like bonsai trees, dotted the space. At first Choco-Ra took them for weed growth, but when he looked again he saw them for what they were.

"I mean, it wasn't even his plan," the voice said again, "but he thinks he's the scuttest one around."

This time Ra pinpointed it as coming from one of the closer hedges. He stayed where he was. He really wanted to just rattle a hedge and see what was in there, but the plan didn't seem prudent. Not until he knew what was in there, at least.

A small figure—its head would have reached Ra's ankle—came out of the hedge. Soon it was joined by a second.

They looked very similar. Both were tiny men, as yellow as one of T.C.'s ripe bananas. They wore identical knee shorts, hiking boots, and wide-brimmed hats, all in the same dark brown. Antenna sprouted up from the sides of the hats, and

Ra could make out that their tiny hands had a small, pinching claw along the back toward the wrist. The men were, Ra realized with a blink, tiny half-insect men.

The one that had come out of the hedge first suddenly stopped moving and talking. His antenna waved wildly and he looked right at Choco-Ra.

"Giant!" he screamed at his companion, and took off running.

Ra sighed and knelt down as the runner's friend considered taking off with him.

"I'm not a giant," Ra said, lowering his voice—he remembered how loud Gigantic had sounded. "Well, not normally. Now relax."

The little yellow man nodded and stood still. He was, however, visibly shaking. Ra closed his eyes for a second, wishing he could roll them.

"All right," he said to the little man, "run."

The figure didn't need any more encouragement before he too ran off shouting about a giant. Soon enough a host of the little guys, all dressed alike, were approaching slowly. There had to be, Ra estimated, a hundred of them. One of the ones in front, the only one with a mustache, must be their leader, Ra figured. The others were prodding him enough, certainly.

"Are you a friendly giant or a mean giant?" the mustached man asked.

"If I was mean," Choco-Ra said in soft tones, "would I tell you?"

"Of course," the little man answered.

"Well, if you're that gullible, then no, I am nice. You work out if that means anything. Look, my name is Choco-Ra. I'm just passing through. Is that going to be a problem?"

"No problem, though if you are a good giant, maybe you can help us."

"I would really rather just pass through," Ra said, giving them all a shrug.

"A really friendly giant would help us!" the man declared, mustache quivering.

"Oh come on now, are you serious?"

"Scutting right I am, Mister Giant!" The little man stomped a foot to show everyone exactly how serious he was.

"My name is Choco-Ra," Ra said. "Stop calling me giant."

"Well fine then, Choco-Ra, will you help us?"

"Yes," Choco-Ra said with a sigh, giving into the trap.

"Scuttastic! We're the Scuttles!"

"Of course you are," said Choco-Ra. He honestly didn't care. Then again, he reminded himself, it wasn't like he had anywhere special to go. He didn't intend to go back home without finding Cherrygiest, but he also wasn't sure he wanted to deal with Wereberry or T.C. for a while.

Maybe he could strike out on his own and get more done. Until they realized they needed him as their leader, at least. He felt it wasn't too much to ask. He was the best person for the job. He had the most experience and he was, unquestionably in his mind, the smartest.

"Exactly!" exclaimed the Scuttles' leader. "I'm Father Scuttle."

"Hi."

"This is Smart Scuttle, Happy Scuttle, Playful Scuttle, Dancy Scuttle, Woodsmith Scuttle...." as Father Scuttle spoke he pointed to seemingly random Scuttles. Ra saw no way to work out who was who, and so he resolved to just make up names and call them out, or possibly mumble, and see how it worked.

Father Scuttle started to walk as he continued to drone on with name after name. The other Scuttles broke apart their formation. Some went along with Father Scuttle, but the rest just walked off back to whatever they had been doing before Ra's arrival.

Ra took careful notice of the hedges and made sure he didn't step on any of them. They probably, he thought to himself, wouldn't appreciate wanton destruction from someone who was supposed to be helping them.

Father Scuttle stopped in front of a large hedge. The hedge came midway up Choco-Ra's calf. Father Scuttle started to enter and then stopped, shaking his head and laughing.

"Scut me, you can't fit even in our biggest house, can you? Of course not! My apologies! I guess I'm just scut today."

"That's fine," Ra said, sitting down on the grass. He looked around as he sat, making sure he wasn't sitting on anybody's house or, even more importantly, anybody.

"Well, I wanted to tell you about the help we need. Maybe give you some nice fresh scut tea," Father Scuttle said, laughing again. "But even a pot wouldn't make a difference, would it? Scut, you are large."

"I'm fine, just go on and tell me the problem."

"Well there's this wizard. He wants to use us Scuttles to make a powerful potion," Father Scuttle explained, "one that would make him rich."

"That's it? He's a powerful wizard who just wants to be rich?" Ra asked. The economy in this world must be in shambles if that was the driving force behind this guy, whoever he was. Anyone powerful enough to use people to make a... what kind of potion did someone make to turn them rich, anyway?

"That's it. Well, sometimes he says he wants to eat us," Father Scuttle said, thinking, "but I'm not sure about that."

"What kind of potion would make him rich, anyway?"

"A golden one. It would turn the simplest of rock into pure gold! But he needs the spirit of a Scuttle to make the magic work."

"That's it then? You want me to get this wizard guy to stop trying to melt you down into a potion, or possibly eat you?"

"Well there's also the evil Princess."

"There's an evil Princess?" Ra asked, feeling a stress

headache start. Evil Princesses weren't in the original bargain. There was a spot of trouble, they'd said. Choco-Ra had thought maybe they had a big cat around, or some field mice even. But a wizard and a princess? This was getting silly.

"Yes!" exclaimed Father Scuttle. "She makes us build shoes!"

"Or else what? What happens if you just say no?"

Father Scuttle stopped and looked around at the other Scuttles. They all seemed perplexed, to a Scuttle. "Why, you know, bad things."

"So you've just never tried to say no to her, have you?" Ra asked.

"Would you?" a random Scuttle asked, eyes gone wide.

"Oh yeah. Yes, I would. Easily so."

"Then tell Her no for us!" a few Scuttles shouted at once.

Choco-Ra stood. He was growing impatient with this madness and wanted out; he just didn't see a good out open to him. Sure he could've just walked right out of the area and left the Scuttles behind. What, exactly, could they have done to stop him? Shouted a lot?

Something stopped him, though. He couldn't put a finger on exactly what it was. Their openness, their insanity... it called to him. The fact that they had a leader who didn't lead, that certainly nagged at him a bit.

Whatever the sum total cause was, Choco-Ra didn't walk away. Instead he found himself standing there and giving the village a good once-over.

"Well," he began, "if I tell her no for you, then when I leave she'll just take it out on you, if she's as bad as you say."

Ra watched the Scuttles' faces drop. They saw what he was saying and realized it was right. That was, he decided, a good sign. They weren't dumb, or completely naïve. That would be a help. But in order to do this right, Ra thought to himself with an internal grin, he would need a small army. He had, in fact, a small army. If they could be roused and led, at least.

They seemed to be good at following a leader, and if their leader backed the change, it could work.

He looked around him. The Scuttles were all looking at him. Even Father Scuttle was simply waiting for Ra to continue and explain himself. He started to plan right then. He laughed, loudly, causing the Scuttles to startle.

"Sorry," he said with a wave of his hand, "I know what we can do." Ra took in a deep breath and nodded to himself. This would work.

"You do?" Father Scuttle asked, full to the brim with hope.

"We'll march to her front door and demand what you need. You might be small, but an army is an army with the right general." Ra spread his hands, as if waiting for benediction. He waited for the Scuttles' triumphant reaction.

"We don't have generals!" some of the Scuttles said fearfully. The stood, looking around, wondering what the giant could really mean.

Ra started to sigh but turned it into another laugh. A quieter laugh this time, so the Scuttles wouldn't jump, or worry about his sanity.

"You do now," Ra said with a bow.

5 • Convergence

THE CASTLE STOOD TALL AND PINK in the bright sunshine. Its spires glinted with reflected light. The windows, all set tastefully into recessed arches, flashed like prisms. The castle was large, covering acres of land. The grounds around it were carefully trimmed and perfectly tended. People bustled around, checking on flower beds and doing other small jobs. The shadow cast by the castle dropped over the land and smothered the nearby tree line.

In other words: the castle loomed, but prettily so.

There was only one road leading up to the castle's front gate. It was wide and sunny. Though a dirt road, it was tamped down firmly so that almost no dust rose when travelers trod along it. The road went in a straight line away from the castle for a few miles before it split into no less than six separate paths. Each path then wound its way to different locations, splitting and resplitting, until they touched almost every single road there was.

No one had walked all of them to make sure that this was a fact, but those who wanted to try to prove or disprove it had spent days or weeks walking, just to give up and shake their heads and agree with the concept as fact in the end.

There were always people on the road that led up to the castle. Visiting the castle, and the Princess that lived there, was a popular thing to do. People had favors to ask, duties to perform, and deliveries to make.

When a small herd of Buffaloves appeared on the road, no one really noticed. They meandered, accompanied by T.C., who chatted in low tones and brushed various Buffaloves as he walked.

The Buffaloves looked proud and happy with their new companion. They carried their heads slightly higher for the company and they swayed from side to side, showing off their well-brushed fur. Together they started to hum. It was a happy, wordless song that made the people they passed smile. They were going to go see the Princess and it was exciting and fun.

A whistling joined into the humming. Some of the Buffaloves looked back to see who had joined them. They smiled large. T.C. glanced back as well and caught a sight he wasn't expecting.

"Were'!" T.C. exclaimed. He felt a rushing wave of gladness at seeing his friend. It was tinged, slightly, with an undercurrent of worry. He didn't want to leave the Buffaloves, but also didn't want to leave Were', and that mash of emotion swirled around inside him.

"T.C.!" Wereberry said, blinking. There was no way he could have guessed that his friend would be leading a herd of tiny buffalo. That simply wasn't the sort of thing you counted on. It was great to see him again though, Were' thought.

"Are you headed to see the Princess, too?" T.C. asked, halting the Buffaloves. He didn't command them, or even really suggest it to them; he just stopped walking. The Buffaloves stopped with him, not really wanting to leave his side.

The Fuzzticuffs looked at Wereberry, not sure how he knew this strange-looking man. They still walked with him though, the Buffaloves and Fuzzticuffs soon mingling and blocking the road.

"Well, yeah," Were' said with a smile, drawing closer to T.C., "I think she might be Cherrygiest."

"What? Why do you think that?" T.C. wasn't sure which shocked him more: the thought that this Princess they were going to visit could be their long lost friend, or that the idea hadn't really occurred to him.

"Hey, who's your friend?" Victor asked, cutting Were' off before the werewolf could speak.

"Oh, hey guys, this is T.C. He's one of the friends I told you about. T.C., these are the Fuzzticuffs. Bernie, Sam, Patricia, Jennifer, Kevin, and Victor." Were' gestured to each Fuzzticuff as he introduced them.

T.C. nodded and smiled at them. He waved a hand around at some of the Buffaloves. "These are the Buffaloves," he told Wereberry, "but I think your friends know mine, huh?"

"Seems that way," agreed Were', looking at the two groups mingling.

"So what was that about the Princess?" T.C. asked.

"Well," Were' began, "think about it. She wears a lot of pink, she came to this place out of nowhere, seemingly, and is said to haunt the castle she lives in. Sounds possible, right?"

"I suppose," T.C. offered. He wasn't sure at all. It would be great, but it felt too pat to him. Then again, life could be pat, he reasoned, and Were' was generally smart.

"Hey if we came here and we're pretty sure she did too, why couldn't she end up a Princess?"

"True," T.C. wrapped his head around it, trying the idea on for size. It fit, if a bit roughly.

"Are you guys going to ask the Princess for stuff?" Patricia asked the purple Buffalove.

"We want help for T.C., he's one of us now. He's good to us, you know. You guys could come comb us too sometimes if you wanted."

"Uhhh, yeah we could," Victor said with a laugh, "but we have things to do a lot. So maybe soon?"

Wereberry unslung his bag and dug out a strawberry, popping it into his mouth and chewing it thoughtfully. He used a full mouth as an excuse to listen instead of talk. The Buffaloves and Fuzzticuffs were happily discussing trading services. The Fuzzticuffs could easily brush some Buffalove fur when needed if the Buffaloves could come help them do some light construction. Harnessing walls to their backs and lifting and such were things the Buffaloves did pretty well, all told.

T.C. mostly watched his friend. The Buffaloves were fine; they didn't need to be watched every second. They had been fine before he came along, after all. So instead, T.C. focused on studying Wereberry. There had been no words given to his departure, no apology or explanation. It might as well not have happened at all, from the way Were' was acting so far.

And maybe that was fair, T.C. felt. There wasn't a good way to get into the problem, just then, surrounded as they were. Besides, what could be said? An apology, certainly, but wasn't that understood by the friendship and warmth, the joy Were' showed upon seeing T.C.? T.C. watched Wereberry chew, watched him get lost in his own observations of those around him, and smiled. Yeah, Wereberry didn't need to apologize, not really. T.C. realized he already knew the apology and had accepted it, without anything being spoken.

The two groups, now acting as one, started to move again. They walked down the road toward the castle, humming and whistling and chatting. People got out of their way, standing on the side of the road while they passed. They made for a large group, one that filled the road completely. Gardeners and people pushing delivery carts tried to move through them and gave up, going off the road and around.

Still, no one seemed to mind much. The party was just too obviously enjoying itself. A bright blue Buffalove was singing a song about the sun in a nice duet with Patricia. Victor and Kevin were whistling a tune that only they knew. Three Buffaloves—one yellow, one blue and green striped, and the other a lush, dark red—all hummed a song they had forgotten the words to.

T.C. and Were' walked together, close to the middle of the madness. They became the eye of their own hurricane. Snatches of the various songs fought for control of their brains while they each ran through their respective plans.

T.C. was sure they would be welcomed with open arms by the Princess—whisked inside and thanked and welcomed and taken care of. He would ask her to help them find Ra, because the three of them did belong together, and then they would all ask for her help finding Cherrygiest. Assuming she wasn't Cherry to begin with, the way Wereberry thought. If she was, that just made the whole mash of events seem even brighter.

Wereberry was fairly certain that the Princess was Cherrygiest after all. And once they met back up, they could all go home if they wanted. They could find Ra, help people, do whatever it was they felt like. And if she wasn't, by some chance, who he thought she was, well then it would still be all right. She was the ruler of the land; she had to know where people were. Hell, he thought, she probably already knew they were coming. Maybe she'd even had lunch put out. Lunch would be a great boon. A royal lunch must be a great spread.

Their thoughts were interrupted by the rhythmic thumping of a march. It came from behind them, sounding military and serious, all the more so for the brightness of the day. They turned around, the noise gaining.

A horde of tiny yellow men, each with a broad hat, marched in lockstep down the road. They chanted as they went. It wasn't a chant of words, more simple sounds, but it was still effective. People got out of its way, fast. Although the marchers were ankle high, there were enough of them that they came across as dangerous as a swarm of locusts, if not moving half so fast.

Behind them, Choco-Ra marched along. He was moving slower, of course—a leisurely stroll, due to the difference in stride length—but he looked twice as imposing as any of the Scuttles that walked before him. T.C. and Were' looked at the marching army and then at each other. They were both surprised. Well, they were also both completely unsurprised.

"Ra," Wereberry called out, "what are you up to?"

"Wereberry! T.C.! I see you found each other. Good. You can join us," the mummy said, trying not to sound too overtly commanding.

"Uhm, Ra," T.C. said, trying to sound gentle, "we were just going to go ask the Princess for help. See now, asking was the idea. You don't look like you plan on asking things."

"No," Ra agreed readily, "we're demanding them. You need to, sometimes, with that type."

"And what type," Were' asked, "is that?"

"The blindly demanding ruling type," Ra answered. His column of Scuttles was still advancing.

"The irony isn't lost on me," Wereberry said with a small laugh.

The Scuttles caught up with the road-blocking group that had been, until recently, merrily wandering down the road. The Scuttles swarmed through the mass of Buffaloves and Fuzzticuffs. They came out the other side and reformed their column. Choco-Ra started to make his way through as well, having a more difficult time of it.

"I see you've found some new friends," Ra said as he reached T.C. and Wereberry.

"As have you," T.C. said.

"Every good general needs an army," Ra pointed out grandly.

"Now, Ra," Wereberry said, shaking his head, "you're getting just a bit too into this here."

"No, Were', I'm not. They have a grievance with the Princess. In return for helping them sort that out, they will help me—help us, now—with our own goals."

"Except I think the Princess is who we're looking for," Wereberry said.

"Doubtful," Ra said, waving his hand in dismissal and looking down the road toward the castle. "From what I hear she couldn't possibly be."

"You're also leading a charge of very very tiny men," Were' said.

"What does that have to do with anything?" Ra demanded.

Wereberry laughed, "Nothing, really, I just wanted to point it out. Look, I just think that going in there guns and tiny men blazing is the wrong move."

"And so you aren't doing that. I, however, think it is exactly the right move. Which is why I am doing it."

"Why don't we work together?" T.C. suggested. "We could start working together again, huh? And you could drop the army maybe, Ra, and—"

"Oh sure, here we go again! Look, the both of you! I'm the best leader we have, and maybe it's about time the two of you listened to me and understood that I, at the end of the day, I can—" Ra was cut off by a blast of colorful energy.

Patricia and Kevin watched Choco-Ra stumble a bit and try to find the right words again. They shook their heads a bit sadly.

"You don't need fisticuffs when you have the Fuzzticuffs!" they said cheerfully, and then turned back to their previous conversation.

"What was—" T.C. started to ask.

"Oh, I should've warned him, huh?" Were' said, smirking. "Yeah, the Fuzzticuffs don't like it when you get excited. Uhm. Hey, Ra?"

"Yes, Wereberry?" Ra asked sleepily.

"You feeling all right there, man?"

"Oh sure," Ra agreed slowly, "just a bit—"

"Sleepy? Yeah, sorry about that. I know you'll be mad later, but it really wasn't intentional." Were' kept looking at T.C. as he talked to Ra. It wasn't that the whole thought of Ra acting this soft was funny to him... no, it was that exactly. He wanted to laugh. He wanted to be in a place where he could laugh about it and lose himself in the humor of the situation.

"Why would I be mad about it?" Ra asked. "Nooo, I don't feel mad at all. Nope. So we should go and," Ra thought for a few seconds, dropping into silence before continuing. "Talk to the Princess. Softly."

Wereberry clapped a hand on Choco-Ra's shoulder and nodded. They both started to walk, without hurry, to the head of the gathering. T.C. went with them, still a bit shocked over Ra's behavior. He wondered if the Fuzzticuffs would lend him their ability to do that. Both Were' and Ra needed it from time to time. To be fair, T.C. figured there were times he needed it as well. He was sure. Sometimes.

The Buffaloves and Fuzzticuffs started moving again, right behind the Scuttles. The Scuttles didn't know what to make of it. They seemed to have gained more people to make their case, and yet the newcomers all seemed so happy. The singing reminded the Scuttles that they loved to sing and dance too; why, it was only since Choco-Ra had laid out his plan that they had started to sing deeper marching-type songs. Maybe, they thought and whispered to each other, Choco-Ra was wrong.

Father Scuttle didn't believe that, and passed word to that effect. Choco-Ra was their general. For this plan to work, he needed the Scuttles to remain firm and strong. To show the world, for once, that they weren't just tiny men with big hats, and that they could be a force that needed to be listened to.

Wereberry, T.C., and Choco-Ra gained the front of their irregular column. The castle's gate was in sight now, and the three friends all studied it. Were' looked deeply, trying to see if the design fit something Cherry might have liked. T.C. wondered when they stopped making castles with moats. He would've liked a good moat to take a dip in. Ra wondered why he was so calm and thought the gate looked very nice and solid.

In fits and spurts Choco-Ra came back to his right mind. He grew more and more annoyed with the simple fact that he wasn't feeling annoyed.

How dare, Ra thought, Were' let those little furballs drug him like that. No, that wasn't quite fair. Wereberry hadn't told them to; they had just seemed to react badly to his display of emotions. Still, it angered him and he wanted to take it out on someone. Ra did realize, of course, that taking it out at all would simply make the Fuzzticuffs do it again; Ra resolved to let the matter drop. At least for a while.

Up in the castle, people had noticed the large, mixed group marching toward them. Guards looked out windows and told their supervisors. The supervisors told their supervisors, and so on up the food chain. Word eventually reached the Grand Vizier, who decided to have a look out at the crowd herself.

She peered out, considering both the size and makeup of the group. None of them were considered a threat, and certainly not in those numbers. The three out front, though, they were new. They looked like they just might be trouble. The Grand Vizier made a choice. She informed the people near her and they, in turn, told their people, and so on back down the line. The guards at the windows received word. They knew what they were supposed to do now, and it was a job they were perfectly comfortable doing. The castle continued to run smoothly and efficiently.

The trio came to the large front gate of the castle. It was a gigantic pink wooden door that opened in the middle, both halves designed to swing inward. They stood there and looked back at their assorted charges. None of them really knew what to do. Normally, it had been explained along the walk, the guards saw people approach and opened the gates for them.

They stood in front of the gates for a few minutes, considering the issue. The guards had to have seen them. That much was a given. So they either didn't want to let people in or they were just slow today. T.C. looked at Choco-Ra, who looked at Wereberry. Were' looked back at Ra and then at T.C.

Choco-Ra sighed and shook his head. He stepped up to the gate, the grain of the wood only inches from him. He waited another second, sure he was being watched from more than just behind. Ra raised one hand slowly and made a fist. He knocked. Hard. That one loud thump seemed to echo inside the castle.

The door didn't move. Ra knocked again. And again. He stopped and looked back at Wereberry and T.C., who stepped up to stand next to their friend. Ra knocked a fourth time.

Silence followed the boom of Choco-Ra's knocking. Then, the gate creaked. Gradually, it started to open. The three friends each took a step back as the gate swung.

Several guards stood, blocking the entrance, while the gates opened. They didn't look overly happy, really. Each guard carried a tennis racket. None of them wore armor. Instead, some of them were dressed for a game of tennis, while others looked ready to go to a party in their sweater-vests and slacks.

Were' turned to the group behind them, the Buffaloves, Fuzzticuffs, and Scuttles, and addressed them as one. "Guys, you just wait here. We'll take care of this and everything will be just fine," he told them. He turned back to see that the guards hadn't moved.

"Excuse me," Choco-Ra began, "we were needing to speak to the Princess. It's important."

The guards stood immobile. Except for one, who was apparently their leader. His tennis racket was shinier, and his tennis shorts and polo shirt were both a muted shade of pink.

"The Princess isn't accepting petitioners now," he said. "Please disperse while you wait. We can't have you blocking this road." The guard's pristine blonde hair didn't flinch in the gust of wind that whipped up as he finished speaking.

"No, really," Ra said, fighting his own impatience, "it's important."

"It is. We don't want any trouble, if that's the worry," Wereberry put in.

"We're sorry, sirs," the head guard said, "but the Princess is not seeing any petitioners, as I told you."

"But we came pretty far, and we just want to—" T.C. was

cut off by a wave of Ra's hand.

"Listen," Choco-Ra began, setting his shoulders, "we don't intend to stand around and wait all day and we don't intend to disperse. The Princess can make time for us. She's reasonable, I'm sure. And as a good leader, she should be willing to hear her own subjects speak to her."

"Sir, I have to ask you to leave," the guard said, twirling his racket idly in his hand, "right now."

"I think not," Ra said, flashing his eyes brightly.

The guards moved forward as one, raising their rackets. They all looked passively annoyed. None of them seemed mean, or even angry. They were fine just standing there. They would've been happier, it seemed, to not be standing there, but as long as they had to, that was going to be okay by them. They also didn't seem to mind if they had to enforce their boss' word.

Their commander held a hand up to stop them, looking at Choco-Ra. "This is your final chance, sir," he said.

"No," Ra said softly, "it's yours."

Were' rolled his eyes. He knew his friend was about to get them into a fight that wasn't strictly necessary. On the other hand, there was no good reason for the Princess to not see them. At the very least they could've been given a reason.

Behind them, the mass of various people was all a-twitter with what was going on. Had Choco-Ra really threatened a guard? Was the Princess truly unwilling to see them? Neither event made sense to any of them. Both were completely unprecedented, to their recollections. Maybe, whispered the Scuttles, it was the presence of the outsiders that made the difference. The Buffaloves disagreed, putting forth T.C. as perfectly fine to see a Princess—after all, he was always nice. The Fuzzticuffs wondered aloud if they would need to step in and stop silliness from happening until cooler heads could prevail.

The guards were also slightly confused. No one had

threatened them in a very long time. Then again, they hadn't been asked to bar entrance to anyone in quite a while, either. The day was shaping up to be a memorable one.

The head guard took a step forward and started to put a hand on Choco-Ra. "I'll have to ask you to come with me," he said.

Choco-Ra grabbed the guard's wrist and pulled down sharply. The guard dropped to his knees in surprise, managing to yell a quick "Arrest them!" before Ra pinned him to the ground with a foot.

The other guards raised their rackets and rushed forward. Wereberry became a pink furry blur, moving deeper into the guard's ranks, getting in between and behind them even as they moved forward. T.C. simply stood his ground. He didn't want to hurt anyone, but he also wasn't relishing the idea of being hit with a tennis racket.

Wereberry leapt at two guards, falling as he grabbed both of them from behind. They went down in a tangle of fur, limbs, and rackets. Only Wereberry stood back up. The other guards were unsure of what protocol was here. They could turn their back on the rest of the fight to deal with this one furred one, but then—they gave up thinking and did whatever felt right.

Choco-Ra pushed another guard to the ground easily. Wereberry tripped one and stood on him. T.C., having no good choice, threw a guard back through the open gate. And then the world turned to color. Bright colors mingled and splashed over the guards, T.C., Wereberry, and Choco-Ra. It hit a few of the Scuttles who were moving to help.

"You don't need fisticuffs when you have the Fuzzticuffs!" yelled all the Fuzzticuffs in unison.

Wereberry sighed, sleepily. You just couldn't have a fun brawl with these guys around. Not at all. The guards that were down stayed that way. The ones that were still standing dropped their rackets to their sides, not interested in fighting anymore. T.C. and Ra both took deep breaths and looked around calmly.

The head guard stood back up, sluggishly, and surveyed the battlefield, such as it was. "I'm sorry," he said wearily, "but I still have to take you three in. The rest of you can go, if you want. That's fine. Thank you."

The Buffaloves nodded, and the Fuzzticuffs gathered up the sleeping Scuttles and, en masse, started to move back down the road. Wereberry, T.C., and Choco-Ra all just nodded. Ra motioned for the guards to lead the way.

6 • The Strength of Your Convictions

BY THE TIME THE FUZZTICUFFS' blast started to wear off, the three friends were being put into a holding cell. The guards took their bags from them and led them each into a cell. The cells were connected end to end, but the extra space made them feel separated. The bars didn't hurt the feeling of separation either.

The doors were closed and locked, each one making a clanking noise that spoke of finality. The guards retreated back to the hallway. Wereberry, Choco-Ra, and T.C. all sat in their respective cells and felt their anger at the situation start to rise.

"Why," Ra asked with growing tension, "did you bring those drugging little furballs along?"

"Hey, when I set out it wasn't with the intention of getting into a fight," Were' pointed out.

"And maybe we shouldn't get into one now, either," T.C. said, standing. He paced the length and width of his cell. Seven by nine and containing a bed, toilet, and sink, the cell didn't impress him much at all. He ran the sink anyway, splashing the tepid water over his skin.

"All right," Were' conceded. "We should concentrate on getting out of here. Ra, do you want to do that slipping through the bars trick again?"

Ra nodded and stood. "Might as well," he said. Sucking in his breath, Ra shrunk in width again. He walked toward the bars and started to move sideways between them. He didn't get very far. As soon as his arm passed into the space between bars a bright pink flash set off, throwing Ra backwards into his cell and onto his ass.

"Right then," Ra said, standing again, "that won't work."

The three of them studied their cells and thought. Wereberry noticed a food slot at the bottom of the bars. If things couldn't pass through the main bars, certainly they had to be able to slide things through that slot, or else they couldn't be fed. Assuming the guards couldn't turn off whatever protection was going on.

Gambling, Were' dropped to his stomach and slid a hand through the food slot. It passed through easily. He wiggled his fingers a few times, outside the bars, before withdrawing his arm.

"Can you fit through the food slot?" he asked Ra.

Choco-Ra shook his head, staring at the slot. "No way. I can get slimmer, sure, but I can't exactly—well maybe there is a way," he said, sitting down to think.

Slowly, the bandages around his finger started to unravel. Underneath them was empty space. A finger vanished, then his hand. Wereberry and T.C. looked on, jaws slack.

"There's nothing under those?" T.C. asked. He hadn't ever seen Ra sans bandages. Were' hadn't either. They both thought there was a person under there, though, T.C. realized, it would make no sense how he could shrink himself widthwise if that were the case.

"Nothing at all," Choco-Ra said. His voice was strained, the effort of unraveling himself obviously taking a toll. "Except my eyes, of course," he added after another minute.

The bandages that were once Choco-Ra's right hand dangled limply from his wrist. He lowered his arm to the floor and pushed them through the food slot. The bandages sat limply on the other side of the bars.

"Now," Ra said, mostly to himself, "if I can reform them—"

"Why couldn't you?" Wereberry asked, unable to stop himself. He was fascinated by what his friend was up to. Always another surprise in that bag of tricks, Were' thought with a proud grin.

"Well it isn't something I do daily, now is it?" Ra said testily. He took a deep breath, calming himself. It was no good to get annoyed with Wereberry. He was curious, was all. Ra knew it, and he stole a glance at his furred friend. The look on Wereberry's face made Choco-Ra want to burst out in laughter. Were' was so obviously amazed and proud. Maybe, Ra thought, he had misjudged them both. They knew that Ra was the best leader, in most situations. That qualifier of "most" was what Ra had to learn to keep in mind. The best leader doesn't always lead. Choco-Ra shook his head and emptied it. This was no time for startling self-realization.

The bandages on the outside of the cell twitched slightly. They shivered and jumped in slow motion. The very end of the bandage rose into the air, coiling upward from the ground. It twisted in on itself and started, little by little, to wrap into a coil.

A finger formed, then part of a palm, and then a second finger. Long minutes passed in silence. Choco-Ra's eyes dimmed to almost nothing in steely concentration. Wereberry and T.C. stayed as silent as proverbial mice, watching their friend reconstruct himself. The fingers that sat outside the cell twitched and moved, flexing. They shook under the strain, but held together.

More of his palm reformed, and then a third finger. Choco-Ra didn't want to admit that he was afraid to unravel too much of himself at once. He figured a hand could be followed by an arm and so on, until he was outside the cell, but he knew it would take a dangerously long time. Seeing no better options, however, he kept at it.

None of them paid attention to anything but Ra's slow progress. The world didn't exist for them outside of those three, almost four, fingers that twitched and waggled in slow motion.

Which is how they missed the approach of the guards.

A foot came down on part of Choco-Ra's limp bandage. Ra reacted instinctively, trying to yank his hand back into the cell. The foot pressed firmly and the bandage just yanked in futile motion. Ra looked up, pinned, and his eyes blazed with found fury.

"Do you mind?" he spat out. His voice was deep and regal, a sure sign that he found no amusement in his position. Wereberry and T.C. tensed for some unknown, desperate gamble. Neither of them knew what would happen if Ra's bandage ripped, and there wasn't exactly time to check and find out. So they took the worst case scenario, that he would lose his hand for good, and started working out a way to prevent it.

"Get back in your cell," the guard said, moving his foot. Ra yanked the bandages and partial hand back through the food slot quickly.

Standing up, Ra locked eyes with the guard and lifted his again-unraveled hand. He grabbed the edge of the limp bandage in his left hand and seemed to just twist the bandage in the air quickly. The missing hand reformed instantly and tightly. Choco-Ra flexed it firmly, managing to make the simple motion of opening and closing a hand come across like the threat it was meant to be.

The sound of clapping came from farther down the hallway. "Bravo," a voice rang out. It had the pitch and timbre of a girl's voice, but carried the steel of a much older woman. The guards stood at attention and the one standing opposite Choco-Ra took three steps backward, giving the bearer of the voice room.

The Grand Vizier strolled into view. Ra turned his gaze on her, eyes flashing a red glow that dimly lit against the far wall. Wereberry and T.C. turned to see her as well, their faces betraying nothing but bottled frustration.

She was only a few inches shorter than Wereberry, but much younger. She appeared to be a little girl. A little blonde girl with her hair done up in a wide bun that trailed a ponytail from the center of it. She wore a knee-length purple skirt with a long-sleeve shirt tucked into it of the same purple. The sleeves of the shirt turned colors, however, as they went down her arms to her wrists. Rainbows of color traversed the arms of the shirt. The color pattern matched the wide metal belt she wore. Her white socks were rolled at the cuff, sliding into thick, rainbow-colored hiking boots that matched the sleeves of her shirt.

Cradled in her arm was a black peg board. Some of the holes were filled by colored plastic pegs. They flashed, colored lights coming on and off, pulsing in an unknown rhythm.

"Thanks," Ra said, bowing, "now, if you'll let my friends and I out of these," Ra looked around him, "cages," he spat, "I'll be happy to show you other tricks."

The Grand Vizier shook her head and laughed a clear, tinkling laugh. "I'm so sorry, but I just can't do that," she said with a smile. Her eyes locked with Choco-Ra's.

"Can't, or won't?" Ra shot back.

Wereberry and T.C. stood in silence, watching the exchange. They didn't know exactly what was going on, but it looked like Ra had met some sort of match in this strange woman. Even more, they both seemed to be, on some level, enjoying it.

"Oh, well, all right then," the Grand Vizier said with a soft chuckle, "won't. You win. I could let you go. I just don't see why I should."

"We want to see the Princess. The person in charge," Choco-Ra explained, "and that is not, sadly, you."

"I wouldn't say 'sadly,'" the Grand Vizier said, "but no, I am not the Princess. I am her Grand Vizier."

"Ahh, very well," Ra said, "I am Choco-Ra. That," he tilted his head, "is Wereberry and that is T.C. Your name?"

"You may call me the Grand Vizier. But it is good to know who I am caging. Now the question is why. Why did you three move to attack the castle?" she asked. "And why, in Heaven's name, would you drag those innocents into it?"

"We didn't attack the castle," T.C. piped up quickly.

"Yes, we did," Ra pointed out to him, turning back to the Grand Vizier, "but we were left with no choice. We wanted to meet, peacefully, with the Princess. So did our other companions. Your guards would not let us."

"You would have let a mob through the gates if this was your castle?"

"I would've if they were peaceful," Ra said.

"Fair enough," she said with a slight nod, "and I tell you what. I will even give you what you wanted. An audience with the Princess."

"Thank you," Choco-Ra said, bowing slightly.

"Of course," she continued, "it will be for sentencing, but why split hairs?"

The Grand Vizier took a step back, looking at the guards. Ra didn't bother to argue. He went so far as to glance at both Wereberry and T.C., getting their silent agreement to play along so they could at the very least see the Princess.

Three guards stepped forward, one to each cell door, and unlocked them. They rested their hands on the doors, not opening them.

"If you try to escape," the Grand Vizier said, "…well, don't."

The guards ushered the three friends out into the hallway, where other guards joined them. There were three guards behind each of them, and one alongside and one in front of each.

In formation, they were marched along the hallways of the castle. Inside it was more opulent, and pinker, than it had looked from the outside. Massive doors lined the hallway, each door with a sign stuck to it. Four of the six doors they passed were labeled "Wardrobe" followed by a number, each sign white with pink cursive engraving.

T.C. wondered what one person needed with that much clothing. Maybe though, he gave the Princess the benefit of the doubt, they were also for her staff and friends. She did seem to have a lot of guards to clothe, after all.

Wereberry ignored the doors and their signs completely, watching the way the guards moved. They weren't paying too much attention to what they were doing; they were simply counting on strength of numbers. Not that getting into a fight was something Wereberry wanted or looked forward to. He still thought the Princess could be Cherrygiest, after all. No, Wereberry was simply keyed up from the previous fight, added to his basic dislike of being locked up. It made him edgy, and being edgy made him prepare a bit faster, a bit cleaner, for the less hopeful possibilities.

Choco-Ra simply watched the Grand Vizier. She was so obviously in charge, it couldn't have been clearer with a big sign around her neck. That board she cradled, he wondered, what was that for? What could it do and why was it so precious that she carried it gently, and yet wouldn't have left it behind in these so obviously guarded halls?

The Grand Vizier took the lead of the unseemly parade and thought about the prisoners. They were not, she knew, from around the castle. She would have heard about them before now. Her board would have told her something of their presence. The idea that they were from somewhere else, somewhere outside this world, wasn't fully shocking. It had happened before, though very rarely. She wasn't going to tell them that, of course. Still, the board hadn't even warned her that they were coming, much less arrived. That worried her, but only internally. On her face she showed nothing but her normal, happy reserve.

They turned a few corners, left then right then right again, and began to climb a long, sweeping staircase of pink-veined marble. It was wide and shaped like a square, leaving a large space in the center. It lent the entire march a note of serenity, the pink muting down to softer shades.

Wereberry, if he moved slowly enough, seemed to blend into the walls at times. His fur fit the castle perfectly, as if he was manufactured to belong there. The pink was close to the color that Cherry loved to wear, as well. The coincidence did not escape Were's notice, though he wasn't sure if he would chalk it up to coincidence anyway.

At the top of the stairs they came to a large foyer. It went straight on toward a set of doors, almost as large as the castle gates. The foyer was lined with couches and chairs. In between those sat plants in large gilded pots. Windows were set along one side of the foyer, and T.C. caught a glimpse of the courtyard they had entered through.

"Keep them here," the Grand Vizier said, opening one of the large doors just enough to slip herself through. She shut it behind her.

The guards formed up in a circle around their prisoners. They looked calm and ready. Then again, perhaps they simply looked bored and uncaring. Their faces didn't seem to handle too much expression, and a lot of the finer points were left up to the observer.

T.C., Ra, and Were' stood together, facing the large doors. They ignored the guards. What was, Ra considered, the point to really paying attention to them, after all? If they wanted to attack and do harm, chances were that they would succeed. Acting frightened and wary in front of them would only encourage any odd behaviors they already possessed. Were', without asking or checking, was in perfect agreement with Choco-Ra and knew it. T.C. realized what the other two were doing, but not necessarily why. He went along with it because he didn't see a better option. He also didn't intend to debate strategy in front of their jailers. That, he knew, would be counter-productive to the highest degree.

The large doors swung open inch by inch, without a sound. Choco-Ra cleared his throat and stood a bit taller. His friends followed suit. The guards didn't flinch or noticeably pay any attention. They were already on their best behavior. From all anyone could have gleaned from their rigid appearances, they could have been solid blocks of people instead of breathing bodies.

The Grand Vizier walked down the length of the foyer, nodding at the guards as she approached. They moved from their formation, coming to rest behind the prisoners and to their sides. The Grand Vizier approached the three friends and looked them over as if she hadn't seen them in months instead of minutes.

"You will be taken into the Princess' presence now. You will," she said, holding up a hand and ticking off each point on a finger, "not speak unless spoken to. You will stand where you are told to stand and not move from that spot. You will remain standing for the duration of your interrogation and sentencing. When you leave you will bow, turn toward the door you entered through, and wait for the guards to escort you out. Is that all clear?"

Wereberry looked at T.C. T.C. looked at Ra. Ra shrugged.

"Sure," he said blandly, and faked stifling a yawn. He was bored with these games. He was sure, already, how this audience would go. They would be tried for nothing, convicted of everything, and never be given a chance to do anything about it. Shouting out defenses would only compound the problem. Very well, he concluded for himself, if they want a kangaroo court they would have one.

The Grand Vizier signaled to the guards and they marched forward. The prisoners walked as well, being given no choice in the matter.

7 • Presence for Everyone

THE THREE FRIENDS ENTERED the throne room, followed by their entourage of guards. In front of them walked the Grand Vizier. Her head was held high and her step was relaxed. She had no worries. Worries were for people who didn't know their fate. She had gone to great lengths to know hers.

The throne room itself was well-lit and open. Plants and tapestries littered the walls, but the main area of the room was left empty. It managed to feel both imposing and friendly at once. Large chandeliers hung from the high ceiling. They cast crystal-fractured light in every direction, giving the room a brightness and sparkle that opened the space up even further.

At the front of the room was a throne. It was high-backed, well-carved, pink, and simply everything a throne should be, and yet also extremely gaudy. In the throne sat a woman who was, in the simplest terms, exactly like her throne. A Princess to the point of perfection, withholding the gaudy.

She was tall, easily taller than Choco-Ra, but not gangly. Her blond hair cascaded down to her elbows in straight tresses that curled at the end. Her slender shoulders and arms were covered by a bright pink-and-gray silk dress. The arms came down to slender points that draped over the backs of her hands. The dress continued down her body, a subtle white belt accenting her waist, until it enveloped her legs and fell along the floor.

On her head sat a simple silver tiara. It had a clean flower design in the center. Her earrings were silver and cast in the same design as the flower. A silver chain lay along her slender neck. At the apex of the chain hung a silver pendant of the same flower, the design filled in with pink gemstones.

The bright blue of her eyes contrasted with the darkness of her red lips. Her eyes held merriment and joy. Her lips were pursed to show displeasure. She nodded her head, the slightest of inclinations, at her Grand Vizier.

Wereberry's heart fell when he saw her. Though she was beautiful and regal, she was not Cherrygiest. Not in any way at all.

"Milady, may I present the prisoners," the Grand Vizier said, giving a sweeping bow. She turned and addressed the travelers. "State your full name for the records of the court."

T.C. nodded and looked directly at the Princess. "I am The Creature From the Fruit Lagoon, but you can call me T.C. In fact, please call me T.C. Thanks."

Wereberry choked back a small burst of laughter and raised one eyebrow. "I'm Wereberry," he said.

The Princess looked at him and smiled. She had a twinkle in her eye and seemed to see him for the first time.

Ra took a step forward and bowed before the guards could react. "I am Choco-Ra, sovereign of my own land, and I come to you as an equal."

"That will be enough," the Grand Vizier said crisply. The guards started to step forward to deal with Ra but he moved back to where he was supposed to be quickly, a smirk visible along his bandages.

The Princess studied all three strangers intently. She nodded at her Grand Vizier and drummed her fingers against the arm of her throne.

"Well, bring me the pink one. He is incredibly cute. He stays here. The others can go wherever. They don't seem like trouble makers, but if they are, then they are. I can't very well change their natures." Her voice was sweet and light. It collected the ideas of royalty and distilled them into a timbre that could be heard by all.

"Ex—" Wereberry stopped speaking, remembering the

rules and raised his hand instead, feeling perfectly foolish.

The Princess stifled a girlish laugh and smiled. "Yes?"

"I would be happy to stay and entertain you, uhhh, Princess, but if my friends were locked away then I would be too sad to be of use." Wereberry flashed her a big smile, his muzzle stretched so it didn't appear hungry or angry, simply genuine.

"Oh," the Princess said, "I hadn't considered that."

"Princess, please," the Grand Vizier jumped in, "don't listen to him. He obviously wants his friends free with him so that they can plot escape."

"Not true," Wereberry said simply. "We truly did not come to cause trouble. We do not intend any now. You locked us up. That was you. We have no reason to cause trouble and no desire to."

"Princess," the Grand Vizier said, "you have no reason to trust them."

"And yet," the Princess said, "I find that I do trust this Wereberry. Not just," she said with a light laugh, "because he's cute. No, we will try it his way. Him and his friends will remain here with me. So will a contingent of guards, just in case."

"This is unwise, Milady," the Grand Vizier put in.

"Consult the Board of Truth then, if it concerns you so."

The Grand Vizier sighed and nodded. "Yes, Milady," she said, defeated.

The Princess smiled, "Dear friend," she said softly, "don't take this as criticism of you. Go and have Steve work with you to find some new shoes, maybe some earrings. Seriously, you've done well. Take a break, have some fun."

"I'll try, Milady," the Grand Vizier said, hiding her true feelings. She was far from pleased. Very far. But there was nothing that she could outwardly do yet to rectify the situation. So she left the throne room, along with one of the guards. The rest of the guards stayed behind and took positions along the walls, while the once-prisoners stood in front of the Princess and wondered what they were supposed to do now.

"Come here," she said to Wereberry.

Wereberry looked around, making sure the Princess meant him. He nodded and walked forward until he stood in front of the throne.

"Princess?" he asked, unsure of what she wanted from him.

"Over here, by my side," she instructed. "You look very cute. I love that shade of pink. Is your fur soft?" She started to pet his head as she talked.

Wereberry was at a loss. She stroked his head as if he was an animal, a pet. It wasn't intimate at all, but distracted and mechanical. She liked the feel of his fur so he, as a subject, should stand there and be used as a petting zoo. T.C. shot him a look and Wereberry rolled his eyes, after a quick glance to make sure the Princess couldn't see.

T.C. and Ra both resisted the urge to sigh. They stood there and waited. Not that Choco-Ra was intending to wait for long. He was, he figured, biding his time for now. Let the Princess coo over Wereberry until she became completely comfortable. Then they could find their way toward information. T.C. didn't relish the idea of being imprisoned again, but he also felt like the throne room was just another kind of jail cell. A very gilded one, and easy to mistake for a freedom of place. T.C. knew different. He could feel it with every breath he took.

"Uhm, Princess?" Wereberry asked carefully.

"Yes?" She didn't stop petting him, scratching her nails gently along the top of his head. It felt fine to Wereberry, if creepy and possessive.

"Why didn't you let all of us in when we first asked? Why, I mean—" Wereberry really wished he could turn and look her in the eye while speaking, but instead he stood where he was, watching his friends "—why would you even have us arrested at all?"

"Well, I didn't," she said with a soft laugh. "Why would I do a thing like that?"

"Well, but you did," Wereberry pointed out.

"Now come on, I already told you I did not. Are you saying your Princess is telling lies?" Wereberry couldn't see her eyebrow arch, but Ra and T.C. certainly could. And did. And they worried that their friend was about to step in problems for all of them.

"Princess, if I may," Choco-Ra said quickly, before Wereberry could even open his mouth.

"Of course, you poor thing," she replied, nodding at him.

Choco-Ra didn't ask why the "poor thing" was there, he just charged forward. "I think what Wereberry meant to ask is why your Vizier—"

"Grand Vizier," the Princess corrected.

"Grand Vizier, my apologies, did these things. He realizes that it was not you, per se, but her acting on your behalf. He isn't," Ra confided, "royalty, as we are."

"Of course," she laughed. "Well, the Grand Vizier watches out for me. She cares a lot, you know. Why, sometimes she won't even go shopping with me for fear of dereliction of duty, the silly."

Choco-Ra nodded. Wereberry shot Ra a look of gratitude. Ra nodded a second time and otherwise stood very still.

"If you go shopping soon," T.C. said abruptly, "you could buy the Buffaloves more combs for when they visit. They do love a good brushing."

Ra and Wereberry both shot T.C. a look. He wasn't exactly sure what they meant by their looks, but he got the gist of it. They didn't want him to push her, not yet. They probably thought she was, well, T.C. thought to himself, as bad as Ra could be.

"The who?" the Princess asked. A smile lit her face as she

remembered, "Oh yes! Well I suppose I could, if I have any left over. We could go shopping now, in fact!" She stood up, moving away from Wereberry, and looked ready to clap and dance.

The guards came to life, stepping back toward the center of the room. They made sure they could get to the Princess before any of the recent prisoners could, just in case. Inwardly, many of them also groaned. They knew what a shopping trip could mean. Some of them took deep breaths, bracing themselves for what was to come.

"Come on, Steve," the Princess addressed the nearest guard. "These three are coming with me today. Do you have enough men with you?"

Steve nodded. The twelve guards should do. He really hoped they would do. He considered sending for reinforcements just in case, but decided against it. Seeing more guards would only make the whole event take longer.

"I thought," asked Wereberry, "the guard that left was named Steve."

The Princess nodded and pointed around the room at each guard in turn, "He was. These twelve are, now let me remember, Steve, Steve, Bob, Steve, Duane, Steve, Steve, Steve, Bob, Steve, Steve, and Bob." She nodded and then frowned and looked at the nearest Steve, "Was that right?"

"Yes, Milady," Steve said. Generally, he found, if she got a name wrong it was one of the Bobs. Sometimes she thought he was named Duane. Which was, Steve thought, silly, since Duane was named Duane and Bob was named Bob, but then royalty operated under different pressures, he supposed.

"Shopping?" T.C. asked. "Right now? But where?"

"In the Castle, of course," the Princess said, striding across the throne room.

The guards surrounded her. One in front to open doors, four on each side, and one in back, between the Princess and her three fellow shoppers. They moved briskly down the foyer and hurried down the staircase.

Once at the bottom again, the Princess directed them to a different wing of the castle, far from the holding cells. The guards almost felt bad for the three strangers they were escorting. They were better off than they had been as prisoners, to be sure, but a shopping trip wasn't exactly a picnic. It was an endurance test.

The Princess took a sharp right and started to climb another large staircase. It was shaped exactly like the first one they had seen, and Wereberry fought a sharp pang of déjà vu. He took each step in turn and focused on watching his feet. He just didn't want to know if the walls were exactly the same too. Somehow the feeling that so much of the castle was duplicated bothered him deeply.

Leaving the staircase only a few floors up, the Princess stood in front of a door marked "Shopping Center" in large white cursive letters. Her procession stopped smoothly without running into her. Long since adjusted to where she wanted to go and how fast she moved, they always stopped exactly when she did.

The Princess gave in and clapped lightly. "Here we are!" she exclaimed merrily. The guard in front of her, Steve, grabbed the handle of the door and pushed hard against it. It started to move gradually, but once started momentum kicked in and the door glided fully open.

On the other side of the door was a huge chamber. Incredibly high vaulted ceilings flew over walls that were spaced far enough apart that Choco-Ra wondered how the room could be the size it was and not be the width of the entire castle. There were endless pillars along the length of the room, as well as hanging lights, plants, and fans.

Discounting all of that, the room was cluttered and full beyond rational possibility. Clothes hung off of hooks that dotted the walls and pillars. Shoes sat on shelves that stretched as far as the eye could see. A make-up counter ran all the way along a section of otherwise clear floor. Toward the far end of the room, Wereberry could see what looked like vehicles.

People bustled back and forth across the expanse of space, re-hanging items and unwrapping new ones to put on display. Old items were carried away in carts, or pushed further back into the room. Wereberry, T.C., and Choco-Ra just stared. The guards fought sighs. The Princess laughed happily.

"You," she said, turning to face T.C., "wanted to find combs, right? Let's go get some combs if there are any!" Grabbing Wereberry's hand in hers, the Princess darted off down an aisle. The guards and Were's friends ran to catch up, ducking between displays and workers.

A glass counter with silver trim was the Princess' destination. It was filled with combs and brushes of all types, many of them pink, white, and silver. The Princess let go of Wereberry, set her hands on the glass, and gazed down at them. Wereberry stood where he was, pretty sure he hadn't been dismissed, rather simply put aside for a moment.

"Oh! These are wonderful!" she exclaimed. She looked around, but no one was behind the counter. "Miss?" she called out, searching for someone to help her.

Ra wondered why she didn't just go behind the counter; this was all quite obviously hers, considering it was in her castle and all. T.C. was wondering the same thing, but he put the question aside as he looked at the brushes and combs and tried to pick out the ones that Buffaloves would love the most.

"Miss?" the Princess called again, a bit shriller. It wasn't like the shop tenders to be so... absent. She wasn't sure what to do if one didn't come quickly. She could go look at shoes and come back, she supposed, but she really felt that they should be managing the store, since it was open.

A girl came around the counter quickly, moving some stray hairs off of her flush face. "I'm sorry, Princess," she said quickly, smoothing down her green dress, "how may I help you?"

The girl looked like a younger version of the Princess. Softer, her cheeks still held traces of baby fat. The two looked very much related and yet also somehow obviously not related. Wereberry couldn't figure it out. He shook his head and watched the Princess to see how she would react.

"Oh good, you're here. That's all right, I'm sure you were busy. No harm done, right? Of course not. Now. We're here to see some brushes and combs." The Princess peered down into the case.

The girl stole a moment to smooth her dress and straighten her hair while the Princess studied the case again. She put on her best smile and nodded at no one.

"Oh yes, we have the very finest. What kind of thing are you looking for, might I ask?"

The Princess laughed merrily and started to point. "We'll take this one, and that brush, and certainly the silver comb with the sea horse back, oh and the horse hair is a must, and that little white brush in the corner and those two pink combs on the lower shelf and the porcelain one over there." She spoke quickly and clearly, but managed to list off her wants in a single breath.

The store girl was already pulling combs and brushes from the case, grabbing each one as it was listed and pointed toward. She set them all on the counter and started to rummage for boxes and tissue paper.

"Excuse me, Princess?" T.C. asked meekly.

"Yes?" she replied.

"Which of those are for the Buffaloves? I think they'd like that one shaped like a sea horse."

"Oh no, that wouldn't do for them at all. No, they'd get tangled in the design. Well, let me think about it. Really none of these feels quite right for them, but I'll sort through later and find some, all right?"

T.C. nodded and let the matter drop. Externally, at least.

Internally he considered the Buffaloves and how unbrushed they looked. They were still happy and accepted the way things were, but he started to think he could understand exactly how things worked here.

He shook his head sadly and watched the shop girl pack up each brush and comb in a separate box. Every box was lined with pink tissue paper and then tied shut with a snip of pink ribbon. Maybe, he thought, at the very least I can steal some of the ribbon and tie bows in their fur for them. They'd like that, he smiled to himself, not as much as combs, but it would still be something.

As soon as the boxes were tied and put into shopping bags, the Princess moved on. Duane took the bags and carried them, the Princess already halfway down another aisle. She studied some shirts carefully, picking up the hems and rubbing the fabric. Pulling one off the rack she held it up against her, nodded, and then held it out to her side.

Steve grabbed it from her and followed closely. She handed him other shirts, some slacks, a few skirts, and a pant suit. Soon she headed for another counter where a shop girl was already waiting. This shop girl looked much like the first, except she had light brown skin and curly hair. Otherwise they could have been sisters. As it was, Ra guessed, they had to be cousins, at least. The shop girl boxed and bagged the purchases and handed them to Steve.

The Princess headed over to a display case of rings and necklaces. Wereberry looked into the case and laughed lightly.

"I had that ring!" he said happily, spotting a strange bulbous ring with a face that turned.

The Princess looked at him oddly and shook her head, "Impossible," she said simply. "That ring is brand new, and custom made like everything else here."

"No, it's a decoder ring, right? I had one of those, that exact model, even. A friend gave it to me years ago," Wereberry said, thinking back. "He kept one for himself and we used to send silly messages. He had a lot of fun little toys, actually."

"But it wasn't this ring," the Princess repeated.

"No, it was. I mean not that exact one, obviously, since how could it get here, right? But the same ring, if you follow."

The Princess shook her head and just moved away from the case. Everyone followed to see where she would go.

Scarves were next, and a different Steve stepped up next to the Princess, a hand out, waiting. She draped scarves over his hand without even looking to make sure he was there. Wereberry thought some of the scarves would work wonderfully as new wrist bands for the Fuzzticuffs, but unlike T.C., he didn't ask. He had a feeling that she would say they weren't quite right. Instead, he planned to see if he could grab some later from whatever closet she kept them in. Given the number of scarves she was piling up, there was no way she would notice a few gone missing.

The shopping trip continued apace. The Princess would run off to a new department in the store and grab items off shelves and racks, sizing them up and making her choices. A guard would be there to take each item from her and then they would head to a counter where another shop girl would wrap everything up. Every shop girl seemed to be related.

Maybe, T.C. thought around the fifth counter they stopped at, it was a family-run store. A large family, made up of mostly women. It made as much sense as anything else.

The Princess didn't talk, except to ask if some item or another was cute. Whenever she asked, a guard would agree that the item was perfect. The Princess didn't seem to care what was said—she made her choice often before an answer could be given. Any other attempt at conversation was ignored.

Wereberry started to feel funny after a few hours of shopping. At first he chalked it up to the whirlwind shopping trip itself, fatigue or dehydration, maybe. But the funnier he felt, the more he examined what it was. Then he realized what was happening and tried to not panic. He tapped both Ra and T.C. on the shoulder and leaned in close to whisper to them.

"Guys, I think I have a problem," he said.

"What's wrong?" T.C. asked. Choco-Ra looked Wereberry over, trying to spot the problem.

"Well, it's been a while since—" he started to say when Ra interrupted him.

"Fur's already thinning some," he said quickly.

Wereberry looked down at himself and sighed. Ra was right, his fur was thinning. Quickly. His fingers were starting to shorten as well. He could feel, without touching, that his muzzle was smaller. This was, Were' thought, not good at all.

The Princess turned around, reaching over to pet Wereberry, "I'm so glad you guys could come shopping with me! Isn't this just a good time? And you," she smiled directly at Wereberry, "are just so cute and furry." She ran her hand over his head and then stopped.

Looking at his head and then at her hand, the Princess felt something was off. She petted him again and frowned. "Your fur seems thinner," she said, growing concerned. "Is everything all right?"

Wereberry was beyond listening. He had ignored what he was feeling for too long and now it was simply too late. The pain had started. He howled once, loud and clear, the sound sending shivers down the spines of a few of the guards. Choco-Ra and T.C. each took a step, moving to stand at their friend's side. The Princess gasped and took a step backwards, turning to Bob.

"Quick! Get the Grand Vizier, she'll know what to do!" she yelled in horror.

"There's no need for that, he'll be fine in a moment," Ra said calmly, if quickly, trying to take control of the situation before it got out of control. He knew, too, that the Grand Vizier would turn the situation into a power play for herself.

Wereberry dropped to his knees and curled in on himself.

Everyone but his two friends took another step back. Bob turned and ran toward the front of the store, shouting for the Grand Vizier. Ra sighed and shook his head. Were' grunted and shook. He changed and grew smaller.

Everything stopped. Wereberry stood up, arms and legs shaking minorly. He was furless, a normal human man, with a shock of close-cropped pink hair. He was wearing a tan, short-sleeved shirt and slacks, with no shoes. Shaking his head to clear it, he looked around the store at the number of people who were staring intently at him.

"Uhm, well, I'm sorry about that," he said nervously, "so we were looking at shoes next, right?" he asked, trying to deflect interest away from his sudden change. No one bought the distraction.

The Grand Vizier ran into the room, board cradled under her arm. "Arrest them!" she shouted.

8 • Human Behavior

THEIR JAIL CELLS WERE EXACTLY as they had left
them. Steve and Steve and Duane each slammed a cell
door shut and locked them. The Grand Vizier stood nearby,
shaking her head. She had a gleam in her eye—not evil, simply
hungry for profit. Choco-Ra recognized it and saw even more
clearly what the power structure was inside the castle. The
Princess stood off to her Grand Vizier's side, her eyes full of
sadness and betrayal.

"How could you?" she demanded of Wereberry.

"Princess, if you just give me my bag back, I can—" he
started. He was upset, too. Not just because they were being
imprisoned again, but also because he truly didn't want the
Princess to be this upset over something that he felt was so
minor.

"Nice try," the Grand Vizier said, stepping closer to
Wereberry's cell, "but we will not be returning your items
simply so you can trick our Princess again."

"All right," Wereberry said, running out of patience, "what
is your problem? I mean, exactly. Like chapter and verse.
Explain it to me?"

The Grand Vizier's eyes narrowed as she shot dagger-like
looks at Were'. Her lips tightened, growing pale with the lack
of blood flow. The Princess, behind her, felt like defending
her closest friend and ally but found she couldn't. She wanted
to see, she realized, what would happen if events were left to
their own devices.

"Oh, I can do that," Choco-Ra said grandly before the
Grand Vizier could answer for herself. "Little Miss here," he
said, nodding toward her with a grin, "is so afraid of losing

any inch of power that she won't let the Princess have friends. Isn't that right, dear? Aren't you just a scared little thing, at the end of it all? So afraid you might be tossed aside, with your useless little board there, that you have to lock up innocents and besmirch the very throne you say you are protecting?"

Ra realized he had gone a few steps past too far by as soon as he stopped speaking. Taking in the looks of everyone in the jail, his friends and those on the other side of the bars, he wondered how bad he had just made things. Then he wondered if he cared.

The Grand Vizier visibly shook with anger. She shifted the light board to the crook of an arm to rummage in her pockets, and came back with a fistful of small colored pegs. She slid the pegs into holes along the board and considered it seriously, still fuming with rage. Her finger slid up along an edge of the board and, finding the switch there, flicked the board on.

Light dazzled from the board, lighting the room every which way. Colors burst and washed everyone in rainbows of warmth and force. "You dare," the Grand Vizier raged, holding the board aloft, "to speak to me that way? To speak of the throne that way? You dare?"

The light hurt Ra's eyes. He blocked most of it with a hand and looked as directly as he could manage at the Grand Vizier. "Pretty much," he said simply.

"Look," T.C. said, "the thing is, we still don't want to hurt anyone. We never did. Wereberry just... he's a werewolf, right?"

"The moon!" the Princess exclaimed. She was lost to direct sight by a wash of color, but her voice pierced the blinding lights cleanly. "There is no moon risen! Werewolves change under the light of a full moon, that's how you know they're werewolves!"

"Sure, I guess," Were' said, "but I change because of the scent of strawberries."

"What?" the Grand Vizier asked, laughing. "That makes

no sense."

Were' sighed and shielded his own eyes, growing tired of the excessive light. "And blinding us does?"

"This is the Board of Truth! You cannot lie before its light," she said, giving the board a shake.

Choco-Ra wanted to laugh. That was the silliest idea he had heard in a while. He started to tell the room he was secretly made of ponies but found he couldn't give voice to it. Wereberry found the same thing out when he tried to tell the Grand Vizier that he dyed his fur.

"Then you know I'm telling the truth," Were' said, "if I can't lie and I'm saying it now. You know it's true. It's the scent of strawberries! I don't know why I am the way I am, but locking me up because of it? Real nice."

"That isn't the point!" the Grand Vizier said, furiously.

"Yes. It is," T.C. put in, wanting to laugh. This whole situation was ridiculous to him. They were locked up because Wereberry wasn't furry anymore? They had only been released because he had been? How did that make sense to anyone? The Princess didn't seem daft or mean—she just lived in her own little world. Still, he wanted to get through to her.

"So if you smelled strawberries you'd be a pink wolf-man again?" the Princess asked.

Were' nodded. "Exactly."

"Princess?" T.C. asked, not caring about the fur debate, "the light is hitting you, too, right? So, I guess you can't lie, and I don't think you would anyway, but," T.C. paused briefly to gather his thoughts, "what do you do with all the stuff you collect? Can't more of it go to help others?"

"Well," the Princess said, looking around, "I do help others. But I need the newest fashions to be the best Princess I can be. I just also need to keep the old ones, in case they come back into style. It's not easy, you know."

"But," T.C. sighed, "so many more could be helped if you didn't have to hold on to everything like you say..."

"That's just the way it is," the Princess said. "But the light is simply reflected back here, I mean, I don't have to tell the truth. I am, of course, I just don't have to."

"What good would a truth potion be if it worked on the questioner," Ra thought out loud.

"Do you intend to harm me?" the Princess asked quickly.

"Of course not!"

"No."

"Why would we? No."

The answers came quickly and without thought. The three friends looked at the Princess and her Grand Vizier expectantly.

"So, can we go, then?" Were' asked. "Since we don't want to harm you and never did and you can be sure of it now?"

"Do you intend to harm me?" the Grand Vizier asked in return.

"No."

"What? Nope."

"If I have the chance I might consider it."

"Ra!" Were' and T.C. yelled in unison.

"It makes me tell the truth," Choco-Ra said with a shrug.

"You see, Princess?" the Grand Vizier asked her boss. The Princess sighed and nodded. These people, the ones she thought could be her friends, weren't. At least one of them planned to try to hurt someone near and dear to her, and she couldn't allow that. They had to understand.

Wereberry sat down in his cell. There was no way they were going to get out now. Ra and his temper had backed them into a corner. Then again, he thought, if he had been open to the Princess, or perhaps just said he wanted a damned strawberry, they wouldn't be in this predicament anyway. So it was, he reasoned, his fault as much as anyone else's.

T.C. stood and considered his cell. The bars would be impossible to get through, but the food slot was still their weak point. Maybe once everyone left he could find a way to use that to help them get free. Since everyone was focused on the other two he thought he had the best shot.

Choco-Ra cursed himself inwardly. Some leader he was turning out to be, ensuring their incarceration. He knew he had been forced to tell the truth, but it still bothered him. He should've been able to lie, or hide his feelings, or something. At the very least he should've been able to see the question coming, but he hadn't. He had underestimated the Grand Vizier, and that was the root of the problem. He realized he had just assumed he was a step ahead of her without giving it enough thought to be truly sure.

"Princess," Were' said. "Listen. We won't hurt anyone. Of course Ra is mad, he's been unfairly imprisoned. We're just looking for our friend. That's it. If she isn't here, and I'm pretty sure now that she isn't, we'll be moving on."

"What friend?" the Grand Vizier asked. "This is a new twist, isn't it?"

With the light still splayed all over, shining directly on the jail cells, Were' gave her the same answer he would've regardless.

"That's why we're here. We're not from this place at all, as I'm sure you," he nodded at the Grand Vizier, "have known. Our friend, she's about my size? Wears pink, is a ghost? Ring any bells?"

"None," the Princess answered before the Grand Vizier could tell her not to. "She is not here, and I have no memory of her. And you, my Grand Vizier? Have you seen this woman?"

"Milady, I may have," the Grand Vizier said truthfully. She wouldn't have admitted it, but she tried to not lie to her liege. "But it was long ago, and she hasn't been seen by me since. If it even was the one they're looking for."

The three friends perked up at this. Were' stood up again, a renewed sense of urgency tugging at him. "Then you have to let us go so we can find her. Please!"

"Milady," the Grand Vizier said, "I do not trust these men, as you know. Consider staying your leniency. I fear no good shall come of it."

"Can you turn off the light show, at least?" Ra asked.

"So you can lie?" the Grand Vizier shot back.

"So I can see," Ra said simply.

T.C. grinned at that. Well played, he thought. The situation was far from perfect, but Ra seemed less angered and more like his old self, smooth and working an angle. It was an angle T.C. couldn't see, but he had a sense for Ra, considering how long they had known each other.

Were' flexed his hands and glanced down at them, wondering why his claws didn't extend. Then he remembered, seeing bare flesh, that he was in his other form now. It was a form he didn't like much; he felt no real use for it. It didn't give him any advantages that he had discovered. In fact, it seemed to be just the opposite. He felt weaker, he had no claws, his senses were dulled—being human was no picnic for him at all.

The Princess moved forward, putting a hand delicately on her Grand Vizier's shoulder. "Perhaps we can turn off the Board of Truth now," she said simply.

"But, Milady," the Grand Vizier protested.

"No, I think this is over for now," the Princess said, a note of sadness in her voice.

"So can we go, then?" Were' asked, trying to keep from sounding too hopeful.

The Grand Vizier flicked the board off, the light vanishing in an instant. Everyone blinked several times, clearing their vision in the suddenly dim room. She hoped the Princess would at least keep the trio locked up. She didn't see anything to gain from letting them go. Of course, she had to admit she didn't see anything to be gained by keeping them prisoner, either. She just really didn't like Choco-Ra.

"No," the Princess said, "not with everything still so

unclear."

"What's unclear?" Were' asked quickly.

"You say you don't mean harm, and that you just want to find your friend, but you could have told this all to me before. Yet you hid it. If it is harmless, why do that? No, I'm sorry." The Princess nodded once and turned to leave.

"You heard your Princess, keep them imprisoned," the Grand Vizier said as she turned to follow. The guards nodded and moved toward the door, standing watch.

9 • Breaking

RA, WERE', AND T.C. SAT in their cells. Wereberry, still human, considered their options and didn't find anything readily apparent. He wasn't strong enough, in his current state, to break out of the cell. That much he knew. Also, the bars wouldn't let him pass through—the only way out was through the food slot, and that was too small to be workable.

Choco-Ra was thinking along the same lines. He knew he could try to unravel himself again, but it was a slow and ponderous process, one sure to be noticed by the guards. Which put it right out of the realm of useable tactics.

T.C. wondered if he was strong enough to rip the gates upward. He thought he might, at the outside, just manage it, but never fast enough to avoid the guards' notice. He sat and thought.

Wereberry, meanwhile, had a sudden idea. He glanced at Ra and T.C. and patted the air next to him, asking them to just wait and be quiet. He needed them to back his play, but couldn't risk talking about it in case the guards could hear.

"Excuse me, Bob?" Were' called, pretty sure that Bob was the guard standing closest. He was right and Bob turned to him, question on his face. "Yeah, Bob, hey how are you? I know we're prisoners and we can't be let out, but I wondered if you could do me a favor?"

"You know I can't," Bob said, and he turned back to stare off into space.

"Come on, we spent all day shopping with you, you know us. I just want one favor, it won't get you into trouble," Were' said, knowing it would, in fact, get Bob into trouble. He felt bad for that, but was pretty certain he could live with the guilt.

"What is it, then?" Bob asked, slumping his shoulders some.

"Our bags. I don't want to keep them and all the stuff, but we packed some books, you know? And at least we could have the books. As long as we're locked up and all. Couldn't we?"

"I don't know," Bob said, "I'll ask Steve."

"Thanks, Bob!"

Bob walked off, replaced by Bob, and hunted down Steve. Steve was in charge of this detail, and was spending his time going over duty rosters for the next week. Having to keep prisoners meant he would be stretching his men thin for the foreseeable future.

Bob and Steve talked a while and considered Wereberry's request. On the one hand they couldn't just hand the bags over, but they did like the three guys, so they wanted to help if they could. They were prisoners, no doubt, but they weren't exactly evil. Steve sent Duane to go get the prisoners' belongings.

Duane came back to the cells, carrying the three bags. He handed them to Bob and left. He didn't think this was a good move, but he had been ordered to so he did. Still, he had a feeling that his tennis racket might come in handy soon.

Bob stood before Wereberry's cell, three bags in hand. "Well, which one am I digging in, then?"

"Oh let me," Were' said meekly. "Look, like this I'm no threat, not that I would be anyway, given how many of you there are. Huh?"

Bob sighed and considered, looking back down the hallway. There were a lot of other guards, after all. Surely it wouldn't hurt any to let the little guy out of his cell for a second to grab some books. So long as he agreed to the terms.

"I'll let you rummage, if you do it for all of your friends. I can't let you all out, you understand."

Wereberry pretended to pause and think about it. "No, that's fine," Were' agreed.

Bob unlocked his cell and put one hand on his racket. Wereberry took a single step out of his cell, blocking the door from swinging shut, and opened his bag. He started to dig through it, making a show of looking for books. While he was, he hid his movements from Bob carefully. Slowly he opened the bag of strawberries inside and bent for a closer look. His nose almost in the bag, he inhaled deeply and then went back to searching for books. He grabbed one at last, before Bob got too suspicious, and then proceeded to look through T.C.'s bag.

While he was searching, he felt the scent take effect. His skin tingled and started to burn. Now all he had to do, he knew, was find a way to stay outside the cell while he changed. He grumbled to himself, seeing the fastest route, but not enjoying the prospect too much. Still, he reasoned, an out was an out.

Wereberry leapt at the guards with a weak cry. They grabbed their rackets and started to swing, even as he landed short of them. He went down under a press of bodies.

T.C. and Ra resisted the urge to cry out or struggle against their bars. They had both seen Were's movements and realized his plan. So they stood near their cell doors and waited.

A howl sounded and the mass of guards slowed down as they tried to process the noise while swinging their rackets down again and again against Wereberry. Steve went flying. Then Bob, then Steve, Steve, and Duane. Wereberry stood up, covered in pink fur, long muzzle pulled back in a grin, and flexed his claws.

"I don't want to hurt you guys," he said seriously, "so please, just stay back."

Running over to Bob before the other guards thought to sound a general alarm, he grabbed the bags and Bob's keys. He unlocked the cages and tossed each of his friends their belongings.

"Nicely done," Ra said, grinning.

"Wow, Were', that was great," T.C. added, slinging his bag onto his shoulders.

"Hurt like hell. Let's get moving, I don't want to hurt anyone."

"Else," Choco-Ra said.

"Hmm?" Were' asked as they started to run down the hallway, pushing guards out of their way, or leaping over them in Wereberry's case, but trying to not engage them.

"You don't want to hurt anyone else, you meant," Ra clarified.

"Don't start, Ra," Were' said over his shoulder.

Choco-Ra shrugged, but kept running. The three took longer than they would've liked getting to the staircase, which presented a problem. Guards filled it, running down to meet them. Without the high ground of leverage, the three friends considered their options. Then they simply charged, taking the stairs as hard and fast as possible, shouldering guards left and right but trying to not knock them off the stairs.

Alarm claxons sounded. Wereberry yanked both of his friends toward the banister. Their momentum stopped and guards started to shove into them, rackets swinging wildly.

"Oh, good plan, stopping," Ra said sharply.

"Shut up and climb on my back. T.C. and I are agile enough to do this, you aren't," Wereberry said, taking a racket blow on his shoulder.

"Were', we're going—"

"Yeah," Were' said to T.C., "up."

Choco-Ra grumbled a bit but held onto Wereberry. Were' and T.C. climbed over the railing and faced the open pit formed by the square, sweeping stairs.

Then they leapt.

Up and across they sailed, arms extended. Choco-Ra clutched Were' tightly as they crossed open air. Claws and webbed hands grabbed the bottom of the railing on the opposite side of the staircase, half a flight up. T.C. and Were' turned themselves carefully and leapt again. The guards realized what the prisoners were doing, far too late to reverse course fully. They started to shout upwards, trying to warn the guards above them, but Were' and T.C. kept jumping, switching from side to side as they ascended the staircase.

The last bit of railing was grabbed, creaking under the weight of the three bodies. Were' and T.C. scrabbled up and over the railing, finding their footing on the stairs again. Ra dropped off of Wereberry's back and took a deep breath. Guards were starting to come up the stairs after them, of course. There were more already coming at the staircase from the hallway they faced.

"Another run?" T.C. asked, snatching some moisturizer from his bag and slathering random parts of his skin as quickly as possible.

"Let's," Wereberry said. Choco-Ra nodded and the three friends took off like a shot. Their shoulders came down as guards approached, then sharply up once they hit something solid, throwing the guards to the side. They tackled, crunched, and displaced every guard they met.

It wasn't, to be fair, that the guards were truly useless. They just didn't ever get to face an actual threat. The last time the guards had found themselves doing more than carrying the Princess' shopping or nicely telling a Fuzzticuff it was time to go home, well, they couldn't even remember the last time. They tried to keep up with drills, but daily castle life always interrupted, and many of them just didn't see the point in too much practice.

Ra found himself juking and dodging guards, not because he didn't want to throw them around more—that would've been fine—it was just faster. Were' and T.C. followed suit. There was only so long any of them could keep up the pace they'd initially set, and that time was already behind them.

"Where to?" Wereberry asked over the din of footsteps and yelling.

"No clue," Ra answered, "T.C.?"

"I've never been here before," the merman said.

"This way!" Wereberry shouted, turning down another hallway toward a fresh staircase.

"Why that way?" Ra asked, following.

"Scent, remember?"

"Oh, good one," Ra said, laughing.

The stairs were blocked by a host of guards that, to the trio, looked meaner than any they had dealt with up to that point. Some of them had rackets raised and others had baseball bats and hockey sticks, all ready to stop the escapees.

Choco-Ra stopped his friends and simply walked closer to the guards, alone. He nodded at them and let his eyes glow brighter. The glow filled the space, dousing the guards in bright red light. The rackets dropped slightly, the bats seemed to quiver, and a hockey stick chattered against the floor. The guards didn't back down, but their fear was a physical thing. Wereberry could smell it, and T.C. could sense it deep in his gills.

Ra turned quickly to his friends and nodded. Were' and T.C. sprang forward, calling on every reserve of strength they could find. They reached the guards just as they were snapping out of it. The floor was soon littered with their unconscious bodies, though the guards did deal out a few bruises here and there.

"Fear vision?" T.C. asked, panting to catch his breath.

"Exactly so," Ra said, rewrapping a hand quickly.

"I didn't know you had fear vision," Were' said, bent over with his hands on his knees.

"You learn something new every day," Ra said, looking around. "We don't have long, what's the plan?"

"I was thinking we go talk to the Princess," Were' admitted.

"Talk to her? Are you serious? She won't listen now, I can tell you. Though maybe if we pretend," Ra looked at both of his friends, "to threaten her, we can get passage out of here."

"Pretend only, right?" T.C. asked.

Choco-Ra nodded. "Of course, I have no interest in harming her. Just in getting out of here."

They took the stairs at a sprint, coming quickly to the door at the top. It was large, pink, and made of heavy wood. There was no label on it, but Wereberry could smell familiar scents behind it. The door was locked, but three shoulders took care of that after a few blows.

Past the doors, the room was opulent. Plush pink furniture decorated the floor, and giant tapestries decorated the walls. A chandelier hung far above, casting clean white light in all directions.

The Grand Vizier and the Princess herself stood at the far end of the room, surrounded by a small contingent of personal guards. Wereberry could hear the Grand Vizier speaking in quick, hushed tones.

"Milady, I say again, there are reports of an uprising outside as well. This is not random—" but she broke off when the door caved in, turning instead to look at the three who entered.

"We'd like to leave," T.C. said simply.

The Grand Vizier spun and glared at the trio. The guards moved to intercept them, weapons raised. The three friends stood still, though. They made no move to attack, retreat, or even sit. They just stood there, watching.

"Please don't attack us," Wereberry said, "we don't want to fight. We just want to leave."

"You'd like us to think that, wouldn't you?" the Grand Vizier said. "Now that your armies are outside the castle while you attack us from the inside, you would just love it if we let you go to lead them, hmm? Do you think we're stupid?"

"No," Choco-Ra said, bowing slightly, "not stupid at all. Simply misinformed. We don't know of anything going on outside."

"You would say that!" the Grand Vizier fumed.

"Because it's true," T.C. pointed out.

The guards took another step forward, acting on their own initiative. The Princess held up a hand, stopping them. The Grand Vizier looked at her, not sure why her liege would want to listen to these people. It was perfectly obvious that they were behind all of the recent troubles.

"Again, we do not know what is going on outside," Ra said, shrugging.

"There are forces rising against us," the Princess said. "My Grand Vizier was just informing me of them. You knew nothing of this?"

"No, of course not," Wereberry said. "Why can't you understand that we never meant you harm at all? Not even now. We simply want to leave."

"Do not listen to them, Princess, there is a horde of Scuttles outside demanding that we let them in." The Grand Vizier looked at each of the travelers in turn, searching their faces for guilt.

Choco-Ra laughed, as good an admission as any. "All right, in a round-about way that might have been my fault. They were desperate for change, change in how they were treated. I told them to demand it."

"So you admit that you are responsible for this?" the Princess asked, a note of sadness in her voice.

"In a certain way, I suppose so," Ra said, shrugging again.

The Princess didn't know what to do. She did like these three strangers, and tended to believe them. But her Grand Vizier had always looked out for her and kept her safe and happy. They simply couldn't all be right. The Princess found herself forced to choose between friendship and instinct. She found she couldn't. Not quickly, at least.

"The Board of Truth will tell us if they lie, Milady," the Grand Vizier said, lifting the board in front of her. She grabbed in her pockets for some pegs and started to fit them into various slots.

"That thing gives me a headache," Ra said genially.

"Well I am very sorry," the Grand Vizier replied with a sly grin. "Milady, we must discern the truth here and stop the uprisings."

"But," the Princess said, "what if they are right?" The concern in her voice hit home with T.C. He understood that she truly did mean to help the Buffaloves; she just got distracted too often. She was as genuine and good as she appeared. The Grand Vizier, he felt, truly meant to do good as well. She just had a funny way of showing it. Then again, so did his friends sometimes.

"What if," Wereberry asked, "the Grand Vizier is behind this all?"

"What?" said the Princess, echoed by the Grand Vizier, T.C., and Choco-Ra.

"Just an idea, sorry," Were' said, grinning sheepishly. "Maybe, then, it simply is what it seems to be. We want to do you no harm and just leave. The Scuttles just want to be heard. No one wants trouble, but there's only so long you can stand being ignored."

"I do not," the Princess said flatly, "ignore my subjects."

"Sometimes you do, Milady," T.C. said softly, "even if you don't mean to."

The Princess' face washed over with shock. T.C.'s words had hit home. Maybe she wasn't giving enough to the others, maybe she should get out of her castle and visit them more. Still, she had to run the place, too. There were only so many hours in the day.

"The Board shall tell us," said the Grand Vizier, raising the board and facing it toward the three. Her finger slid upward along the side, searching for the switch.

Choco-Ra sprung from where he stood, leaping across the room at her. His hands fell on the board, grabbing at its sides. Wereberry and T.C. ran after him.

"How dare you?" fumed the Grand Vizier. "Let go of the Board! The Board is sacred!"

"Ra!" Were' shouted, finding that he, too, had a grip on the board. "Come on, let it go!" He wasn't sure who he was trying to yank it away from, but he thought that if he had it himself, then he could give it back to the Grand Vizier.

T.C., on Ra's other side, also grappled against the board. His webbing bent around a corner of the board as his fingers grabbed it.

All four of them struggled, yanking the board back and forth in a massive, four-way tug-of-war. The Grand Vizier all of a sudden fell backwards, hitting her ass against the hard stone floor of the room with a gasp. Wereberry and T.C. stood close to Ra, hands still on the board.

"That's enough, Ra, we won't solve anything like this," Wereberry said.

"I'm just sick of this damn board," Ra said, yanking it back toward himself, trying to wrest it away from all other hands.

T.C. and Wereberry held fast, though. Forces sharpened and strained against the black finish of the board, and a thunderous crack was heard. The Grand Vizier screamed as if the pain was her own. The Princess gasped, hands flying to cover her mouth in surprise. Were' and T.C. caught each other's eyes and exchanged a quick glance of worry.

The Board of Truth rent apart. Pure white light spilled from it, growing in the air where the Board had been, even after Ra dropped the halves he held. Pegs of all colors popped out and rolled along the floor, tiny tinkling sounds ringing out loudly in the room.

The white light grew again and then stopped. The three friends looked at each other, recognizing what was happening. They found themselves with just enough time to start and turn, trying to dodge the appearance of the hole in space, before the light exploded outward and then contracted into nothing.

When the air was still and clear again, the Princess stood, watching in silence. The last of the pegs bounced on the floor. The Grand Vizier openly wept. The guards shook their heads and rubbed their eyes to clear their vision.

Other than that, the room was empty.

INTERLUDE TWO

THE WHITE SPACE ADMITTED the three friends once more. They floated aimlessly, wordlessly, for a few minutes. Or hours. None of them knew for sure.

Wereberry forgave Choco-Ra quickly. Nothing had been done that he wouldn't have done himself, if he was honest about it. He just hadn't given in, whereas Ra had. That didn't make Choco-Ra bad, it just made him Choco-Ra. Were' wondered what was going on in the castle now. Did the Scuttles get their time to speak to the Princess? Was the Grand Vizier all right? He had no idea, and let himself float for a while, thinking.

T.C. hoped the Buffaloves were doing all right. He hoped the Princess would remember the combs and brushes and think through her actions more often. Maybe her first step would be to invite the Buffaloves over and comb them. He didn't care if she gave him any credit for it, it wasn't about that. He just wished them well and wondered if he would ever manage to go back and see them.

Choco-Ra sulked as he floated. He started to wonder how often his choices would lead people into trouble. It wasn't intentional. Patterns of his own behavior formed, and he took the time to look at them slightly differently for a change.

Gray mist started to pool off to their side. They watched it but swam no closer. Slowly, it seemed to form trees and grass. The color drained from the apparitions, and they appeared to simply blow away on an unseen and unfelt wind.

They watched the mists form other things, as much as they managed to form before they, too, dissipated. There was no discernable rhyme or reason to any of it, not that the three could work out.

The mists were, however, growing. Ra noticed it first, waving and pointing until the others saw. It spread, starting to surround them. T.C. grabbed his friends and swam clear, not wanting to touch the mist and not wanting to be trapped by it. Once clear, they watched again. The mists now covered a substantially larger area. The visions within that area seemed to grow sharper every time they formed. Color became clear. The apparitions lasted longer.

The three travelers found themselves curious, but felt that curiosity tempered by fear. Were' knew that Ra would want to explore it, and he felt that he could deal with that, if the matter came up. Ra, however, remembered last time as well. He didn't want to force a choice that could obviously endanger the others without discussing it in more than hand signs.

Choco-Ra turned away from the mist and saw a spot. Once again, it seemed to his eyes a rainbow in an otherwise white space. Wereberry, a tap on the shoulder making him turn around, smelled it as soon as he saw it: the scent of grass, thick in his nose. He wondered why he hadn't smelled it before. Ra also nudged T.C. who, as soon as he turned, felt the pull of a current toward the spot.

T.C. grabbed his friends and swam toward it, letting the current pull him as much as he moved under his own power. They reached the spot easily enough, not finding themselves distracted by the mists this time. They swam around it to the other side and pushed against it. Nothing.

The three friends went back to the side they had first been presented with. Their hands pushed through the empty space easily. As they touched it, each one of them noticed something.

Wereberry turned and looked over his shoulder. The mists thinned and wisped away as he watched. The scent off the spot grew stronger, overpowering him. He pulled his arm out of the spot and the scent died down. T.C. and Choco-Ra did the same, having felt that exact odd shift in the fabric of whatever it was they floated in.

As soon as their arms were out of the spot, the intensity of their feelings toward it dimmed and the mists, utterly gone, started to reform. They looked at each other, unsure. Ra jerked a thumb toward the spot, shrugging as he did. The other two nodded and they dove through the spot, leaving behind nothing.

PART THREE
Flicking Off the Safety

"There is nothing so likely to produce peace as to be well-prepared to meet the enemy."

–George Washington

1 • Hard Pressed

ALMOST EVERYONE DOVE for cover in the first minutes of the attack. Blots of green light flashed through the sky, impossibly arcing back toward the ground in exactly the way bolts of light didn't. They hit and exploded whatever they touched. Dirt flew up as bolts grazed the ground, half-vaporized half-heated dust. Walls crumbled and trucks exploded. Chaos reigned over the land as the enemy attacked.

People ran for cover, or crawled for it, and some dug for it. Normally, an attack like this would be met head on, pound for pound and explosion for explosion. This time, for a change, honest surprise carried the day. There was no way to return cannon fire with a pistol, no way to charge forward bravely when to do so meant you ran up a hill against superior firepower, exposed.

"What're they after, Chief?" Firepot Jones asked. Jones was the nominal explosive expert, and he was itching for a way to get to his bag of goodies. As it was, Jones sat behind a large rock, next to the new recruits.

"No clue, Jones!" yelled Chief. Chief Keller, one of the largest men in the service, found himself hunching his six-foot-six frame behind the edge of a jeep. His sunglasses were smudged with dirt and his hat was missing. Chief always had his hat on; it was as obvious to the men as the sun rising. They thought he slept with the thing. To see him there now, sans hat and shiningly bald, lent an air of desperation to the proceedings.

Chief stood, nodding at Firepot Jones, and ran toward the armory. He was intending to answer this challenge in the form of gun fire, and answer it with prejudice. A few of the other men joined Chief in his mad run. The sounds of battle rang out around them, covering whatever they yelled to each other.

The air split with the scream of high-powered jet engines. Five sleek, black jets tore across the blue sky, menace in each and every angular gleam. They dipped low and were out of sight almost before anyone had a chance to recognize them. Then the sound of the engines came back from different quarter. They were circling, looking for easy targets. Black bombs disengaged from the jets and threw themselves violently toward the ground.

The loud, flat thump that followed each bomb's impact tossed men to the ground like rag dolls and threw up plumes of dust and rock. The shockwaves themselves were visible in the hot afternoon, shimmering through the air. Each shockwave gave the men just enough time to see the force heading their way before it picked them up and turned them end over end.

Chief, and the few men with him who still stood, made for the door of the armory. Firepot Jones caught their success out of the corner of his eye and whooped triumphantly for them. Now, Jones knew, the tide could turn. He looked at the recruits near him and pointed toward the armory.

"See, now you'll see what the BOBs can really do," he said proudly, ducking back for cover as more fire swooped down from the sky.

"Besides hide and cower, you mean?" Choco-Ra asked.

"We're biding our time," Jones said seriously. He didn't understand why these recruits were so blind to the obvious.

"So Chief will bring us weapons?" Wereberry asked Jones. He lifted the rifle they had handed him earlier and shrugged. It was fine, he supposed, and after giving it a few test firings earlier that day he'd had to agree that the weapon did fire bolts of light. It just didn't seem like fighting to him. But that was the way these folks did things.

"No, Were'," T.C. said, his own rifle slung across his chest, "they're probably going to go out in one of those big armored things."

"A tank?" Jones asked. "That would be cool, huh?"

"Uhm, sure?" T.C. shrugged. He didn't think getting shot at was really cool, although he did admit to himself that the jets were cool. They were very black and shiny and went along at an incredible clip.

"All right, so why are we just hiding here?" Ra demanded. "Couldn't we, oh, I don't know, do something?"

"Look," Firepot Jones said with a shake of his head, "you three are just recruits. You can't drive, you can hardly shoot, and you just got here, for gosh sakes! I don't like being held back from combat myself, but I was assigned to keep you three safe and back from the action and that's what I'm gonna do, gosh darn it!"

"So shouldn't we be somewhere safe?" Were' asked. He was sick of all the questions. Worse, he was also quite sure that if they would just let him go and head toward the enemy that he could figure something useful out. Being stuck hiding like this rankled his fur.

"You're perfectly safe here," Jones said, looking around, "besides, if I'm right, this was just a quick skirmish anyway. HAVOC knows it can't win a prolonged battle with us. They're probably just trying to disorient us, or something. Once we show our own force back, they'll run. Like they always do."

"So they just come down here, to your firebase," Ra said, looking around him, "and shoot you up, and then run instead of pressing the attack?"

"They know we'll turn the tide and win if they try that," Jones told him.

Wereberry laughed. "So what do they really hope to achieve?"

"Well, I guess just to set us back to having to repair the damage, and of course," Jones grew serious, "killing our men, if possible."

"I haven't seen a single medic though," T.C. said.

"Hey, he's right," Were' agreed.

"We've been really lucky this time," Firepot Jones said, "that's all."

The jets circled back again, but as they started their pass over the firebase, a heavily armored, multi-wheeled vehicle burst out of the armory. The armory shook and collapsed in on itself in the vehicle's wake, tent ballooning down over shelving. The vehicle was a dark olive green and sat low on its ten wheels. Two massive turrets sat on the top of the thing, each one rotating 180 degrees. They began to swivel, and through the few slits in the armor eyes could be seen, scanning the sky.

"Ha! It's the new Beatbox-15!" Jones yelled triumphantly, pointing at the impossible-to-miss craft. "Now HAVOC is in for it!"

The Beatbox-15's guns turned and aimed, the craft aligning itself for a good field of fire. Dual blasts of bright yellow light, each blast as thick as a person's body, lanced out into the sky. Two of the jets were hit instantly, the third banking hard at the last second to avoid taking fire. All three jets turned toward home, two of them smoking badly. They left dark trails through the sky. The BOBs started to cheer, people coming out of hiding to jump and yell in victory.

The top hatch of the Beatbox-15 swung open and Chief popped out, arms raised in triumph. A fresh new hat sat on his head and the metal-rimmed brim caught the light, sparkling into the afternoon.

Firepot Jones left his three charges and ran over to join the celebration that was going on around the Beatbox-15. People were laughing and throwing their fists in the air. There was a rising chant of "Go BOB!" forming, and Chief picked it up too, screaming it loudly into the smoke-filled air.

Choco-Ra, Wereberry, and T.C. stood up and looked

around. The ground was pitted heavily and smoke rose from almost every hole they could see. Buildings were similarly pitted, if not missing whole walls. They could see no injured men at all, however. Not a single person so much as limped.

They wandered over to the mess hall, undamaged in the fight, and looked around. Men started to stream toward them, still celebrating. The three friends moved away from the door, letting the press of bodies enter first.

A small, bug-eyed man stepped aside as well and stood next to them. His uniform was crisp and clean, and the normal BOB emblem on the chest was modified by a jagged blue line, like a shock of electricity running through it.

"Morning, boys," Shocker said with a nod of greeting.

"Sir," Were' said, answering for all three of them. Shocker had been the one to find them out in the field a few days ago.

At first he had thought they were HAVOC agents, and took them prisoner. They hadn't fought, mostly because they weren't sure where they were, but also because they didn't see any harm in following the little man. When they arrived at Firebase Alpha 6 later that day, they were taken prisoner, locked up, and interrogated separately.

Chief quickly realized they weren't enemy agents, and that they were brave and seemed fairly resourceful. So he offered them jobs. They said yes and found themselves rushed through orientation and given weapons, and a watch dog in Firepot Jones.

Wereberry agreed to join up if only because everything looked very, very cool. The chance of getting into a good clean fight didn't hurt, either. He didn't love violence, but it often helped settle his nerves. He also thought that once they gained access to the large information stores the BOB had, they could hunt Cherrygiest down easily.

Choco-Ra found himself saying yes in order to get his hands on the information as well. Though he did relish the idea of having a command of his own. A chance to prove, to himself too, how good a leader he could be. Everyone seemed surprised when he spoke, though, and gave him a wide berth for reasons he still didn't quite understand. When he asked they laughed and shook their heads, convinced he was messing around with them by asking.

T.C. said yes because his two friends answered first. He couldn't say no, he knew, and stay with them. He didn't resent them for their choices—he just found within him no good reason to want to join an army. A few days watching the BOB's tactics had started T.C. thinking, however. He was planning on speaking to someone very soon about a few ideas he had. He realized he wasn't the tactical mind that Were' was, or the strong leader that Ra embodied, but T.C. was convinced that he had something to offer. Which was odd to him, realizing that he actually did have something to offer this army he had randomly joined.

Shocker studied the faces of the three fresh recruits. They didn't seem worse for wear, given the pitched battle of only moments before. That was good, he felt. A true sign that they would make great members of BOB and do the entire service a credit. Shocker found himself proud of them; they were his discovery after all, even if Firepot had ended up leading them around. Shocker understood the reasoning there, too. A man like Shocker, with his responsibilities, couldn't very well lead three fresh faces around by the nose all day.

"You guys seem to be getting on all right," he said to them as men streamed into the mess hall.

"Yes, we—" Ra started. He stopped when he caught the look Shocker gave him. Once again he was flat out surprised that Ra had spoken.

"Choco?" Shocker asked.

"Call me Ra."

"Choco," Shocker repeated, "are you sure you're all right?"

162

"Perfectly."

Shocker shrugged, apparently swallowing his concern, and looked at T.C. "And you, Creature?"

"Call me T.C., and I'm just fine. We weren't hurt."

"It wasn't," opined Wereberry, "even scary, really. Just a lot of noise and dust."

"A lot of noise and dust!" repeated Shocker with a hearty laugh. "That's why you guys'll do fine here! You're unflappable in the face of danger."

"We can be flapped," T.C. said, his tone betraying the seriousness of his flippant words.

"Oh, Creature," Shocker began, waving a hand before T.C. could correct his name again, "don't worry. You guys did fine, Firepot took care of you, everything is grand. We made those HAVOC fools turn tail again, right?" Shocker nodded for everyone and jerked his head toward the door. "Now why don't we get some grub and I'll introduce you to a few guys, real good guys, too."

Shocker went through the tent door, holding the flap up for his three fellows. They entered the mess hall and got in line. Trays were slapped against the railing and all four of the men lurched forward inch by inch. Ra left his tray empty, standing in line to stay with his friends, who both piled up food and drinks happily. Shocker noticed Ra's empty tray but didn't seem to think it odd at all.

He led them over to a crowded table where room was made for the four new additions. Five men and one woman shifted their trays around and scooted over without complaint. Shocker remained standing while the three new recruits each sat.

"Hey guys," Shocker said merrily, "lemme introduce you around to this gang of malcontents." That got a piece of bread thrown at his head, but he continued on with a laugh. "This is Still Water," he said, pointing at the bread thrower. "That's Lugnut, Ears McGee, Full Bore, and this here," he pointed at the woman, "is Captain Violet."

The assembled troop nodded, waved, and generally greeted the three recruits. They were always happy, if occasionally wary, of new blood joining the BOB. More hands to help meant a better chance against HAVOC, after all.

"Hi, I'm Wereberry," the werewolf said.

"T.C.," T.C. told them, "and really, that's my name. Just T.C."

Ra looked around the table at the different faces that all considered him carefully. "I am Choco-Ra," he said, "but most people just call me Ra."

The BOBs around the table looked at each other. Lugnut and Full Bore leaned close and whispered. Captain Violet stared openly. Ears McGee shot a strange look at Shocker, as did Still Water. Shocker just shrugged.

"What?" Ra asked. "Why is it that whenever I speak, everyone looks around? I don't get it. I really don't." Ra waited a few beats and then sighed, "And don't, please, just laugh as if I secretly do understand, because I swear to all that you hold dear I do not. Were', do you understand it?"

"Not at all."

"T.C.?"

"I don't have a clue, but it is funny, you have to admit."

"No," Ra said, "I don't."

"The thing of it is, uhh, Ra?" Captain Violet said, "is that ninja don't normally talk as much as you do. That's all."

"Ninja?" Ra asked, looking around.

"You are a ninja, right?" Full Bore asked. The other BOB members around him nodded, certain that Ra was a ninja. Certain down to their bones.

"No," Ra said, which drew gasps.

"But you look like a ninja," Still Water complained, "why would you dress like one if you ain't?"

"I'm not dressed like anything," Ra explained, "I'm a mummy. The bandages are... I mean they just... look, the

164

bandages are normal."

"Yeah, he's always been like this," T.C. added.

Everyone sat and considered this bit of news. He wasn't a ninja after all, but claimed to be a mummy. And yet, he looked just like a ninja. It didn't make sense, frankly. Finally Captain Violet stood up and waved across the mess hall.

"Let's get Silent War over here to decide," she said. The others nodded and agreed. Silent War, the resident ninja, would know another ninja if one showed up. Hell, if Ra was a ninja he had probably trained with Silent War, and maybe that was why he didn't want to admit to anything. He needed to feel out how Silent War was accepted first. It didn't explain the verbosity he displayed, though.

Silent War caught sight of the wave quickly and wandered over to the table. He stood a good six feet tall and was dressed in head-to-toe black. The only visible part of him was his eyes, peeking out of a full face mask. Twin swords hung from his sides, and an Uzi hung against his back, long silencer attached.

"Hey, Silent," Full Bore said with a casual wave. The two men went on missions together almost as often as Silent War and Captain Violet did.

Silent War nodded his head a fraction of an inch. He stood over the table, trying to not loom and failing miserably. He cast a long shadow, and though the BOBs weren't afraid of him, knowing he was on their side, they would have each admitted to being intimidated by him at times. Except Captain Violet, who shared part of a secret past with the ninja.

"Silent," Violet said, "one of our new recruits here says he isn't a ninja. What do you think?" She gestured toward Ra and waited.

Silent War and Choco-Ra looked each other over with critical eyes. Ra had to admit he understood why, if you went on simple dress choices, they might think the two men were similar. Except for the whole bandages versus sleek battle suit issue, of course. Room for error, he figured.

Silent War shook his head and shrugged. Violet nodded. Everyone at the table nodded.

"He says if you are a ninja you studied under someone else, but he doesn't think you are one," she said.

Were' wondered how she had gotten so much out a nod and shrug, but figured there were nuances at work that he simply didn't understand.

Ra sighed deeply. "I am not a ninja. I've heard of ninja, but am not one."

"But you can fight, right? Or use a sword?" Full Bore asked, interested in where this might be going.

"I can fight, sure. I've used swords before, too," Ra answered.

"Then how aren't you a ninja?" Full Bore asked.

"Look, this guy," Ra jerked his thumb at Silent War, "is a ninja, right? And he says I'm not one. So doesn't that convince you?"

Silent War raised one hand and made complex gestures with his fingers at blinding speed. Captain Violet nodded and looked Ra over. "He says he can be wrong sometimes, but you never know."

Were' laughed and stood up. "Guys, Ra here can fight, sure, but he's no ninja, all right? He can't even leap good. Much less hide in shadows or anything. Isn't that what ninja do?"

Everyone at the table nodded, except Ra. Choco-Ra looked at Wereberry, not sure if he should be thanking him for standing up for the non-ninja side or annoyed that he seemed to be implying that Ra couldn't really fight all that well.

The sound of a claxon put a rest to the discussion. The BOB members all gathered their gear and ran from the table. Were', Ra, and T.C. were only feet behind them, knowing that a claxon almost never heralded great news.

The group ended up forming a loose mob outside of

Chief's tent. Chief himself came out moments later, bullhorn in hand. His uniform was freshly pressed and his hat shone. He tucked the bullhorn under an arm and pulled on thick brown leather gloves, watching the crowd. It gave stragglers time to join them, and Chief waited until he thought there were enough people gathered.

"All right, lissen up!" he shouted. The bullhorn distorted and amplified his voice until meaning's edge started to blur. "You all did great today," he paused to let the crowd react. React they did: a ragged cheer went up. Waiting until it died back down, Chief continued, "Take the rest of the night off, and enjoy it, people! Tomorrow we'll hand out new assignments and redeploy. We're gonna take those HAVOC clowns down for good, once and for all!"

Another cheer went up. People screamed and raised fists in the air. Chief stood there, letting the noise wash over him, bullhorn tucked back under his arm. He turned and strode back into his tent, letting his people wander off to enjoy the night. Of course, he knew, some men were still on patrol and sentries would be active. There was no way to ensure that everyone got the whole night off; it just wasn't possible while running a military operation. He did the best he could, though, and he knew it. He swelled with pride at his team and sat down at his desk to go over tomorrow's deployment plans.

Everyone else went to go party. Ra, Were', and T.C. were swept along as a social gathering started outside the mess tent. Firepot Jones rejoined them and shook Shocker's hand. Everyone milled around, chatting and spreading rumors about the upcoming day.

"I heard they have the Beatbox-16 almost ready," Captain Violet said, tipping her glass back and taking a deep draught of clear liquid.

"Wasn't the 15 what they used today?" Ra asked.

"Well sure, but the 16 will be even better," someone that Ra couldn't see said loudly.

"But the 15 only saw action today, right? Had it been used before?"

"Of course not," Full Bore put in, "then it wouldn't have been a great surprise!"

"But then…," Ra trailed off, thinking.

"Why not just use it again?" T.C. picked up for his friend.

"They'd see it coming!" someone said, "and then what? No, the 16 will be way better. I also heard they're gonna pull out the Warhawks tomorrow."

"Already?" Ears McGee asked, laughing. "I didn't think those were ready yet!"

"I hear they are," the voice replied.

"Yeah, well I heard that we'll get new rifles tomorrow, better ones," Still Water said seriously.

"That'd be great," Violet agreed. She looked around and spotted Silent War, moving away from the group to join him.

Wereberry weighed the conversation so far and softly asked, "Do they upgrade the weapons here a lot?"

Everyone laughed at that, including Ra. He already thought he knew how this worked. Of course they would give out new weapons as often as possible. Even if they didn't need them. Possibly especially when they didn't need them.

"As often as possible," Still Water said, "anything that helps us win, well it helps us win, doesn't it?"

"I suppose," Were' said, uncertain. He didn't see the point of using complex things only a few times if they were still good to use. Then again, he also didn't understand why anyone would want to use a gun when they could really fight against another person. If you had a problem with someone, he reasoned, what better way to truly solve it than to meet them head on, face-to-face, and deal with them as an individual?

It made the entire concept of war smaller and easier to cope with. At least for him, and that was what he was going with. Knowing your enemy and looking them in the eye let you understand them and figure them out. Sometimes it even made the fighting unnecessary. All the better, Wereberry thought, was a fight that was headed off. Mostly, anyway.

The revelry continued deep into the night, soldiers fending off the possibilities of tomorrow by living life to the fullest the night before. None of them seemed bothered by mortality or danger; they acted like they drank it in through every pore.

Eventually people wandered and staggered back to various barracks. The crowds thinned and thinned until only a few people were left standing around, telling stories of their own. Some shared private details, others talked and bragged about old battles. Every single one of them, however, truly felt a part of the whole. Including three new recruits, getting their first taste of how bonded the BOB were to each other. They fell asleep smiling, accepted, and, for the moment, not questioning anything other than what their orders would be in the coming morning.

2 • Orders to the Contrary

WEREBERRY, CHOCO-RA, AND T.C. SAT with their command group in the briefing tent. Their command group seemed to bear no weight on who went where in terms of missions, as they had already learned. More, it was simply the group that they sat with while they got their orders.

It wasn't the most efficient thing anyone had seen, but it seemed to work well enough to get orders handed out, explained, and taken care of. Which was, when the three friends thought of it, all that really mattered.

"Now, you three raw recruits," Chief started, "will go with Still Water, Silent War, Captain Violet, and Firepot Jones. We have reports of some strange activity out by the swamp in sector 18-G and we're sending you guys in as a way to flush it out. If there's something strange, I expect you all to find out what it is and report back. If needed, stop it. Now go join the rest of your team and move out!"

Having seen others given their orders already, all three of the travelers knew how to react to being told to move out. They leapt to their feet as one and yelled out a hearty "Go BOB!" before turning and marching out of the tent.

Violet found them as they left the tent with Firepot Jones. She had Silent War with her, to no one's surprise. They rounded up Still Water out by the vehicle deployment area, where he was talking with Lugnut. Lugnut was tearing apart an engine, trying to see why it wouldn't work. They said hi to Lugnut and requisitioned a large jeep.

They checked out their new rifles on the way out of the firebase, hitting the road as fast as possible. People were streaming out of the camp, everyone forming up in their teams and leaving quickly.

The jeep bounced along the road, throwing up dirt and the occasional splatter of mud. On its side was plastered the BOB logo, a series of four bright yellow stars describing an arc above the word "BOB." Below the stylized letters of the acronym, the words "Battle Operations Battalion" ran along the lower curve of the logo's circle.

They drove for miles, the sun shifting in the sky, with no words exchanged between them. Each BOB was lost in his or her own thoughts and concerns for the upcoming mission.

Firepot Jones was running a checklist in his head, making sure that he had everything right. He thought his bag would have enough explosives to carve out a landing zone if need be, if they needed rescue. He patted his vest self-consciously, checking to make sure the blasting caps were secure. He didn't pat too hard, not wanting them to go off prematurely and end the mission right there in the jeep.

Captain Violet sat on the back on the jeep, next to Silent War. Her long, inexplicably blue hair streamed behind her like a flag. She just hoped that her team ran into resistance. Violet was always on the lookout for some HAVOC members that needed shooting. She still sought revenge for the loss of her best friend, Mongoose. He had died a few years back, on a mission with Violet and Silent War. It had cemented the bond between herself and the ninja, their shared loss.

Mongoose hadn't died of enemy fire; in fact, the mission had been perfectly successful. That didn't matter to Violet. Death during a mission was death during a mission, even if it didn't happen during the fighting part. It was as they returned to the firebase that everything had gone wrong. The boat they were on hit a bad patch of weather and Mongoose was thrown overboard and hit by his own rifle. The blow knocked him out and he slipped under. Both Violet and Silent War dove after him and grabbed him, but not before too much water had been swallowed by their one-time commander.

Chief took over after that, and though neither BOB member had a problem with their new leader, it still pained them at times to see him standing where their best friend once had been.

Silent War sat next to Violet, thinking about the same day she recalled. He also wondered if he would meet his opposite number during this mission, as he had during so many others over the years. It was only fitting that the two ninja, one good and one evil, one in black and one in purple, should find each other so frequently. It was their duty to their shared sensei that put them on a collision course, which, each knew, would last the rest of their lives.

Still Water concentrated on driving. The jeep was hard to control over the ever-shifting surface of what passed for a road out here. The old sailor knew that they wouldn't face sea warfare again soon, but he still wished for it every time they went out. His boat, the Wave Killer, sat in the firebase's hanger. It itched for deployment, as did its pilot, but it wasn't to be, not for far too long now. The problem was, Still Water reflected, when he'd applied for transfer to this branch of the BOBs he hadn't read the situation map right. What he had taken for lakes ended up being swamps. Lakes would've been fine. Something to ride a boat across, to use depth charges in, and to maybe even fish in if there was no mission near the lake zone at the time. He scratched one of his many marine-themed tattoos and drove on.

Wereberry kept waffling about how he felt. On the one hand, he was looking forward to a fight. On the other, he really did wish there wouldn't be any violence. This internal duel was familiar to him. It was easy, he knew, to lose yourself in a fight when it happened. When there was no other good choice you might as well, he always figured, enjoy yourself. But when a choice presented itself, well, hoping for a fight never seemed right.

Until you thought about how much fun the fight could be.

At least, he decided, this time the fight couldn't be avoided, so he might as well enjoy it. Grinning, he leaned back a bit, bouncing along with the ride.

Choco-Ra gripped the side of the jeep tightly, trying to bounce as little as possible. He found the seats padded far below what he would deem appropriate for a person of his stature, hardly a luscious chocolate throne. He hoped the rest of his team found it in themselves to move away from thoughts of him as a ninja so they wouldn't expect him to go off and work with Silent War in some strange martial arts sub-mission.

Truthfully, Ra just wanted the mission over and done with. Having seen his first tank, he realized that he was smitten with the idea of the thing. A large, impenetrable vehicle you could command from, as well as simply rolling through the enemy's forces? He wanted command of one, if possible, but he would have to test them out first. Something that he couldn't do, he knew, while he was being sent off to a swamp in a painfully bouncing jeep.

T.C. hoped the swamp was watery enough to tip the scale. Swamps, he always felt, were either too thick or perfectly thin. There weren't often middle grounds where swamps were concerned. Swamps that were too thick were just that, with packed mud and bits of water pooling around your feet, making it hard to walk. Nice, thin swamps were like slightly muddy lakes, and a slightly muddy lake would be acceptable to him. Something to swim in a bit, and maybe he could find a way to help the mission while under water.

T.C., truthfully, didn't want to get into fights with any enemy, doubly so when he didn't even fully understand why they were fighting each other in the first place. But he was there and had said he would help out, so he intended to.

The jeep rolled on, but the land underneath it grew damper and damper as the motley contingent of BOB moved on. Still Water slowed the jeep down as they got closer to their insertion coordinates, which was simply shorthand for "stop and get out here," but BOB felt that their term made things seem classier and more efficient.

The insertion coordinates reached, Still Water stopped the jeep and hopped out. He grabbed his new rifle, the metal already dulled to a careful degree so it wouldn't reflect light and give snipers a heads-up, and swung it around into his waiting hands. The others jumped out of the jeep as well, all of them bringing weapons to bear, each as carefully dulled as Still Water's.

It made Violet wonder, yet again, why BOB didn't just dull them out of the gate instead of making the soldiers do it. Maybe, she thought, they simply wanted to make sure people were on their toes, and if they weren't, oh well. But that never felt like the right answer.

Silent War swung his Uzi around until it rested against his back again. He never took the offered fresh guns, demanding instead that he use his own. As the company's ninja, he was allowed odd perks. He felt no immediate danger, though, so he felt no need to walk around with his weapon pointing at a few trees.

Captain Violet wanted to do the same, but knew that if she did, everyone would. While Silent was fast enough to bring his weapon around in a crisis, and everyone else should have been as well, she didn't want to bet their lives on that.

She held up a fist and circled it in the air a few times. Everyone took the signal and formed up around her. Their faces betrayed anxiousness, but no fear. The team was ready for her orders, some of them outright restless for them, in fact. The mission would allow them to put a big hurt on HAVOC, and that made any risk ripe for swallowing. Violet nodded as she searched each of their faces and grabbed up a stick so she could draw their secondary deployment tactics in the soft mud near the edge of the swamp.

The orders were drawn out quickly, and people wandered

off with their assignments. T.C. and Silent War were to go off and check the area for enemy booby traps. Firepot and Violet would stay where they were, taking care of the majority of the mission: laying down traps and picking out likely enemy paths to wire up. Wereberry, Ra, and Still Water found that they were the winners, marching out to what was assumed to be the entry point for the enemy and laying in wait for them. Just in case.

Were' and Ra followed Still Water out, traipsing through the mud and muck. Still Water took some strange turns along the way, knowing that he was moving directly toward a possible enemy meet up. He also realized they were moving out before Silent had had a chance to check for traps. Mentally he laughed, seeing it as standard operating procedure for the army: check for traps after you've been through the area. So long as it looked good on paper, you would have some General convinced that the idea was sound.

Still Water knew that wasn't really fair of him to think, but the mission annoyed him. He thought they should be delivering a final blow to those HAVOC clowns, not just laying some surprises for later. He was far more of a direct confrontation sort of guy.

He unslung his rifle and held it at the ready, indicating to both Were' and Ra that they'd better do the same. They got the message and did so, gripping the rifles tightly, even if they were unwanted.

The three men reached their designated wait point and each picked out a spot to settle down in. They needed places to hide where they could each easily see anything coming, as well as each other. They also needed a place that they could settle into but that, when the need arose, they could also each get out of without being cramped from crouching.

They sat and waited in silence. Nothing else seemed to be moving in the swamp except for a few insects. Those buzzed around, landing on exposed skin and seeing if these new additions to their world were tasty. Unfortunately for Still Water, he turned out to be the only tasty person crouching there, and found himself slowly beset by a small horde of winged bugs. He moved carefully, brushing them off as best he could, but his need for at least some stealth meant that he discouraged almost none of them.

Meanwhile, T.C. found himself lying on his stomach in thick mud. Silent was nearby, in the same position. They were searching for booby traps and other nasty surprises that HAVOC could have left behind. The swamp itself made the entire process twice as annoying. Instead of simply looking for traps and considering terrain, they found themselves digging carefully into muddy banks and sifting through gunk at likely spots.

T.C. started to wonder why the mission was shaped the way it was, but not for the same reason Still Water wondered. No, T.C. wanted to know why no one seemed to have sent a pure recon force forward to see what the enemy was really getting up to at any given moment. Sure, both Silent War and himself were good at what they were doing right now, finding traps and digging in mud, but T.C. was sure their abilities could be put to better use. Despite his overall dislike for the army and for fighting, T.C. found that he liked the idea of doing a good job and getting it done, regardless.

Violet followed Firepot Jones around, handing him various items as he asked for them and helping him run cable. He was in his element, wiring things to explode, and didn't think for an instant that the Captain found any less enjoyment in the job than he did himself. He was also wrong on that front. Violet sighed and handed another foot of wire over. She wanted to yawn, to check her watch, to work out whether maybe someone had stashed a magazine in the back of jeep—anything other than to be a golf caddy for the explosives expert.

The work needed doing though, and Firepot couldn't manage it by himself. Plus, having two people know where the traps were laid was far safer than having just one. And if a fight should break out, she could protect him. No, it made sense for Violet to be there and she knew it. She still didn't like it, however.

Up at the manufactured front line, Were' sniffed and caught a human scent. He signaled to Still Water, who brought his rifle up to bear. Using the scope as makeshift binoculars, he scanned the area ahead of them with care. Sure enough, there was a contingent of HAVOC agents on the march.

No vehicle was in obvious sight, but Still Water assumed they had walked the last while for the same reason the BOBs had: stealth. Which also meant, he knew, that there was a chance that HAVOC had known all about today's operation. It opened a bad can of worms for Still Water, but he pushed all of it down to be dealt with later. Right now his only concern was how to stop the eight advancing soldiers cleanly and quickly, without giving rise to a pitched battle.

Signaling to Were' and Ra, Still Water studied the enemy. Eight of them, all armed with new-looking rifles and a bandolier of grenades apiece. One of them, he saw, carried a large backpack. It set him apart as their own demolition agent. Which meant they might simply be here for the same reason as the BOB, that the entire meeting was pure chance. Still Water filed that away for later as well and waved Ra and Were' over.

The two friends managed to form up around Still Water without betraying their position. They leaned in close to converse and plan in whispers. But first, Still Water sent a series of light flashes using the BOB communicator, signaling the quick details of the trouble without giving himself away. Everyone's communicators flashed simultaneously with Still Water's encoded signal message.

Violet and Firepot kept working, as did Silent War and T.C. The message wasn't emergency status, it was simple information. If things went south, both sub-teams were now prepared for it, but there was no reason to drop everything and run, not yet.

"Look, let me ditch this rifle and just go take them out," Wereberry was whispering.

"That's a no, soldier," Still Water told him, "I can't risk you being hurt, or the mission exploding into a huge firefight."

"Still, you must admit," Ra said, rattling his rifle, "we're new at this. We'll be pretty bad shots, chances are. Let us fight the way we're used to."

"No way," Still Water said emphatically, his voice starting to rise above a whisper, "operational methods are there for a reason. You aren't a ninja, right? Then you fight like the rest of us."

Wereberry sighed and shook his head. Then he bent over, raising his own rifle toward the enemy. Sighting trough the scope, he searched for a way to make this work to their advantage, where "their" was himself and Ra, first and foremost.

"All right, look," Were' said softly, "let me go out and around them, I'll bring the rifle. When they get close enough, Ra can push over a tree…," he looked at Ra for confirmation. When Ra nodded he continued, "It'll seem natural, a tree falling, this one here is fairly old. They'll startle and assume it's an attack, but when we don't do anything after it, they'll simply go around or over. Chances are they'll go around, toward the clearing right next to it. When they do, we attack."

Still Water raised his eyebrows, impressed if not convinced. "Then why do you need to get behind them?"

"Because when they move around the tree and get attacked from the rear, you guys gain the upper hand. They'll be out of formation and trying to turn around."

"Go BOB," Still Water whispered, giving his blessing. These new recruits were possibly crazy, but they had guts—he gave them that much. Also strength, if that one guy could really just push over a tree. He was willing to bet on them, seeing as how Chief had sent three fresh faces on such an important mission. That would never have happened if Chief didn't know something special about these guys.

Were' moved off at a quick clip, keeping out of sight of the HAVOC agents. The mud slowed him down some, but Were' found ways to compensate; years of being friends with T.C. had taught Wereberry a bunch of tricks for running on mud.

He passed around the HAVOC agents with them none the wiser for it. One of them almost saw him, but Wereberry grabbed a bush and skidded to a messy halt, sending the spray of mud directly into the bush to hide it. Were' stood behind the bush, crouched low, until the enemy moved a few more feet. Curving well outside of their lines of sight he took off again, looping around behind them and to the right. Then he simply followed them in.

Choco-Ra planted his feet near the tree and rested his palms on it. He would, he knew, have to push hard enough to knock it over, but at just the right variations in speed to make the entire event look perfectly natural. Nothing impossible, but certainly not a boring walk in the park either.

The HAVOC agents drew closer, unaware that anything out of the ordinary was going on. They counted no visible BOB forces. This was, they guessed, a walk in the park. Enter the damned swamp, check on the traps that they had left behind the last time they had passed through, and then go back to base. It was simple and easy and they loved it for that.

Suddenly a tree creaked, right along their preferred path. The field leader signaled for a full halt, and as the HAVOC agents stopped, the tree gave way and fell with a resounding crash, splattering mud every which way possible.

"Good timing," the field leader said through his face mask, "if we'd passed through here a few seconds later we would've had a problem. All right, men, let's go around."

That was Wereberry's signal. He leapt out at them, arcing high above their heads. His claws were fully extended and his teeth bared. The regulation rifle slung across his back didn't bother him at all, but he knew he should probably bother to fire it once or twice at some point; that was the standard operating procedure, after all.

The HAVOC agents let loose volleys of fire in response. The blue bolts of light arced up against the sky and sidled right past Wereberry, who landed among the men and started to punch, kick, and throw anyone he laid hands on.

Within seconds, Still Water and Choco-Ra joined the fight. Still Water fired his own rifle, exchanging large bursts with HAVOC, but every shot from both sides missed its mark by slim inches. Ra grabbed rifles from the enemy and smashed them against trees, the ground, or the enemy themselves. He wasn't anti-gun, really—he just wasn't pro-being-shot-at.

Still Water landed a roundhouse punch right into a HAVOC faceplate, sending the agent down into the mud. Still Water grabbed his leg and yanked him further down into the mud before dropping down to land blow after blow on the guy, hammering away until the face plate cracked and the agent dropped thankfully into unconsciousness.

Wereberry and Choco-Ra continued the assault as well. HAVOC agents struggled to get back up and run, landing some hard, solid blows of their own in the process. Were' found himself falling, sent sprawling to the ground by a massive body blow. He struggled to get free of the mud as soon as possible, but took another two hits in the process. Rifles came up and Were' lunged just in time, the bolts missing him and splattering heated mud through the air instead.

Unfortunately for the HAVOC soldiers, that particular near-miss made it personal for Were' and he renewed his attack, fighting harder than before. Still Water stood and, as Wereberry and Ra knocked out the last of the enemy, sent flash signals to the rest of the team. The all-clear flashed across everyone's communications device brightly. With that done, Still Water resumed his watch position, giving Ra and Were' hand signals to do the same.

"We're not out of the woods yet, guys," he said softly. "They may have more men on the horizon. Still, nice work back there. Non-regulation, but nice."

The two friends nodded and took up their positions, keeping watch. Wereberry ached all over, but he managed to sit watch just fine. He spent most of the time listening, sniffing out scents, and cataloguing his bruises. There was a rib he thought he might have cracked where he'd been slammed by the butt of a HAVOC rifle, too.

Ra sat and rewound some of his bandages, making sure to keep his work out of Still Water's line of sight. He didn't need the BOB officer realizing how non-normal he truly was. They seemed like alright guys, but there was a limit to how much some people would accept. People around here, at least. Choco-Ra had first caught sight of it a few days ago, but the feeling gnawed at him continually. They didn't dislike the different, or necessarily fear it; they were just constantly wary of it. He heard it in the way they spoke of something called the Mu-Corps.

No one would give him specifics; they all just spoke around whatever it was. All he could glean was that the Mu-Corps was definitely not full of normal soldiers. And he didn't want to end up there himself, or end up having to leave because he refused to be segregated.

Another hour passed before their communication devices flashed in unison again. Still Water glanced down and nodded at his wrist uselessly. Then he looked for Were' and Ra, spotting them easily enough. Still Water stood, stretching, and jerked his thumb back the way they had originally come.

"That's the sign, we're moving back out. We're done here, boys. Good work." He started walking without another word or glance. Were' and Ra fell in easily behind him, and together they marched back to the rendezvous.

Captain Violet and Firepot were waiting for them, Firepot

packing up the last of his bag. "Watch your step, gentlemen," Violet said with a grin. The three new arrivals to the area froze in their tracks. None of them knew where the new traps were laid out.

Firepot Jones laughed softly and shook his head. Then he directed them, slowly, through the dangerous area. Once clear they all stood and waited for Silent War and T.C.

Silent signaled his all-clear to Violet just before she sent the general recall order. He and T.C. were taking their time getting back, making a last sweep. They joined up with the others after a few minutes and were waved through clear sections by Firepot Jones.

T.C. wanted to laugh when he saw the amount of mud dripping off of Ra and Wereberry. The latter's fur was plastered down, and only small streaks of pink showed through the caked-on brown. T.C. could see that Choco-Ra was starting to have trouble moving freely, the mud seeping into his bandages and starting to dry.

He blinked when he realized that both of his friends had the same look in their eyes that he had himself, that barely stifled laughter. Then T.C. looked down at himself and saw he was covered in mud deeper and thicker than either of his friends.

The three friends drew together and pointed, smirking, at each others' predicaments. The whole team made its winding way back to the jeep and mounted up, showing utter disregard for the amount of mud that found itself living inside the vehicle. They drove off back to the firebase, bumping and rattling the whole way.

3 • Special Forces

THE BOB FORCES ALL RETURNED to the firebase around the same time, and the news was all very similar. Each of them had met resistance, but all the missions were being deemed successful. People threw helmets in the air and cheered. Cries of "Go BOB!" rang out. Chief came out and congratulated everyone.

Choco-Ra noticed that this didn't seem to be the one final blow to HAVOC that everyone had been led to believe it would be when they set out. He also noticed that no one seemed to care. Shrugging, he dropped the matter without even bothering to bring it up to Wereberry or T.C.

The revelry died down in due course and the troops went back to their normal duties. Much of which seemed to be handing out new rifles and getting new vehicles ready for combat. Someone poked their head into the barracks where Choco-Ra, T.C., and Wereberry sat around, finally mud-free. He handed them each a new rifle and told them to report to Chief's office as soon as they were presentable for duty.

Given that it didn't sound to terribly important that they therefore rush like mad, Were' took the time to let his fur dry while Ra rewrapped himself tightly. T.C. went back for a second shower while that was going on, enjoying the spray of cool water over his skin.

As soon as they were all ready, they made the short walk to Chief's tent. Were' pulled the flap aside and held it open for his two friends. Inside, the tent was spacious and spartan. A cot sat in one corner, made up in pristine military fashion. A desk took up much of the room, covered in maps and papers.

Folding chairs sat in a pile, folded neatly, for visitors to use. Ra handed them out to his friends and the three stood by their still-folded theirs until Chief welcomed them and told them to sit and be comfortable. They unfolded the chairs quickly and sat.

"Thank you for coming to see me, boys," Chief began, tipping his hat back a fraction of an inch. "Of course, I did make it an order," he said, chuckling to himself. The three friends chuckled too, honestly and openly, not feeling the need to force fake laughter on their commander just yet.

Chief looked at each of them in turn. His stare, even from behind sunglasses, was piercing. He saw to their core, as far as they felt, and judged what he found there.

"That was some fine work out there today, boys," Chief continued after a few moments, "I heard nothing but good things. Wereberry, Choco-Ra—Still Water said you two had some great plan that really made his job easy. He told me all about it and I gotta say, sons, I'm impressed."

"Thank you, sir," Wereberry said quickly, "it was refreshing to get a chance to implement a plan of action like that, sir, and—"

"No need to butter me up, son," Chief said with a smirk, "you have a good head for a fight. I'm gonna suggest that the next battle plan in your team be run by you first. Really let you stretch your legs on this some, son."

"Thank you, sir," Were' said, sitting up a bit straighter.

"As for you Ra," Chief said, "word got to me that you have a thing for tanks?"

"Well, sir," Ra said, making extra effort to interject the proper "sir" at the end of sentences, "I would like the opportunity to learn to drive one, yes. I think they're fine vehicles."

"How about I do you one better?"

"Sir?" Ra asked.

"There's an opening coming up, having to do with tanks.

We have some new ones. They take a driver and a Mu-Corps specialist to run. Would you be interested?"

Ra's heart sunk. He felt like he'd been kicked. That was it then, Chief's big plan. Toss the guy who doesn't fit in into the special section reserved for freaks. He didn't understand these people. They had no problem with werewolves or mermen, but he could sense their dismay at a mummy from a mile off, and that was before they knew what was or wasn't under his bandages.

"With all due respect... sir," Ra started cautiously, unsure how he could possibly phrase this to sound good in the least.

"You don't want to be working with the so-called freaks of Mu-Corps? I thought better of you, Choco-Ra. Truthfully, son, what's your problem with them?"

"What? No, I figured you had a problem with me, you see," Ra started, tossed onto unfamiliar ground.

"Because I asked you to work with Mu-Corps? That makes you less of a person or something?"

Ra sighed and started again, "No, sir! I thought you had a problem with me, and that the Mu-Corps was generally treated as less than the rest of us, though I don't know why they would be. But, sir," Ra said, his old commanding voice coming back to him, "that was why I thought this was some sort of punishment."

Chief laughed, slapping the surface of his desk in surprise. These boys were special, they were, he thought as he brought himself under control. "No, Ra. The Mu-Corps is very special. Not to be slighted, but respected. Working with them is a privilege not everyone gets."

"In that case," Ra said, smirking, "I'd be happy to take the job, sir."

Chief nodded, shaking his head to rid himself of the last vestiges of laughter. "And as for you, T.C., I heard that you had some ideas about deployment?"

"Oh, yes, I do!" T.C. said quickly, leaning forward. "Sir!

Yes, sir! I mean, well I was thinking that, you know how you sent Silent War and I out to look for traps? Well, why weren't we sent off to recon the enemy and find out what they were doing well beforehand?"

"Hmmm?" said Chief.

"You know, quiet recon work, sneak up and spy sort of stuff. I'm sneaky—"

"He is," 'Were' put in with a nod.

"—and I could be of great use that way, I think, sir."

Chief sat back and scratched at his cheek while he thought. "Well, son, we aren't generally very big on sneaking around. The BOB is a machine for attacking, for making a difference and really getting the job done. Understand?"

"I do, sir, but—"

"No, I see your point, I just don't think it's what the other boys would think of as soldier's work, really. But why should that stop us? I'll talk to Silent War as well, and see if he would be willing to work with you to put together the type of mission you think we need to try out. That sound fair? We'll give it a test and see."

"That's more than fair, sir," T.C. said. He felt his pride rising on acceptance.

"All right then, soldiers," Chief barked at them, settling back into his chair, "dismissed! You'll get your new orders in a few hours, I'm sure."

The three friends stood, refolded their chairs and made to leave the tent. On their way out, Choco-Ra caught sight of a photograph hanging from the tent's support strut. He stopped and stared at it, his friends already moving past him without notice.

"Sir?" Ra asked, turning back to Chief.

"Ahhh, caught sight of her picture did you? She's a beauty all right." Chief smiled warmly.

Choco-Ra felt something go cold inside him. The picture depicted a woman, reclining against a tree. She wore a loose white summer dress and had her hair piled about her shoulders in soft curls. She was the spitting image of the Princess.

"Do you know her?" Ra asked, growing wary.

"Everyone does, don't they?"

"Well, I think I might know her, yeah," Ra admitted. He wasn't sure if this was some sort of trap. He wanted to trust Chief, had every reason to in fact, but seeing her here made him wonder if the Grand Vizier was around too. "The Princess, yes?"

That made the Chief laugh. "Princess? Well, I'm sure some have called her that, or stronger. But come on, seriously now, you don't recognize the most popular pin-up girl around?"

Ra took a deep breath. This place had to be where the Princess came from. But it wasn't where she was, and she probably had no interest in coming here. She couldn't do anything to him even if she did. He knew that, and wondered why the image had affected him so strongly at first. He gave the Chief a quick nod and moved to catch up with his friends, putting it aside for later.

Together again, the three friends stood under the wide-open sky. None of them could really tell which of them was the most pleased. They had each gotten what they wanted, but they also knew that they had each of them earned it, too. They rejoined the rest of the soldiers at the mess hall, bumming around and trading more stories until orders came in. It took a while, which nobody minded. Wereberry and Firepot Jones found they had a lot of things in common that neither had really thought the other would enjoy.

Choco-Ra carefully asked about the picture that Chief had, and found that everyone knew of her but no one had ever actually met her. They didn't even know people who had, although most of them quickly told stories about friends of friends who swore they'd run into her once or twice. Ra was careful to let the conversation steer itself in case anyone noticed he was pushing after information.

T.C. noticed Ra's questioning and asked after some of the stories, gathering information of his own to try and see what Ra was up to this time. The picture T.C. built for himself told him fairly quickly, and he backed off to let Ra dig deeper as best he could.

Captain Violet strode into the mess hall and nodded at the three new recruits. "Come on, boys, saddle up. Time to get your orders."

They disentangled themselves from various conversations and followed after her. Along the way T.C. whispered to Ra, asking about the picture. Ra brushed it off as paranoid nonsense, and they continued to march after Violet.

"Wereberry, you're here," Violet said, pointing to a large flat tent. "Hand-to-hand and tactics center. Nothing big, your new mission will start when we all move out next. Until then, Chief wants to see you helping out other BOBs with their capabilities."

Wereberry nodded and waved to his friends. He took off at a slow jog and vanished inside the tent. The others continued onward.

Around the next bend they came to a large tent. Marked off for experimental weapons, the tent was the most used in all the camp. Violet nodded at Ra, "That's you, Ra. Go pick up your new commission. T.C., you're with me."

Ra nodded at Violet, then T.C., and then marched over to the tent, throwing the flap aside and ducking in. Violet and T.C. continued on. They reached the officer's tents and Violet held her own tent flap open for him.

"We're in here, go on," she told him.

T.C. nodded and ducked into the tent, not sure what to expect. He hadn't been told that Captain Violet was part of his briefing, but then, she did seem to be the only one who truly communicated with Silent War. So he supposed that made sense. Inside, Silent War was seated on a chair, having tea. Violet handed T.C. a cup and gestured to another chair, then took one herself.

"So talk to us about sneaky," she said with a wild grin.

4 • Missions Possible

WEREBERRY SPENT THE EVENING going over hand-to-hand combat with a large group of BOBs. Some of what he showed them they simply couldn't do. Very few of them could leap the way he could, and they had no claws. Still, he taught them some new tactics, based on ideas he'd thought up years ago playing with woodland creatures outside his home. He didn't bother to tell them where he had developed these strategies, of course, but it made him smile to himself.

That self-same smile made the troops slightly nervous. They enjoyed the teachings, taking notes and planning on reviewing them as much as necessary, but some of them still wondered if those claws might accidentally stay out this time, or if some other accident might endanger them while they practiced.

Wereberry, for his part, was reveling in the activity. His bruises—and uncracked rib—were sore, but stretching them out certainly helped. He also guessed that not telling these people that he was a bit slower than normal and in pain was a good thing. Some of them didn't look very proud of themselves, and Were' tried to make sure they knew that they were very capable, just new to this.

After a while, when his body started to really complain, he took to the sidelines and started to pair up BOBs against each other to let them test out some of the things they had just started to learn.

Off in a different part of the base, T.C. sat around a teapot with Captain Violet and Silent War. He sipped the strange green tea that Silent brewed and explained his ideas. What

T.C. didn't understand, and what neither Silent nor Violet could really explain, was why BOB seemed not to use this sort of mission more often in the first place. It made too much sense, and the more he explained the more they agreed with him.

"So, see," T.C. said, resting his tea cup on a knee, "if we just crept in and knew how they generally detected enemy threats—"

"Radar, sentries, the usual," Violet told him.

"Well then, don't you have ways around them?" he asked, looking back and forth between her and Silent War.

Silent nodded, his fingers dancing across his forearm. Violet watched, nodding and frowning in alternate seconds.

"Silent says that's the general problem," Violet translated. "We can get around them most times, if we try hard enough, but the vehicles we use to do so get upgraded along with their weapon detection systems and there just never seems to be a good window of opportunity. He's right, too," she added, "I mean there's just never the right mix of equipment and resources and timing."

"But I'm talking more about doing it by hand. Not relying on machines—come on, Silent doesn't need a machine to tell him how to move quietly. And if we knew the limits of the radar system we could just go in under or around or above it," T.C. said with a shrug, "or whatever."

"It might work. Here," Violet took out a stack of papers, "look at these."

While T.C. studied the diagrams Violet showed him, Choco-Ra was investigating something completely different.

The experimental weapons tent had a door latched into the dirt floor. Ra was shown over to it and a scientist-looking type opened it for him, explaining that the Mu-Corps was based down below. Choco-Ra shrugged and descended the stairs.

As he went down, the place started to remind him of his

home. The air grew cooler, and flecks of dirt occasionally found their way loose from the walls. He trailed a hand along one wall, feeling the texture there and reminiscing.

He reached the bottom of the flight of stairs and took stock. The room was full of animals and people. Both moved around unimpeded. The animals all seemed to have spots of metal on them in different places. Some had tiny antenna leading away from their metal-shod sections, but most didn't.

The humans kept leaning down and talking with the animals. That didn't strike Ra as strange. It was when the animals talked back that he got slightly confused. Ra had seen the animals of this world and knew that they didn't talk. Wereberry had tried that. The humans around here didn't think it was unusual. Quite the contrary, really. Animals here did not, Ra was certain, talk. At all. Not in ways that other beings communicated, at least.

Yet here they were. A few cats, rodents, and the rare dog, all walking around, in other respects like perfectly normal animals of this world, talking to humans. Ra stood and stared for a full minute, until someone noticed him.

"Hello there," the man said, tugging a white lab coat closed over his military uniform, "you must be Ra. Yes, we heard you were assigned here, or rather sort of assigned here. Yes, yes, I'm Doctor Kasugai, I'm supposed to introduce you to what we do here." The doctor walked away without checking to see if Ra was following. Choco-Ra stood still for a moment, waiting for some signal, but when none was given he caught up with the doctor quickly.

"We at Mu-Corps are charged with designing human/animal co-pilot systems. The animals, you see, the Mu-Corps themselves, are enhanced so that they are smarter than average animals, and able to communicate. Yes, well, it may seem a bit odd to you, I'm sure, but trust me, it is all for a good reason. The animals' instincts and reflexes are key. They make superb co-pilots."

"So why not do this more often, I mean," Ra looked as one of the cats passed by, offering the doctor a greeting, "if it doesn't hurt them and it's so great."

"We want to, but for now it must be kept a secret. The Mu-Corps links up pilots and co-pilots, but nothing is said of it in battle. The enemy must not find out about our work here, because the day will come when this will be the project to win the wars once and for all and stop HAVOC for good!" The doctor calmed himself down after he finished speaking, rather sheepishly lowering the fist he had raised into the air, and stopped to adjust his glasses and smile nervously. Chief had talked to him, personally, about being too prone to emotional outbursts.

Choco-Ra looked both amused and interested, which was good enough for Doctor Kasugai. Ra looked around again and saw that the animals were more than just milling around; they were helping to do work on the vehicles, none of which looked quite like the conventional ones Ra had seen earlier.

"Ah, yes, and Chief said something about a tank?" he asked, willing to give this a go.

"Yes, yes, of course! The Mark VII! We were looking for a good, willing pilot for it, and Chief said he would deliver. He has once again, it seems." Doctor Kasugai led Ra over to a corner of the lab and stood before a large mass draped with a sheet. "Let me present to you the Mu-Corps tank Mark VII, code name Wallsplitter."

The doctor gave an edge of the sheet a good hard yank and it drifted free of the tank. The vehicle itself was smaller than most tanks, sporting a large, single cannon mounted just off-center, a small cannon mounted along the side, and a strange dual tread system with treads like most cars had tires, front and back. Ra could see that each set of treads could turn independently, and he grinned a bit. This was going to be fun.

His co-pilot apparently agreed. A grey mouse, the size of

an adult rat, ran around Wallsplitter, whiskers quivering with excitement.

"This," Doctor Kasugai said, "is your co-pilot, Little Fella."

"Little Fella?" Ra asked, bending down to study his new partner. "That's... I mean, you let them call you Little Fella?"

"It's not like there was a form to fill out," Little Fella said, his voice high-pitched but firm, "where I could ask for something like Bruiser or Manly McStudly. They tell me my call sign is Little Fella. I can take it or bite them and quit. I like the idea of a damn big tank, so I let it wash over me."

Ra stood up, laughing, "I think we'll get along just fine, but I can't call you Little, and Fella doesn't work right for me."

"Al," Little Fella said, "my name is Al. Just don't use it in open comms or they'll bitch."

"Deal. I'm Choco-Ra," Ra said, holding out a finger for Al to shake as best he could with his tiny paw.

"And you think Little Fella is odd?" Al asked with a grin.

Ra shook his head and leaned down to offer Al a hand. Al hopped up into it and climbed his way to Ra's shoulder, perching there while they were shown what their new ride could do.

Back in Captain Violet's tent, T.C. pored over detailed maps and plans for buildings. He handed them back to Violet and Silent War, nodding in thought. Violet rolled them back up, storing them away somewhere that T.C. couldn't see. He wondered where she had gotten them from, and if she was even allowed to have possession of them.

Those weren't his main concerns, though. "So, if those are right—" he began, cut off by a swipe of Silent's hand, cutting through the air like a guillotine.

"They're right," Violet said as way of explanation, "don't doubt that. But go on."

"Well if they're right then I could get in easily enough, if you told me what to look for," T.C. said, the words coming quicker and quicker as he spoke.

"You and Silent could get in, maybe I could, as well."

"No," he shook his head, "the best way is underwater, fully. You two would need to breathe, right? And that would cause bubbles, I'm sure. I don't have that problem."

"Ahhh. All right, so how do we sell this to Chief?" Violet sat back, intrigued, amused, and above all impressed.

"That's your department, I think." T.C. raised his cup of tea to them both and downed the rest of the now-tepid liquid in one shot.

Silent wanted to laugh. He couldn't, of course, his vocal chords long since severed, but his shoulders still shook with mirth as he watched this new recruit truly come into his own. T.C. possessed some interesting plans, Silent felt, ones that could change the way BOB did business. Chief told everyone that each battle would be the time they turned the tide and took down HAVOC for good; that was just the way their leader did business. Everyone humored him—hell, most of the guys probably believed it on some level.

Silent War had spent too much time working with BOB, over too many years, to ever truly believe that one thing would, one mission could possibly end a war by itself. Winning was, he felt, something that happened gradually and then simply increased as you went until the enemy realized that there was no option but backing down before they were completely destroyed. Still, what this one recruit was saying, it really might turn a tide or two and mark a discernable start toward the end.

Silent refilled T.C.'s cup and peered at him through the steam that rose to twist away toward the top of the tent. This one, Silent knew, bore watching closely.

Which is what Ra thought about Al as the two of them climbed into their new tank. Choco-Ra sat in the main cockpit, a thankfully well-cushioned seat surrounded by

camera screens, readouts, dials, and levers. Two steering levers
rose up in front of the chair, each one capable of directing a
side of the tank treads forward or back. When turned to either
side in unison, however, the front two treads would turn to
that side, giving him even more options for maneuvering.

All of that certainly interested Ra, but what truly had his
attention was the mini-cockpit that lay in his line of sight.
Nestled forward and below his own seat was a small, enclosed,
transparent sphere. In it sat Al, surrounded by his own sets of
screens, knobs, levers, and dials. Al could control the entire
tank the same way that Ra could, and either one of them could
do any function solo. Together, on the other hand, they could
seamlessly split duties, switching off at a second's notice.

What it would take, Ra realized, was perfect teamwork.
If they both tried to turn the tank at once, or aim the canon,
disaster would strike. Nothing would work. The scientists of
Mu-Corps dealt with this in a fairly unique way, at least to
Choco-Ra's thinking. Each pilot settled a small earpiece/mic
in place. This way they could whisper, or talk at a normal
tone even, without having to worry if the other half of the
team could hear. Then they put the animal half of the team
in charge.

Counting on, it was explained to Ra, the animals' faster
reflexes, they would make the control choices, giving the
human pilot control of whatever systems they felt were best at
the time and switching that set around as needed.

Which put Ra both in and out of control at the same
time. He had to trust Al, utterly and without hesitation, or the
plan would never work. But that simply wasn't what Ra was
used to, and he knew it.

For his part, Al realized that his new partner was accustomed
to being a leader. Al was very quick at noticing hierarchy rules
in social groups, dominance being nothing to sneeze at for a
mouse. He thought Ra had it in him to work with a partner,
though, and was willing to give the stranger a try. Worst case,

he could boot him out and find a new partner.

He didn't like to talk about it, but Little Fella had already worked his way through four partners. He was, they said, too bossy. Too stubborn and commanding. Al saw it as his job. That was why they set him up as primary, he reflected—because he could be a good leader. Silly humans, far too worried about their status and not worried enough about making the partnership last.

But Al had to admit, somehow or another, Choco-Ra came to the party with an inherent respect for rodents that spoke of some history Al didn't know about but intended to pry out of him before long.

5 • By the Light of the Moon

BOMBS BURST IN THE AIR, sending dark clouds of debris out in all directions. The flak made the jet paths harder to navigate, and as it drifted down toward Earth the stuff hit soldiers in the head and shoulders. It wasn't a good time for anyone involved.

BOB found itself deployed for reasons initially unknown. They were to hold a line. Hold that line for what, they did not know. All they knew was that they simply had to hold it, and furthermore, if they could turn the line while they held it, that would be simply fantastic.

Firepot Jones hit a switch connected to his vest. A signal traveled down a white wire all the way to the charges he had strung out back at the beginning of the now-pitched battle. Dirt, dropped personal items, and bursts of shrapnel took to the air at supersonic speeds. The blast shape described a perfect arc, right at the advancing HAVOC trooper lines. There was cheering along the mass of soldiers near Firepot as the HAVOC troopers backed away quickly, not sure what was going on aside from the ground exploding at them.

Wereberry looked back at the other troopers who seemed inclined to work with him on this. They weren't the best hand-to-hand combat trainees, but they were certainly brave. Silent War stood by Were's side, as did Lugnut and Still Water. They watched the advancing line of HAVOC agents grimly.

"Wait for them to raise their weapons," Were' said softly. It was a potentially dangerous tactic, but one Were' felt confident about. Once they raised guns, they expected the same in return. Seeing a few people simply leap toward and around them would give them pause enough to make a difference, he was sure. He was willing to bet his life on it.

The enemy surged forward and reached for their rifles. "Cry HAVOC!" they shouted as one, bringing their rifles up and around toward Wereberry's line of men.

"Now!" shouted Were', already leaping. A cry of "Go BOB!" rose a split second after, and the other troops leapt at the enemy. They engaged as hard and fast as they were able.

The HAVOC agents paused, as Wereberry thought they would, and the first wave of them went down in a mass of unprepared flesh. Silent War hit one with an extended side kick that made Wereberry almost jealous. Were' grinned and pounced on a HAVOC trooper, knocking him down and throwing him back before the guy had a chance to react to the idea of a large, furred pink beast attaching itself to his chest.

HAVOC soldiers fell on all sides, but they also started to fight back. Bolts of energy from their rifles cut through the mass of BOB members, but they somehow kept missing. They adjusted their sights and fired volley after volley. Dust and debris were kicked up by the blasts, causing confusing clouds that only made combat more difficult for both sides.

Were' and his troops fell back through the clouds of crud. The plan was simple, a mixture of Chief, Wereberry, and Choco-Ra working together to create a very simple, but effective, way to hold the line. As Were' fell back, clearing the field of battle, Ra and Al rushed forward, driving the Wallsplitter at top speed right into the HAVOC troops.

One of the HAVOC agents yelped, diving under the tank to avoid being hit head on. Al manned the large top canon, and Choco-Ra drove. The canon fired, a huge blast that scattered troops and separated them from their commanders.

HAVOC simply had no idea what was going on. The day had started normally, some training missions, a few disciplinary actions, and a lot of yelling and swearing. Then, out of the blue, BOB had attacked one of their firebases. Explosions rocked the sky, jets zipped overhead, and the entire day pretty much went to hell in a handbasket. Lunch was, most certainly, not going to happen. From the look of the vaporized mess hall, a gift from Al and his canon, dinner was off as well.

It made no sense. The BOB weren't advancing. They were just creating a line, slightly inside the perimeter of the HAVOC firebase. And they were holding it. HAVOC had no where to retreat to; they were already inside their own base. Their weapons were being knocked out before anyone could get to them. There couldn't be any decent advancement, between the BOB tanks and jets. When they did try to send troops out en masse, they were knocked back in hand-to-hand combat; even the regulation rifle action that BOB loved so much was mostly missing.

HAVOC Commander, a short, gray-faced man with a polarized monocle, sat behind his desk looking at possible battle plans.

"Impossible!" he shouted to his lieutenants. "What is BOB up to?"

"We don't know, sir," replied Destructo, his second-in-command. "They appear to be simply antagonizing us for no good reason."

"Well," raged HAVOC Commander, "destroy them!"

Destructo nodded and turned to leave his CO's tent. He turned along the dirt path outside, hearing the sounds of battle in the not-so-far distance, and strode to the side of his jeep. He wasn't sure what he could do, but he also knew he had to try something or it would be his head taking the roll for this.

T.C. grinned when Destructo failed to wander behind HAVOC Commander's tent. Not that he possessed a single reason to go for a stroll, but still, it made T.C. happy when people did what he thought they would. Now, he knew, all he had to do was get HAVOC Commander out of the tent for a few seconds and the mission could be accomplished.

The sounds of war came to T.C., and he knew that Were' and Ra were working with BOB to do their part in things.

Keeping HAVOC distracted and confused for a while would let him complete the real mission: retrieval of a select set of documents.

T.C. took a small, black object off of his rifle strap. About the size and shape of a roll of quarters, T.C. thumbed the switch along the top and pushed the thing under the very edge of the Commander's tent. He counted to seven and nodded to himself when the inside of the tent grew warm and dark.

Mere seconds later, HAVOC Commander came running out of his tent, screaming, demanding a response team to find out what was on fire in his tent and to put it out. T.C. knew he only had a few seconds before the Commander went back, or sent someone else, probably, to grab the documents on his desk.

Before that could happen, T.C. wiggled under the flap and grabbed the documents, stuffing them into the watertight pouch that hung against his hip. Hearing approaching sounds, he scattered a fistful of ashes from the same bag over the desk and dove back out. He caught sight of a small safe as he made the dive, and wondered what that could contain. He forgot it for the moment, concentrating on getting out alive this time.

The fire that his device caused was, in fact, mostly smoke and heat. It was just enough to start a small fire, only large enough to ensure some level of believability when the documents on the Commander's desk were found to be ashes. The fact that nothing else of his was really harmed would be puzzling—seeing as how T.C.'s device consumed itself to start the fire—and hopefully wouldn't be worked out for a while yet.

Now things got tricky—T.C. faced a gauntlet back to the shallow lake that would be soon overrun by HAVOC officers trying to put out a tiny fire. Luckily for him, he had counted the bushes and memorized their spacing on his way in. He dove for the first, rolling until he came up against it. A HAVOC agent ran past, glancing toward the blur but discounting it: the screams and demands of his commander overrode curiosity.

T.C. breathed a sigh of relief and retraced his careful stages all the way back to the water. He slid into the lake on his stomach, the water covering him by only a foot at best, and pulled himself hand over hand along the lake bed until he was clear of easy sight.

He short-burst a series of flashes to Captain Violet and Silent War, signaling the completion of his mission. T.C. still had, he knew, a ways to go before he was safe, and even a small war as a distraction would no longer help him.

Silent War and Violet looked at their communicators and then at each other. They were busy fighting, side by side, stopping an advancing wave of HAVOC agents by laying suppressing fire down, but they both took their fingers off their triggers. Violet raised a fist in the air.

"Go BOB! Retreat! We're done here, boys!" she yelled, as much for HAVOC's benefit as for her own men.

Al and Ra exchanged a disappointed sigh, turning the tank around for one last pass through some fencing. The tank knocked it down, splintering the hold posts and mashing the wire deeply into the ground. Al switched over to driving and handed Ra control of the canon for a while, letting him take some quick shots at retreating soldiers.

Wereberry slid off the soldier he was in the middle of wrestling to the ground. The guy looked at him, uncomprehending, when Were' simply punched him, cracking his HAVOC-issue faceplate and knocking him out.

BOB went into full retreat, covering their tracks by laying down a line of fire. Before the HAVOC troopers were even fully aware of the retreat, BOB was gone, like it had never even been there. Except for the wide swath of destruction they left behind, that is.

The Wallsplitter came up alongside Wereberry, pacing him for a second. Were' recognized the vehicle and hopped onto its side, holding the side canon for support. Ra laughed and told Al all about his friend as they drove back to base.

Halfway home, Silent War turned the jeep he shared with Violet and rocketed down a sloping side path. Skidding to a halt, he sent up a spray of gravel and plume of dust that T.C. walked through, coughing slightly. T.C. climbed in the jeep and they took off again, speeding toward Chief's tent directly.

Chief met the force just inside the base, megaphone held high in victory. "GO BOB!" he screamed, his amplified voice echoing out through the roads. It was a statement and a challenge.

6 • The Downside of Downtime

RA DROPPED WERE' OFF at the edge of the celebration and went to go park his tank. Al took over the driving controls as they entered the tent, which annoyed Ra a bit.

"I can drive," Ra said into his mic.

"True," Al replied, "but I felt like it. That's my job, see? Doing whichever job I want and having you cover the rest."

"Whoa there," Ra said, "the entire time we were out there we worked great together, wouldn't you say?"

"Yeah," Al admitted grudgingly.

"Then why the attitude now?"

"Look, think about it. We're going to go park Wallsplitter, right? And then you'll go join your friends and celebrate. I'll wander around the basement and talk to the other Mu-Corps about the fight. So sure, we'll both celebrate, but separately. Me and... my kind... we're not allowed out on base, as I'm sure you realized," Al spat out.

He didn't tell Ra that the fight had been the first time Al felt that he had worked with a partner truly worth working with. The other BOB were all right, but they seemed to resent being lead by a mouse. Choco-Ra, he reflected, showed absolutely none of that, and that acceptance, that raw, blind allowance, made this even more annoying for call sign Little Fella.

"I," Ra started and then stopped. What could he possibly say? He wanted to tell Al that of course he would stay and celebrate with him. But then, there were his other friends, too. He was caught, and there was no good way out of the trap. "I wish," he said eventually, "that wasn't the case. You have to know that."

"I do," Al admitted, sliding Wallsplitter into its berth.

"Now go party. Get. It'll be fine. I'm just cranky."

Choco-Ra left the Mu-Corps basement glumly, rising up into the experimental weapons tent and watching other BOB do the same. How many of us, he wondered, work with Mu-Corps and never speak of it at all?

Ra wandered over to the mass of BOB that were still chanting and celebrating. Forcing himself into a good mood, Ra spotted Wereberry standing by Still Water and wandered over to join them.

"Hey man," Still Water said, slapping Ra on the back, "nice work out there today!"

"Thanks," Ra said, "you too."

Wereberry watched Ra and knew that something was wrong. He had no clue what it could be, but he tried to cheer Ra up with stories of the fight. Slowly, Ra managed to let go and enjoy himself. Were' smiled and looked around for T.C. Both Were' and Ra knew that T.C. had been involved in some other part of this battle, but they hadn't seem him at all.

T.C. left the documents with Violet and Silent War in Chief's tent and waved to them. "I'll see you guys later, we can make plans for the next raid then."

"Next raid?" Captain Violet asked, raising an eyebrow.

"I saw a safe I simply couldn't get to in time," T.C. explained, "I had no way to open it or move it, and the distraction wasn't long enough anyway... I dunno, I think we can get that safe next time if we really want it."

Silent's hands became a flurry of motion that Violet watched like a hawk. "Silent's right," she said, "you think big. But if you're sure we can do it, HAVOC Commander's safe? Damn. That would be huge for us. Let's digest what we have first, and then we'll plan for that. Now go celebrate, T.C. You earned it, six or seven times over."

T.C. smiled and stood a bit taller as he left Chief's tent. He earned it, he thought, replaying Violet's words over and over in his head. This sneaking stuff was second nature to him,

and it really was a boon here. He was becoming important.
No one else quite had these skills. He smiled even wider and
went to find his friends.

Were' and Ra waved to T.C. and untangled themselves
from the group conversation they had found themselves in.
The three friends walked off, laughing and talking together.
They found a quiet spot in the back of the barracks to sit
and go over the day. After a while devoted to recounts and
recollections, however, the talk turned a corner.

"Cherry was never here," Were' said. The subject broached,
they all leapt in.

"How can you be sure?" Ra asked.

"I just know, so do you if you stop thinking and just feel it
out for a second," Wereberry said, leaning back on his hands.

"Let's assume you're right," T.C. broke in, "what do we
do?"

"Move on."

"Not yet," T.C. said. He looked at his friends and fumbled
around for the right words. "We can still do a lot of good here;
I have to come up with a plan to get HAVOC Commander's
safe and—"

"They gave me a tank," Ra said with a laugh, "I don't want
to walk away from it just yet."

"We don't belong here," Wereberry insisted. "It's fun, I
know that too. But something's off, and either way we don't
belong here."

"What do you mean, 'something's off'?" Ra asked.

T.C. nodded, though. "Have you ever seen someone get
hit here? By gunfire, I mean. Were's right."

"Well, the HAVOC goons are just bad shots," Ra said
loftily. "I know that we hit a bunch of things with Wallsplitter
today."

"Buildings? Tents? The ground maybe?" Were' asked.
"But people, Ra, how many people did you shoot?"

Choco-Ra stood up and paced. He thought back to the

battle and tried to recall every shot fired. He was a good shot, he knew, and Al was even better. Given that, of course they had shot a number of HAVOC troops. Except, when he replayed the scenes in his head, he realized that somehow they hadn't hit a single one.

"Coincidence," he stated.

"Nope. BOB don't shoot people, HAVOC can't shoot people—that first day we saw two planes get hit. They flew home afterwards. They flew home. But they had been hit pretty badly. How do you account for it?" Were' asked.

Choco-Ra let that sink in as well and stopped fighting the facts as he saw them. "And all they do is build new weapons," he said softly.

"Because they think those will work," T.C. muttered. "New rifles every mission, new planes and vehicles. They just keep building and building, but none of it really does the job." He sighed and leaned back against the wall, frowning. "But that's the point. We're changing things. Were', you're showing them how to be effective, leaving the useless guns behind. I'm showing them how to sneak around—I mean, we're changing things here. We could end this."

"How long?" Wereberry asked.

"Until we end the fighting? I don't know," T.C. admitted.

"Right, so you want to stay here and just devote ourselves to this place, this world? We're not here for that. We're searching for Cherrygiest. Last I looked, searching for someone didn't include sitting around where they aren't and playing games!" Wereberry's fist found the floor in frustration and he scowled at his friends.

"I understand where you're coming from," Ra said, "but what if you're wrong and she was here or even is still?"

"She isn't and you know it!" Were' raged. "At least be honest about why you want to stay."

"Fine, I like it here, I like my new partner. I like the job,"

Choco-Ra shrugged. "We can move on later."

"And how much harder will it be to find her then?"

"But Were'," T.C. offered, "we really could make a difference here."

"We could've made a difference with the Princess, too. Do you think we should've stayed there?"

"Maybe?" T.C. ventured. He thought of the Buffaloves and sighed. He hoped they were doing all right.

"No, you know why?"

"No, O great and wise one," Ra spat, "enlighten us."

"Oh come on," Were' said.

"What?" Ra asked, trying to reign in his urge to sneer. If Wereberry had something to say, some big important correction to make, then Ra wanted to hear it. Even if he wouldn't agree with it.

"No, I don't want to play this little game where I get upset and you egg me on and—" Were' sighed, frustration eating at him. He didn't want to give into it, but Ra had a way of setting him off. It had worked like this between them as long as he could remember, so he wasn't sure why he was surprised this time. If he was even truly surprised, not just disappointed.

"Just spit it out," T.C. said.

Were' lost it. T.C. siding with Ra over this made his heart break. They couldn't see what they were doing, what they were losing. "We're not heroes!" Were' yelled, then continued, softer. "We're not going around fixing everyone's lives. We're looking for a dear friend who is missing, we don't know if she's all right, or hurt, or trapped, or any of it. But instead of aiming toward our goal, you two want to play solider and help people win a fight that they aren't smart enough to win by themselves."

"That's not fair," T.C. said, "they just don't know what's up, they don't know the score. We do, and that gives us an advantage they could use."

"So you'd rather save them than Cherry?" Were' asked. He

didn't get it. He was having fun, too. He liked it here, but it wasn't what they needed to be doing and he simply couldn't parse how the others were so blind to the truth. Didn't they see, he asked himself, that their lives couldn't be spent fixing every problem they came across?

"Of course not," Ra said, glancing at T.C. The merman nodded in agreement.

"Then we go. Sooner than later." Wereberry stood and stalked off, fur bristling. He didn't want to hear them fight against it anymore and was determined to treat it as a done deal.

"Were'," T.C. called after his friend.

"Let him go blow off steam," Ra said, "he needs it. Listen, he is kind of right, I suppose. We have been losing ourselves here."

"Speak for yourself," T.C. said testily, "I've been finding myself here."

"Oh, so now you're the big bad super spy? Loving war and the spoils?" Ra laughed. "T.C., you like to hide at the bottom of lakes. You love peaceful days on the shore. Since when do you love fighting in any form?"

"Since I found out I could be actually useful!" T.C. shouted before he knew what he was even saying. In the silence that followed he stood and stared at Ra, silently asking him not to continue, to just let it drop. T.C. wasn't sure how he felt about what he had said; it repulsed him and warmed him all at once. He needed to think. He needed to get some fresh air, maybe have a swim. Alone.

Watching T.C. walk off in a daze, Choco-Ra hit the wall with the back of his head a few times. This had to get easier, he reflected, because if it didn't he wasn't sure he could deal with it. He considered splitting up with them for good, this time. Still, it hadn't worked out so well the last time, and something felt wrong with the idea. It was Al, he reflected. A partner, not a group of individuals. Not someone who just did what he

209

said, but someone who worked with him, cleanly.

Yet, they had started this trip together, focused and ready for what they had thought would be thrown at them. Every day, it seemed, they were proven to have no good clue what was to come. Something had to change. Someone had to take charge and really lead them. Maybe, Ra reflected, I can. Not through force, that didn't work, he remembered, but through partnership.

Ra was sitting, thinking everything over, when he heard a noise. Turning to locate the source, he spied a single, tiny gray ear. He stood and walked toward the door, acting for all the world like he had seen nothing at all.

Just before he yanked the door open, Ra turned and spotted a flash of tail. Laughing now, he turned his back to the door. "You can come out, Little Fella."

Al slunk clear of his hiding spot and sat in plain view of Choco-Ra. "I want to come," he said, whiskers twitching.

"Come where? I was just going to see if—"

"I heard everything. I'm also not stupid. Not from this world, you don't match anything we're ever heard of, but most people pass it off as some experiment or accident. Whatever. You aren't from this world at all and you're leaving. And I want to come along."

Ra sighed, sitting with his back against the door to block outside entry. "Impossible." He wanted to take Al. He knew it then that he had been hoping the rodent would want to come. Ra just wasn't sure how to sell it, how to make it work, and really, when he thought about it, how to rebuild a friendship to be better than before when he would be focused on a new one. New loyalty fought with old, and Ra found himself siding with old instantly. He smiled inwardly at that.

"And here," Al said, "I thought we were partners. Come on, you aren't dumb either. There's nothing for me here except helping in secrecy. With you, I don't know, I can do something cooler, more fun, better suited to me."

"You don't know what you're asking," Ra said softly. His eyes dimmed. He wanted to say yes. He just didn't know how it would work, with the friction that already sat between him and his friends. But he wanted to find out.

"So tell me. Then let me come along. Partner."

Ra took a deep breath and nodded. "I might have some ideas on how we can do this," he admitted. Ra let Al climb into his bag and they wandered out of the barracks to find a spot for the two of them to talk and plan.

7 • Planning for the Worst

T.C. HEARD THE START of the battle behind him and
knew it was his signal to move. The operation timed
itself out carefully, stage by stage, and there would only be one
chance at the goal. He closed his eyes for a second and gathered
himself up, narrowing his focus down to the job at hand.
Everything else was left behind, except trust that his friends
would do their part. He moved into the night silently.

Wereberry was in the middle of a tumultuous burst of
sound and force. Buildings to the left and right of him were
being obliterated one after another in a ceaseless display of
destruction. The fire pattern left only one path clear, the one
Were' was on. He signaled to the men with him and they
charged, as one, into the breach. HAVOC forces were laying
down suppressing fire, but Wereberry ran right into it, praying
that his theory about the gunshots always missing was right.
Nothing hit him, though the people on either side of him
stared in awe.

It wasn't a theory that Were' would ever develop fully, and
he found it didn't matter. What mattered then was pushing
the line back. More than simply back, however, his goal
entailed pushing it back in steadily timed increments. Which
meant he had to marshal his hand-to-hand fighters to strike
forward two inches and then retreat one, somehow leading the
HAVOC troops into thinking they should advance that inch.
The strategy needed to work every time they attempted it, or
the timing of the overall operation would be off.

A hand signal told Lugnut and Still Water to fall back. The
HAVOC forces grew confused and stayed where they were,
ready to simply hold the ground they found themselves on.

Were' sighed and shook his head. He bent down and grabbed a small rock, which he threw with enough speed and accuracy to crack one of the HAVOC troop's faceplates. That got them advancing again. Wereberry's troops, for they really were his to lead in combat now, held and then bit by bit started to advance again, pushing the HAVOC forces back. He stopped for a second to chew a strawberry and consider his plan.

"Cry HAVOC!" one of the enemy troops yelled, bravely stepping into the fray and landing a solid blow against Lugnut.

"And let slip the wolves of war," Still Water muttered as Wereberry launched himself at the HAVOC trooper, who was soon down with a pink werewolf on his chest. Were' stood back up. The trooper didn't.

Inside Wallsplitter, Ra and Al drove in slow patterns and targeted any shelter standing. No building was safe from their sights. Other tanks took out buildings as well, some Mu-Corps, some not, though Al didn't tell Ra which were which. Of course, it didn't matter, which was the point of not knowing. They were all, honestly, simply working with BOB to fight HAVOC. Everything else was icing.

Al switched the controls around, letting Ra know simply by saying "One." One meant Al drove and Ra worked the gun. Two was the reverse. It saved time and energy, increasing their reaction time and reducing the amount of chatter they used. It also made Ra feel like they were somehow dancing amongst the carnage. It wasn't a bad feeling at all.

T.C. snuck behind the latrines, one of the few buildings in the same line as Wereberry's forces. He knew Ra and the other tankers wouldn't be firing along that line today. HAVOC Commander's tent was off to the right and should be fired on within minutes. Until then, all T.C. had to do was wait. Wait and think.

He hated war, in theory. He didn't like to fight. It wasn't part of who he thought he was in the least. T.C.'s entire life, he remembered, constituted someone who would rather hide than attack, unless attack was truly necessary. For friends, of course he would dive into trouble. For a really good cause, he felt the same. He wasn't a coward, but he wasn't a fighter.

Except, he realized, he enjoyed the hell out of this. Spying, sneaking—those were his elements. Using them in a battle, well that made battle something he'd discovered that he kind of liked. It clashed with his sense of self, and he was starting to stitch a new sense of self together.

Pushing that all aside, he leapt and rolled into the cover of a fallen tarp. Within reach of the Commander's tent, he crouched and waited, taking his own problems out to stare at again. Not being who you knew you were was something new for T.C. He itched at it in his mind as though he were poking a sore spot in his mouth with the tip of his tongue.

Wereberry counted to ten silently and signaled for another forward surge. Still Water went down; the butt of a rifle met the side of his head, and his head lost. Were' started to leap to his defense when a man dressed much like Silent War leapt in front of him. Why, thought Wereberry, did no one think to mention that the other side had a ninja, too?

The enemy ninja kicked out at Wereberry, who countered, spinning, with the side of his arm. They traded a series of blows at speed, neither gaining a clear edge. Silent War, had he been there, would have leapt in and claimed the fight for himself. Sadly, Silent was off covering a tiny corner of the battlefield to ensure T.C.'s safe retreat. Were' was on his own.

He slid to the ground and grabbed for the ninja's ankles, missing by seconds. The ninja landed from his small leap and kicked at Wereberry's head, connecting with a dry thump. Were' snarled and crouched. The ninja dropped into stance. They faced off like that, eyes locked, and time seemed to stand still.

Wereberry knew the ninja could outfight him. He could think of no clear strategy to win the fight, and in that moment he stopped trying to. He let go of everything: of the fight, of his own fear, of his search for Cherrygiest, of his stress over his friendships. Wereberry took a breath, and when he released it: he was simply and fully the animal.

The ninja saw, in Were's eyes, that he faced a being of pure animal consciousness, desire, and ability. He flinched internally, but his body betrayed nothing. That internal flinch proved to be enough. Wereberry could smell the slightest edge of the ninja's fear. Were' leapt, taking the blows that the ninja rained upon his body, blows that would ache tomorrow and the day after but which didn't stop him now.

Claws rent at clothes and skin. Teeth sank into soft flesh. Strong arms and legs encircled and twisted the ninja's body in different directions. Before he could counter any one move, the ninja found himself confronted by another. No sane guiding force controlled them, only the purest animal concept of combat. The ninja sank to the ground, Wereberry still attached to him.

Choco-Ra targeted the HAVOC Commander's tent and blasted it to smithereens. He made it look like just another shot, another building blown to bits. He managed to, however, aim very carefully, hitting the tent at the farthest point possible from the safe. Wallsplitter rolled forward, blasting a few shots that purposefully went wide around the tent. Dust and smoke rose from the new holes in the ground, giving T.C. a chance to scurry under the fallen tent.

Ra whispered "Two" and gave Al control of the guns. Al made, Ra admitted to himself, a better shot overall. The mission depended on a few perfectly placed and timed shots, and Ra didn't want to mess them up because of his desire to do it himself.

Choco-Ra considered the idea of teamwork again. He thought of himself as the pilot and Al the co-pilot, but Al was the one who made the choices. Ra could request a change, as he just had, but it wasn't his job to do that. Al was the pilot, not Ra. Ra was his co-pilot. What Ra kept thinking of as a partnership, where both he and Al made choices to direct the team, was false. Al ran things, not Ra. And yet, Ra thought, and yet it felt like what Ra thought a partnership would be.

Al fired several shots in quick secession, covering T.C.'s use of explosive charges. They both saw the tent flap blow up from the force, but Al was already firing just clear of the tent, causing it to balloon even higher. The shot was one Ra simply could not have made. Ra, with a spreading grin, realized he had a lot of things to learn from his new friend. Perfect aim was only one of them.

Wereberry came to his senses as T.C. started to move out from under the tent. He unslung his rifle and started firing shots all across the tent, covering T.C.'s retreat while Ra and Al moved on to other—perfectly false and useless—targets.

Lugnut blinked; he couldn't remember Wereberry ever firing the rifle before. It showed—his covering fire was sloppy, throwing up tufts of dirt all over the place. Lugnut gave a hearty "Go BOB!" and joined in, firing his rifle all through the Commander's tent.

The two of them covered T.C.'s escape perfectly, destroying everything left under HAVOC Commander's tent, ensuring the blown safe would look like just another victim in the raid. Were' glanced at Lugnut and nodded.

T.C. reached Silent War, as planned, and handed him the contents of the safe. The plan, from there on, was for T.C. to go with Silent and for everyone else to pull back. Then the jets would come in, give a single bombing run pass, and turn toward home. HAVOC would be left without any plans at all, no one to blame it on, and BOB in possession of a lump of secret files.

Which is not how it went at all, when the moment came. T.C. handed Silent the stack of documents from the safe. Turning, he called, "I have another snatch-and-grab to try for," and he sprinted back into the rubble of the HAVOC base.

Silent stood there, documents in hand, not sure what he was supposed to do. Well, he knew what he was supposed to do: take the documents and retreat. Still, he considered tracking T.C.

Wereberry sent Lugnut back to base with the rest of the troops. Signaling for the general retreat before the bombing pass, he told Lugnut that he'd be right behind him. Lugnut turned, starting to help the rest of the troops retreat along the proper retrieval lines. When he turned back to ask Were' a question, he found that he was alone; there was no one behind him at all. Not a bit of pink fur in sight.

Then Wallsplitter almost ran Lugnut down, passing by close enough that Lugnut had to fight the urge to raise a fist and shake it. The tank rumbled off deeper into the HAVOC camp, not even firing its canon.

Ra turned the tank sharply, heading for T.C.'s reentry vector. T.C. leapt out of hiding and grabbed onto the side of the tank. Ra swung the tank around again and picked up Wereberry the same way. Their communicators were flashing messages, asking where they were, what was going on, and general warnings that the jets were already on their way so perhaps they wished to be somewhere else just then.

Only T.C. messaged back. He sent a message only to Silent and Captain Violet, explaining that they had a quick side mission that they weren't sure they could return from. He tried to ensure that no one thought them traitors. Not because, T.C. knew, the trio didn't want to be thought of as traitors, but so no one would doubt the information T.C. had stolen for them.

If they were traitors, that information was suspect and the entire mission was for nothing. If they simply had other orders from above Chief, then everything was fine. T.C. really hoped they believed it. He could think of nothing else to do or say. T.C. unstrapped his communicator and dropped it on the ground as they sped along the HAVOC base.

They met very little resistance. The jets could be heard in the distance and the HAVOC troopers were in bunkers or had withdrawn away from the field of fire. Still, Wallsplitter drove on. It drove right through the edge of the HAVOC base and out a bit further. The land here was green and lush, somehow untouched by the base camp right next to it. Unscorched by bombs or pulse fire, everything looked and smelled new and crisp. The tank growled to a halt, its side passengers dropping off to land on the soft ground.

Inside the tank, Al climbed into Choco-Ra's bag and hid. Ra flipped the main canon to emergency overload and hoped out of the vehicle, landing near his friends.

"All right," he told them, "we have about three minutes before it blows. How close do you think we should be?"

"Wait," Were' said, "what about your co-pilot? Will he be all right?"

"Sure," Ra said, waving a hand dismissively, "don't worry about him. So, how far?"

T.C. wondered about Ra's sudden indifference but passed it over in favor of dealing with an exploding tank. "Are we even sure this will do it?"

"Nope," Ra said happily, "but it should."

"I can't see why it wouldn't," Wereberry added with a shrug.

"Well, lots of things have exploded here, why would this one poke the hole we want? Why hasn't anything else?" T.C. wondered.

They all took a few steps back from the tank and listened as the jets roared overhead. Bombs started to fall from the sky, not on top of them, but close enough for the noise to be annoying and the clouds of dust and debris to sift through the air nearby.

"Gut feeling," Were' said. He looked at both of his friends and sniffed, catching another scent. Looking around, he tried to place it, but left it alone as another bomb went off nearby.

"True enough. Maybe we're all wrong and this tank goes up, and we watch and then go back to base. But maybe we're right," Ra said, studying the tank. "Didn't you feel something before that Board of Truth went up? In the pit of your stomach, or along your spine? That familiar tingle, like the White Lands?"

"Some?" T.C. said, not really sure. He stopped to think about it and to feel, and realized that he did feel something building. He hoped it wasn't simply nerves. "Yeah, I can feel it."

"We have nothing else to go on," Were' said. "Thank you guys for this."

"For what?" Ra asked, shaking his head. "You were right, I'm... I'm sorry we all got caught up in this."

Wereberry sighed and nodded, looking toward T.C.

"I'm sorry too," T.C. said. And he was, but for more than only what Ra had been talking about. T.C. was sorry that he found himself caught up in enjoying and discovering sides of himself that he was still coping with. He wasn't sorry that he had made yet more friends in the worlds, though he was truly sorry to have to leave them yet again.

Wereberry caught many of the unsaid things that T.C. meant and clapped a hand on his shoulder warmly. "You guys are my best friends, you know."

"Of course we are," T.C. said before Ra could speak, "who else would put up with you?"

"Oh, are you stealing my lines, T.C.?" Ra asked, pretending to be shocked.

"Hang out with you long enough and they just become obvious," T.C. said, smirking.

"That's low," Ra said.

Wereberry laughed. "How long until the big boom?" he asked, wondering if a few more steps away might not be a bad idea.

Ra looked at the tank and then at Wereberry. "Less than before. I stopped counting. Damn. Let's take another step back, I guess."

They all did. Wereberry and Choco-Ra took off their communicators, still flashing questions, and tossed them into the tank together.

"Hey, before we go," Were' said quickly, "do we want to explore the White Lands any?"

"Oooh, asking before we end up there, good idea," T.C. said with a soft laugh.

"Well, for once we're planning it, right?"

"True," Choco-Ra said, "and why don't we, just a little."

"T.C. seems the least affected by it," Were' pointed out, "so T.C., you decide when we should leave them. Agreed?" Wereberry knew Ra would want to linger and that he himself would want to rush through. Letting T.C. decide was the only middle ground Wereberry could think of.

"Agreed," T.C. and Ra said simultaneously.

Jets circled, taking another run. They were, however, slightly off their own planned course. Bombs dropped closer and closer to the three friends and one hidden passenger.

"This could suck," muttered Ra, watching the jets.

"Shouldn't have stopped counting," Were' pointed out.

"Fair enough," Ra admitted, eyeing the tank.

Wallsplitter hissed and started to glow, the cannon issuing a trail of smoke. The jets' carpet-bombing continued, drawing ever closer. A race between explosions was on.

The lead jet released the last of his bombs. They disengaged from under wing with a soft click, heard by absolutely no one. Air parted beneath them, whistling past the rounded metal casing. Fins popped out from the sides of the bomb as it fell, controlling its descent so that it nosed down and aimed directly at the ground. It fell, drawing closer by the second.

On the ground, a sharp metal ping sounded from the engine of the tank. Then it exploded. In the air, the falling bomb got caught in the shockwave and exploded prematurely, pushing its own concussive force against the tank's. The air between them shimmered with conflicting force waves and vaporized, new air rushing back into the space with a thunderous clap.

The three travelers saw the start of the tank's explosion. White space blossomed outward toward them, riding the shockwave of the blast. The blast picked them up and threw them backward. Soaring uncontrollably through the air, ass over elbow, the travelers had no way to see the white light catch up with them and engulf them utterly.

The bomb would go on record as having destroyed the tank. The whereabouts of the four BOB soldiers would never be resolved.

INTERLUDE THREE

THE THREE FRIENDS HURTLED along in the empty white space. T.C. found a current and swam into it, righting himself along a line that he decided was up. Grabbing both of his friends, he slowed them down and righted them as well.

The mists flowed around them, faster than before. The scent of grass and trees hung heavily in the non-air. The grass was still gray and dull, but the trees started to gain color as they watched. Nearby a lake started to form, gray water lapping at brown shores.

T.C. urged them on toward the lake, deciding to take a chance. The mists were still forming out of nothing and coalescing into shapes. Color was leaking into creation at an even slower rate, behind scent. They touched down on the brown, muddy shore of the lake whose water was just starting to discover blue.

The ground beneath their feet didn't feel quite right. It was too spongy, the mud behaving like a solid, yet gel-like, mass. All three of them stomped on it for a while, testing it. Choco-Ra's foot came down on it and passed through. He yanked it free and the ground reformed around the hole he had made. When he tested it again, everything was a bit more stable. Still, he didn't stomp so hard the next time, just in case.

Wereberry noticed the spot form closer to where they stood than it generally had in times past. He pointed it out with taps and gestures, and they all regarded it for a moment before going back to their exploration.

At least, they all knew, they weren't trapped. They had an exit they could use when they needed to, but for now they felt free to explore this strange between-land that had no name, or seeming purpose.

Wereberry picked some of the grass, but it crumbled back into mist and seeped through his fingers. He sniffed the mist as it went past and caught no scent at all from it. He plucked a few more blades of grass, sniffing them before they could dissolve: grass. They smelled exactly like grass should while they lost color, while they started to fuzz along the edges, even. Then they lost their scent and became pure mist again.

T.C. touched a webbed toe to the surface of the lake. The water there didn't give, feeling as spongy-solid as the mud he stood on. Still, it rippled and moved like water should. The confusion between the look and feel of the stuff sent a shiver along T.C.'s spine.

Choco-Ra watched T.C. and began to wonder: The mist formed things that were familiar to them, but gradually, and only getting things partly right. It found direction from somewhere and carried out its imperatives, but what was directing it? Whatever the guiding force, the mist didn't seem to know what it was doing. To Ra's mind that meant only one thing could be directing it. Him and his friends.

He tapped Wereberry's shoulder and tried to explain. They used the code signals of BOB, adapted for physical touch instead of light strobe. Wereberry watched, his jaw going slack as he absorbed what Ra told him. Choco-Ra went on to tell T.C. while Were' experimented some.

He looked at a patch of mud and thought spiraling thoughts regarding mud at it. The texture, the give, the smell and taste of it, even. How it ran along the ground and how it stuck to you. He put everything he could find about mud in his experience and directed it in thoughts straight to the patch of mud in front of him.

Carefully he touched a clawed toe to the ground. The toe sank into the warm mud, coming back from it with mud stuck on. It was mud. Real mud, or at least the stuff was behaving in a real way. Were' showed T.C. and Ra his achievement. They nodded and then T.C. worked on a patch of water, trying to get the same results.

The water flowed and washed up on the shore, leaving trails in Wereberry's mud. They smiled at each other and played with the mist—the thought-stuff, as they now considered it.

More and more mist formed, blotting out the white emptiness as it trolled along to join the land the travelers were creating. T.C. looked around and then stopped. The spot, their exit, the safety zone they were relying on, was obscured by mist. He pointed it out and all three looked at it, not sure what that meant for them.

Choco-Ra tried to will the mist clear of the spot, but, thinking of it as a wall that impeded them, the mist gradually solidified instead. Wereberry, seeing it solidify, tried to focus his intent on the mist being simple air, and the wall swirled and swayed, but remained solid. T.C. took their hands and tried to swim off, finding that the ground they stood on was, in fact, acting like ground, and that he couldn't just swim off into the non-sky any more.

Thoughts full of curses, Choco-Ra leapt off of the area of ground they stood on, trying to launch himself clear of it entirely. He managed it, but found himself floating away in the wrong direction. Still, it was enough, and Wereberry and T.C. followed his lead and leapt after him. Once clear, T.C. grabbed them and started to swim around the wall.

The wall was easily passed, but once beyond it there was no spot. No opening back out of the world, not that they could see. T.C. spun, swam around the wall a few times, and then stopped. He felt out for the current that always lead him, drew him, really, to the spot. Slowly it came into focus.

The current lead T.C. straight back to the wall. Using signals, he explained the problem as he saw it to his friends. They sighed. The spot was still there, that much was certain now; Wereberry could smell it and Ra could see hints of the rainbow of colors leading to it. It was simply inside the wall itself.

They had managed, they each realized, to lock themselves in. Punching the wall didn't hurt it, though it swirled around some. It seemed to be made of solid gray air now, and though it did twist and turn, it never broke, shattered, or cracked in the slightest.

They tried to think it away, focusing on the mist, on the idea that it could dissipate. Nothing. Finally, Wereberry waved his friends off and decided to try something else. He focused hard, not on the wall but on the spot. He tried to draw it out from the wall instead of moving the wall from it.

They could all sense the spot getting closer to freedom. Each of them started to try and will it loose. They visualized it, they felt it, pushing and pulling itself free of the trap the spot had found itself in. Moving the spot was far more work than reshaping the mist, and sweat broke out on their brows.

Deep in Ra's bag, Al had no idea what was going on. The world, to him, hadn't changed. It was simply quiet. He knew to wait for Ra to free him, as they had agreed. Choco-Ra wanted to wait for the right time, but also didn't want to toss Al into the White Lands with only a half-thought-out and ill-informed warning to guide him.

Ra wondered briefly, thinking of Al in his bag, whether a fourth will would help them. He was certain it would, but had no way to work Al into the mix this late in the game. Frustration drove him harder and he threw everything he had into the spot, tugging at it with his mind.

The wall shattered, breaking apart into shards of mist shrapnel that floated away into nothing. The spot sat heavily in the nothing, glowing at them. Each one of the three breathed a deep sigh of relief. They didn't need T.C. to tell them when to go; they all agreed, without asking, that the time was now.

But they had learned some about the White Lands, and that was worth it, Ra felt. They were truly starting to move forward with purpose, and it was a change that Ra found worth fighting for.

The spot allowed them access, letting them sink deeply in and pass through to the other side. Behind them, the small island of mud and water they had worked on so hard stayed, not dissipating at all; solid, if half-formed. Half-colored, but behaving much more like water and mud and grass than one would first guess upon seeing it.

The island remained, and waited.

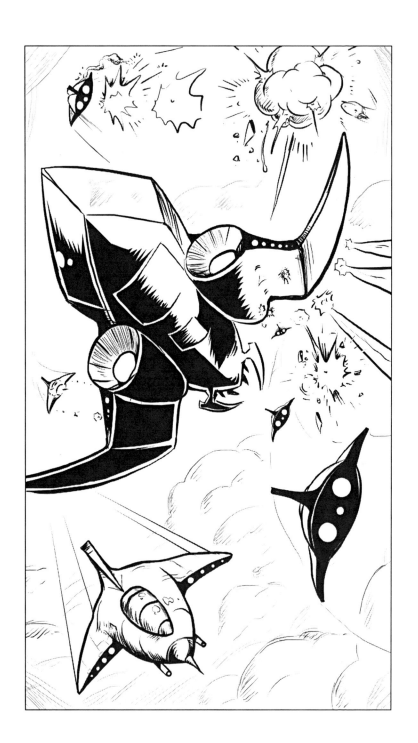

PART FOUR
All Together Now

"The achievements of an organization are the results of the combined effort of each individual."

–Vincent Lombardi

1 • Confirming Membership

THE SIGN READ "WELCOME TO..." ignoring the need for an actual place name. The three friends just stared at it for a few minutes in silence. Beyond the sign lay a road. The road itself branched and branched again, until it became a grid of streets that described a small suburb. With no name attached to it, the place somehow declared itself nowhere and everywhere at the same time.

Wereberry shrugged and looked past the sign into the suburb. Buildings of all sizes and shapes littered the landscape, each sitting in its own large plot of land. A veritable mile separated each building, the suburb widely spaced and yet also seeming crowded. Spires eighty stories tall fought for the sky, while smaller buildings described ovals, pyramids, and other shapes.

Choco-Ra identified it as a suburb, just from his gut feeling. The thing that gnawed at him was simple: what was this a suburb of? He didn't know, but felt the only way to be sure would entail asking. Which, by extension, suggested entering and finding people to ask.

Before that, though, he knew that he still had something he needed to do. Unslinging his bag and setting it on the ground, he started to open it. Were' and T.C. turned to watch, not sure what Ra needed right then. The bag open, Ra held out his hand and Al climbed onto it. Ra set him on the ground and looked at his companions.

"Uhm, Ra?" Wereberry asked, staring at Al.

"Yes?" Ra asked, acting indifferent.

"What is that?" Were' asked, pointing.

"You mean 'who,'" Al said, "I would assume. I'm Al."

231

Wereberry and T.C. exchanged glances and then turned toward Al and Ra. They both knew about Al, of course; Choco-Ra had told them all sorts of stories about the Mu-Corps and the secrets that it held, but they simply weren't expecting to see him here.

"Hi," T.C. said to Al, giving him a small wave.

"Glad to meet you," Al told him.

"Whoa, hold on, before we get to the greetings and all that, Ra, what happened to working together?" Were' tried to remain calm while he spoke. He wanted to believe this was all some sort of misunderstanding, or something to that effect. Maybe Ra had simply mentioned it in passing, or Al had snuck along, or—

"Well, we're still together and still working, right?" Ra asked. "Al needed to leave, is all."

"And when were you going to tell us?" Were' demanded.

"Were', maybe we shouldn't be fighting," T.C. cut in.

"I'm not fighting," Wereberry snapped, "I'm just asking a question."

"The truth is that Ra agreed to take me along, that's it," Al said.

"Without telling us," Were' said, wondering if he would have to keep repeating himself.

"I didn't tell you because you might have said no," Ra said at long last. He wanted to leave it at that and not get into it any deeper. He wasn't yet comfortable with the rest of his reasons.

"And then we could've discussed it," Were' said.

"With what time?" Ra asked. "Last I remember we were pulling off a plan that we weren't even sure would work at top speed at the last minute because... look, let's drop it. I'm sorry."

Wereberry started to answer sharply and then stopped, processing Ra's words. He didn't apologize lightly, or often, really. There was a note in Ra's voice that spoke volumes to Were'. A vocal pitch that he wanted to save for later, to deconstruct.

T.C. caught the tone of voice as well but thought he knew exactly what the issue was. He knew the sound of loneliness very well and caught it quickly in others. He looked at Al and wondered about the friendship that had built so rapidly between the two of them. He found he didn't care why they had bonded so close and so fast; he only knew that he was glad for it.

"Well, what's done is done, Were'," T.C. said, "so we might as well say hi to Al and keep moving. Agreed?"

"Agreed," Were' said, after one last quick glance toward Ra. "So where now?"

"Seems obvious," Al said, scurrying off down the road. The other three watched him go and hurried to catch up.

They walked along the road for a while, just sight-seeing. No one building grabbed their attention over any other. Every now and then deep rumblings could be heard, and then things would leap forth from one of the buildings: jets, cars, tanks, and other vehicles. They were always brightly colored and always gleamed brightly in the light. After the third set launched, no one paid any attention to them.

The light started to fade as night crept up on the travelers. Wereberry suggested they stop at the next building they came across and the others agreed, especially Al. Along the way, Were' and Al had managed to find some time to talk. Wereberry admitted to himself that Al was a good guy, and was more than happy to have him along. Al was smart and small, two things that could come in handy. Plus he just seemed nice in the same way Ra was. Under a rougher exterior he really did seem to care about things. His friendship with Ra was important to him, and that made it important to Wereberry.

He still wasn't happy with the way things had unfolded, but at least, he reflected, Ra had managed to bring along someone good—though if pressed, Were' would admit that Choco-Ra was a better quick judge of character than either himself or T.C. The equation, all put together, meant that Wereberry was going out of his way to be nice to Al, and he recognized and appreciated it when he saw that Al was doing the same.

Ra allowed himself to smile at the turn of events. He had worried, he admitted to himself, that Were' and T.C. might not get along with Al, and that meshing of personalities was important to him. He didn't want it to be, or so he told himself, but he knew it really was.

They came to a short green lawn with a strange, bright-red rock walkway, leading up to a building that looked like a squat onion. Deciding it was as good a bet as any, they went up the walkway and approached the door. T.C. knocked and all four of them waited, trying to be patient. After a few minutes passed, T.C. knocked again. A minute later the door, a large metal thing the same red as the walkway, opened a crack.

"May I help you?" a tall, reed-thin man asked them. He was dressed in an impeccable black suit and somehow managed to block the wide entranceway through personality alone.

"Ahhh, yes," Wereberry began, "we were just wandering down the road and were hoping you knew of somewhere we could stay for the night."

The man patted down his suit and harrumphed, obviously about to rebuke the foursome when he stopped and studied them. He scrutinized them and hmm'd and huh'd to himself, ignoring their looks and confusion.

"Which team are you, again?" he asked, warily.

"We're not a team," Ra said, "we're just friends. I mean, I suppose in some senses that might make us a team."

"I see, yes, you are missing a member. Have you simply not found one yet?"

"No, we're looking for her," Wereberry blurted excitedly.

"Oh dear," the man intoned softly, "I'm very sorry, yes, come in."

He ushered them inside the building, which T.C. imagined

was full of rooms with round walls and strange dimensions, given the exterior onion shape. Instead, the foyer they entered took up the entirety of the visible dome. Incredibly high and curved, the ceiling itself gave off a soft glow, lending the area light. A few rooms poked out against the far wall, but other than that, they saw nothing.

The butler led them to the far side of the foyer. They could see that the rooms there were sparsely decorated and mostly for waiting. One of the rooms, though, could be seen to contain two other doors.

They were led to a simple sitting room and the butler vanished out, asking them to sit and wait. Al leapt down and followed him briefly before reporting back.

"That room? One of the doors is an elevator," he told the others. Al paced, circling the chairs that the others sat in. "Which tells us where the rest of this place is, at least."

"But not," T.C. pointed out, "what it is."

"A base of some sort," Wereberry said. He sat, chewing a dried strawberry from his bag and thinking.

"What makes you say that?" Ra asked.

"Most of the buildings we've seen have launched some sort of craft, right? And he thought we were a team. This must be some team's base. He's their guard, I guess."

"Butler," Al chimed in. "I know a butler when I smell one. He's a good one, mind you, but he butles."

"So what do we do?" T.C. asked. "I think we should pretend to be a team."

"Why pretend?" Ra asked. "We are one, and like he said and as Were' here already told him, we're missing a member. It isn't a lie if it's true."

"In some sense, at least," T.C. muttered.

"Even better, then," Ra told him.

The butler came back into the room and the foursome grew quiet. They weren't sure if he had heard them or not, but whatever damage they'd caused was caused. No one intended to cause more, however.

Before him, the butler pushed a cart of tea and sandwiches. Wereberry instantly saw the usefulness of a butler. He never needed anyone to open his door for him, but someone to make sandwiches was a great idea. He wondered how one went about getting a butler as the man handed out cups and saucers.

The butler filled Wereberry and T.C.'s cups, Ra declining. Then he put a saucer down for Al and filled it with tea as well. Next came the sandwiches, a variety of them. Wereberry chose a nice cucumber job, and T.C. opted for a sandwich filled with some sort of jam or paste. Al took the same and the three of them ate and drank as the butler watched.

"I do," he said, "apologize for the delay, sirs. Continent Strike Team Five will return shortly."

"Thank you," Ra said.

"Oh dear," the butler said, shaking his head sadly, "I never did introduce myself. Yes. I am Orin. I work for—"

"Continent Strike Team Five?" Ra ventured with a nod.

"Yes, of course. Very good, sirs. Now if you will excuse me, I have other matters to attend to. Please don't wander off. Thank you."

"And thank you, Orin," said Were' and T.C in unison.

"Of course, sirs," Orin said. He left the room, leaving the tray behind and vanishing, they supposed, back into the elevator.

Al began to pace again, his saucer empty and sandwich half gone. He didn't leave the room, choosing instead to pace every inch of the one he was in. By the time Wereberry and T.C. had finished eating, Al had the layout of the room memorized. Every obstacle and possible entranceway, mouse-sized or other, locked itself away in his head. Not that the room was huge. It wasn't. Still, he thought it better safe than sorry.

"So what," T.C. asked, "do you think this Continent Strike

236

Team Five is?"

"Rich, for one," Were' said. He leaned back in his chair and linked his hands behind his head. "I don't think you get an underground building with a butler just because you have a cool name."

"You think it's cool?" Al asked. "I thought it was rather clumsy."

T.C. laughed and nodded in agreement. The entire place was making him oddly nervous. At first it seemed shiny and different, like so many places he sat in these days, but the longer he stayed, the more he felt that he simply didn't belong. He couldn't pin down why. He thought about the look of the place, but discounted that quickly. It was nice, but it wasn't so nice that the interior made him twitch. No, it was something else. He put it aside again and sat forward in his seat, resting his elbows on his knees and watching the others.

"I don't care if it's a clumsy name," Ra said, "but they sound military."

"They do," Were' agreed, "which would be good, we can deal with military."

"I suppose we can, but do we want to?" Al asked. Al's history with the military worked, understandably, to put him off the idea somewhat. He thought about it and knew that he would go along with his new friends, Ra especially. Still, a military group often looked upon the small as weak, and then gave them jobs to do anyway. They just didn't give them the credit afterwards.

"Not much of a choice, I'd say," Were' said, "I mean, you saw all the buildings around. They all look kinda like this one. All the ships launching, I'd say this whole area is going to be the same thing."

"We're getting far too comfortable with this," T.C. said.

"With what? The military?" Ra asked. "T.C., I'm sorry that the military end of things hit you the way it did, but—"

"I meant the travel," T.C. said, turning to Ra. "And it isn't as if I was the only one affected and you're some stone-cold guy who just happens to sneak a friend along even though he's not affected."

Choco-Ra sighed. He hadn't meant to anger T.C., or anyone else for that matter. A glance at Wereberry told him that anger them both he had. Or whatever. Ra wasn't good at caring that others were upset, not due to faults of his own. He also wasn't sure why T.C. had felt the need to snap at him like that.

Were' wanted to laugh. T.C. wasn't one to snap like that, but it had been perfectly said. He knew there was more to Ra's choice than he had let on, and that was fine as far as it went. Still, he wished that Ra felt easy enough to open up some. Not that Ra had ever really been that guy—which didn't stop Wereberry from wishing he could be, once in a while.

"We do travel a lot," Were' said, "so I guess it's about time we got used to it."

"Still," T.C. said, accepting the topic shift away from Ra. T.C. didn't mean to upset anyone, but when Ra started to tell him that he was weak... no, that wasn't fair, T.C. told himself. Ra had never said that. He had been trying to be sympathetic, T.C. saw, but when the words came out, T.C. had just flinched and slapped back.

"Still," Ra repeated, "you worry we're getting too cynical about the whole thing?"

"I don't see what the issue is," Al said, the earnest note in his voice defusing the words. "I mean, how is that a bad thing?"

"I'm not saying it is by default," T.C. explained, "it's just that I feel like we've gotten too used to it. To the point that, sure, nothing takes us by surprise now, but maybe—"

"We've lost a sense of wonder?" Were' asked.

"I guess," T.C. said, "though I certainly don't think I'd put it like that. I don't even know what I mean. Look, ignore me, I'm babbling."

The choice to let it drop or not was taken from the quartet's hands when they heard the elevator open. They all grew very quiet and watched the doorway nearest them.

Five figures stepped into the room quickly. They weren't rushing, Were' noted; they simply walked quickly. They weren't anxious so much as just generally feeling busy, he realized. We're just, he thought, another thing to deal with.

Each one of them, the members of Continent Strike Team Five, stopped and stood proudly while they looked over their guests. They each wore a form-fitting jumpsuit and held a helmet in their hands. The jumpsuits were each of a different color, but they all had the same white racing stripes running down the arms and legs into their gloves and boots, which were white as well.

"I'm Rick," a young, happy-looking man said. With the others standing slightly behind him, he seemed to be the leader, and he wore a mostly yellow jumpsuit. His lean frame was topped by a thick shock of unruly black hair.

"Hi, Rick," T.C. said. The merman stood, and Were' and Ra stood just after him, in support. "We were really just, I mean hi. How are you?"

"I'm Mint!" shouted a small boy in a bright green jumpsuit. He wore large, thick goggles that rested on his forehead, just below his matted short yellow hair.

Rick and the others laughed. "Yeah, you are, kid," said a taller man standing near Rick. His perfect black crew cut matched his deadly serious face and dark blue jumpsuit. Even though he laughed with the others, his stern demeanor shone through.

"I'm Wereberry," the werewolf said, "and these are my friends. We're traveling together. This is T.C., Choco-Ra, and Al." Were' gestured to each of his friends as he spoke. They each nodded in turn.

"That's Scott," Rick said, nodding at the man in blue, "and that's Biggun back there," an overweight but obviously well-muscled man in black nodded, "and that's Princess." Princess, her long blue hair flowing down along the back of her purple jumpsuit, smiled warmly.

"So you'd be Continent Strike Team Five, then?" Ra asked.

"Of course!" Rick said. "This is our base, after all, so we'd better be. Orin took good care of you, I assume?"

"Very good care," T.C. said with a smile.

"Oh good," Princess said.

"Rick?" Mint piped up. "Can we show them the hanger? Can we?"

"Whoa there, Mint, let's see what they want first before we go showing them all our secrets, all right?"

"Awwww," Mint kicked the floor lightly, "sure, Rick."

"We were just looking for a place to maybe sit a while, stay the night, that sort of thing," Al said quickly.

"Yeah we just wanted—" Were' began.

"Hey, where's your fifth?" Biggun asked, his low voice full of concern.

"Well, we're looking for her," Ra put in before Were' could go off, "if you've heard anything, that would be a big help."

"Now can we go to the hanger, Rick?" Mint asked again, the whine in his voice grating instantly on Al's nerves. "I bet my hover tank could find her for them! I bet it could!"

"All right, Mint," Rick said. He smiled at the strangers, a "what can you do?" look creasing his face. "Let's go to the hanger. We can look for your friend while we're down there. Come on."

Rick turned and walked through his group toward the elevator. Continent Strike Team Five formed up behind their leader and followed Rick in. The travelers walked right behind them, if slower.

The elevator itself had five circles on the floor with a good amount of space between each. Rick stood in the center space and the others each stood in a circle that was ringed with colors matching their jumpsuits. Were' wondered what they would say or do if someone stood in the wrong circle.

"Hanger level, no rush," Rick spoke to the air. The elevator doors closed but, aside from a slight electric hum, there was no sense of movement. The elevator doors opened again, a second later, and the view outside was decidedly not the entranceway any longer.

The hanger was huge. Big enough that looking directly toward a wall gave Were' a pang of vertigo. He decided not to risk looking up, guessing the effect would be even worse.

Equipment of all sorts lay on work benches across the space. Bits that looked like they could be engines or weapons sat with pieces of side panel and fuselage. Each work table was a little island of chaos in a calm storm. A runway dominated the center of the space, red and white lights blinking down either side. The runway curved sharply up near the edges of Ra's vision, and from there it vanished somewhere they couldn't see. To the left of the runway four vehicles sat, lined up in a perfect row. They were each the same color as one of the team member's jumpsuits.

A bright yellow jet, looking futuristic compared with the BOB jets the four friends were used to, sat low on its wheels. Two large cannons, one under each wing, looked like big toys, due mostly to their color. Next to the jet, a small blue racecar pinged, the engine still cooling. A purple motorcycle came next, followed by a green... something. The green thing was shaped like a rounded-off pyramid, though it bristled with tiny gun barrels. It sat directly on the ground, no means of movement visible.

On the right side of the runway sat a huge airplane. Each of the black beast's wings alone were bigger than the yellow jet. The black plane sported no visible guns or armament. Its massive size worked as a threat by itself. The engines on the black jet were massive as well, making Al wonder how it took off without setting fire to everything else in the hanger.

Each vehicle had a stylized CST-5 logo painted on the side, layered on top of another number. The black jet was number 5 and, Were' noticed, the yellow jet was number 1.

"Here's my hover tank!" Mint cried out, running toward the green lump. He touched the side of it and a panel slid down to form an entrance. Mint leapt in, and the door slid shut behind him. A powerful hum started up seconds later. The lump lifted off the ground quickly, hovering a few inches above the surface of the hanger.

Ra hid a small laugh behind a hand. He knew, now, from tanks. That was no tank. It was a metal blob that moved around above ground. Then again, he thought as he glanced back to the black jet, he wouldn't have guessed anyone made planes that size, either.

The hover tank slid over to the group and Mint's voice squeaked out from a hidden speaker. "Your friend," he asked, "was she wearing a locator, maybe?"

"Of course she wasn't, kid," Scott said, "if she had been they could've found her by themselves, huh?"

"Oh, right, sorry Scott," Mint said. "All right then, well maybe I can scan for anyone lost, or without a team or something. I'll set up a search."

The four strangers nodded. They weren't sure what they were really agreeing with, but it sounded good.

Inside the hover tank, Mint hit a series of unmarked, glowing buttons and stared at a split-screen hopefully. On one side of the screen he had a view of the hanger; the other scrolled with glowing symbols that ran down the screen almost faster than the eye could follow. He hit another button and spoke into the mic that sat near him. "Nothing so far, but it'll get back to me."

The hover tank lowered itself to the ground and Mint leapt from it deftly, landing in a crouch. He stood and ran back to his team, standing proudly. "If she's out there, the hover tank'll find her."

"Don't make promises you can't keep, Mint," Biggun said.

"Awwww c'mon, Biggun, don't be like that!" Mint protested. "You'll see!"

"So yeah," Rick said, ignoring Mint, "this is the hanger. The heart of the team."

"Speaking of, you guys never told us which team you were," Scott said darkly. "I don't remember hearing about a team with a mummy on it, much less a mouse, werewolf, and fish guy."

"We're, uhhh, new," Were' said, "we go by uhhh—"

"The Foursome," T.C. put in quickly.

Al sighed and mentally counted down from ten. He liked T.C., and appreciated the merman, but he made a mental note to talk to him about speaking before thinking.

"Four?" Princess asked, "I thought you were missing your other member? Wouldn't that make you five, not four?"

"Yes, well," Al said, "he meant Fivesome. We call ourselves the Fivesome." Fivesome. That, Al thought, had to be the dumbest name ever invented. It ranked right up there with Little Fella. At least Little Fella hadn't been his own damn fault.

"Fivesome?" asked Biggun. He wanted to laugh—that was a terrible name—but he was afraid that if he laughed, they would make fun of his name in return. He hadn't wanted to be called Biggun, but when he had joined the Continent Strike Team Five as their mechanic, Mint had started the name going and never stopped. Though he was grateful to be part of the team and pilot of the *Black Angel*, Biggun still rankled at his name, regardless. Hearing of a team named the Fivesome helped ease that, at long last. In the silence after he spoke, Biggun whistled softly, hoping that it would somehow magically change the subject for him. Instead, an alarm claxon did the job for him.

It rang out loudly in the hanger, and the lights went red

and started to flash. The members of Continent Strike Team Five started to run for their ships. Biggun looked over his shoulder at the Fivesome members.

They were standing around, waiting for the other shoe to drop. They had each flinched when the alarms went off, but now they were just standing around watching for some reason. No leaping into action, no running for uniforms. Missing a member was really upsetting them, Biggun thought, and he decided to help.

"Hey, you guys can ride with me in the *Black Angel*," he shouted as he climbed the ladder into the nose of the ship.

Choco-Ra shrugged and walked toward the ship. Wereberry laughed and ran past him, nudging his friend's shoulder as he went. T.C. and Al hurried with Were', the three of them climbing into the ship quickly. Ra shook his head but picked up his pace, climbing in only seconds after his friends.

2 • Flight of the Bumblebee

THE *BLACK ANGEL* WAS a huge ship; that was without question. Its cockpit, though—that was fairly small. There were five seats, each one at a different duty station, and an elevator in the back.

Biggun told the four to grab seats and strap themselves in. Al alone wondered what he should do. He crawled up into a seat but knew there was no way for a belt to protect him. Instead he wedged himself into the crack of cushion between the back and bottom of the seat itself and hoped for the best.

"Prepare for take-off," Biggun said, his voice deep and commanding. Ra realized he wasn't speaking to them so much as the rest of his team.

The various vehicles all shot down the runway at full speed. The *Black Angel* was the last to go, taxiing forward behind Mint's hover tank.

The *Black Angel*'s engines whirred and whined as they came up to speed. The large black jet ambled down the start of the runway as the hover tank gained speed and took off. Biggun's hand rested lightly on the throttle, easing it forward inch by inch.

The hover tank clear, Biggun jammed the throttle to full open and the engines roared to life. The four passengers were thrown back hard against their seat cushions. Al found himself wedged deeply in and took slow, careful breaths as best he could manage.

The hanger zipped by at greater and greater speeds. Wereberry and Ra were the only two who could see out of the cockpit as the plane rocketed toward take-off. The tunnel grew smaller as they went, the flashing lights becoming a pure, glowing blur as they watched.

Suddenly they could see the end of the runway, an open hole pointed at the sky. Were' felt the jet start to lift off its wheels just before the plane left the hanger. Clear and free now, Biggun eased the *Black Angel* into a steep climb, gaining altitude as well as speed. The engines vibrated the ship hard, their noise drowning out any words that could have been spoken.

Biggun eased back on the throttle precisely and nosed the plane back to level. The noise settled down to a constant, dull roar, and Wereberry shook his head to clear it. Al struggled to unstick himself some, just enough that he wouldn't be swallowed by the chair. Ra unbuckled himself and reached over to help. T.C. looked bluer than normal.

"I don't feel good," he said softly.

"Oh, take-off is always fun," Biggun joked, "you'll be fine. If not, there's a bathroom downstairs in the ship's hanger."

Biggun put the *Black Angel* through its paces, swooping down out of the sky to keep an eye on the team's ground-based vehicles. Rick came on the radio, telling them all to keep sharp. He mentioned something about a Garuda ship entering their airspace, and the obvious need to stop it.

His team members radioed their agreement, and the vehicles kept their current course. Soon a large cloud formed, as dark and foreboding as only unnatural clouds can manage. "That's it!" Scott shouted over the radio. No one doubted him at all.

The cloud started firing multicolored beams, each beam drawing closer to one of Continent Strike Team Five's ships. The CST-5 ships juked and dodged with skill. Beam fire rained down, blasting and smashing pockmarks into the ground. Ra watched as Scott's racecar found itself hurtling toward a series of holes far too dense to drive over. Flames flared from the back of the car and it leapt into the sky, flying a short distance over the mess onto clearer ground.

Rick's yellow jet was taking heavy fire, dodging between beams, twisting and turning every which way. Rick pulled up into a power climb, heading right for the cloud, his own guns loosing beams of deadly energy. Holes in the cloud steamed away, but none of them could be sure that whatever lay in the cloud itself had sustained damage.

"Biggun, we need to get rid of their cloud generator to reveal them!" Rick shouted. "And we need to do it fast!"

"Right, Rick," Biggun said calmly. The *Black Angel* broke out of the pack and started to climb. The angle of ascent was steep, throwing everyone hard into their seats. The engines roared again as Biggun's hand worked the throttle. The sky around them started to darken as he climbed, the atmosphere waning as their height grew simply dangerous.

At the apex of his climb Biggun yelled "Hang on!" and nosed down just as the engines started to sputter out from lack of air. The dive proved worse than the climb. Biggun's four passengers truly felt like they were hurtling toward their doom as the *Black Angel* dove, spinning, toward the cloud.

Biggun released a barrage of missiles at the cloud, and, unseen by anyone else, prayed as he aimed his ship to use it as a weapon. The nose of the ship parted the cloud cover and Biggun turned on the afterburners. Between the missile explosions and the close passing of the hypersonic jet, the cloud cover ripped from the Garuda ship. Gray smoke wisped every which way around yellow explosions and raging fire.

The *Black Angel* continued to hurtle toward solid ground at speeds too great to bother recording. Biggun pulled back heroically on the control stick, putting all of his strength into the action. The stick didn't budge.

"You... might want to... pull up," Choco-Ra said, finding it difficult to breathe. His body had flattened itself out almost entirely in response to the g-forces being tossed around inside the ship.

"Trying...," Biggun spat out. Every muscle strained, all

focused on one tiny stick. Sluggishly it twitched, starting to move. The nose of the *Black Angel* eased up and they leveled out. Wereberry didn't mention to anyone else that he was sure he could count the blades of grass on the ground just before they pulled out. The image would stay with him, though.

The *Black Angel* climbed again, but at a reasonable rate. The Garuda ship, revealed now, sat proud and heavy in the air above them. Large and colored a gleaming orange, the ship resembled nothing less than a gigantic hawk. Metal wings segmented and actually beat at the sky, the tips firing deadly red beams of destruction.

The nose of the ship, the beak, opened wide and a beam as thick as a tree trunk lanced the sky, the air shimmering around it. Rick's jet spiraled out of the beam's way just in time. The nose of the Garuda ship turned to follow the jet—the next section of the ship, the hawk's neck, was also segmented, allowing it to articulate. T.C. wondered why anyone would really go to the trouble of making a ship resemble and move like a bird. There had to be, he reasoned, easier ways to build weapons.

"We can't take it out alone," Scott yelled over the radio.

"We need to use the full power of the *Black Angel*!" Princess joined in.

Biggun acknowledged the plan by starting another dive. Not as low as the last one, Biggun cruised the ship down and flew directly over Princess, Mint, and Scott's vehicles. Each of them leapt into the air on short jet bursts and, to the eyes of everyone on board, vanished. The team members came in through the elevator and stopped as they saw there was no where to sit. The *Black Angel* climbed and Rick's jet met up with them as well. His jet mated with the *Black Angel*, and soon he too was in the crew chamber.

"We'd leave, but we're kind of stuck here," T.C. said apologetically.

"We need to man our stations so we can destroy the

Garuda ship," Rick said.

"Do you want them to win?" Scott yelled.

"Enough," Wereberry said, "with the yelling." He undid his seatbelt and stood. "Do you have anywhere we can sit and still be safe?"

Princess looked around the room and noted the absolute lack of other chairs. "Well, there is the Skimmer," she said.

Scott and Mint turned to Princess with mirrored looks of surprise. "But what if we need it?" Mint asked quickly.

"We won't," Princess told him simply. She was sure that the escape vehicle wouldn't be needed. The team never used it, as a point of pride. Most of the time they pretended the small escape warship didn't exist.

"Fine, go man the Skimmer, it's in the lower bay of the ship," Rick said quickly, "take it out but stay clear of the fight, understood?"

"No problem," Ra sniped. Standing, he held onto a chair's back with one hand while he grabbed Al with the other. T.C. and Were' joined him and they hurried to the elevator. CST-5 belted themselves in, flicking on monitors and bringing systems on-line without another word.

The elevator traveled a short distance down, coming to an abrupt stop almost before it started. The doors opened and the four friends made their way into the *Black Angel*'s internal hanger area, weaving from side to side as they tried to walk despite Biggun's sharp evasive maneuvers.

The four other CST-5 vehicles were parked in the hanger, each one tethered firmly in place and facing the hanger door. Set away from them, its tethers a bit older and darkened, sat a small, bubble-shaped craft. It looked like a UFO might, a see-through dome covering most of its surface area, leaving the rest of the ship a silver-flashed color. A small CST-5 logo adored it, but no number was superimposed behind it.

Were' and T.C. undid the tethers as quickly as they could manage. They fumbled with straps and hooks and locks, not sure how any of the strange equipment worked. While they freed the Skimship, Choco-Ra and Al sat inside the ship's one compartment, easing the engine to life.

Twin guns slid from a hidden compartment at the front of the ship. Ra and Al looked at each other and nodded. Some more switches were switched and toggles toggled. A twin set of guns slid out of housings at the back of the ship. Al glanced toward the hatch from his perch on a control panel as Were' and T.C. boarded. "We're armed, the engines work, and... no, I think that's about it," he said.

There were five seats in the small craft, two in the front where the flight controls sat, two in the back to man guns there, and one on the side opposite the hatch, a bank of screens and keys in front of it. The four friends each took a seat, leaving the center one empty. Wereberry stared at it for a second before turning to face the rear of the craft, thinking how obvious it was now that they were missing someone. Before it had been a search for a missing friend, a missing love, even. Now it became more and more apparent that they were missing some part of themselves as well, and that part was tied up and into Cherrygiest. None of them, he reflected, would be whole until they found her.

Al was a welcome addition and, Were' thought, in some sense Ra's attempt at filling their communal void, but all he did was highlight the fact that they were still missing something more. It wasn't Al's fault. If anything, Were' felt bad for the mouse now. He was nominally supposed to fix the situation, but not only did he bring it into sharper focus, he had also become one of the people missing something. The worst part of that was that he didn't even know it, or her. Al missed a part of himself he hadn't even met.

Were' sighed and grabbed the targeting control for one of the rear guns. T.C. grabbed the other, stopping to look over at his friend. "Good luck," T.C. said.

"Luck?" Were' asked. "T.C., we shouldn't even need

guns. We aren't joining in the fight, we're sitting it out, remember?"

"That's the plan, at least," T.C. said, "but how often has that worked out for us?"

"Point," Wereberry said, and he checked his ammo levels a second time.

Ra found the switch for the radio and flicked it on. "Biggun, we're departing, open the hanger for us?"

"Sure thing, stable for take-off in three—" Ra started the ship's engines and taxied it so that it pointed at the hanger door. He threw the brakes on the wheels and started to throttle up the engine. He had no idea if this was how you took off from a moving ship—he honestly hadn't even flown before, but it seemed right enough. "—two—" The ship's engines roared in the hanger, sound bouncing off the walls and flames spitting out behind them, "—one—"

The hanger opened and Choco-Ra released the brakes. The ship shot forward, clearing the bay quickly. Open air swallowed them, surrounding them in their bubbled ship. The *Black Angel* pulled ahead of them in the blink of an eye. The ship's engines thrust hard. The ship itself started to drop, losing altitude fast.

Ra worked the controls quickly, refusing to panic. Al sat nearby and offered suggestions, never bitching or demanding, just advising in a tone that Ra managed to not take badly. Between the two of them, they managed to level the ship out and start it flying under decent control.

"Hey, Ra? Al?" Were' asked.

"Were', what is it?" Al asked in return.

"There are some ships back here, flying directly at us. Just wanted you to know. Look, if it's alright with you, T.C. and I'll shoot 'em down. You two just fly this thing if you have it under control now."

"Sure thing," Ra told Were' over his shoulder.

Behind them, three ships closed in. They were all the same

color as the Garuda ship, but where that ship was massive, these three were small, one-man fighters. Their long bodies and swept wings gave them a look of menace as well as speed, maneuverability, and grace.

Wereberry and T.C. opened fire. Beams lanced from their guns, tracking the movements of the enemy ships. The ships dodged the fire, zipping around the ship at speed.

"Coming around on both sides!" T.C. yelled.

Al was ready for them, leaping back onto the control surfaces whenever the acceleration threw him back into his seat. A blast nicked the wing of one of the ships, sending up a spray of smoke. The ships broke formation and turned.

"They're coming around for a second pass, get ready," Al told Were' and T.C.

Choco-Ra struggled to fly the ship, teaching himself how it behaved as he went along. A few sloppy, random turns and strange dips managed to work in their favor as the enemy ships opened fire.

A stray shot scorched the clear dome of the ship, causing T.C. to flinch. The dome didn't crack, but where the beam impacted, a hole was partially melted through the clear surface.

"Evasive would be a good idea," he said over his shoulder while he took a few shots at the enemy ships.

"Right," Ra said, "working on that. Just keep firing, and hit something."

A bark of laughter escaped Wereberry and he let fly with a barrage of fire. One of the ships, caught in mid-turn, exploded. It showered the ship nearest to it in debris, and that ship wobbled as it hit afterburners to move clear.

"Got one," Wereberry said as the sound of the explosion died down.

"We guessed," Al told him, bringing his own guns around.

The remaining ships stepped up their attack. Blasts of

energy splashed against the Skimship's dome, smearing and melting it in increments. Choco-Ra fought the controls, trying to get the ship to respond faster. The throttle was pinned at max, but he put a hand on it anyway, trying to jam it even higher.

He dodged and turned, trying anything he could think of. It simply wasn't much, and certainly not enough to deal with two enemy ships whose pilots were, quite obviously, professionals at this sort of thing.

A whistle started as a pinhole section burned all the way through the dome. Wereberry, T.C., and Al all fired without relief, and Ra concentrated on avoiding any more shots.

"We have to land," Al said, furiously lobbing shots toward the enemy ships.

"I know, I know," chanted Ra, looking below for a likely space. He throttled back to take the edge off their speed and started to descend. "Brace yourselves!" he shouted as they approached the tree line much faster than he'd intended.

The Skimship cruised lightly against a few leaves, still dropping. Branches scraped the bottom next, destabilizing it. The ship tipped to the right, smashing along trees, cracking them apart. The impacts dropped their speed considerably and far too quickly, sending the four jostling in their seats and crashing back and forth against their instrument panels.

Wereberry's head smashed into his gun grips, firing a salvo that took down trees that had otherwise managed to avoid their destructive descent. T.C. leaned into his seat, tightening the muscles of his stomach and back, hoping to stay as upright as humanly feasible. His hands gripped his guns tightly and he squinted, attempting to sight along them to blast one of the enemy ships out of the sky even as the Earth rushed up to greet them.

The enemy ships continued to fire, their blasts missing more and more as leaves and branches found themselves tossed into the air in the Skimship's deadly wake. Climbing free, the enemy ships watched the rest of the descent from a distance, prepared to strafe anything that climbed free of the soon-to-be wreckage.

A tree trunk broke under the force of the Skimship's progress, cracking the already weakened dome. The dome shattered, sharp edges of unknown materials adding their own threat to the mix. The ship overturned and then trees were slapping against each of the four, battering them senseless. Choco-Ra held on to the controls, working them in pure desperation, hoping beyond hope that he could do something. The control stick was dead in his hands, however, unresponsive on every level.

Another tree impact flipped them yet again, and with a final twist, the ship kissed the ground hard. It hit sideways, digging a trench as it dragged along, slowing to a shuddering, final, halt. Smoke rose from the Skimship as it sat, dug-in and quiet.

Wereberry slumped, bleeding from cuts and scratches, unconscious, dangling from his seat. His safety harness kept him in relative place as best it could. Drops of his blood fell to splash gently against T.C.'s head, not stirring him. His hand webbing was ripped and torn in several places, his limbs dangling limply from his seat.

Al lay dazed, stuck deeply into his seat. He appeared unhurt, but a branch as thick as his body sat on top of him— the impact had knocked him out. Choco-Ra moaned in his impact-caused slumber. A sharp branch, ripped and torn against the ragged edge of the dome's remains, stuck out of his chair. It ran from right next to his head down to his waist. A pile of bandages fluttered in a breeze a few feet below him— the unraveled mass of his right arm, bandage torn angrily from where it met his shoulder by the branch that had almost taken his head off instead.

The enemy ships circled a few times, waiting for signs of life. They spotted nothing and radioed the Garuda ship.

Recalled to help in the final stages of the battle being pitched against the *Black Angel*, they peeled off, leaving the crew of the Skimship to their fate.

3 • In the Hall of the King

AL WOKE FIRST. He looked around and realized quite quickly that he possessed no idea about where he was. The walls were white and the soft thing he found himself laying on matched. Rolling onto his legs he stood, only a little shakily, and looked around.

Wereberry, T.C., and Choco-Ra all lay in beds, covered by sheets up to their necks. The crisp white bedding seemed to shine in the all-white room. His friends were all asleep, or worse, Al thought. Al himself realized that he sat in the middle of a pillow that had been crammed into a wicker basket.

Machines beeped and booped all around, creating a constant background noise that ate away at Al's peace of mind. Healthy people weren't surrounded by machines, he knew that. The last thing he remembered, when he tried to search for a chain of cause and effect, was the ship going down hard. Flashes of trees filled his memory, along with bursts of pain and dirt and sky. Much like the crash landing, he realized, his memories were all a-jumble.

Flexing his legs experimentally, Al guessed his muscles were up for movement. He scurried down to the floor, slower than normal but recovering quickly, and climbed Wereberry's bed. The werewolf looked pale, his breathing shallow. Al nudged him, squeaked into his ear, and finally bit him on the nose.

The bite did it, waking Were' with a start. He sat up quickly, bewildered, and threw Al toward the foot of the bed. His blood pressure couldn't keep up with the sudden movement, however, and Wereberry fell back into a prone position with a heavy thwump.

"What," Were' asked, lifting his head dizzily, "the hell was that?"

"Sorry," Al said, climbing back up Were's body. "I was worried. I just wanted to wake you up, you know?"

"Was I asleep?"

Al laughed, "We all were, they still are. We're... somewhere else. As dumb as that sounds."

"Well what happened?" Wereberry laid his head back down and closed his eyes. Waves of dizziness washed over him and left him weak. He could feel the aches and bruises from the crash, each one demanding attention. Wiggling his fingers, he realized two of them didn't move. Brushing them with his other fingers, he felt the splint there and realized they were sprained.

"We crashed—"

"I remember the crashing part. After that?"

"I have no idea. I woke up here and woke you up, since you were the closest."

Were' nodded and opened his eyes. The room's light created a dull ache just behind his eyes, but he fought past it. Carefully Wereberry worked himself to a sitting position. He looked around and frowned.

"We should try and wake the others. When we can move," he told Al. The mouse nodded and started to scurry toward the edge of Were's bed. "Don't bite them," he added with a grin. Al laughed and climbed carefully down the sheets to the floor.

A door in the far wall opened with a whisper. Al stopped in his tracks and Wereberry considered flopping back down on the bed and pretending to be asleep. Until he realized that quick movement would probably make him feel even worse, that is. Resigned, he sat there and watched the door.

A young man entered the room. He boasted a black jumpsuit with silver highlights running along it. Silver gloves and boots added to the accents, and the silver collar set off his short black hair and dark eyes. Seeing Wereberry awake, he

---

---

made a bee-line for the bed.

"You're awake! That's fantastic," the man said, a smile playing across his face.

"So am I," Al said, climbing back onto Wereberry's bed.

"Even better!"

"Who are you?" Wereberry asked quickly. "Not that we're not grateful, we are, I just... we don't remember anything past the crash. Where are we? What's going on?"

"I'm Roy," the man said, nodding, "and of course you have questions. So do we."

"We?" Al asked. His whiskers twitched and he glanced behind the man, looking for companions.

"The rest of Powerbot Force, of course," he explained without explaining anything.

"Uh-huh," Were' said, "and?"

"Oh, right, well we found you at the crash site and took you back to our base so you could rest and heal," Roy told him, still smiling. "Nothing sinister at all. Though I do wonder, how did you get Continent Strike Team Five's escape ship? Did you steal it?"

"Of course not," Al said with a laugh. "No, we were working with them and they needed to do something in the *Black Angel* and, well, here we are."

"I see. Well, I'll have Chunk radio them to confirm it, no offense."

"None taken," Were' said, shrugging. "How are our friends?"

"They should be able to be woken up, if you'd like. There is the matter of your wrapped friend, though—"

"Ra?" Al said, voice raising a pitch from its already high starting point.

"If that's his name, then yes. There's nothing under the bandages, which is strange enough. But it looks like something ripped them, and, well—"

Al took off like a wobbly shot toward Choco-Ra's bed.

He climbed the bedding quicker than he should have and managed to nudge the blanket down Ra's body with his head. He tried to ignore the dizzy spell and bit back a yelp as he saw Ra's shoulder end in a tattered bandage. "Did you find the—"

"Other end of the bandage?" Roy asked. "Yes. We have it, but don't know what to do with it."

"I'm sure he will. We should wake them," Were' said decisively. He didn't want to end up deciding Ra's fate. Wereberry thought back over all the time he had known Choco-Ra. He pictured it in his mind, flashing from moment to moment, covering as much ground as possible. Unraveling was one thing; everyone who knew Ra eventually saw him rewrap part of himself. But a break? A tear? That didn't happen. Were' wasn't sure it had ever happened before.

He thought of tape, of sewing and glue. Could Ra grow new bandages? Were' just didn't know enough to guess, and that made him more frightened than anything else.

While they were fretting, T.C. woke up. He seemed fine, alert, and ready to go for a walk. He found his hands had already healed and the rest of his body in fine shape. Though he was, he noticed, a bit parched.

Roy brought in a pitcher of water and several glasses while Were' and Al caught T.C. up to date. They knew that really they should wait for Ra to wake up to avoid having to retell the story yet another time, but while they all agreed that they simply had to wake Choco-Ra before much longer, none of them wanted to.

Finally Al insisted, and Roy went over and shook Ra awake. While Choco-Ra came to, Roy went around flipping off the machines to avoid telling the mummy about the missing arm situation.

Choco-Ra, when Were' told him about his arm, simply sighed and looked at the ragged edge of bandage drooping from his shoulder. "They saved the rest, I hope?"

"We did," Roy said, coming around and handing Ra a tightly rolled segment of old cloth.

"Thank you," Ra said, shaking the roll out with a snap. It stretched down off the edge of the bed and he shifted around, seemingly uncaring.

"Uhm, Ra?" Were' asked, watching.

"Yes?"

"Is that gonna be, I mean, will you be all right?"

"Of course," Choco-Ra said imperiously. "You don't get to be an ancient creature if you can't fix your own arm. Although," he studied his shoulder, "some help would be appreciated."

T.C. got out of bed and stood next to Ra. "What's up?"

"Could you just tie a solid knot in the ends there?" Ra asked.

Everyone stood still and watched Ra. Then the laughter started. It warmed the room up and made Roy wonder how sane they all were. He joined in anyway, but the thought nagged at him.

T.C. tied a tight knot in the ends and clasped Ra on the shoulder, "All you now," he said, and stepped back.

Choco-Ra grabbed the far end of the loose bandage and spiraled it in his hand. Faster than their eyes could see, the bandage took the shape of an arm, a wrist, a hand and fingers. At the shoulder the knot protruded a bit, but other than that, Ra looked fine. He flexed and twisted the arm and hand, testing them out. "Seems good. In a bit I'll need to undo that knot. The fibers will have knit by then, I'm sure. They always do."

"So this has happened before?" Al asked, eyes large with wonder.

"Sure," Ra said, "life happens." He shrugged and looked around. "So now, someone catch me up, huh?"

The story got retold and catching up was done. Nothing new was added, no new wrinkles or insight given or found. Choco-Ra stood and, together, he and T.C. helped Wereberry up. Al hopped up to perch on T.C.'s shoulder, and they all followed Roy out of the room.

Al wanted to sit on Ra's shoulder, as per the usual, but found that he was still nervous about hurting his friend. So instead he sat on T.C.'s, finding the clammy, almost slick skin an interesting change of pace. Also, Al reasoned, as he grew closer to them all, he shouldn't single Ra out quite so much. That kind of behavior normally ended up, Al knew from experience, causing more rifts than it avoided.

Roy took them into an elevator and up a number of floors. They exited into a large atrium, windows looking out into the world beyond. They could see other spires reaching toward the clouds, ships launching with regularity and, behind them, the occasional pitched battle.

"Sit, relax," Roy told them. "You just got out of bed, huh? I'll be back in a second with the rest of the team and confirmation of your story."

Wereberry sat down too quickly on a large purple couch. He held his head in his hands and shut his eyes tightly.

"You all right?" Ra asked, sitting down next to him.

"Yeah, I'll be fine, just a dizzy spell."

The others sat too and looked around. T.C. counted the trophies that lined a shelf sitting just below the start of the large windows: forty-seven. Each one was a different shape: rocket ships blasting off, men and women with guns drawn, planets circling each other. The trophies spoke highly of the team, and also spoke volumes about their egos.

The elevator door opened again and Roy stood there with his four teammates. They all wore suits lined with silver like Roy's, though the body colors all differed. Roy smiled at the four on the couch and started walking toward them, his team following right behind.

"Fivesome," Roy said, nodding, "I'd like to introduce the rest of Powerbot Force. Your story checked out—of course it did—but why didn't you tell me you were the Fivesome?

We will, of course, help you find your missing member. I understand that your headquarters was destroyed as well? Well, we can deal with that, too. Won't we, team?"

Each member of Powerbot Force nodded and introduced themselves. They were: June, in red, who stood proudly with her long pink hair trailing behind her; Chunk, in white, the large mechanic whose tool belt sat heavy and full; Bobby, the youngest member, who stood nervously on one foot in his blue suit, and Steve, in gray, who was trying to give off an air of anything but impatience and failing.

The introductions went both ways and the groups mingled. A lot of questions came about, centering on the Fivesome's missing team member. Answers were dodged, the Fivesome all very in synch about keeping information close to the vest.

"But what about your headquarters?" June asked.

"Hmmm?" Choco-Ra replied. He wasn't sure when their headquarters had found itself destroyed, mostly because he wasn't aware they'd ever had one.

"Well, Continent Strike Team Five told us that your headquarters were destroyed," she explained, "and I was wondering if that's when your other member went missing? You can't locate her at all?"

"Oh," Ra said, "no. We can't."

T.C. glanced over at Ra before turning back to the conversation he was having with Steve. The reticent man in gray kept talking about weapon systems and spy techniques. T.C. found himself interested, but only up to a point. This guy, he thought, is obsessed.

His mind wandered while Steve described a new, ultra-tiny camera in use. They all, T.C. thought, push their expectations on us. Everyone here is a team, they all have headquarters, they all fight the same fight, so of course we do too. It was strange, he mulled. Everywhere they went, people seemed to accept them without questions, assuming all sorts of things from the small all the way to the humongous, but they didn't want to listen to the truth. They chose instead to push forward with the information they decided on, throwing out the plainly stated. It made T.C. start to wonder if he and his friends did the same, and, if so, how that may have tripped them up.

Steve stopped speaking, just staring at T.C. He waited for the merman to notice, but T.C.'s thoughts enveloped him deeply. Steve sighed and tapped his foot. No change. Finally he cleared his throat, and T.C. blushed and stammered an apology.

"Well, we each have our own ship," Chunk was saying to Al while T.C. blushed.

"Of course you do."

"And they're all shaped like animals, see? I have to keep them running. It's easy mostly, except the transform joins. Those can be a pain. Well, and the Dimension H engines. We don't even really—" Chunk stopped and peered at Al. "Don't tell, all right?"

"I won't," Al told him. Who, exactly, would he tell, Al wondered? His own teammates? Well of course he would tell them regardless. Chunk's team? He had to assume they knew, so why bother? It was easy to agree with a smile.

"Well, we don't even really know how the Dimension H engines work. I can fix them, to an extent, but really they work on some other principle."

"Other principle?" Al blinked several times.

"Some force that we just don't understand," Chunk gave a massive shrug and then leaned in conspiratorially. "I hear that a few of the teams have engines like that. It hasn't been a problem much, but I'll tell you, chum, there are days it worries me."

"I can see why. So the ships, wait, they're shaped like animals?"

"Of course," Chunk laughed.

"And they have transform joints? What are... they change shape?"

"Well no, they link up to form Powerbot."

"Oh, well, of course they do," Al said, wondering what a Powerbot looked like, if it was made up of animals. Something very strange, he decided.

"Hey, Roy?" Bobby asked, dragging Wereberry behind him. "Do we still have the Manimals?"

Roy laughed and nodded, "Of course we do, Bobby. Why... oh! I see now! Yeah, that's a great plan! Come on, team!" Roy started for the elevator without another word. His team broke off their conversations and followed him, leaving the four members of the Fivesome standing there looking quite confused. Roy waved to them from the elevator, Bobby's small frame leaning against the door to pin it open.

Choco-Ra, Wereberry, T.C., and Al hurried over and hopped in. The elevator doors closed with a clunk and the car they stood in whisked them down at high speed. The door opened on a huge hanger.

Inside the hanger were vehicles of all sorts. Mostly though, centered in spotlights, the hanger featured five large, very shiny metal animals. A red swan, gray cat, blue dog, white gecko, and black rhino each gleamed in their respective floodlights. Roy waved a hand in their direction proudly.

"Fivesome, may I present the Powerbot Ships!" He paced down part of the hanger and found a switch dangling from a cord. Yanking it, other lights came on, illuminating the rest of the huge space. "Over there are the Manimals."

Five small vehicles, each one shaped like a man sitting down and wearing an animal mask, sat in their own smaller lights. Ra felt an affinity for them. He felt convinced that at least one of them, wearing a gleaming hawk mask, came directly from his home. Nodding in approval, Ra turned to Roy. "So we could borrow these, to help us find our friend?"

"Well," Steve started, frowning, "I don't know about that. Continent Strike Team Five lent you their Skimship, didn't they? Look what happened to it!"

"That wasn't our fault," Wereberry insisted. He still felt woozy, but less and less with each passing moment. "We were attacked."

"And what if you get attacked while in the Manimals?" Steve demanded.

"You could show us the controls, something Continent Strike Team Five didn't bother doing," T.C. shot back.

"Fair enough," Chunk broke in. "Steve, give them a chance, I like them."

"So do I," June added.

"And me!" Bobby chimed.

Steve sighed and muttered something about lax security before turning away. The other team members ignored it, brushing Steve's behavior off with obvious experience. Chunk walked the Fivesome over to the Manimal ships, smiling as he did. He was proud of the ships.

"Ya see," he said as they approached the nearest ship, which wore a cat's mask, "the original Powerbot used these ships. They were great, but not as maneuverable or fast as the new ones. When we upgraded to the new systems, we couldn't just leave the Manimals out to rot." June and Bobby nodded along with Chunk's story. Roy watched, smiling. "But the Manimals, they still work, you'll love them," Chunk added quickly.

Wereberry nodded and ran a hand along a section of the Cat Manimal. The metal was slick to the touch, but warm. Raising an eyebrow, he studied the surface closely.

"Yeah, the metals are strange. They aren't living, they're just metal, but the Dimension H engines inside give them a strange almost-life that we never figured out. We did learn to trust it, though. Why don't you each get in and we'll take 'em for a spin?"

Roy showed them where the access panels were and each of the four Fivesome chose a ship of their own. Wereberry chose the Cat Manimal, while Choco-Ra went right for the

Hawk. T.C. noticed that one of the ships had a fish mask on and made a beeline for it happily. Al, however, sat on the ground, looking up in frustration at the access panel on a ship wearing a mantis mask.

"Oh hey," Bobby said, coming over, "sorry about that. We just need to configure it for voice commands." He opened the hatch and climbed into the Manimal ship with a deft hop. "Come on in," Bobby called from inside. Al clambered up into the ship quickly.

Inside the ship, Bobby sat in a large, well-padded control chair. A bank of instruments stretched around him in a wide arc. His fingers played over switches and dials as lights flashed on and off in response. Al wondered how he would fly the ship, seeing as how he couldn't even glance out the viewport if he sat in the chair.

Bobby flipped a few more switches and stood up. The chair flattened out and sunk into the floor. A pedestal rose up, padded deeply, with a small ladder leading up to it. The seat stopped rising when it was much higher than the cockpit chair it replaced. Bobby gestured to it and Al happily climbed the ladder and sat.

"The ship should be reconfigured for non-human control now," Bobby told Al, "just give it your voice print when it asks, and then you can use voice command from there."

"Does it have to be voice-based?" Al asked. He wasn't sure how he could fly combat by demanding sharp turns and shouting for guns. He was, of course, willing to try anyway, and the system he found himself handed constituted a vast improvement over nothing at all. Still, if he had his druthers, Al knew, he would love a way to control the thing by hand.

"Some of it, yeah," Bobby told him, "the doors, for example. The flight controls can be voice-based or target-based."

"Target-based?"

"A heads-up display that tracks eye movements. Otherwise how could you hope to fly combat?"

"That was my concern," Al admitted.

"Makes sense. Well anyway, just give the ship your name and let it know you."

Al nodded and turned to the bank of instruments. "Identification Al," he said, realizing that he wasn't sure if a key phrase was needed.

"Confirmed, Al. Welcome aboard. Please confirm with a voice identification from a member of Powerbot Force," the ship said with a smooth, if metallic, tone.

"Identification Bobby," Bobby said, mirroring Al's command phrase, "Al is confirmed as controller of Mantis Manimal. Confirm and reroute full control to voice-print Al."

"Al confirmed," the computer said.

"Well there you go," Bobby told Al. He smiled down at the mouse and made for the hatchway. "You'll be fine. Enjoy!"

Outside the Mantis Manimal, everyone was climbing into their ships and preparing for take-off. The Powerbot Force ships hummed with available engine thrust and the Manimals all rose slightly off the ground, their strange sitting shape making them look like floating monks in party masks. Bobby ran for his dog ship and leapt in, slamming the hatchway after himself. In seconds his ship matched the others, bracing for action.

The Powerbot Force ships took off first. Their hover capabilities meant they didn't need a long runway, and the tunnel ramped upwards quickly, opening into clear skies. The Manimals, four of them, followed suit.

Wereberry sat back in his chair, looking over the control panel. The basics were easy enough for him: pull back on this, push that forward. He wasn't sure about the rest of it though, the combat flying, the weapons systems, or, honestly, the landing. He still felt fairly sluggish from the crash and, he thought, there couldn't be a good reason why he was piloting a ship. He knew, he could feel, that he simply wasn't up for it, but everyone else seemed to be, and if he'd declined they would've either left without him or not gone at all. Neither answer struck him as right, so he sucked in a breath and pushed through the slight dizziness and mounting pain, aiming his Manimal for the sky.

T.C. flipped switches, laughing to himself. Flying a ship was something he had never done; he could find no good basis for the experience in his memory, either. Still, he went for it as much as possible. The entire ship, something bigger than himself, swimming through the air under his control. A giant beast all his to point and steer through clouds. The idea excited him as much as the reality of it did.

Choco-Ra made sure his ship followed Wereberry's lead. He knew that his friend was shaky and so he went out of his way to fly nearby, just in case of trouble. That's what Ra told himself for the first few minutes, at least. Better to stay back, to take it easy, for Were's sake. It sounded good and made enough sense that he even believed it himself for a bit. But eventually he had to admit, like it or not, that after the crash he was finding himself a bit gun-shy. Choco-Ra didn't want to lose another ship, demonstrate his lack of ability, or hurt anyone while flying again.

T.C. and Al flew to either side of Ra. A mixture of concern for Wereberry and desire to look like a good, solid flying formation made their choices for them. Wereberry, now in the lead of a short V formation, followed the Powerbot Force ships to higher altitudes.

Clear sky greeted them. Free of any Garuda ships, or anything else that wanted to open fire on them, they flew slow, easy patterns in the sky. The Fivesome learned how to handle their ships and the Powerbot Force logged some airtime that didn't consist of battle.

Roy and the rest of Powerbot Force talked the Fivesome through more difficult maneuvers: twists and turns, breaking and reforming formations, and other tactics that would come in handy if battle became necessary. Not that the members of the Fivesome thought it would, or hoped it would. Best case scenario they flew around a while, landed, and thought out their next move.

Sadly, as the Fivesome knew all too well, best case scenarios didn't happen very often. Six enemy fighters screamed down out of the sky, sunward, preceded by a rain of blaster fire. The Powerbot Force ships broke formation and took off after them.

4 • Dog's Fighting

"GET CLEAR!" Roy shouted over the radio to the Fivesome in their Manimal ships. The others were ready to follow the suggestion, but something in Wereberry refused to let him leave. He turned his ship toward the battle and accelerated.

"Uhhh, Were'?" Ra's voice crackled over the radio.

"Yeah, Ra," Wereberry said clearly, "we're helping out."

"This isn't smart," Al pointed out.

"I know," Were' admitted, "but neither is letting people who helped us fight by themselves. Now less talk and more not getting hurt."

"Last time—" T.C. started.

"That was last time," Ra said, his voice growling, "and we can't let that be this time. Were's right."

The Manimal ships swept into the fray in a tight formation. The six enemy ships were swarming around the Powerbot Force, obviously not a match for them in firepower, but outclassing them in terms of speed. Two of the ships closed in on June's red swan. She twisted and turned but couldn't shake them.

Suddenly one of the enemy ships exploded in a ball of fire and superheated metal. Four large, metal men, sitting and wearing masks, peeled off, climbing again to get a better view of the battlefield. They rose in time to see six more ships enter the skirmish. Breaking formation, the Fivesome scattered, giving the enemy no clear targets.

"Decided to join in the fun?" Chunk asked over the radio.

"Looks like," Were' replied. "Who are these guys?"

"Toggoth ships. They're an advance force," June said. She sounded like a schoolmarm, reading off cool facts. Nothing in her betrayed the fact that while she spoke she was also dodging fire. "They tend to run in packs of twelve, the thirteenth will be whatever the Toggoth have dragged up from the pits. Some genetic thing."

"A genetic thing from the pits?" T.C. asked. "I can't think that's good."

A fighter slipped behind T.C., firing as it tailed him. T.C. dove, banking hard, and crossed paths with Al, who opened fire on the Toggoth ship, shearing a wing right off it.

"Bobby," Al said, "thanks for the systems work. This thing controls great."

"Glad you approve. Mind moving to my sector and giving me some cover, then?"

Al didn't bother with a reply. His Mantis Manimal spitting out flame as the boosters engaged, he simply intercepted Bobby's vector and moved to lay cover fire for him. Bobby took the critical seconds Al bought him and used them well, diving and looping under the Toggoth ship, coming back up smartly next to Al. The pair opened fire at once, and the Toggoth ship didn't stand a chance.

Wereberry fought against vertigo. Pulling his Manimal ship into a steep climb, the first part of an inverted loop, he found the g-forces did anything but help how he felt. He closed his eyes and tried to will himself back to perfect health. It didn't work. His vision swam and then blacked out for a second.

He came to in the midst of shouting and smoke. A Toggoth ship was on his tail and had already put a small hole in his ship. Choco-Ra and T.C. headed directly for Were', shooting past and around him. The Toggoth ship couldn't break clear without getting hit.

"Were', you all right?" T.C. asked quickly.

"I'll be fine. Thanks guys."

"No problem," Ra said. "When I say 'go,' I want you to bank hard left. Got it?"

"Got it."

"Go!"

Wereberry banked left as hard as he could manage. Ra stopped firing just long enough for Wereberry's ship to slip clear, and then both he and T.C. reopened fire on the Toggoth ship. The explosion buffeted all three Manimal ships, shaking them.

Inside his ship, Ra's eyes shone brightly. The inside of his ship reflected the red back at him, sinking everything into the same wash of color. He tracked Toggoth ships, cursing himself every time his reflexes weren't quite fast enough. He didn't want to be the best of the best; he just wanted to win. To prove himself.

A gray ship in the shape of a cat crossed Ra's path quickly, drawing off enemy fire. "Pay attention or get out of the way!" Steve barked over the radio. Choco-Ra fumed, his eyes flashing hotly. He took his ship up and over, spotting a Toggoth ship heading toward Chunk's.

Taking careful aim, Ra shot the Toggoth twice before the enemy pilot had a chance to realize he was a target. Chunk barked his thanks and cut left in a tight circle to finish off the ship.

The remaining Toggoth ships quickly broke off from the air duels and started to climb, right back toward the sun. Were' and Al started to cheer on the radio, happy in turning a tide of sorts. They stopped cheering abruptly when the sun itself was blacked out by a large mass.

"It's Kragen!" Roy yelled across the radio. "Quick! Powerbot Force, form up on me! It's time to unleash Powerbot!"

The Powerbot Force ships flew directly at each other. As they drew toward collision, Roy yelled "Powerbot Force, go!" and the ships were engulfed in a blinding burst of light.

The Fivesome members each squinted, watching as best they could. The giant monster Kragen lowered himself from the sky toward the transforming Powerbot, unconcerned with the goings on.

Inside the light burst, the Powerbot ships changed and melded together. June's swan lengthened and met Roy's rhino. The rhino stood in the air, legs retraced, while the other ships all connected to it in different ways. The head of the rhino grew and turned, even as the horn lengthened, glowing with energy. The light burst faded and Powerbot stood in the sky, a giant robot made up of different animals. A swan and gecko for legs, cat and dog for arms, the strong rhino body acting as connecting torso and head.

Kragen came into full view. As big as the ten-story tall Powerbot, Kragen's body was covered in deep purple slime that dripped down onto the ground far below. His twin tusks sprouted from a lizard's head, and gigantic bat wings flapped in a slow and steady beat. He lifted a gigantic cutlass in one slimed hand and roared.

Powerbot raised both metallic arms like a boxer, and foot thrusters moved him closer to Kragen. The two clashed, Kragen's sword swinging down at Powerbot, glancing off an arm with a huge shower of sparks. A kick sent Kragen sprawling backward, crashing him down into the ground. Earth shattered and exploded in every direction as Kragen's back dug a trench half a mile long. Standing slowly and drippily, Kragen roared again and lowered his head toward Powerbot. His tusks pulsed with energy, shooting thick, deadly beams of destruction up at the robotic defender.

Powerbot was ready for the attack, however; the rhino's horn flashed and shot its own beams. The beams collided in the air, straining against one another, neither gaining ground at first. Defiantly, inch by inch, Kragen's dual-powered tusk beams forced Powerbot's horn ray back, inch by inch and foot by foot until the beams collided with the menagerie robot, sending him to the ground as well.

Another shower of dirt and dust colored the sky as Powerbot skidded to a halt. He stood, creakily, from the ditch that his body had created, looking across the open field at his enemy. Dirt showered down off of his body and the gleam of his metal skin restored itself.

The Manimal ships sat on the ground, watching. They had landed after the first round of blows had landed. Knowing they were unable to really help, the Fivesome had made the conscious choice to wait and see what would happen. If they saw an opening in which to help, they were ready. Engines were powered up, weapon systems primed. They could take off and be in the thick of things in a matter of seconds. Until they were needed, though, until then they knew they couldn't be in the way. Their ships, smaller and slower, were no match for Kragen. All they could do was watch and hope.

Powerbot brought his fists together with a resounding clang. Over the radio, the others heard Roy shout, "Powerbot, form energy sword!" The massive robot's fists separated, but where there was only air before, now there was a blue sword, blazing and crackling with raw energy.

The robot hero curled his legs underneath him and launched himself at Kragen, a mighty leap that covered the distance between them in mere seconds. Kragen was ready, though, already bringing his cutlass up to defend himself. Kragen's cutlass met Powerbot's energy sword with a blinding flash and deafening bang. The two faced each other from mere feet apart, both of them looking determined enough to topple the other from sheer willpower.

Powerbot pulled back, the sword held one-handed but firmly in what was once the dog ship's mouth. He swung, a great and powerful swing that Kragen met with his own cutlass. The cutlass didn't stand a chance—the force of the blow shattered it, metal shards flying everywhere. The sword continued its trajectory, slicing a mortal wound into Kragen's body.

Kragen's tusks lit as he died, shooting the last of his deadly rays at Powerbot's sword arm. The rays punched holes in the ship, and the dog's mouth went slack, dropping the blazing sword to the ground where it clattered and dimmed. Bobby screamed over the radio, a toe-curling scream of pain. The dog ship crackled with flames and electricity, darkening in color deeply. The rest of Powerbot Force screamed as well, and with a final kick sent Kragen down to the ground for the final time, only seconds too late.

5 • Picking Up the Pieces

DISASSEMBLED, THE POWERBOT FORCE ships lay scattered in a rough semicircle. The Manimal ships flew in close, landing roughly. People streamed from vehicles, all of them converging on the blue dog ship. It lay silent, the hatchway closed, smoking fitfully. The fires died out, smoke coughing from ragged holes in the ship's hide.

Roy and Steve rushed forward and tried to open the hatchway, but the electrical systems of the ship wouldn't respond. Chunk and June joined them, both crying, and together the team dug in to force the hatch open.

The metal plate refused to budge. Powerbot Force strained and screamed, tearing at the metal hatchway to no avail. The Fivesome joined them, adding their strength to the task. Eventually the hatchway started to move under the combined efforts of the two teams.

Their pushing, clawing, and tugging at the hatch eventually won out, the metal panel sliding down fully. Dark smoke gushed out of the opening. Roy and June ran into the ship, heedless of the choking lack of air. They came back less than a minute later, Roy holding Bobby cradled in his arms.

He set the youth down on the ground and the two teams stood, mesmerized by the limp form of the young man in his blue uniform, the silver piping smudged by soot. No breath moved his chest—no sign of life shifted his body at all. Powerbot Force circled the body, unconsciously pushing the others away.

Choco-Ra agreed with the move. He didn't think that anyone else belonged there. Grief like that, the loss of a friend, it deserved to be private. The problem, he thought, was a social one. Though the team might want to be alone, there remained no good way to leave. Just getting back into ships and flying off would be disrespectful in the greatest way. Standing around on the edges and seeming to wait for the team to simply be done with mourning so things could go back to normal wouldn't send the right message, either.

Wereberry found a tree to lean against. Somehow, despite the incredible forces tossed around during the battle, it still stood. Were' appreciated that, giving the tree a secret smile. He knew how it felt. His legs felt like they were going to go on strike and dump him on his furry ass at any second, but, despite that, they kept holding him up. Losing Bobby hurt some, even though he hadn't known the kid that well, but Were' still found that the tree's survival meant a lot, too. He leaned against it for strength, for hope, and for a way to not fall over.

T.C. replayed the fight again and again, wondering if he could have made a difference. If they'd used the Manimals, the team could have helped in the fight after all. Maybe, he considered, their small help could have saved Bobby's life. Realistically he figured that they would have hindered the Powerbot Force and probably caused even more death by jumping into the middle. Regardless, part of him tried to work out ways Bobby's death could have been avoided. He couldn't find one, but that didn't stop him.

Al felt tears rolling down his small cheeks. Bobby was a good kid. He'd helped Al when everyone else had forgotten about him. A good fighter, Bobby didn't deserve death. Of course, Al couldn't pick a team member, on either team, who did deserve to die in that fight. There wasn't a better choice—there wasn't even a good choice. The truth didn't make the events easier to accept. Al looked at the faces of everyone around him and steeled himself to his plan.

"Uhm," Chunk said, turning to face the Fivesome, "I think we'll, uhhh, meet you guys back at—"

"We understand," Ra said softly. He moved to place a hand gently on Chunk's shoulder. The large man nodded once, his face wet with tears. "We'll catch up later. Give you all some time alone."

"Thanks," Chunk whispered. He turned and left the Fivesome alone again.

Without a word between them, Choco-Ra, Wereberry, T.C., and Al returned to their Manimal ships and climbed in. They took off and flew away slow and low, making as little disturbance as possible. Wereberry took the lead again and lead them all off, far out of sight, before he put his ship down in a clearing.

He left his ship quickly, watching the others land and exit. They stood in a wide clearing, old trees and lush grass on every side. The sky above gleamed, not caring about the troubles of the world below.

"I didn't think that—" T.C. started.

"He would die," Were' finished. "Me either."

They stood staring at each other again.

"We should be more careful, huh?" T.C. asked.

"What?" Ra asked, shaking his head.

"This could have been any of us, instead." T.C. explained.

"No, I got that," Ra said, "I was asking if you were serious. We could've died a hundred times by now. This whole trip, we could've died."

"We still could," Were' pointed out, "and some day we will."

"Yeah, but—" T.C. tired to argue.

"We don't have to be more careful, we just have to make sure we don't waste our lives when we do go," Wereberry said. He took a deep breath and thought for a second. "And we should go, huh?"

"Yeah," Al said, giving the mouse equivalent of a shrug, "I was going to say something later about that."

"Oh?" Were' asked him. He sat down on the grass, leaning

back to enjoy the sun. The others followed suit, as if finding permission to relax in his actions.

"Is she here?" Al asked his three friends, looking into each of their eyes.

Choco-Ra sighed and shook his head, "No, she isn't. And we've known it, I think."

"Not at first," T.C. said. He took off his bag and dug around in it, coming back with his moisturizer. He started to slather his head and chest, squinting up at the sun.

"With all the... everyone here has a full team. Maybe she joined one. We don't know," Were' said. He wouldn't look at his friends, instead staring up into the trees.

"When did you start telling yourself lies about that one?" Ra demanded.

"I'm not. She could be here," Were' insisted.

"Were'," T.C, said, shoving the bottle of moisturizer back in his bag, "come on."

"What?"

"Look at me," T.C. insisted.

Were' dropped his head, opening his eyes. They were redrimmed with sadness. "What?"

"Exactly," T.C. said softly. "You're the one always saying how we have to feel for it and when we don't, we know. Well I don't feel her here. Ra doesn't feel her here. You don't either, do you?"

"No," Were' admitted, "but we've come so far. We've done so much."

Choco-Ra laughed. "Now, see, that would be the injuries talking."

"No, it isn't." Wereberry closed his eyes again, face lifting toward the warmth of the sun. "I mean, sure, I'm still messed up. I won't deny it. But I'm just tired, outside of that."

"You weren't a while ago," T.C. said. "What changed? What is it about this place that changed you?"

"I did," Al said softly.

T.C. and Ra looked at him, confused. Were' sighed and laid down on his back.

"Wereberry's figured out the same thing I did, didn't you, buddy?"

"I don't know what you mean," the werewolf muttered.

"Exactly so."

"Well I have no idea what you're talking about," T.C. said.

"This whole thing here, these teams—you guys aren't whole. You need her, or something like her. And maybe some of you," Al looked at Ra sadly, "hoped I was it. But all I've done is make Wereberry notice how much I'm not it."

"S'not true."

"All right, furball. Whatever you say. But I think he realized the same problem I did. I don't get quite why he's the one who's this upset about it, but there you have it."

"Explain," Ra said, eyes glowing brighter.

"You three, you tear through worlds. Why don't other people?"

"They don't know how," T.C. said simply.

"Bull," Al countered. "You've told me about it. I was there for one of them, hell. Blowing up a tank does it? Then why aren't people leaping around all the time?"

"Maybe they are."

"They aren't. It's intent. That's the trick. It's all intent."

"I don't know if I buy that," Ra said.

"Oh, well sure, the explosions, the key force in the world, that's a lot of it too. But without intent it wouldn't work." Al walked closer to Ra, looking at him sternly. "I've been thinking about this."

"So what does that have to do with you?" Ra asked.

"You need, if Were' and I are right—"

"Don't drag me into this," Were' said softly.

"Don't bullshit me," Al snapped, "this is pure tactics. It's a way out of a tight spot. Don't try and pretend you didn't go here, too."

"Shut up."

"It's a question of key force and intent."

"Key force?" T.C. asked.

"A tank in a world of war. An artifact in a world of artifacts. A collective in a world of collectives."

"Powerbot?" Ra asked, leaning forward.

"Manimal," Were' whispered.

"Yup," Al said over his shoulder, "we know it can transform. It's our ship, now. It's the key force, I think. So it can move you forward."

"What do you mean, 'you'? You mean 'us,'" Ra insisted.

"One of us has to pilot the ship." Al sighed and sat down heavily. "But why is he the one who's upset about it?"

Wereberry muttered something none of the others heard. Ra stood up, shoulders thrown back, looking every inch the angry ruler. "What was that?" he demanded.

"I knew how upset you'd be," Were' repeated, louder.

T.C. flopped backwards into the ground and laid there.

"You can't do it," Al told Were' sadly.

"I know! I get that, that's the problem. But Ra, he's been so alone. Even with us. How can I say that she's not here if that means what we know it does?"

Ra stood defiantly, but internally his heart was breaking. He knew that he had snuck Al along with them just because he had wanted a friend. Were' and T.C. were closer than friends, of course, but Al was different. Across all of Ra's time, he had had subjects. Animals that did what he demanded of them. Al wasn't one of them, and the difference—mental, not physical—made Ra realize how much he had always wanted it. All the subjects in the world meant nothing to him in the face of one equal.

"We started this," Choco-Ra said, summoning every erg of ruling power he could, "to find Cherrygiest. No matter what." He looked around at his friends, none of them looking at the others. "No matter what," he repeated again, forcefully.

"And that's the choice Were' didn't want you to make," Al said with a soft smile, "but you wouldn't be you if you couldn't make it. And if you weren't you—"

"We can find another way. Get someone else to do this. You can come with us," Ra insisted.

"Someone has to take Bobby's place," Al said.

"And someone else will," Ra countered.

"Ra, don't fight me on this," Al told him sternly, "please."

"This isn't an acceptable loss," Ra spit.

"Isn't it? You just thought it was a second ago," Al pointed out.

"Guys," T.C. said from his place on the grass, "we can fight about this until we grow old or we can do what we all know is right, and very wrong."

"And if we're going to do that," Were' said, sitting up, "we can at least enjoy the time we have."

"What?" Ra asked, growing furious. But Wereberry was already opening his bag up and pulling things out. He set out plates and took out containers of food, setting them on the grass.

"A picnic," Wereberry said simply. "We had one before we started, knowing we might not ever return but hoping we would. I still hope we will. This time? We hope we'll be back here to get Al again. But until we do have to leave, let's celebrate friends present and friends still missing."

The others just stared at Wereberry a moment. They weren't sure if he was being daft or was simply perfectly correct. Correctness won out and they set to, eating and telling stories and having as good a time as possible while events loomed over them. Still, the sun shone brightly, doing its part to dispel the shadows that crossed the minds and bodies of those present.

In time, the food ran low and thoughts returned specifically to the future. Choco-Ra stood and walked toward his Manimal ship. "How do you think we need to do this, then?" he asked.

"We have to work out exactly how they merge," Al said as he, too, returned to his ship.

"It can't be that hard, I'd think," T.C. said, leaving Wereberry to pack up the remains of lunch by himself. "They have to be able to pull it off mid-battle, right?"

"Good point," Ra said.

Were' crammed things into his bag and opened the hatch of his ship. "So let's do this, then."

The others climbed into their ships as well, and the four Manimals rose into the air. Wereberry took them up, cruising the sky and chasing clouds. They flew idly for a while, plotting no specific course at all. Al convinced the ship's computer to read off a list of instructions for transformation. Were' brought the ships lower as Al explained the plan.

Fifty feet above the ground, they were ready. They each found the unmarked red lever on their control panels. Throwing them, the ships started to rumble ominously.

"I don't think we're close enough together," Were' said nervously. There was a power spike on his readouts but nothing was happening—it was just building and building.

The four ships drew closer together. Dangerously close, T.C. thought, fighting to keep his ship from colliding with Ra's. The energy built further, still finding no release.

"Have you tried the voice command?" Al asked.

"That's just silly," Were' insisted.

"Hey, the ships have it for a reason, right? Let's try it."

"Fine," Wereberry sighed, "Manimal force, go," he said unenthusiastically.

"If you're going to do badly at it, don't do it," Choco-Ra said with a laugh.

"It's ridiculous," Were' complained. "But fine, fine, you want it done like Powerbot Force did? Fine."

"That would be great. Anytime before we crash would be perfect," T.C. said.

Inside his ship, Wereberry fought back the urge to grumble. He grabbed the control stick with both hands and tried to really mean the words. "Manimal Force, GO!" he shouted into the radio and at the ship.

Light burst from the ships and they felt the control sticks go slack. Around them, inside the ships, pieces started to shift. A wall here, a viewport there—the ships came to life and moved around them. The cockpits stayed where they were, but tunnels opened up where they joined together. Small, single-person tubes whistled with rushing air.

The shifting stopped, the light faded, and Manimal stood on air, fifty feet above the ground. It stood on one leg, however; the four ships were one short of a complete set. Manimal lowered to the ground. Wereberry found that he controlled most of the systems from his seat now, though each crew member also controlled their own limbs. There were overrides and secondary systems just in case, all laid out in the new control panel that Wereberry found himself facing.

"Al, come on up," Were' said into the radio. Down in the leg, Al left his seat, jumped into the air tunnel, and zipped away toward the center of the ship. He floated there, kicking off of thin air to land at the floor beside Wereberry.

"Now what?" Were' asked, wondering how Al would pilot the robot.

"Bobby showed me, actually. Here's what we do...."

T.C. and Choco-Ra left the ship, traveling by air tube down to the leg, where they left by a hatchway in the foot. Wereberry joined them a few minutes later. He moved surer than he had been, steadier. He loped over to join his friends, nodding at each of them. His eyes spoke volumes that he didn't bother to try to express with words: sadness, loss, and hope all mixed together in a giant blender.

Choco-Ra read all of it from Were's eyes and took off at a sprint. He ran at the Manimal robot and dashed as quickly as possible up into the heart of the thing.

"Al!" he shouted as he left the tube.

"You should be on the ground, Ra," Al told him from his perch in front of the controls.

"They can wait a second. Listen, I just wanted... you...."

"I know," Al said, "now go back down and get going." Al turned and looked at his friend.

"Thanks, Al," Ra said, eyes dimming in sadness.

"No problem."

"For everything."

"A pleasure," Al said, nodding. "And hey, Ra?"

"Yeah, Al?" Ra turned, a glimmer of hope that an alternate plan had been found.

"Thanks to you, too."

"Anytime," Ra told the mouse. He took a deep breath and knew that this was as close as either of them would get to saying goodbye.

"Just do me a favor?" Al asked, turning away from Ra to look out the robot's portal again.

"Name it," Ra said, taking a step backwards toward the tube.

"When you find her, tell her about me."

Choco-Ra laughed, a loud and strong laugh that bounced off the ship's metal walls. "As if I wouldn't?"

"That's right. That's exactly right. Now scram."

Ra didn't reply—he simply took another step backwards, falling into the air tube. He fell on a cushion of air, landing back in the leg of the robot. He strode out, clamping down on his feelings for a minute, needing to simply exist and not think.

"Hold on to your... whatever you want to hold on to," Al's voice boomed from Manimal's speaker. "Manimal sword, go!" he shouted.

The robot's fists slammed together hard. It teetered, having only a single leg to stand on. The fists separated and when they did, a one-handed sword appeared. It glowed with energy, much like Powerbot's, but, of course, much smaller.

The arm holding the sword swung upwards quickly and paused there. It hung in the air, crackling with power. The crackling grew, as did the light thrown off by the weapon. Al charged the sword to maximum before slicing at the air.

The sword swung, cleaving open sky. A wide rent tore open there, harsh white light flooding through. The three friends stood there, watching it. Wereberry, T.C., and Choco-Ra each considered the light, their travels, and their future. They each had a brief moment of doubt, a second thought, that they didn't want to tell the others about. Instead they leapt, clean and true, into the light as it started to fade.

They vanished, and the sky was whole once more. Al shut down Manimal's system after sending a quick S.O.S. to Powerbot Force. They would come to investigate soon enough, and Al waited for them on the grass, staring at a spot in the sky that now looked like every other spot around.

INTERLUDE FOUR

ALMOST-EMPTY SPACE GREETED the travelers as they fell into nothing. A spot of greens and grays and browns hung out there in the nothingness. They made for it, T.C. once again taking his friends and swimming through the emptiness.

Color flooded the island as they drew close, and the green edges expanded outward in all directions. The water lapped at the muddy shores and the trees' bark smelled of sap. They stood on the island created, they were convinced, by their own thoughts, and marveled at it.

A cloud formed above the island, white and full. It hung there, drifting in a slowed-down loop, never leaving the area of the island. Ra grinned and considered the cloud, and slowly the white space between the island and the cloud settled and thickened. A patch of blue blossomed around the cloud, sunlight from an unseen sun reflecting and hitting the water.

Wereberry sniffed the air and took a deep lungful of it. It tasted like air, a bit flatter than normal in some way he couldn't quite work out, but it was certainly breathable air. He whistled, forgetting that they couldn't make sound in this eerie, strange land. The whistle rang out clear and shrill, and the three friends stopped and stared at each other.

"This will sound stupid if you can—" Ra started, but stopped as he heard his own words. "Well, I was right, it does sound stupid, but did you just make noise?"

Wereberry and T.C. both laughed. Choco-Ra joined in, and all three realized how deeply it had bothered them to be unable to make or hear noise.

T.C. splashed some of the water around, enjoying the

sound of it but realizing that it wasn't quite right. It behaved like real water, though. He lifted his hand, still wet, and licked the tip of a finger. The water tasted like nothing, not even water—there simply was no taste at all, not in any sense of the word.

"It's like if we don't think about it specifically, it isn't here," he said, standing.

"Which makes no sense," Ra said, "even if it does seem to prove out. What is this place?"

"Nothing at all. Everything there is. Both at once?" Wereberry offered.

"Oh great, that's kind of useless, isn't it?" Ra said, shaking his head and grinning.

"Yup," Were' said with a shrug. The White Lands, as he still thought of the area, made Were' nervous. There were so empty, and so malleable, that he felt uneasy just standing around. A single thought, he considered, could do all sorts of harm. Harm to what, he wasn't sure, but he identified it as harm.

T.C. studied the water and found thoughts along the same line of reasoning Were' was following. The potential, for anything, was overwhelming to a degree that bothered him. It wasn't, he thought, the idea of power. It certainly wasn't that nervous feeling T.C. would get in the pit of his stomach when he knew he had an incredible opportunity in front of him, that amazing brief pause before an act of creation. This was something else. Something to fear and respect.

"I think we should just go on," T.C. said. Wereberry nodded in agreement.

"We never fully explore this place," Ra said. "Why not?"

"Nothing to explore," Were' said, "big, empty, white. All right, we're done. What else is there?"

"Oh I don't know," Choco-Ra said, looking all around, "the fact that we can create anything we want? The nature of this place? How about that?"

"Power, is that it?" T.C. accused.

"No," Ra insisted, "I just think we shouldn't be too quick to throw away a chance to explore this place."

"We keep coming back, though," Were' pointed out, "regardless of our intention. This is a... space between other spaces, I guess."

"What if it's more?" Ra asked.

"Then we find Cherry and come back. Deal?"

Choco-Ra nodded and ran a hand down the side of the tree. The bark felt almost perfectly right to him. The sky above, though it was only a small slice of blue, looked like sky should look. The area not only responded to their intentions, it did so faster every time they found themselves here. Ra considered the possibilities. They felt endless.

"So we leave. Where's the exit?" Ra asked. He turned around and around to look for it, but saw nothing.

Wereberry sniffed, trying to locate it by scent. T.C. felt for the current in the space. They looked with their eyes as well, but found nothing more than Ra had discovered. Their exit point didn't seem to exist.

T.C. jumped off their island, gravity ceasing to exist outside of its borders, and swam around in empty space, searching. He tried to speak, but no longer inside the bubble of sky, sound didn't move. He sighed to himself and floated free. There was, no matter how deep he searched, no desire in him to return to this place. He wanted to leave and find endless ground underneath his feet and water to swim in. He didn't want to have to create both himself. What happened when they grew tired? Or forgot something?

T.C. shuddered slightly, wondering if their idea of sky missed some critical component of skyness that made it unhealthy. He didn't know what chemicals went into proper drinking water or fish. T.C. took a deep breath and contemplated the incredible responsibilities that faced them just by existing in this empty land.

Back on the island, Wereberry watched T.C. float away. Up and down stopped mattering again off this little slice of land, he considered. What if he concentrated and wanted up and down to reverse—would they? Why stop there? Why ever stop anywhere, he wondered?

The more he considered it, the less he liked it. The place was wrong on a lot of levels. His fur bristled and he sat down on the grass, putting his back to the tree in hopes that Ra wouldn't notice.

Choco-Ra didn't notice in the least, caught up in studying the island with a critical eye. A bit of work, some dedication, and this could be something really worth sitting in. Still, he did see the others' points. They came at him with a host of reasons to leave, but Ra thought that they all boiled down to fear, spoken out loud or not. This sort of control was frightening and addictive, he knew. He was familiar with it and, he considered, the best suited to dealing with it because of that selfsame experience.

Either way, the others would take convincing, he knew, and in the meantime they did have to find Cherrygiest. How could T.C. even think to assume Ra's desire to explore was based in a need of power? Childish, that's what it was, he thought. He wanted to find Cherry as much as any of them. He'd left Al, one of the few friends he had ever met, because of their plan.

Did they somehow think that he didn't feel the pain of that loss? That it wasn't something he missed already? No, he consoled himself, of course not. They were frightened. He reminded himself of that as he turned to watch T.C. search for an exit.

T.C. spun around and considered. He cast out his feelings deeply and caught an edge of the current that always seemed to lead him to the exit. It led right toward the island the others sat on.

T.C. returned to them and explained the situation. They

looked at him and then at the ground they were on top of. T.C. dipped his face into the lake, but the exit didn't hang there, either.

"I think we have to destroy the island," Wereberry said finally, giving voice to T.C.'s initial thought.

"What? Why?" Ra asked stubbornly.

"If the exit is... remember the wall last time? If this is the same thing, we have no choice. You know it too, Ra."

"I don't like it."

"Do you think it's a wrong-headed choice?" T.C. asked.

"No, but I don't like it anyway," Ra said, shrugging.

"Fair enough," Were' said. "Now how do we do it?"

"It stayed after we left, so it can't be easy... that wall was a pain, too." T.C. pointed out.

"All right, we leave the island and try from outside it," Choco-Ra said firmly. He leapt off the island without another word. He floated there in empty space, upside down to Were' and T.C.

They leapt after him, T.C. grabbing Ra and Were' once they were all free of the confines of the island. The three concentrated on unmaking their island. None of them knew what that felt like. Making the island was instinctive: a non-simple matter of willing things to be. This was the opposite, and Were' wasn't sure how you thought about a non-island. He considered it like being told to not think about an island, perfectly maddening and impossible. Still, he tried.

They all tried, each consumed by variations of the same problem. Slowly, the island lost color. The water, even from their distance, lost some intrinsic thing that made it water, reverting to a solid mass that simply looked like water ought to.

The sky vanished, the cloud hanging in space again as it dissolved. Gray grass turned to smoke and blew away on breezes that didn't exist. The dirt and mud boiled away into wisps of nothing. Soon only the bowl of the lake was left. It sparkled as it grayed out and vanished.

The spot revealed itself. It hung in the space that wasn't, rotating. The trio headed toward it without hurry. Touching one side, T.C. found it to be solid. They tried the other and Ra's hand sunk into it. As his hand started to vanish, they each felt pressed on, suffocated. Ra drew his hand back and looked at his friends.

Were' sank his hand into the spot and the three felt the same enclosing, crushing sensation. Looking around as Were' yanked his hand back, Ra noticed what seemed to be the outline of an island.

Quickly, he communicated with them, using the adapted BOB code signals again. The island started to reform around them each time they touched the exit spot.

Rolling his eyes, Wereberry grabbed his friends tightly to him and threw them all through the spot. They winked out of existence. Behind them the island started to reform, getting as far as an outline before vanishing again.

PART FIVE
Find the Princess

"Of course the game is rigged. Don't let that stop you—if you don't play, you can't win."

—Robert A. Heinlein

1 • World 1-1

THEY RAN ALONG THE ROAD. That was the thing of it, the road. Cobblestone and mortar, laid out like any other ground surface, the road didn't have the decency to end. On and on it went, relentlessly.

The cobblestone hurt Were' and T.C.'s feet. They both longed for thick grass and soft dirt. Choco-Ra found he didn't care nearly as much, being used to hard stone floors to begin with.

There was no way off it, either. They had tried that, early on. Wereberry punched out again in frustration and, as it had every time so far, his hand glanced off some invisible force just off the edge of the road. It hung in the sky, to make matters worse, so while they could see freedom all around them, all they could do was run down the road.

The blackness behind them also served as prime motivation toward running. Every step they took, it moved closer. They had started to run, initially, when they found that the faster they went, the faster the blackness went. It might stop when they did—there was always that chance—but so far they felt no need to test that theory. Instead, they just ran.

When T.C. had first noticed the blackness that loomed behind them, a large, solid-looking wall of something that simply absorbed light, he had touched it. His hand still hurt.

The road was not simply straight and endless—it also contained outcroppings and denizens to contend with. The small mud and wood obstacles could be leapt with relative ease, at least. Useless hurdles that were swallowed by the blackness along with everything else, Wereberry wondered at their purpose. All they did was slow down the running.

Maybe, he thought, that was their purpose. Whoever had laid out the road had also put the blackness behind it, he reasoned. It could be some sort of test, some torture chamber of immense expense. And if, he thought grimly, you built a road like this simply to force people to run, why wouldn't you add some obstacles along the way just to make it interesting?

The other inhabitants were a different story. They didn't speak, not even to scream when they were swallowed up by the blackness. They were silent wanderers, walking both ways along the road. Some paced, trapped by heaps of wood, unable to leap. Others walked back past the trio, right for the blackness.

Choco-Ra tried to stop them, but touching them hurt like hell. After only a second of contact, Ra found himself being carried by Wereberry. He recovered, enough to run at least, but the memory of the touch still stayed with him, ghosting in the core of being, a memory of hurt that stung almost as sharply as the hurting itself had.

Instead, the little beasts: tiny, knee-high gryphons, slow-moving slugs, and quick-footed rabbits, were all leapt over. There was, of course, no going around on the road. The road was just wide enough for one-and-a-half people to run down. If they were Siamese twins. The trio's order changed every now and then, based on some metric they didn't feel the need to vocalize.

T.C. ran ahead, a few feet in front of Wereberry, who loped along just in front of Choco-Ra. Wereberry didn't watch the road. He didn't pay attention to anything other than T.C.'s legs in front of him. When they leapt, he timed a leap. When they ran, he ran. Were's world narrowed in focus to the movements of two legs in his line of sight and nothing else. He trusted T.C. completely, just as he trusted Ra when Ra took the lead.

Choco-Ra was doing the same thing with Were' that Were' was doing with T.C. It kept them saner, only one of them at a time really needing to pay attention to the world. The rest of the time, mind detached from the strange and unrelenting surroundings, they could try to think of a way out.

Ra, in the rear, figured that the road had to end sometime. It simply had to. Nothing, he reasoned, went on forever. Even he, Ra admitted to himself, wasn't eternal. Sure, he was the closest thing to immortal he knew of, but one day he would return to dust, and if even he would stop existing one day, then the road must do the same, he reasoned. He just hoped the road didn't dead end, that it wasn't simply a cruel joke made by some fool.

Wereberry wanted to stop running, but he still couldn't quite convince himself that the black wall wouldn't move if they didn't. It hadn't, he thought, been moving when they'd first appeared on the road. It didn't move any faster than they did themselves. Therefore, it made simple sense that it wouldn't move if they stood still. Sure, it probably wouldn't retreat, but at least they could stop running for a while.

As it was, they had stopped talking amongst themselves to save their breath for running. Which meant, Were' knew, that they couldn't come to any real solutions. Individually they could each think of an idea, but if they refused to share them, much less act on them—well, if they had learned anything from their travels, it was that they were better off together than apart. Except, running behind T.C., Were' wondered if they had learned anything at all. He laughed at himself for giving into pessimism and chided himself appropriately.

T.C. felt about ready to drop back in line again. He hated leading the charge. His hand still hurt and his feet ached in ways he never knew feet could ache. But he knew the others were just as tired as he was, so who was he, he thought, to whine and ask for downtime? T.C. pressed on and shoved all thought to the back of his head, as much as possible at least, and concentrated on when the next jump would be. A mini-gryphon strolled along the road in front of him, headed right for the three travelers. T.C. counted steps and judged distances, bracing for the jump.

A rail-thin man sailed over the heads of all three friends and landed squarely on top of the mini-gryphon. The gryphon vanished in a burst of blue light, and the man just stood there.

Not sure that he could leap a six-foot tall man, T.C. stopped, his feet sliding on the cobblestone, and hoped the blackness would too. He managed to stop just short of hitting the stranger. Wereberry dug his claws in and, aside from feeling like they might rip out, they stopped him just fine. Choco-Ra found himself with enough time before the dead stop to see it and adjust. They stood, alternately staring at the man and glancing back to make sure the black wall had, indeed, stopped gaining.

The blackness did, actually, stop. It stood, fiercely, a few feet behind Ra, looming with the weight of strangeness. Ra tried to look directly into it and found that it hurt to stare into. His gaze tried to slide off the flat black surface, but found nowhere else to land until Ra turned away again to look at the stranger in their midst.

Tall and thin, the man's red hair flowed down to his shoulders in thick waves. He wore a uniform of white and gray. Dark, shining buttons ran down one side of his jacket, gleaming like the wall behind them. His boots seemed to be made of the same stuff, coming up to his knee. White pants tucked into the tops of the boots, discolored by gray swirls that ran up along them and continued onto the jacket. The spirals wound their way down his sleeves to his gloveless hands, each pitted and scarred. His skin looked as dry as old leaves, calluses cracking along his palms. His piercing green eyes studied the trio even as they took his appearance in.

"Well now," the man said, "who are you?"

"We might ask the same question," Ra said, sliding in front of T.C.

"You might. M'name's Jonas," he told them, giving them a

small bow. "Now, what are you doing upon the road?"

"We don't know," Were' said, "we don't even know where it goes, or where else we could go."

"You don't," Jonas said, considering the matter, "end up on the road for no reason. So there's no need to disassemble for. You're trying to find the Princess, aren't you?"

"Uhm," T.C. said, "excuse me?"

"Yes, we are!" Were' shouted before anyone could stop him.

"Princess?" Choco-Ra asked quickly.

"Of course," Jonas told him, "of course I have to save the Princess. And obviously you want to do the same."

"What does she look like?" Ra asked nervously.

"As if you didn't know!" Jonas laughed heartily. He stopped to point out a slug creeping up behind the trio. "Quick! Jump!" he cried. They did, each in turn, and Jonas leapt over it as well, landing with another laugh. "Those slugs. Anyway, yes, you wanted me to tell you about the Princess, though I can't imagine you don't know."

"Humor us," Wereberry pleaded.

"Very well," Jonas said with a curt nod. He thought for only a second and when he spoke, his eyes found a point in the distance and stayed there, seeing something only he could see. "She wears the most wonderful pink flowing gown ever created. Her hair is lush like the fields, her eyes pierce your very soul." He closed his eyes, turning away from the empty air. Opening them, again he studied the trio's reaction.

"Do you think that maybe," Were' started to ask Ra.

"Possible but unlikely," Ra tossed over his shoulder. "I'm worried that she's someone else we know."

"The Princess Princess?" T.C. asked. He wasn't sure how he felt about that.

Choco-Ra, on the other hand, knew one hundred and twenty percent how he felt about that possibility: all bad.

The Princess herself wasn't even the true problem, Ra

admitted to himself. It was that Grand Vizier of hers. He just couldn't see a way for the Princess to travel without her Grand Vizier, and so where there was pink smoke there would also be rainbow fire.

Choco-Ra gave it honest thought in the few seconds he had. He didn't fear the Grand Vizier. He didn't even consider her a match for his own skills. Something about her just set him off: her casual way of dismissing things, the way she simply looked down on him no matter what, her reliance on guards to do things for her. Some of the reasons he found reflected back on himself, he knew, and some didn't.

Part of him wanted to meet her again, of course, and he admitted that to himself as well. His own waffling nagged him even worse. Ra took a deep breath and pushed the thoughts back. He didn't have time to dwell, and it couldn't be her anyway.

"It couldn't be," Ra said blandly.

"Then why say that?" T.C. asked, turning away from Jonas and concentrating on Ra. "Really?"

"Just a thought I had for a second," Choco-Ra explained.

"But it could also be—" Wereberry said.

"No, it doesn't sound like her," T.C. said.

"We thought the other Princess could have been her, right? And so this one could be as well." The note of hope was so strong in Wereberry's words that even Jonas, who wasn't sure what the hell these three strangers were talking about, caught it.

"No, Were'," Ra said sadly, "you thought she could be. I don't think either of us ever truly believed it."

"It could have been," Were' insisted, "and just because that wasn't doesn't mean this isn't, see?"

"Well," Jonas broke in, "she certainly is special. And she needs saving! Which is what I'm having to do. You lot, well I don't know why you're here."

"To save someone, too," Were' said sadly.

"Before we run off again though, "Choco-Ra said, "where does this road lead? It just seems to go on forever."

"Not quite forever," Jonas laughed, "though it is quite long. It ends at the castle."

"The Princess' castle?" T.C. asked.

"The one she's trapped in, at least."

"Then that's where we're going," Wereberry said, determination rising to the top.

"Well of course it is," Jonas laughed again, "the road only goes in one direction, after all. Where else could you go?" Jonas liked these men. They were determined, full of steel and fire—things Jonas could respect. He felt the need to warn them about the trials ahead, but decided there would be time enough. If they traveled with him, if they could truly keep up, they would learn along the way. Jonas didn't have time to adopt friends, he knew that much, but a bit of assistance certainly wouldn't hurt while it lasted. "Stick close," he told them as he started to run.

The wall tried to keep up with Jonas, despite the three travelers' lack of movement. Quickly they ran after him. T.C. cursed Jonas under his breath for not giving them more warning. He settled in line, behind Were' but ahead of Ra. T.C. watched Were's legs as his friend went into a constant, easy lope, and tried to not get lost in the repetitive scraping sound of Were's claws against cobblestone.

Wereberry felt hope burst bright in his heart. Something in him told him that the Princess was Cherrygiest. Sure, he had felt that same thing before, and been wrong, but this time it burned even brighter. He knew he should squelch it, push it down and just move forward with the normal levels of hope and excitement. Somehow he couldn't, though. Something inside set him off and convinced him that this time, this time he was right. And despite himself, Were' followed that beacon of hope. His legs moved of their own accord, not feeling the stress of the run anymore. His feet stopped hurting and his third wind kicked in.

"Shouldn't be long, now!" Jonas yelled over his shoulder. "We just have to get past the homunculus!"

Choco-Ra didn't like the sound of that. He had once controlled a homunculus, and remembered the problems it had given him. Not a full golem, the homunculus was a fabricated man but small, miniature in every respect. Perfect for small, odd jobs, Choco-Ra had used his to clean a few air shafts in the pyramid.

The thing was far stronger than it looked, however, so when it had decided, of its own accord, to destroy some air shafts because they simply wouldn't get clean enough, Choco-Ra had spent a good solid three days fighting his homunculus in the tiny air shafts.

"Why," Ra asked, shouting to be heard by Jonas, "is there a homunculus?"

"Well it's more of a golem, I suppose. I don't know," Jonas said, "but he's there. He guards the end of the road."

"Oh," Ra replied, "that's comforting."

They ran along the road. What felt like miles vanished behind them, all swallowed by the ever-present wall of blackness. Slugs were hopped over and the sky was passed under. Heavy clouds sat in the blue field above them, tempting and taunting them with their freedom.

The castle appeared before them. The spires reached impossibly high, and the fact that the building still stood miles off made them wonder exactly how tall the castle was. Pink and white, flags flying from every rampart, the castle shone in the sunlight, casting sparkles into the eyes of the tired runners.

Jonas picked up his pace, forcing the others do to the same. They wanted to grumble and groan but saved their breath for running. The road took a small hill, the first they had encountered, and as it dipped back down they could see the homunculus standing there.

"Got a plan to deal with him?" Were' asked Jonas, his breath starting to come in ragged gasps.

"Jump on him a lot," Jonas said with no hint of amusement. Were' thought that maybe he was kidding, but the tone nagged at him. No, Were' decided, he was serious.

The homunculus started to run toward them, not giving the runners a chance to prepare. Jonas leapt, bounding up into the air. As he came down, both legs straight and aimed directly at the homunculus' head, it reached up and grabbed Jonas' ankle, throwing him.

Jonas screamed in pain and flew over the heads of the three friends. Were' explained the plan, such as it was, to his friends and then leapt himself. The homunculus raised its arms, ready for Wereberry to come down on top of it. Were' had other plans, though, and went sailing straight over the beast while T.C. and Choco-Ra both leapt at its head.

Turned to follow Were's descent, the homunculus didn't notice the two pairs of feet rushing toward him. T.C. and Ra both hit the homunculus' head squarely, thumping onto it. The beast fell and Were' leapt again to come down on its head a third time. With a puff of smoke, the beast vanished into nothing.

Jonas walked up, limping, as the trio celebrated their victory. "Nice work, men," he told them, nodding at the last of the smoke wisping into the sky. "Now let's go save her."

The castle stood before them, though they hadn't really taken notice of it yet, having been too busy dealing with things to pay much attention to the scenery. White, with dashes of pink, the castle stood at least eight stories tall. In the front them sat an archway. Black and wide, the archway hung in the face of the castle like a mouth. A spiked gate that was set into it, raised so that only small points trailed down into the archway, acted as teeth.

Jonas started running again, and the other three took after him out of necessity. He reached the archway and dove into it. Were', T.C., and Choco-Ra looked at each other and considered. They had no way of going back and the road led nowhere else. They ran into the castle, hoping they could just stop running for a while.

2 • World 1-3

THE THREE FRIENDS LANDED in a dark tunnel. They didn't drop down into it, nor could they leave it; the wall behind them was perfectly solid and made of the same metal that the other walls and floor were. All they had done, Ra thought, was walk through a door. Walking through a door at ground level should not drop you off in an enclosed tunnel, he knew. Except that, well, it had.

Fair enough, then, Choco-Ra thought, they were in a tunnel. At least there wasn't a wall of blackness behind them, and the tunnel did have some light. Raw, flickering bulbs hung from the ceiling, each of them casting a small puddle of yellowish light onto the steel floor.

The wall at the end of the tunnel held a door. The door's perimeter flashed with red lights, outlining it brightly in staccato beats. The three travelers looked at one another in confusion.

"Where'd Jonas go, do ya think?" Wereberry asked.

"Into the castle," Ra said.

"Then where are we?"

"Somewhere else," Ra answered. "I don't know either, but it seems like a good guess. Still. Door. Do we have another choice?"

"Forward it is," T.C. said, taking a step toward the door.

As T.C.'s foot hit the floor, a single step forward from where they all stood, a door in the ceiling slid open and three men dropped to the floor. Each of the men wore a brown jumpsuit and green protective eye gear. Rifles gripped in hand, the men took aim at the three intruders in their midst.

"Take 'em out!" Wereberry shouted.

T.C. turned his next step into a dive, heading right for the legs of the nearest attacker. Wereberry leapt, claws out, at another. Choco-Ra ran forward, planning on taking out the third. Bullets shot out of gun barrels, the noise thunderous and echoing in the small metal space.

T.C. curled his legs under him as he dove, the bullets passing him by mere inches. Wereberry got lucky; the man firing at him was simply unnerved by the sight of a pink werewolf descending quickly toward his head. Ra fell backwards, three bullets ripping clean through his bandages, front and back. He laid on the cold steel floor, unmoving.

Neither T.C. nor Were' noticed the fall of their friend as they were busy disabling the men they found themselves on top of. Dispatching them with relative ease, the two stood up to find the third man aiming directly between them, his finger curling on the trigger and arm already starting to swing in a spread.

T.C. reached the man first, grabbing the gun out of his hands and using it to smash the man's face, shattering the goggles he wore. The man slumped, and T.C. hammered at him again, knocking him out.

Behind them, Ra sat up slowly, shaking his head. He looked at the holes in his front and sighed. Reaching over, he pinched one of the holes together tightly.

"Damn it, Ra, are you all right?" Were' asked, spotting him.

"I'll be fine, just come pinch the holes on my back so they knit, will you?"

T.C. and Were' did as asked, but kept an eye on the room. The ceiling door stayed closed and the red lights around the door in the opposite wall went out. The room was silent, except for the breathing of the three friends.

Choco-Ra stood and inspected himself. "Good as new. Actually, I should undo the knot at my shoulder, too."

"I got it," T.C. said, deftly working the knot out. It curled back into itself and settled smoothly, the seam gone to the naked eye.

"That is so lucky," Were' said.

"How do you mean?" Ra asked him.

Were' paced around Choco-Ra, looking his friend's body up and down. "The whole healing trick."

"You heal, too," Ra pointed out. He didn't enjoy feeling like a specimen to be examined.

"Not as quickly. Those bullets could have killed me. Easily, in fact. But you, what? You pinch your skin together and you're fine."

"And you get to have internal organs and eat food. We're all so happy for you, too." Ra walked away from Were' and T.C. and grabbed one of the fallen men's guns.

"I didn't mean—" Were' started.

"No, you didn't," Ra said, checking the gun over, "I know. I'm sorry."

"Whatever," Wereberry said with a smile, "wanna get out of here?"

"I know I do," T.C. put in. He knew that Were' and Ra sniped at each other and that they never really meant it. It just got old, some days.

Choco-Ra walked over to the door and nudged it with the barrel of his new rifle. The door swung open easily—too easily, he thought. On the other side there was only blackness. With a shrug, he stepped through.

The others followed him and the door swung shut behind them on its own. As soon as it closed, the lights came on in the new room. It was a mirror image of the room they had left.

Turning around, Were' sighed as he saw that the wall behind them was completely solid and sealed. "It's like there never was a door here," he told the others.

"How much do you want to bet," T.C. asked them, "if we take a step forward, some guys drop down and try to kill us?"

"No bet," Ra said, "but this time let's be ready for them."

Choco-Ra knelt down and raised the rifle to sight through. T.C. nodded and crouched, ready to leap. Wereberry nodded and took a quick step forward, bunching his legs under him as he squatted down immediately after taking the step.

The ceiling opened and three more men, all wearing the same brown outfit, dropped through. They didn't even get a chance to hit the ground conscious. Ra shot one as soon as he appeared, Were' launched himself into the air to tackle and intercept the second, and T.C. followed him for the third. The lights on the door at the other end of the room winked out and Ra looked at T.C.

"Ideas?" he asked.

"Me?" T.C. asked, looking at Were'.

"We can go through that door," Were' said, "and possibly repeat this process. But you're the sneak here. Got a better idea?"

"Can we force the ceiling door somehow?" T.C. asked. "Maybe it'd be easier to go through whatever it up there."

"Wouldn't there be a whole lot of guys up there, waiting to drop down?" Ra asked T.C.

"Might be," he said, "if we assume they just sit up there all day waiting for us. But then we'd have them all at once, and funneled. But if it's a system of free rooms up there that they just deploy into, we could avoid them easier with more space."

"Fair enough," Were' said.

None of them could reach the ceiling. Choco-Ra brushed against it with the butt of his rifle, but that was as close as they could get. Were' waved T.C. closer and climbed up his friend carefully, standing on his shoulders. The ceiling door was smooth and didn't want to budge.

"No go," Were' said, dropping down. His claws skittered on the hard metal floor when he landed, causing them all to look down.

"Claws couldn't even get purchase?" Ra asked him, staring

at Wereberry's feet.

"Nope," he answered, "the thing is sealed tight." He knelt down by the one of the felled attackers. "They had to have a way to get out if they killed us, though."

"You think they'd go back up?" T.C. asked, watching.

Wereberry patted the guard down, searching his pockets thoroughly. "I can't see where they wouldn't have wanted the option, at least. Retreat should have been in their plans." He pulled out a black box with two buttons. Holding it up with a grin, he pressed a button.

The red lights that circled the door set into the far wall came back on. Were' looked at his friends and hit the same button again. The lights went out. Nodding at the box, he hit the other button. The ceiling door slid open and he laughed.

"Shall we? Give me a boost, T.C." Were' climbed back up T.C. and grabbed the edge of the hole in the ceiling. He pulled himself up in one fluid motion, vanishing into darkness.

Shots rang out, causing T.C. and Ra to try to reach the opening themselves. Choco-Ra was on T.C.'s shoulders, fingers grabbing the lip of the hole, when a rifle sailed past his head to clatter on the floor below. A pink hand came out of the tunnel and grabbed Ra's arm, yanking him upward.

Were's head popped out of the hole and he held out his arms to T.C. "Jump, I'll grab you," he told his friend, grinning. T.C. grinned back and leapt, reaching for Were's outstretched hands. The three soon stood in a wide tunnel, darker than the room they had left. Ra's eyes glowed, augmenting what little light was available.

"They had some guards up here," Were' told them, pointing, "to keep that door protected."

The door that Were' pointed to sat closed and dark. The knob was highly polished and threw back Ra's glow at the group, seeming to scream at the trio to be used.

Nudging a downed guard clear, Were' inched open the door and peered out. "Clear," he told them, and he swung the door wide. The hallway they exited into was well-lit and simple. Flat, tan tiles ran along the walls with darker, wider tiles covering the floor. The metal ceiling remained though, with better lighting strung along it. The hallways looked empty, but a series of doors lined both sides for as far as they could see.

"There's a turn up there," Ra said, relaxing his eyes so that they faded.

"Then let's take it," T.C. told them. "I'll go check it out."

The other two nodded, and T.C. edged along the wall. Were' and Ra stepped back into the dark room and waited for his return. T.C. nodded as he heard the door close behind him with a quiet snikt. Hugging the wall, he approached the corner and peered around it. No less than twenty guards marched in silent formation down the hallway, away from the junction where T.C. stood.

He watched them go and looked around for a good exit point. A door stood near him marked "Stairs," that seemed, he thought, perfectly good. Taking a deep breath and fairly sure that the guards wouldn't suddenly turn around in mid-march, he slid up to the stairwell door and studied it. No wires ran up to it, that he could see, and no lights sat anywhere near it.

He laid a hand on the wall and felt outward. Years of living underwater, playing with fish of all types, had made him fairly sensitive to electrical fields. It paid to know when the electric eel you tickled was about to discharge in frustration. He sensed nothing, which, he admitted to himself, only reduced the chance that it wasn't wired. He wasn't perfect, and a small field could do the job just as well as one big enough for him to notice.

He rested his hand on the knob and waited. No signal rang out, so he turned the knob quickly and quietly, cracked the door open, and peered through the crack of an opening. The stairway was painted in flat, industrial grays, and it was empty. Satisfied, he closed the door and went back for his friends.

Together they stole along the hallway to the stairs and entered quickly. "Up or down?" Ra asked as they stood before the stairs.

"Depends on where we are," Were' said quickly, "which we don't know."

T.C. laughed and shook his head, "Up," he said simply.

"Why up?" Were' asked.

"What's so funny?" Ra asked at the same time.

T.C. jerked a thumb at the sign right behind them. A small plaque bolted to the wall near the door read "B-1". Were' and Ra shrugged and nodded. "Up it is," Ra said, gesturing for T.C. to go first.

The merman sprinted up the stairs to the first turn and glanced around the corner. Seeing it clear, he waved Ra and Wereberry forward. T.C. stood where he was while Were' shot up to the next turn in the stairwell. T.C. watched behind them to ensure no one snuck up on them while Were' checked ahead. Clear again, Were' waved them forward.

The stairwell door sat marked with a giant "1". Wereberry tried the doorknob, giving it a slow, gentle turn. The door popped open silently and he peered out into the hallway. Bullets thudded into the door, the crack of gunfire surprising all three travelers. Were' slammed the door shut.

"I think they know where we are," he said sheepishly.

"And they're quick on the trigger," Ra noted, "So."

T.C. put his head against the wall near the door. Were' nodded and did the same. They listened hard, Ra joining them, trying to count. Boot steps and guns cocking could be heard far too clearly.

"We have about ten seconds before a lot of people come through that door," T.C. said.

"Yup. Ra, T.C., pull the hinges out of the door," Were' whispered.

Choco-Ra stood tall and grabbed the hinge pin at the top

of the door. T.C. knelt and did the same on the lower hinge. They pulled hard, and the pins cracked and pulled free.

Ra moved to stand next to the door, unslinging his rifle and taking a breath to settle himself. He remembered what Al had taught him about aiming, even in close quarters. Taking a deep breath to center himself, Ra relaxed his fingers around the grip of the gun. The trigger sat half-squeezed, and Ra focused his eyes on the point in the doorway where he would fire once it was open.

Were' motioned T.C. to the other side of the door and whispered into his ear. Then he knelt in a crouch behind his gilled friend and waited. His plan should work—he was confident of that. The more fighting Were' saw, the more hunting he thought of, and the better he felt about telling the others what to do.

It was situations like this where Wereberry felt at home, though if you had told him that ages ago he would have laughed and shaken his head. Hunting a rabbit, sure. Hunting men who hunted him, that was significantly different. Though he was seeing, more and more, that they were often the same.

The building's guards tried the doorknob, finding that it turned easily. They unlatched it and slammed into the thing with a shoulder. With no hinges to hold it in its frame, the whole door gave way.

T.C. grabbed the door by the hinge side and turned it in his hands. The door's arc back through the doorframe created a sudden and destructive fly swatter effect, knocking men every which way. Over the door a pink-furred blur flew as Wereberry leapt over T.C. and the swinging door, directly into the midst of the men on the other side. Choco-Ra opened fire on the few who got clear of the door, sending them falling every which way.

Giving the door a final shove, T.C. tossed it into the rear ranks of men. The ones that still found themselves on their feet, that is. Were' was happily using their confusion to decimate their ranks. He saw the door coming and ducked just in time. The duck turned into a low leap that took out the last of the men.

"There'll be more soon, let's keep moving," he said, standing up and stretching. T.C. and Ra didn't answer, simply coming out of the stairwell to join their friend. All around them, the floor was covered with the unconscious bodies of guards. They worked to find clear space to walk, hopping and stepping over limbs. Pointing at a right-angle turn, T.C. took off and the others followed, running down the hallway.

A siren sounded, red lights set into the ceiling flashing rhythmically. The trio ran just a bit faster, glancing at each doorway they passed. Footsteps sounded behind them, followed by short bursts of gunfire. Choco-Ra turned and returned fire, his rifle clicking empty after only a few shots. In frustration, Ra threw the gun at one of the soldiers, cursing quietly as he did.

A door stood in front of them. Above it hung a lit red EXIT sign, glowing brightly. Were' dove for the door, slamming into the emergency release bar with his shoulder. The door flung open wide, crunching badly as the hinges found themselves bent past their turning point. T.C. and Ra dove through mere seconds after, all three vanishing into the darkness that veiled the other side of the doorway.

3 • World 3-4

T.C. DRANK DEEPLY. The water that surrounded them filled his gills and revitalized him. He swam around in a sharp circle, spiraling quickly. Behind him, he saw as he turned, Wereberry and Choco-Ra were drowning.

Realizing the problem, T.C. grabbed them both and looked for a place to swim to safety. Nothing appeared to him. Above him there was only rock, the water lapping right up against it, flooding whatever chamber they were in. Behind them was a wall of blackness, the sight of which gave T.C. a burst of panic and frustration, mingled together as they so often were these days.

In front of them stretched a long tunnel, flooded with water. T.C. saw fish swimming in schools and seaweed along the bottom of the tunnel. He wondered how the water was oxygenated. He saw enough glowing algae to explain the light in the water, but nothing that would let his friends breathe.

He swam forward anyway, in hope, in desperation, and glanced back to see the wall of blackness move with him. Grimly, T.C. swam on, faster than he wanted to, trailing his friends behind him.

Wereberry could swim, though he did hate to be this sopping wet. If he had only been expecting this, he thought, then he could've taken a breath and been fine. But that last thing any of them knew they had been in a hallway—a dry, above-water hallway. Were' concentrated on staying calm and not using up what little air he held, putting his trust and life in T.C.'s hands.

Choco-Ra wasn't doing as well. He didn't need to breathe in the conventional sense at all, so he wasn't so much drowning

318

as he was coming apart at the seams. Filled with water and thoroughly soaked, his bandages were starting to drift apart. He focused on drawing his body together, holding himself in shape, before T.C. wound up dragging one long length of bandages. Ra also knew, and hadn't thought to tell the others, that if he unwound completely they would have to find a way to keep his eyes with him. His eyes were the key. They dimmed now with the sheer force of will needed to retain cohesion.

T.C. spotted something strange in the water and dove for it, feeling Ra's arm go slack in his grip. Refusing to glance back, T.C. tightened his grip and kicked harder against the water that gave him so much life at the expense of his friends.

The oddity in the water looked clear, a giant bubble hanging impossibly. T.C. realized it looked like a giant air bubble and burst through it, hoping to at least afford Were' a gulp of air before the bubble split and dissipated. Instead, the bubble, when entered, didn't break or split. It hung as it had when viewed from the outside, content and whole.

"Holy hell," Were' said, in-between taking deep ragged gulps of air, "where are we?"

"I only wish I could answer that," Choco-Ra said. His body leaked water like a faucet, all of it falling out of the bubble. He grew tall and impossibly thin for a second, wringing himself out as much as possible.

Were' wanted to shake himself out some, get the water trapped in his fur loose, but he decided that Ra didn't need to be wetted down any more than he already was. He looked down, wondering how they were even standing in a bubble that they could swim into so easily.

"Wall of blackness dead behind, by the way," T.C. said.

"Oh, wonderful," Ra said, resuming his normal shape.

"No, that's good," Were' said.

His friends looked at him blankly. T.C. wondered how any part of going from an enemy base into a drowned world was a good thing, especially when the space between them made no sense. There hadn't even been the smell of water from the doorway they'd jumped though.

"Come on," Were' continued, "if the black wall is back and we're in some sort of tunnel, then all we have to do is follow it to the end and leave that way. The same as the road."

"You make it sound so easy," T.C. said.

"He may be right, though," Ra said thoughtfully, "look up."

Choco-Ra pointed and the trio watched Jonas swim by, not even noticing them. He kicked powerfully, his strong, wiry legs propelling him through the water almost as fast as T.C. had gone. They could see he held his breath, staring dead ahead, on the lookout for trouble.

"So Jonas went into the castle and is here now?" T.C. asked.

"We went into the castle and we're here now," Ra pointed out.

T.C. stuck his head out of the bubble and shook it happily in the water for a second. Were' and Ra watched him, both with smiles on their faces. Sure, they were trapped underwater, recently attacked and generally lost, but T.C. looked so happy that they couldn't think of anything other than how good it was to see him that way.

"We didn't see him in the building," T.C. said when he returned.

"And he doesn't see us now," Wereberry said, "but I'd say we're on the same path. The Princess, Cherrygiest."

"We don't know that it's Cherry," Ra said with a note of warning.

"It's her," Were' said confidently.

Ra put the discussion aside, but he really wished there was time to sit down and discuss this with Were', just to make sure his friend was truly braced for possible disappointment. They'd been to a lot of places and searched a good-sized number of lands with no luck so far. Placing all of his bets on this one felt dangerous and foolhardy to Ra. They had bigger things to deal with first, though.

"Regardless," Ra said with a shake of his head, "we go forward?"

"Seems like," Were' said.

"Yup," T.C. agreed.

"Can we assume there are other air bubbles like this?" Were' asked, wondering how long this tunnel was.

"We have to," T.C. said. "I'll grab you guys and—"

"No, we'll each swim," Were' amended.

"That might be a problem," Ra said.

"Then we'll adjust as we go, but we'll want T.C. anything but hindered, just in case."

Choco-Ra sighed and nodded. "Fair enough. So if we don't see another bubble, what do we do?"

"I'll swim ahead some," T.C. said, "and if I don't spot one we'll come back and think it through more."

"Wait," Were' said.

The others looked at him and waited. Wereberry looked around him, noting the bubble's size and position.

"Why don't," he continued, "you try pushing the bubble with us in it, T.C.?"

T.C. clapped his hands together once and dove out of the bubble. Swimming around it a few times, T.C. decided on the best angle of attack and stopped just shy of the air bubble. He knew that passing through it was simple, seamless even. But inside, it felt solid. So maybe, he hoped, there was a way to work that solidity from the outside as well.

He set his hand against the bubble and it fell through as if there was no barrier at all. He pulled it back and concentrated on the bubble being firm. He projected his will at it, demanding that it be firm from the outside, and, as slow as he could possibly move and still do more than just drift on currents, he set his hand against the bubble. It passed through.

Frustrated, T.C. dove through the bubble and rejoined his friends. "Obviously a no go," he told them, "so we're back to the first plan. I'm ready whenever you guys are."

"Now is as good a time as any," Choco-Ra said. He looked out of the bubble into the deep blue water. He didn't dread the coming plan, but he came close. Helpless in this much water, Ra wondered if there was anything he could do that would even approach useful. He decided to, at the very least, keep an extra-sharp eye out while the others swam.

T.C. dove out of the bubble again, kicking off strongly once water surrounded him. Were' and Ra followed, slower and clumsier. T.C. glanced back at them but kept moving forward, ten body lengths ahead of them at all times, scouting for danger and air bubbles sitting plump in the water.

Wereberry swam as best he could, ungracefully. He'd taken a huge breath of air, but even so, his body wanted to breathe badly enough that his lungs already felt cramped. Diving down for a second, he thought, was easier. Your body knew it would only have to sustain the unnatural state for a short time. Surrounded by water with no escape in sight, his body rebelled, not trusting the brain that guided it. Were' fought back the rising adrenaline and swam at a constant rate, trying to remain as calm as possible.

Choco-Ra held onto Were's shoulders, trailing along above his friend. Glancing back, Ra watched the black wall keep pace with them and wondered, not for the first time, what was behind it. There had to be something behind it; that was simply how walls worked. They had two sides.

Possibly the other side was just things they had passed already, the wall just moving and acting as a barrier. Then again, Ra thought, if it destroyed whatever it touched, then the other side had to be something else entirely. Ra looked away from the blackness—it felt like it could swallow his attention too deeply—and studied the fish.

T.C. studied the fish as well, wondering. He was hungry

and could use a bite to eat. But the last time they were on a road like this tunnel, touching anything living was a bad idea. So maybe, he thought, maybe the same held true. He decided to risk it, touching a fish lightly with one finger. Nothing bad happened, so he grabbed it and ate it in a single gulp. Three more followed and T.C. resolved to grab some for Were' when they came across the next air bubble.

The shark almost took his head off, distracted as T.C. was by small, snacking fish. A flash of teeth, a burst of water forcing toward him against the current—T.C. put the signs together at the last second and bucked like a dolphin, throwing himself through the water faster than the shark could clamp down his powerful jaws.

T.C. dodged and taunted the shark, trying to keep its attention away from Were' and Ra. In the middle of a complex, twisting turn that would have won awards at an air show, T.C. spotted the next air bubble. He couldn't think of a good way to tell the others so he swam for it, hoping they would follow. Were' did, trying to also stay out of the shark's notice. The bubble sat temptingly close, but T.C. couldn't get the shark to follow him far enough away to be fully clear of the path Were' needed to take.

Were's lungs were running out of air and he decided to just go for it. With a strong kick, Were' swam as hard as he could, aiming directly for the bubble. The shark, noticing the disruption in the water, turned mid-fight and shot off after the strange, slow-moving furry creature that trailed what looked to the shark like strange, bunched-up seaweed from his back.

Wereberry tried to outswim the shark, racing for a breath of air. His lungs burned and Were' didn't know what he would do if the shark blocked his entry. Luckily for both him and Ra, Were's path was a shorter line. He made the bubble seconds before the shark did. Ra dropped off of Were's back and, as the shark leapt straight through the bubble, punched it in the nose as hard as he could with a waterlogged fist. The shark staggered as it reentered water, circling the bubble for a minute but not daring to enter it.

T.C. took the chance to sneak up on the stubborn animal, pummeling the top of its head with fists and feet until it winked out in a puff of smoke. He entered the bubble and sat down, quickly and heavily.

"Have I ever told you that I hate sharks?" he asked his friends.

"Never even knew you'd fought one before this," Were' said.

"Not something I do a lot, no," T.C. said, "but it's happened before. Hate them. They're all... toothy."

Choco-Ra laughed, wringing himself out again, "Yeah, that's just it. They're toothy. The hundreds of pounds of muscle and raw force? Who cares? It's the toothy that'll get you ever time."

"I'm serious," T.C. told him.

"That's what makes it funny," Ra told him with a grin.

"Wait," Were' said, "you've never fought a shark before."

"Sure I have," T.C. replied with a grin.

"Nope. We would've heard all about it. So...."

"Silent War," T.C. admitted, "he told me about them. I mean, I'd seen sharks before, but never mean ones."

"Still," Ra said chuckling, "they're toothy."

"Exactly!" T.C. said. He looked around and wondered when joking this soon after a fight had become normal to him. "We should go, though."

"Probably, just give us another minute," Wereberry said, stretching.

T.C. nodded and dove out of the air bubble, swimming ahead a bit, mindful of the black wall. He cut through the water, feeling it part around his body and slide against his skin in a constant caress.

His gills expanded and contracted, flushing water through his system. T.C. didn't really want to leave this place. He knew then exactly how deeply he missed sleeping under water, going for long, uninterrupted swims, and generally letting himself be who he was.

Life didn't give him the choice though, and he recognized that. He accepted it, or at least tried to as best he could. The trip back to the bubble, to his friends, rushed by, leaving T.C. wishing he'd had more time to think.

"Come on," he said, poking his head through the air bubble.

Wereberry and Choco-Ra nodded and dove through the bubble into the water. They swam on, T.C. in the lead, and wandered their way through the makeshift ocean.

T.C. saw another bubble, but near it circled two sharks. He shook his head and sped ahead. Further on he saw a staircase. It spiraled up out of sight. Charging back to his friends at top speed, T.C. signaled the dilemma to Were', who passed it on to Ra.

Were' wasn't sure if his lungs would hold out all the way to the staircase, but fighting off more sharks might be more trouble than it was worth if the stairs were close enough to make. Ra agreed, or close enough, as he signaled they should just forge on.

Were' held out his arms and they formed a chain of bodies, Were' holding onto T.C. and Ra hanging off of Were's shoulders. T.C. took off at top speed and Wereberry bucked his body in rhythm with T.C. It wasn't a great way to travel, and they both knew they couldn't sustain it for long. The hope was simply that they could keep it up for long enough.

The air bubble passed by beneath them, and Were' felt his lungs burn even more as he watched salvation slide by. The sharks around the bubble never noticed them, circling around as if they were set to guard the place.

The stairs came into view and Were' gave it everything he had. Ra drifted further and further apart, the best he could do to hold himself together not quite good enough. The current sweeping by made cohesion harder, but slowing down would kill Were'. It wasn't a choice, to Ra. He knew he could keep himself together enough to survive. That made it simple math for him. He concentrated and tried to stop noticing the world around them.

The stairs drew closer and, as T.C. swam up them, Were's foot brushed a stair. Something in his brain didn't trigger right at the touch though, and Were' thought a shark had caught up with them. Letting go of T.C., Were' dropped to the stairs and spun around, looking for the threat.

T.C. noticed Were's departure too late. His momentum took him straight up the stairs for a collision course with the blackened archway at the top of them. He vanished through.

Back on the stairs, Were' stopped looking for sharks and tried to keep consciousness. The world swam red in front of his eyes and all he wanted to do was take a breath. Choco-Ra wrapped around Were and covered his friend's muzzle, trying to stall off what now felt was the inevitable.

They realized T.C. was nowhere to be found and looked every which way. Finally, dimly, Were' realized he must have gone up the stairs. Were' went after him, struggling against breath, forcing some control of his limbs to hold.

The black archway scared him. It could lead anywhere, but Were' knew that if it didn't lead to air, he would die. Going through the arch, Wereberry knew the next thing he would do would be to draw a deep breath. He hoped it would be made of air and not water.

4 • World 6-2

THE GRASS WAS WARM under the watchful eye of a sun high above. The heat from the star fell on the ground and infused the dirt. The dirt trapped the warmth, spreading it back upwards, warming the roots of plants as it went. Even as the sun warmed the air and heated the earth from above, the ground radiated back some of its own heat, warming from the other direction. T.C., Wereberry, and Choco-Ra lay on the grass, soaking up the heat from every direction.

T.C. enjoyed the heat and dry land as a change, but he already missed the water. The relief he felt was directed at his friends, not himself. For their lives, he was grateful they had escaped the enclosed ocean. Still, he already felt his skin drying out by degrees and knew he would be grabbing his moisturizer in a while, a poor substitute for water rushing along his body.

Wereberry's first act upon reaching dry land had been to shake himself long and hard. Water flew in every direction as he forced his fur to release all the water it had trapped. The shake also loosened his muscles, tense from swimming. While he shook he took deep, ragged breaths, huge gulps of air that sent him into a coughing fit. Doubled over, he held his knees and let his body adjust how it needed to. Then he collapsed on the grass and stared at the sky, letting his breathing slow and his body go limp.

Choco-Ra didn't even try to pull himself together, letting the sun dry out his bandages first. They were slack and as he lay, flatter than normal, grass could be seen through his torso and limbs. Ra didn't care. The dry land, the warmth, they all drove the excess moisture from his body. That was enough, for now. Soon, he thought, he would have to concentrate and pull himself together. Soon he would stand up and work out, with the others, where they were. But that was soon, not now. Now he just dried out, splayed along the ground.

The child snuck up on the trio as they lay on the grass. He looked at them and stood nearby, watching the strangers as they did nothing at all. He wore a jumper and matching baseball hat, which he adjusted every few seconds, twitching the brim left and right, trying to find the perfect spot for it.

Were' scented the kid and turned his head slightly to see him. "Hey, kid," he said softly. There was nothing even approaching concern in Were's voice. He sounded sleepy, if anything. His friends idly joined him in looking at the boy, each of them realizing that their break might already be over.

"My mother says Jimmy might be in the big house at the end of the road," the child said. Satisfied, he walked a few feet away and continued to mess around with his hat.

"Excuse me?" Were' asked, sitting up.

"My mother says Jimmy might be in the big house at the end of the road," the child repeated, after walking back to where he'd stood before.

"Well, if you say so," T.C. muttered. He sat up as well and looked at Were'. "Do we care?" he asked, whispering.

"Hey, at least we're not in a tunnel of some sort," Were' said.

"That is interesting," Ra said from where he laid. Sighing then, his bandages started to spin as Ra tightened his wrapping and resumed his normal size and shape. He stood, flexing his fingers. Dry enough for now, he supposed, the rest would happen as it would.

Were' and T.C. stood, joining Ra. Looking around for the first time, other than staring at the sky, they realized they had been sunning themselves in someone's garden. A small red and white house sat behind them, a white fence all around. Next to the house whose garden they stood in, other houses sat. All the houses were similar, one- or two-storied affairs of the same basic colors. The dwellings all lay in a nice simple grid, with wide streets between them and lush grass all around.

Oddly, the streets seemed almost deserted. No traffic moved there—in fact, nothing at all occupied them. They were just wide lanes of gray concrete, paved for people who didn't seem to have a need for them. Giving the empty town a shrug, Ra headed around the side of the house and looked for a door.

The door to the house was cracked open and swung freely when Ra's hand gave it a good push. Were' and T.C. followed, trying to see if anyone besides that one lone boy was around. Of course, the fact that he seemed to be alone told them volumes about their chances of seeing anyone else.

The house inside looked lived in: toys on the floor, a radio playing music, food smells wafting from the kitchen. They headed toward the food, Were's stomach growling at the scent of it. A woman stood by the stove, stirring a pot and humming to herself. Her apron ties sat perfectly in a bow at her back, the color matching the boy's jumper.

"Excuse me," Ra said.

He put the full force of his royalty into the words, hoping that the woman would at least respond to the tone, even if she hadn't noticed three strangers walk right into her house. The woman didn't respond or even seem to notice them, still stirring the pot on the stove and humming.

"Maybe she's deaf?" Were' asked, stepping closer. "Excuse us," he said, louder.

The woman turned around, spinning quickly on her heel. The wooden spoon in her hand dripped sauce onto the floor, but she paid it no mind. "Did you know that there's adventure around every corner?" she asked them.

Her smile grew rigidly along her face, not quite a grimace but certainly far from natural and pleasant. T.C. recoiled at it, taking a hurried step away. Were' stood his ground and nodded at her.

"Yup, I had heard that, actually," he said, hoping to put her at ease.

"Did you know that there's adventure around every corner?" she repeated, then turned back to the stove. Her spoon dipped back into the pot and she resumed stirring.

"All right," Were' said to his friends, turning his back on the woman he now dubbed crazy, "confer in the other room, please?"

Without waiting for a reply, Were' pushed past his friends and made for the front room. He played with one of the toys on the ground, a shiny robot. Its arms and legs moved, stiffly, and Were' lifted them and bent them back, trying to not focus on the woman in the kitchen for a second.

"They're all crazy," Choco-Ra said as he walked into the room with T.C. "Anything else?"

"I don't think so," T.C. said, "this place seems...." he trailed off and looked at Were'. "Why are you playing with that?"

Were' looked up from the toy in his hands and dropped it on the floor again. "Oh, sorry, I have no idea. Anyway! Crazy, yes. I'd agree with crazy."

"So what do we do?" Ra asked.

"Leave town?" T.C. suggested.

"Well there is," Wereberry said with a smirk, "adventure around every corner."

"But what does leaving town get us?" Ra asked.

"Away from the crazy people in Empty Town."

"Aside from that, Were'."

T.C. laughed. "I bet we'll find a path outside the town."

"Which way, then?" Were' asked.

"Well," T.C. said, thinking it over, "let's see which way the town is oriented and go from there."

The others agreed and they set off, not bothering to close the door behind them. The boy, Ra saw when he peeked around the house, still stood there, adjusting his hat every now and again. They left the boy behind, exiting through the only gate in the fence around his house.

The gate led to a road that branched off around the town. Homes gave way to small markets and official-looking structures. All of the doors were ajar, but no one else walked the streets or stood visible through the openings. The travelers left the buildings alone, deciding to err on the side of not running into more crazy people who gave them the creeps.

The roads lay in straight lines, all making right-angle turns to meet other roads along the way. They also, each and every one that the trio walked, ended in a dead end. The town seemed closed off and self-contained.

After an hour of wandering, switching back and retracing steps to follow other roads, they considered going off into the grass that covered the town, but the grass ended in mountains on every side. Large mountains with no discernable path to climb. Foreboding walls of stone, they locked off the town where the roads couldn't.

Eventually they found a stretch of road that looked unfamiliar. Wondering how they could have missed it the first time, they followed it. Mountains rose up around them, and they came to a gate. The gate sat shut, large and painted red, wooden slats filling its form and lending it an air of gatehood.

"Well," Were' said, looking at the gate, "do we go through it or do we keep exploring the town?"

"There's nothing in the town," Ra said.

"That we've seen," Were' corrected. "T.C.?"

"Forward," the merman said with a shrug.

"Forward it is," Choco-Ra said. He didn't think there would be anything in the town, regardless of the woman's claims of adventure. Something, he reasoned, had happened to the town. Not too long ago either, he judged by the general state of things. The place was too nice, too well kept, to have been abandoned for long, but where had the people gone? Maybe, Ra thought, they'd left town and gone somewhere down the road past the gate. They had to have, he felt, gone somewhere.

T.C. opened the gate, pushing it wide. The three friends walked through, staying on the road that wound out of the town and down through the strange land they now saw sprawled before them. Patches of forest sat to either side of the road. In between those clumps, however, the land was barren and desolate. It was startlingly flat, letting them see for miles ahead—the turn in the road they spotted could easily be a day away or three hours. The mismatched land looked endless. They started to walk.

Uneventfully, they walked and watched the land go by. The sun still hung in the sky, though Were' thought it smelled like it might rain later. High grass grew in random-looking patches, contained from spreading by forces none of them understood. Wereberry thought that maybe it was a soil issue. Something about that answer didn't work for him, though, and he couldn't find the right way to explain that feeling, not even to himself.

T.C. was tromping through some tall grass near the side of the road, just enjoying the feel of it rubbing along his legs, when a dark shape leapt out at him. The spider wrapped its legs around T.C.'s head before he could react. He flailed wildly, quickly catching his friends' attention.

Wereberry and Ra grabbed for the spider's body, but T.C. was spinning around and around in panic, making it even harder for them to dislodge the spider. Were' finally grabbed one of the legs where it joined the spider's fat black body and yanked hard. The leg snapped off with the dry sound of a breaking twig and squirted green muck into the air.

Choco-Ra grabbed another leg and followed Were' lead, and between the two of them they pried the spider down to legless and watched it drop to the ground, its body twitching.

"What," T.C. asked, wiping his face with the back of a

hand, "the hell was that?"

"Spider," Were' said, looking down at the carcass.

"There is no way something that big could hide in this patch of grass and not be seen," T.C. insisted, "no way at all!"

"Maybe it burrowed," Ra offered. "Either way, we should be more careful."

"More careful how?" T.C. asked, still upset. "Should we be watching for invisible things now?"

"Always," Were' said, "or at least expecting them. This place's been too quiet. Ra's right, we have to start assuming that it isn't as quiet as it seems."

"You didn't have a spider on your face, suffocating you."

"Thankfully," Ra said, "but I'm sure it isn't the last thing that will try for us."

"That just..." T.C. shuddered, "that was the worst thing yet. Suffocating, something hugging my head like that, I just...."

"It's all right," Were' said. "Let's just move on. You'll be fine, T.C."

"No, I know I will, but... it... gah!"

They moved on without further discussion of spiders, the idea of having one latch onto faces, or anything else of the sort. They stayed clear of the grasses, instead wondering if they should try entering one of the wooded areas for less chance of arachnids.

Wereberry took the lead and walked them into one of the clutches of trees. The canopy above them filtered the light. No birds sang and no insects chattered, though, unsettling all of them. Something had to be alive in the land, they each believed. Wereberry sniffed the air deeply, turning around and half-climbing a tree. Still, he couldn't catch a whiff of anything other than dirt and tree.

He let go of the tree, dropping down to the dirt in a low crouch. The silence pressed in on his skull like a living thing. It distracted him, so only Ra's yell of warning alerted Were' to the large bird that lunged at him from the other side of the tree.

T.C. came from nowhere, to Were's eyes, and grabbed the bird before it could attack and pinned it to the ground. The bird was small and squat, bright yellow, and presented a wickedly sharp-looking beak. The edges around the beak's point were barbed, creating a saw-tooth edge that, Were' thought when he noticed it, could have torn him to shreds.

While T.C. wrestled to keep the thing pinned down, Wereberry and Choco-Ra worked together to knock it out, finding the bird much tougher than it looked. When it was finally unconscious, they stood around and stared openly at the thing.

"That bird wasn't there," Were' said, "I would've sensed it, smelled it, heard it, something!"

"Maybe it burrowed," T.C. said. He realized that he probably sounded bitchier than he intended, but seeing Were' as creeped out by the bird as T.C. himself had been by the spider helped him some. It was an unfair and unjust sort of help, but T.C. took it as something to cling to for a while.

They left the bird, trying to not dwell on it, and walked through the woods until they ended abruptly in a rocky, barren stretch. Each of them kept as alert as possible, scanning the ground and trees for trouble. Despite that, each of them felt perfectly confident that if something was there, they wouldn't notice it until it was too late.

The hard ground hurt their feet after the softness of the underbrush. The sun, too, stung as its rays crashed down onto them, outside the protection of the tree line. Rocks littered the ground, ranging in size from the smallest of pebbles, irritating T.C.'s toe-webbing, to full-blown boulders that cast dark, deep shadows against the ground.

One of these shadows, Ra noticed, was in actuality the mouth to a cave. He pointed it out and the trio considered just walking on. Their curiosity started to get the better of them, and tipped over into complete exploration-mode when Were' heard the crackling of a flame from within.

The cave mouth sloped down, and the air cooled considerably as they descended. The sound of the flame, and the smell of it, reached T.C. and Ra. Were' wondered where all of the smoke went—he didn't see any of it floating past him, and on the surface he'd seen no vent of smoke coming from the ground. He put the puzzle aside and walked on.

In the cave proper, at the end of the ramp leading down, sat an old man. Bald and clean shaven, the man sat comfortably, swaddled in dark brown robes. The robes were darker than the rock around him, and the light from the single torch near him cast sharp, flickering shadows around the cave.

"Er," Were' began, "hello."

The man said nothing, sitting as rigid as the stones surrounding him.

"Hi," T.C. tried, taking a step closer to the man. The flame traced patterns of light and shadow along T.C.'s skin, painting him vividly.

"It's dangerous out there," the man intoned. His voice boomed, rattling around the cave like a living thing.

"Yes, it is," Choco-Ra agreed, stepping up next to T.C., and Wereberry joined them.

"It's dangerous out there," the man continued, reaching under his robe with a spindly, age-spotted arm, "take this." He pulled out a rough-looking sword. Holding it out to T.C., the man simply stared, waiting for his burden to be taken from him.

"Uhm, I'm not sure I really need a...."

"It's dangerous out there," the man repeated, "take this."

"Look," Ra said to T.C., "just take it and let's go, all right?"

"Sure," T.C. said, grabbing the sword quickly.

The three bowed and said their thanks even as they started to back away. As they strolled back up the cave's ramp to the surface, T.C. laughed.

"It's a wooden sword," he told his friends.

"Wooden?"

"Yeah, Were', and hand-carved, I'd bet." T.C. held the sword up and studied it. "I wonder what good a wooden sword will do?"

"None, I'd bet, that's why he gave it away," Were' said, dismissing the entire thing.

"Well, whatever," T.C. decided. He lashed the sword to his bag and stared out into the desolation ahead. Nothing, followed by nothing, followed by trees, stared back. T.C. took out his moisturizer and lathered himself down. He caught Wereberry in the process of chewing some dried strawberry, and he reslung his bag.

They walked on, finding a path and then abandoning it for another. Aimlessly, they wandered like that for hours until the sun started to dip down low in the sky. Once night was upon them, they found a decent, waist-high rock and sat behind it. Two sleeping while one took watch, they passed the night uneventfully. No sounds caught their attention, no movement showed itself. The land was as barren as anything the three had ever heard tell of.

And yet, Were' thought while he stood watch, twice they had found themselves surprised by things that simply couldn't have been where they turned up. Neither the spider nor the bird realistically made sense where they'd appeared. No warning at all, they'd simply appeared. Maybe, he reasoned, that was why people in the town and the old man in the cave were so... squirrelly. If he lived here for long, Were' thought, he'd go nuts too. How were they supposed to be able to get anything done with invisible threats looming simply everywhere they could possibly look? No, Wereberry, decided, their insanity made perfect, horrible sense.

When the sun started to come up, Were' woke the others. T.C. and Were' had a bite to eat while Choco-Ra looked around.

He knew they wouldn't see anything before it appeared, but he hoped to encourage something to show itself, to prove that they weren't alone. That way they could deal with it, and feel like they might be alone afterwards. Which made about as little sense as anything else Ra could come up with, but it made him feel better.

They walked on for hours, sometimes under harsh sun, sometimes under the cover of trees. Nothing stirred—no beast dropped onto them from above or snuck up from behind— they simply walked. T.C. felt that walking ended up somehow more tiring without problems. The boredom, the unchanging process of a step followed by another, compounded his weariness.

When the castle came into view, they almost didn't notice. It shimmered in the heat and T.C. stopped to confirm with the others that they could see it too, that he wasn't simply hallucinating. They agreed that there seemed to be a building in the distance, shaped reasonably like a castle.

They headed directly toward it, not caring if the straight line of their path took them through forest or wasteland. The occasional creature leapt out at them, but their nerves were so completely fried by then that none of the lunges had any affect, outside of violence incurred against the leaping object. A bird here, a spider there. Once a hedgehog of unreasonable size scurried out at them, but a simple kick to the face dealt with it. Choco-Ra wanted to laugh at the sight he knew he presented, kicking a large hedgehog in the snout, but contained himself.

As the castle drew ever closer, the trio found within themselves a renewed sense of purpose and energy. Wereberry could feel it deep in the pit of his stomach. Inside the castle was the princess and the princess was Cherrygiest. That wasn't quite right, he admitted—he couldn't feel it, not really, but he also couldn't not feel it. He simply wasn't sure, which ended up being more sure than he'd found himself for the rest of the trip so far.

It was good enough for him. She was there, she was in the castle and they would go in and rescue her, if she needed it, and finally he would just tell her that he loved her. The trip, all the meandering, fighting, and walking, served only to heighten his love for her. Now he just burned, in some growing part of him, to be able to tell her to her face.

But despite all that, he found many of his memories of her still blurry at the edges. Sometimes she was hard to hold onto, a slippery wealth of happiness. He wondered, idly, if the others had the same problem. So, as he walked, Wereberry concentrated on his memories of Cherrygiest. How the bells she would sometimes wear rattled a song out into the night while he howled at the sky. Her smile, and the way she enjoyed a good lunch.

The sun started to dip as they drew closer to the castle. A path curved toward them that looked to run straight to it, so they shifted their wandering footsteps to walk along it. They stayed away from the grass to either side of them and kept their eyes on the goal.

The castle, once they were close enough to see it properly, was tall, and set into the sides of a mountain range. Painted a soft golden color, it reflected light dimly. A moat ran around the front, dead-ending on either side against cliff faces that rose higher than the castle before they broke off and became part of the mountains they grew from.

The door to the castle, a large steel affair, stood open and welcoming. A dry breeze wafted from the entrance, and they sped up their pace as they crossed the already lowered drawbridge and entered the darkened castle.

5 • World 8-4

THE FIRST THING THEY NOTICED was that the castle's ceiling sat so high as to be invisible. Huge arches reached upward from one side of the room and curved back down on the other, but their apex couldn't be seen. Lights hung from on high, their brightness shining down, but, even squinting, no ceiling could be made out.

The second and third things noticed by the travelers was that behind them stood a wall of mute, deep blackness, the kind that moved forward when you did, and that the room they stood in went straight ahead and opened into another room, much like a road.

Choco-Ra audibly groaned. Were' and T.C. both managed to keep their sighs internal.

Besides a high ceiling and impenetrable moving wall of blackness, the room was decorated quite nicely. Tapestries hung along the walls, and the floor was hewn from solid, gleaming white marble, inset with veins of light blue and soft pink. The stone somehow, Wereberry noticed, felt soft under their feet. Not soft in the sense that it gave springishly, like grass or moss did underfoot, but neither was it hard and unforgiving in the way that stone floors normally tended to be.

The walls, akin to the flooring, held a warmth that raw stone didn't tend to. Running his hand along it, Choco-Ra thought it felt almost like flesh. Hard, strong flesh of stone. That would be useful, he thought, touching and exploring the material. Impractical, Ra laughed to himself, because moving while made of stone would be a long and boring event, with grating and scraping and dust everywhere, but also useful. At least in case of attack.

"All right," Were' said, "we know the drill on this. Shall we?"

"Do we have a choice?" T.C. asked.

"Of course we do," Choco-Ra countered. "We could sit here and do nothing, or we could run into that wall back there, or maybe we could... no that's about it."

T.C. laughed, "Well at least our options are new and exciting. Right then, Were'. Forward it is!"

"Let's find us a Princess!" Wereberry yelled, and he started running down the hall. Choco-Ra and T.C. took off after him, exchanging a glance. Were's firmly held belief both warmed and warned them. They appreciated his dedication and his willingness to launch himself at the goal with such gusto. To be sure, T.C. thought, he wouldn't have Were' lose faith for anything. That spirit in his friend, it fueled them all. There was such a thing as too much, though. Too much of it, well, it could cause the kind of crash that T.C. didn't want Were' to have to face.

T.C. thought back to how he'd felt when he realized that war lived in him as much as anything else did. That kind of self-realization hurt, and though T.C. admitted to himself that it did help in the long run, it just wasn't the kind of thing you hope for a friend to go through.

Choco-Ra worried that Were's clinging to blind hope would backfire on them all and get people hurt. Yes, he felt for his friend, but just then he found himself far more concerned about simply getting through this alive. If they couldn't all focus and push through this to the end, then staying alive might be a pipe dream at best. Choco-Ra needed Wereberry focused on helping them, on all of the wonderful tactical things he knew his friend excelled at. Not, he thought grimly, running chin-first at a fist coming their way.

Doors stood in their path. Wereberry shouldered them open, one after another, running along the castle. Behind him, T.C. and Ra paced him at a distance, in case Were' ran head-on into a problem he couldn't simply charge through.

Their concern became justified when, shoving a door open, splinters from the frame flying through the air, Were' ran straight off a cliff. He yelped, and T.C. and Ra managed to speed up and slow down at once; they sped up to reach their friend, but slowed down almost as quickly, lest they follow him off the edge.

Ten pink, clawed, and furred fingers dug into the edge of the doorway. Beyond it lay a gap in the road. On the other side of the gap the room continued on as if nothing had happened. The gap itself was deep, and heat rose from it in belching gasps. Something in the rising air made Were' want to sneeze. He twitched his nose. A sneeze could dislodge his tenuous grip on the ledge. A simple sneeze could kill him; it made him want to laugh, but laughing, he knew, would lead to sneezing.

T.C. and Ra each grabbed one of his wrists and hauled Wereberry back up to the floor. They set him down, and Were' sat there staring down into the hole. He sniffed the air rising from the gap, sneezing in safety.

"Well, I think I know why the floors are so nice and warm now," he said.

"You have to be more careful," T.C. said diplomatically.

"I know," Were' told him, "and I'm sorry. I just miss her, you know?"

"We do know," T.C. agreed, "but missing her isn't a good reason to get yourself killed finding her."

"Right," Were' said, standing. "Well, I suppose we could take it a bit slower."

"Take in the sights," Choco-Ra said, grinning. "Be tourists?"

"That sort of thing," Were' agreed.

They each leapt across the gap and looked into the next room carefully. It, like the others, sat empty. Were' wondered at that. There was nothing else around but the three wanderers, and that didn't feel right. These weren't the barren lands, or the forest near the city of crazy missing people. Everywhere else they had been, each road upon which they had walked in front of that same black wall had had things to fill it. Creatures to fight or jump over, life of some sort or another.

A sudden burst of inspiration hit Wereberry and he sniffed, sorting out the sulfur and the rich stone smells of the castle, searching for a specific scent. Faint but present, Wereberry found what he was looking for.

"Jonas came through here not too long ago," Wereberry told his friends.

"It would explain why nothing else is around," Choco-Ra agreed.

"So unless he missed something, the way should be clear for us," Were' said. "Barring any more pits or whatnot, at least."

They took off again, jogging through the rooms of the castle and opening doors with more care. T.C. wondered who had closed the doors after Jonas came through, but he didn't dwell on it. Thinking too deeply about that led to thinking about the wall of blackness again. What it was and how it moved with them.

Sometimes life just did things, he felt, and they didn't have to make sense. It helped when they did, and often the sense of a thing was just around a corner, but that didn't mean you ever got to see it. This felt like one of those things that T.C. thought he wouldn't get to see.

A clanging sounded from up ahead. Soon other sounds found their way to the trio's ears: sounds of battle and strife. They hurried up, watching for pitfalls and keeping an eye out for anything dangerous.

They came to a door that looked like the others but, when Were' tried to open it, wouldn't budge. Testing the door again, Were' realized the door had been painted to look like wood, but was, in fact, made of stone.

They stood together, the three, and grabbed the handle of the door, hands overlapping. Then they pulled, each of them planting themselves as a force to not be moved, but rather to move other objects. They heaved, and the door shifted by inches. They strained, muscles and will mingling to produce force greater than either by itself, and the door opened. Begrudgingly, but it opened.

On the other side of the door a battle raged on. Jonas was standing his ground, reaching into a bag at his side. Before him stood a gigantic stone-and-metal golem. It swung mighty arms down against the ground between itself and Jonas, and splinters of stone flung themselves around the room at incredible speed. Some of them buried their way into Jonas, causing him to scream in pain.

Beyond the battle, a cage hung from a length of chain. The chain itself, golden and shining, wound its way up into the ceiling, they supposed. The cage was shrouded in black curtains, keeping whatever lay inside a mystery. The mystery felt obvious to Were', who realized that the Princess must sit inside, quietly and stoically waiting for someone to release her.

They dove into the midst of the fight, Were' grinning a feral grin in reaction to Jonas' surprise. The man's green eyes flashed confusion at the appearance of the three. He had never expected help against the dark beast, not in a thousand years. He started to say so, but Were' cut him off.

"You think we'd miss this?" the werewolf asked.

Wereberry launched himself at the golem, claws extended, intending to wrap around it and find a weak spot to gouge. His limbs were stretched, reaching for a purchase, when the golem's arm swung, too quickly to be seen, and swatted Were' away like a rag doll.

Choco-Ra loosened the bandages on one arm and made as if to punch the beast. When it countered, he allowed the wrappings of his arm to go slack and then tightened them again, entangling the golem's arm with his own. Trapped, the golem started to swing its arm up and down, trying to shake Ra free. Choco-Ra's eyes flashed a brilliant red as he grimaced, feeling the bandages start to fray under the stress.

T.C. took the opportunity of the golem's persistence to slide between its legs and spring up behind it. He wrapped around its head from behind and worked his way toward covering the thing's face. Grimly, he realized how much he was behaving like the spider that still made his skin crawl. He pushed the thought aside and hung on as the golem pawed toward him.

Jonas wasn't one to allow others to do his fighting for him, though—not for longer than it took to find a way to help, at least. From within his bag he produced a few bombs, lighting their fuses and getting ready to throw them, when he noticed that there was simply no way to explode the beast without also taking down these strangers who had only wanted to help.

They struggled while the fuses hissed down, down. Suddenly they were snatched from Jonas' hand, as Wereberry carried them in a dead run to the monster.

"Let's try a BOB tank tactic!" he yelled. T.C. and Ra understood and dropped away from the beast as Were' faked it out, starting to lunge low. The golem lifted a foot to crush him, but instead of a pink werewolf there were only bombs under its massive foot.

The bombs went off under the golem, and the explosion rocked the room. Dust fell from far above, and the walls cracked. The golem fell backwards, shaking the room again as it landed.

"Thanks," Jonas said, striding forward to finish the beast off. A giant stone hand, shod in metal, came out of nowhere and took Jonas off his feet. He hit the wall hard, slid down to the floor, and vanished in a puff of smoke.

The exact same smoke, Were' knew as he sniffed it, that the other things along the road turned into when killed. Jonas was just like them in some respects, it seemed, but his loss would have to be dealt with later.

"T.C.," Were' said, "do you still have that sword?"

T.C. blinked in surprise but nodded, freeing the sword from his bag and tossing it to Wereberry. Wereberry tossed it back with a shake of his head. "It's your sword, T.C., you use it."

"But what will it help?"

"No clue, but that old man gave it to you because he knew it was dangerous out here, right? So maybe he knew something we don't!"

"Worth a try at least," Ra said. He eyed the golem as it stood back up, looking at the thing's feet. They were unharmed by the explosion, and Choco-Ra found himself holding doubts as to their ability to stop the thing.

T.C. grit his teeth and edged closer to the golem. It noticed him and rose a mighty hand to smite him down. The hand never reached T.C., though—it fell to the ground with a flat boom, neatly severed at the wrist by a wooden sword.

"Want to explain this?" T.C. asked, looking at the monster's severed hand.

"Err," Choco-Ra said, fumbling for ideas, "golem made of stone and metal, wood is another element so it hurts it? I don't know, but I know it works, so kill that thing!"

"Killing it," T.C. agreed, and he took a step back. His friends distracted the beast, taking bruises for their trouble, while T.C. moved in to slice his way through the monster. The sword took off its legs and arms easily enough, leaving the golem writhing on the ground in misery.

"Finish it off," Were' said, nodding.

T.C. nodded in return and went to cut the monster's head off. The sword passed clean through its metal-banded neck and bit into the floor of the castle. Once there it wouldn't be budged, no matter how hard T.C. tried to tug it free.

He let the sword go, leaving it sunk partly into the floor,

and joined the others as they made their way to the cage that still hung from the far end of the room.

Black curtains draped over the outside of the cage, its metal ribs showing through in form. Wereberry approached it with a sort of reverence, feeling sure this moment would be the one. Cherrygiest sat in that cage, as far as Were' had decided, and they could free her and go home now.

Choco-Ra found himself unsure. The cage hung obviously at the end of the room, a simple and clear objective. Yet no sounds came from it, and only its gentle sway gave it any appearance of life at all. Ra thought back and realized it had started to sway when the golem first fell, the explosion causing it to rock gently.

T.C. stood with his friends, forcing himself to go blank. He didn't want to get his hopes up, but he also refused to be a pessimist about this moment. Everything could go either way. He watched Were's hand grab the edge of the curtain and tug it down hard.

The curtain fell to the floor, one edge clutched tightly in Wereberry's hand. His face fell instantly as he saw the cage sat empty. An ornate lock clasped the door to the gilded cage shut. The bell-shaped structure was beautiful, built with obvious love and care, but it held nothing and no one.

Wereberry screamed and fell to the ground. He rent the curtain to shreds, kneading his hands into the fabric over and over again. His friends both dropped to their knees to comfort him.

"We knew it might not be—" Ra started.

"She's still out there—" T.C. said at the same time.

"I can feel her!" Wereberry raged. "Am I alone in that? Can't you feel her, inside the cage?"

Both Ra and T.C. stopped and considered. They thought and felt, searching themselves. They each knew they would be honest, either way, regardless of how their friend took that honesty.

346

"Yes," T.C. said, startled, "she is in there, but I can't see her."

"Oh my," Ra intoned softly, "you're right. I can feel her, that sense we've been following since the start, it's right there in that cage. She's there, but then... if she's there, where is she?"

Wereberry stood. Every line of his body spoke volumes of determination. Striding forward like a hero of old, Wereberry grabbed the lock in his fist and rattled it. "She's in there. So we need to remove this lock."

He hammered at it with his fists, but the lock simply shook in place, damaging his hands far more than it found itself bothered by his fleshy pounding. Ra and T.C. each took a turn as well, but the lock wouldn't budge.

Finally, all three of them grabbed the lock and the cage together. Wereberry held the lock in both hands while T.C. and Choco-Ra braced either side of the cage. They pulled together, straining against the metal. It groaned, a high-pitched whine that ran nails along Wereberry's nerves. They pulled again, Wereberry howling in frustration and determination.

The lock snapped abruptly, sending the three friends to the ground in surprise. Wereberry held the broken lock in his fist, the metal hot from the forces that played over it. He threw it away, skittering and scratching along the floor.

The cage door remained closed, and Wereberry, Choco-Ra and T.C. approached it warily. Ra's hand settled on the door and pulled it open, inch by inch. As the door opened, a high-pitched whine sounded in the room, causing Were' to wince and look for the source. The source was the cage itself.

He grabbed the door from Ra's hand and flung it wide, hoping to stop the noise and find Cherrygiest. The door clanged against the side of the cage and the whine only grew in intensity.

Inside the cage a bright white light burst, growing quickly and swallowing the cage. The three travelers only had time to scream before the light swallowed them. It covered the room quickly and then faded again.

After the light faded, the cage sat quietly, still on the end of its chain. The lock, once flung to the far corner of the room, again sat, locked firmly, holding the door of the cage closed. The golem lay dead, a wooden sword stuck into the floor by its severed head. Dust and debris still coated the room and the holes the golem had punched down still marked the floor's surface.

The only other change in the room was the absence of three people.

PART SIX
The Unknown World

"We shall not cease from exploration and the end of all our exploring will be to arrive where we started... and know the place for the first time."

–T.S. Elliot

THEY TUMBLED THROUGH the white emptiness, screaming soundlessly as they flipped end over end in nothing. T.C. and Choco-Ra oriented themselves and looked around, checking to see if an exit hung anywhere visible. Nothing caught their eye; there was only the painful-to-stare-into whiteness, everywhere.

Wereberry simply kept screaming. He curled in on himself and hung there, spinning slowly, sobbing. Everything he wished for, as far as he was concerned, now lay dashed to pieces. Nothing mattered. Nothing, he felt, ever would.

His friends concentrated and watched gray smoke curl into existence. They felt cut deeply by the events, too, but not to the point of breaking. Instead they focused their loss, their frustration and anger, into a shaping.

The smoke coalesced, tendrils growing thicker and thicker until they bunched together, forming something with mass. A small platform grew in the middle of nothing. After a time, it found edges, textures, and density. Though still flat gray, a lake could be seen in the center, surrounded by only sand.

Color filled in, followed by a spot of sky. T.C. and Ra looked at each other, nodded, and grabbed Wereberry. They dragged him to their small creation and set him down. His sobbing became audible in the newly created air. The sand felt almost right, and the water moved close to how water should move.

"Were'," Ra said, kneeling by his friend, "we need to figure this all out."

In response, Wereberry curled in tighter around himself. His sobbing died down, but his shoulders still shook.

"Come on, Were'," T.C. tried, "it's just a setback."

That got a reaction. Wereberry unfolded himself enough

to glare at T.C. "No, it isn't!" he raged. "Don't you see? Are both of you simply blind? She was there and we lost her!"

"I don't think so," Choco-Ra said quietly, "but we can't discuss it until you're able to actually talk and not scream or sob."

"Oh, nice," T.C. sniped, "berate him, that'll help."

Ra turned toward T.C. and sighed. "Cooing at him is better?"

Wereberry stood and walked to the far end of the sandy reef. He concentrated, and more smoke and mist formed out of the emptiness to build grass and the start of a tree. He expanded their perch, walking onto each new section before it finished absorbing color.

"What are you doing?" Ra asked, following.

T.C. joined him and watched. Each time they landed in this space they each grew better at shaping it, he knew. This time, though, T.C. watched in subtle awe; Wereberry was forming stuff out of nothing faster and fuller than any of them could have managed before.

"Getting away from you both," Were' said over his shoulder.

"Enough!" Choco-Ra boomed. "This is simply childish! You can't exactly hide from either of us, you can't run, and there's nowhere to go!"

Wereberry sat down on the grass, watching lush greens seep into each blade. He kept concentrating on it, even as he looked toward his friends. "It's over," he said simply.

The sadness and loss in his eyes was almost a physical thing, hitting both Ra and T.C. in the gut. Theatrics and emotional rages they could deal with. The utter loss of hope they saw in Wereberry's eyes constituted a different matter entirely.

Wereberry sat down heavily. The tree behind him filled in and he leaned against it, staring into the small patch of blue sky above. He sighed, lacing his hands behind his head, and closed his eyes.

"So that's it, then?" Ra asked. "You're going to just sit here now, for the rest of your life?"

"Maybe," Were' allowed. "Look, Ra, I know you mean well and I appreciate it, but...."

"But you've lost more than us, haven't you? That's what you would love to think."

"Ra—" T.C. said, only to be cut off by a swipe of Ra's hand through the air.

"Because not getting what you want is going to destroy you, but T.C. and I, we aren't affected by it. Al? He meant nothing to me, right? Certainly not as much as things mean to you."

Wereberry opened his eyes and looked at his friend. Choco-Ra stood proudly, defiantly even, with his eyes blazing bright. Were' couldn't find anything to say. He knew his friend was wrong, but if so, then why couldn't Were' think of anything to say? He chewed his lip in thought.

"And T.C.," Ra continued, pausing to glance at him, "I'm sure that learning he can fight, learning that his reflexes and lusts were different than he had spent his whole life thinking they were, I'm sure that was a walk in the park, right T.C.?"

"Ra," T.C. said aimlessly, "I don't think... I'm not sure what you think you're getting at."

"This selfish, stupid behavior needs to end, here and now!" Ra bellowed. "Wereberry, we're your friends and we want to help and we're still in this, but only if you stop being so self-centered about it!"

Wereberry nodded and stood. There was no way that a speech like that would simply change his behavior, just a snap of the fingers and everything's all right, but he needed to make a show of it. He didn't think Ra would stop until he got a reaction big enough to count. It didn't matter that his emotions just didn't work that way—he had to run with it until he caught up internally.

"All right, Ra," Wereberry said softly. "So then what do

you expect? What do we do?"

"I'm curious about something," Ra said, glancing between his friends. "You always asked us to feel for Cherry—that was how we would know if she was really where we were. But you never felt for her here. I think she's here."

"We can see she's not," Were' said.

"Ra's right," T.C. put in, "we should at least try."

Wereberry shrugged and closed his eyes. Then he sought out that core feeling, the one constant he traveled with besides his friends: his sense of Cherrygiest and the pitch of her existence's note ringing through the rest of the worlds. As he felt for it, he truly wondered at the ability for the first time. T.C. and Choco-Ra could both do it as well, but what was it about her that let them sense if she was there? Could they do the same with each other?

He fought the questions down, focusing only on the feeling. He spread outwards across the simple sands and grass that had only recently come into being and poured his senses into the whiteness beyond. He opened his eyes.

"She's here," T.C. whispered, "somehow she's here."

Were' nodded and looked at Ra. "How did you know, and what does it mean?" he demanded.

"I didn't know," Choco-Ra said firmly, "I suspected. As for what it means, I'm not sure. Ideas?"

"We always felt when she had been somewhere, and we passed through here a lot," T.C. said, "so I guess it makes sense if she did, too. But then why does it feel like she's still here?"

Wereberry turned around and faced the tree behind him. He focused on it and reduced it to mist. The grass under their feet started to vanish as well. Color leeched from them first, and then form, as the land went back to nothing.

"The exits always hide," he said, "maybe she's hidden, too."

"She wasn't here when we got here, not visibly," T.C. said. "And we need somewhere to stand so we can talk, remember?"

"I think maybe she's gone," Choco-Ra said at last.

Were' stopped what he was doing and spun around to stare at Choco-Ra. There was anger and hatred in his eyes for a second. But only for a second. His eyes softened and he knew exactly what saying those words had cost his friend.

T.C. turned the idea around in his head for a minute before trusting himself to speak. So much of this seemed to boil down to a direct conflict between Ra and Were'; maybe, he thought, if he could find some other route, coming from him it would be listened to without a layer of rivalry added to the process.

If she died, would they feel her as something still living? T.C. added to the mix the idea that she had died here in the white area. They didn't know, put simply, what that meant. For all they could guess, death here meant exactly what they were dealing with now. Then again, maybe it didn't. They had no data to go on and no way to find any, either.

"So if she died, here, her body could have turned to more of the gray smoke, maybe?" T.C. ventured. Choco-Ra and Wereberry looked at him. Neither looked angry, confrontational, or defiant. They both just looked sad. T.C. knew that he wasn't the cause of the sadness, yet it itched at him, like a scratch in his webbing.

"It's possible," Were' said. He took a deep breath and held it for a second before blowing it out through his nostrils explosively. "It is possible."

"As possible as anything else," Ra allowed. "So now what?"

"Do we know she's gone?" Were' asked. "Truly gone? Or are we just guessing because we don't know what else to do?"

"You," T.C. said before Ra could, "tell us."

Wereberry nodded and stretched his senses out again. He felt for her in his gut and caught the tendrils of feeling that told him she was here, just around a corner that didn't exist.

The feeling didn't echo and fade like it tended to when they could feel her moving away from a place. Instead it hung and encompassed large areas, almost drifting. Smoke drifted, he thought sadly.

It was that second that Wereberry knew in his heart that Cherrygiest would never be found. Not because they didn't search long enough or try hard enough. No, right then he knew, as deeply as he knew that he still lived, she would never be seen again.

The sorrow ate at him. He felt like his own heart might stop beating just from acknowledging the concept. The sadness, the sorrow and loss, they were living things, funnily enough, he thought, and they would be his own end.

"She's gone," he told his friends. His voice broke as he said the words, and tears started to dig runnels through his fur.

"Damn," Choco-Ra said, simply and succinctly. He found no joy in being right—just the opposite. Leaving home had hurt Ra. Without him to run the place, he had no idea what could be going on. The place might be just fine without him, but then again, he could have accidentally consigned everything there to a horrible fate. All for the sake of chasing someone that couldn't be found.

Which said nothing of Al. Left behind by necessity, for the hunt at hand, it felt like a meaningless gesture now, a loss with no gain to cover it. Choco-Ra felt the urge to count up those losses in his life that were, essentially, worthless to him now, but dismissed the thought with the severity of a leader scorned. Perhaps they were mistakes, in some sense. The intent behind them, though, the moments of choice themselves, those were beyond rebuke for him, and Ra felt confident that he had indeed done everything he could, both as a friend and a ruler.

"So now what?" T.C. asked. He had ideas of his own, of course, but they mostly arranged themselves into two categories: go home, and go see the Buffaloves. A third idea, one involving going back to work with the BOB again, T.C. didn't want to admit to, not too much.

"Wait a second!" Were' said.

Smoke started to form again and took shape. Small, humanlike, the shape was starting to pull together when Were' felt Choco-Ra violently shaking his shoulders.

"Don't you dare!" Ra yelled at him.

"Why not?" Were' asked. "We can create anything out of this stuff, right? And if she died here then it already has part of her being in it, and I could just... then we could...."

"Damn it, no," Ra insisted, "I know better than either of you what that would be like. I lived with subjects that I controlled, didn't I? Did it ever make me happy?"

"That was you," Were' countered.

"You'll create her the way you wanted her to be. Perfect from your mind. She wasn't perfect! You'd create an abomination, one that looked like her, talked like you remember her talking, but not one that was truly her. It couldn't be her—it would only ever be what you thought she could be. A faint echo at best. At best."

"Ra is right," T.C. said, seeing it himself, "is that what you really want, Were'? A fake version that only reminded you, constantly, that she was fake? It's a bad idea."

"But we could all do it, all of us. Combined, we could make her what she was. Where's the harm? How is that not right?"

"I couldn't make Buffaloves appear, Were'," T.C. told him, "and my memories of them are a lot more recent. I think if we want to truly honor her memory, we have to leave well enough alone. She's gone. She needs to stay that way."

"We could—"

"No, we couldn't," Ra said. "I wish we could. If I thought it would work, Were', believe me, T.C. and I would both be right there with you. We really would. Listen to us on this, please?"

"Then what are we supposed to do?"

Choco-Ra thought hard and a chair formed behind him. Not a throne, though he started off with that idea in mind, the chair was simple and built more toward comfort than appearance. He watched it form and gave it color and softness, a rigid frame and level legs. Sitting, he shrugged.

"Relax for once," he offered.

They started building then. A beach, a bigger lake, with a system of underground streams big enough for a person to travel through, a forest of trees both young and old—they indulged themselves in creation. They used the act of willing things into being to defuse their own emotions, to push past them and lose themselves in the simple process of imagination for a while.

Time passed. None of them knew how much. The light couldn't be agreed upon. Sometimes it was bright and sunny—other moments, night fell and covered the ever-expanding land. Clouds came and went, soft rains traveling with them. A cool wind blew from nowhere, only to be snuffed out on a whim.

They played, as gods might play, and tried to forget their problems. Nothing concerned them but building and adjusting. They didn't speak, each of them simply playing and creating lush lands to explore.

The area they built on grew constantly. Each creation easier than the last, they reconstructed a favorite tree, a familiar sand dune, or a beautiful coral reef only dreamed of.

They slept in beds of their own creation, rising for the day whenever they liked, day and night having no sway over them. They played and tested the limits of their abilities continuously. Boredom didn't occur to them, and so they weren't bored. A vacation, a true break from everything, helped them cope and heal.

They started to spend more time together, building things in concert. Wereberry helped Choco-Ra create a new type of candle wax that replenished itself as it burned. T.C. worked with the others to reinvent the air bubbles they'd seen recently, solid masses that hung in water and yet were perfectly intangible at the same time. The others visited with T.C. at the bottom of his lake, learning to see the world through his eyes.

At times they all lived in a forest, high in the trees. Hammocks hung from branches and ladders trailed down to the undergrowth. The night stars, just pinpricks in their darkened sky, weren't great to look at until they started to make shapes out of them, before willing day back into existence instead.

Time stopped having meaning to them as a concrete thing. Everything lived in the now until they decided it should be different. Then it became the past, though only in relation to their recently created now. The intervals were entirely under their control.

They sat, one sunny afternoon, at a picnic table. The wood gleamed in the sunlight, a rich mahogany. No splinters marred the benches or table, no imperfections lived in the wood at all.

On the table lay fish that T.C. had caught, and a spread of bread and cheese that Were' had served. A cool pitcher of fresh water acted as their centerpiece and the three sat happily, talking and enjoying themselves.

"Remember Gigantic?" T.C. asked, apropos of nothing.

Were' and Ra nodded, laughing with the memory. T.C. chewed a bite of fish and grinning, thinking back.

"He might have been," Were' started and then stopped, starting the thought over. "I would have paid money to see Gigantic deal with the Princess."

"Which one?" Ra asked, to a soft round of laughter. Cherrygiest remained a topic best broached carefully, but some things, the sheer amount of princesses they'd wandered across among them, were exceptions.

"Good point. The first one. You know, The Princess,

capital T and P?"

"She wouldn't have understood why she couldn't simply be as big as he was," T.C. said.

"Oh, it would have been priceless," Choco-Ra agreed.

A short distance away, smoke swirled into existence, finding shape. None of them knew it, sensed it, or considered it as possible. They ate, laughed, and told stories.

"So then," Ra was saying, "the Scuttles decided I should lead them, and wanted to make me an outfit like theirs. I explained that I looked ridiculous in a floppy hat and left it at that."

"Oh, but the knee pants," Were' said, howling with laughter, "how could you have said no?"

"But the Princess," T.C. said, "she was incredible. I mean I don't think she was a bad person at all, just so—"

"Blinded by her Grand Vizier?" Ra asked.

"Pretty much," T.C. agreed.

A sound from the direction of the forest stopped their conversation. None of them had created a person, a decision made without conversation. After the choice to not remake Cherrygiest it had just seemed practical to not make anyone else, no matter how well-intentioned.

At times the choice annoyed them each separately. The one exception was the fish T.C. created. They were a food source, he felt, and thus immune to the general spirit of not creating sentient things. Still, they missed the sounds of birds, even insects, and often considered creating some. But they hadn't. Which left each one of them utterly confused as to what could be possibly making stomping sounds in the forest.

Crashing through the forest, knocking trees over, a giant foot landed near the picnic table. The trio of friends leapt to safety and looked at what revealed itself. The Princess, a giant version of her, laughing and waving her arms around, towered high over them. Around her feet, tiny versions of Gigantic ran. They laughed and explored, each of them pulling something different apart to show the others: a handful of grass, some leaves, fish from the table, whatever they could reach and rip free.

"This isn't good," Ra said.

"Or feasible," T.C. added.

"But it might be the most fun we've had in a while," Wereberry said through a spreading grin.

"Did you do this?" Ra accused Were'. "Did you create them just to get into a fight?"

"What?" Were' asked as he leapt out of the way of the Princess' oversized, fashionable shoe. "No! No way! But that doesn't mean I can't enjoy it!"

Choco-Ra shook his head, dropping the subject. They needed to find out what was going on, not just get into a useless fight. Though he did admit to himself that Wereberry was right. Having to contend with something unknown, some problem they hadn't planned and waited for, had a refreshing edge to it.

T.C. felt the same, knocking tiny Gigantics down as he tore through them to reach the Princess. Little helpless cries of "Gigantic!" squeaked out of the tiny copies as they fell, and T.C. laughed. Battle would never be his favorite thing, but the newness of it, the novelty of a fight here of all places, came with its own appeal.

Were', Ra, and T.C. tackled the Princess as one, knocking her back and sending her sprawling to the ground. She laughed and raged and smashed things with her oversized fists. They moved back while she struggled to get up.

"We have to try to unmake her," Ra said.

"So do that," Were' said over his shoulder, "and T.C. and I will distract her. And hey, Ra?"

"Yeah?"

"Take care of the little mob, too, huh?"

"Sure."

Choco-Ra retreated, focusing first on the Princess. The

tiny Gigantics swarmed around him for a moment, but Ra kicked and tossed them out of the way. Wereberry and T.C. dodged and leapt at the Princess, confusing her and getting her entangled in her own limbs.

Shaking his head to stop himself simply watching his friends buy him some time, Ra refocused, concentrating on his shaping. He had to work in reverse and find the threads of her being from within, turning her back to smoke.

Wereberry and T.C. climbed the Princess' back, making for her shoulders. The Princess swatted at them, trying to not hit herself in the process and mostly failing. Were' and T.C. were too quick for her and far too agile. Her laughter stopped as her frustration grew, but she had yet to utter a single coherent word.

Abruptly they dropped to the ground, falling through her body. The Princess roared in confusion. Bewildered, she lost color and form, melting down into wisps of gray mist.

Were' and T.C. dusted themselves off and all three concentrated on the horde of mini-Gigantics. They puffed out, not quite exploding but certainly not going gently back to nothing.

"What was that about?" Were' asked.

"I think we're getting too good at this," T.C. said, "we were only talking about them. They were like mixes of everyone we discussed."

"So we can't think anymore?" Were' asked, shaking his head.

"No, but I think T.C. is right," Ra said. "We created them without intending to. Maybe we've been here too long, or something."

"Well, then what?"

"Were', I don't know, all right?" Ra said, "I don't have the answers any more than you do. But that's the situation."

"Fine," Wereberry said. "Fine."

Separately they wandered around the remains of their

picnic table, picking up food and plates, broken shards of glass and splinters of wood. Each, lost in their own thoughts, considered the possible ramifications. No answers came to them—no good ones, at least.

"Here's the thing," T.C. said, "the more we do this, the more we, I don't know, indulge in whatever this is, the worse this is going to get."

"It calls into question what this place is," Ra offered, "that it allows us to shape its being, that it's just so damned blank."

"Well," Were' said, sitting on the grass and thinking, "you've noticed how the more we effect, the easier it is to effect another change."

"Yes," both his friends answered.

"And we saw that it can be harder to undo structures that have a deeper stability, not the Princess and her mob, but the ground, say."

"Right," Ra said, growing excited, "and maybe that's it, perfect!"

"Huh?" Wereberry asked. "I was just running down things, I didn't have some great thesis to follow up with."

"I might," Ra said, sitting next to his friend. "T.C., tell me what you think about this, too."

T.C. sat and joined them, nodding.

"What if," Ra continued, "everywhere we've been, every land, is simply something created at some point? From the same space as this, even. But once it gets too firm, too old or solid or whatever, it can't be changed? What if, at the core of the world, this place sits and waits for new spaces to be made?"

"It sounds ludicrous," T.C. offered, "which probably means it makes perfect sense, too. I don't know, though, how do you explain the exits, how we—oh." T.C. nodded to himself. "The exits always hid inside something solid once we built things, didn't they? So—"

"So," Were' said, catching the excitement of a good theory,

"once they're firm, the only way back here is to rip a hole!" He shook his head with a laugh. "Which is all far too simple."

"Pah!" Ra exclaimed. "Saying something is far too simple is a doubter's way of trying to make the world more complex so he won't have answers. It may not be right, but it hangs together correctly for now."

"And when it doesn't?"

"Then we find a better answer," T.C. told Were'. "But Ra's right."

"So we either stay here," Were' said, looking around, "and build things and live here until this place we invent is so solid we can't escape—"

"Without tearing a hole," Ra amended.

"Without tearing a hole," Were' agreed, "or we... what?"

"Wander aimlessly without a home for the rest of lives," T.C. said with a sigh. It wasn't a plan that appealed to him. This place could be paradise for them. It might be lonely at times, but they could solve that too, sometime. Didn't the other worlds have people? So eventually, he reasoned, there would be other people to help fill all their days with.

"You say it like that's some horrible fate," Wereberry said, standing up and starting to pace, "but come on, let's be honest here. We could find an exit here, before we go too much further, find an exit and go wherever it takes us."

"Never stopping or resting?" Choco-Ra asked. The idea appealed in some ways but, like T.C., he thought that there was a chance at peace here.

"You want to go home?" Were' asked.

"I don't think we can," Ra said.

"I don't think we're anywhere but home," Wereberry said.

"Then why would you want to leave?" T.C. asked.

"I didn't say this place was home. I meant you two. Why do we need a bed that never changes, the same woods to stroll through, the same sky to look up at? We have each other, and tell me that hasn't worked so far."

366

Choco-Ra thought about it for a minute. Were' might have something there. They all worked together, even when they fought. He felt closer to the two of them than to anyone or anything else in creation, with the possible exception of Al. And, if they traveled, couldn't they go back for Al sometime? Where was the downside, except in never having a stable place to call their own? And how much did that really mean to him, anyway?

T.C. wrestled with the same problem. He realized quickly that a chance to see the Buffaloves again had opened up. A good lake could refresh him, but alone he would never be happy. His friends, he knew, were as much a part of him as the water. Now more than ever.

Wereberry felt proud and true settling on this particular path. If the others disagreed, though, he would go along with their choice. Staying with them meant more to him than they might have known. He'd lost Cherrygiest—he wouldn't lose them as well.

Hell, he reasoned, they still had to work out why they'd suddenly noticed she had been missing in the first place, when no one else had seemed to. What had made them realize the difference, and what had set them on their path in the first place? There were still answers out there somewhere for him, and he wanted to find them.

"We can always come back here again," Wereberry said, "to relax, recharge, or stay if we decide later we were wrong."

"True," T.C. said, "and if we do go, we can find a way to get Al," he smiled at Ra, "and visit the Buffaloves."

"And watch out for the Grand Vizier," Ra said with a shake of his head. "I don't know."

"Think of the people we haven't met yet," Wereberry said, "think of the doors that are still closed. We helped the Buffaloves, and the Scuttles and Fuzzticuffs. We certainly helped the BOB."

"Oh no," Ra said quickly, "I won't agree to this if we set off to fix other people's lives."

"Yeah, I don't want to just meddle forever," T.C. agreed.

"So we don't go out of our way to, but that doesn't mean we can't explore. How many people get this chance? Hey, maybe there are others, we don't know! But we won't find out here. We won't. We can go out there and see the worlds, all of them, and live a life no one else gets to, or we can build a few houses and settle down here. But," he said with a shrug, "we can't do both. We'll have to destroy all of this in order to find the exit, we all know that. So which is it?"

T.C. and Choco-Ra both thought for long moments, considering their friend's words. Wereberry watched as each of his friends stood up and formed a circle. Ra looked at T.C., who nodded, a smile playing across his face.

"Let's start unmaking this place, then. We have an exit to find."

Never the end

Acknowledgements

Novels begin in strange places and must often travel, collecting debts, along the way to finding a printed life. This one most certainly has its share of wanderings and secret origins. The book only exists because D.J. Kirkbride didn't want to do it. He was searching for novel ideas, and I gave him the kernel of this one to play with. It didn't spark for him, but a few hours later I knew it would be something I had to write for myself. Thankfully it didn't work for his head, because then I would've had to cry. Still, I do sometimes wonder what a Kirkbride version of this book would look like.

Ariana Osborne was there at every stage of initial plotting and writing, acting as a sounding board and advisor. She helped keep me sane when I ran into odd puzzles or had to stop and rewrite whole chapters. She also named the Buffaloves, which is one of those things you should go down in history for. Without her this book would be a darker place.

And then there was a lot of writing. At some point there is always a lot of writing and no one to blame for it. There is, however, a lot of blame to accept, so let me do that right here in the middle. Any mistakes of logic, concept, plot, or personal character are entirely mine. And from here on out I will claim they were also intentional. That's how I roll.

But after the writing comes the editing, and this is where Lauren Vogelbaum came in to the picture. She is a fantastic editor who not only got what I was doing with the story but also understood what I wanted to do and saw the places I missed. Her deft editing makes me look good.

Speaking of looking good, Renato Pastor drew the hell out of the cover and art plates contained herein. Though we (together with Lauren) work on a web comic together (Legend of the Burrito Blade), Renato and I have never met in person. Still, he is a true and good friend who has helped me see visuals of characters that grew in my head.

Finally, but in no way least, Pete Allen took a chance on a strange little book and decided to publish it. I admit to the reader that Mr. Allen was drinking at the time of agreement and leave it up to you to decide if that influenced his decision.

I would be remiss, though, if I did not also thank the childhood that saw me watching too many cartoons and far too deeply steeped in pop culture. Without all of the cartoons, video games, comics, and action figures, I would not be the person I am today.

About the Author

Raised by the glowing light of cartoons, Adam P. Knave still gets excited when he sees the USA Cartoon Express train logo come on. As he grew older, APK realized the perhaps his favorite childhood tales were not quite true. Then he discarded that entire theory as pure hogwash and went on a hunt to become both one of Spider-Man's amazing friends and a member of Mr. T's T-Force.

He failed, miserably, on both accounts. His claim that both Spider-Man and Mr. T beat him up and took his shoes may have been exaggerated. Possibly.

Broken and disillusioned, APK took to the streets and decided to become a one man army force for good, fighting his way through corruption and crime, taking it all the way to the top. That, uhm, well the less details about how that worked out the better. He was also, summarily, rejected from the Holograms.

Since those dark times, he has found his purpose by writing. Be it fiction, non-fiction, or comics, Adam P. Knave strives to write stories that entertain. That's it. Horror, adventure, SF, or a mash-up of everything that falls out of his head, the point is to entertain.

And to join the T-Force, dammit.

Visit *adampknave.com* for more fun.

Breinigsville, PA USA
22 August 2009
222786BV00004B/1/P

9 781894 953597